Down Comes The Night

Down Comes
The Night

ALLISON SAFT

WEDNESDAY BOOKS
NEW YORK

First published in the United States by Wednesday Books, an imprint of St. Martin's Publishing Group

DOWN COMES THE NIGHT. Copyright © 2021 by Allison Saft. All rights reserved. Printed in the United States of America. For information, address St. Martin's Publishing Group, 120 Broadway, New York, NY 10271.

www.wednesdaybooks.com

Designed by Devan Norman

Library of Congress Cataloging-in-Publication Data
Names: Saft, Allison, author.
Title: Down comes the night / Allison Saft.
Description: First edition. | New York : Wednesday Books, 2021.
Identifiers: LCCN 2020040965 | ISBN 9781250623638 (hardcover) | ISBN 9781250623645 (ebook)
Subjects: CYAC: Ability—Fiction. | Conspiracies—Fiction. | War—Fiction. | Love—Fiction. | Fantasy.
Classification: LCC PZ7.1.S2418 Do 2021 | DDC [Fic]—dc23
LC record available at https://lccn.loc.gov/2020040965

Our books may be purchased in bulk for promotional, educational, or business use. Please contact your local bookseller or the Macmillan Corporate and Premium Sales Department at 1-800-221-7945, extension 5442, or by email at MacmillanSpecialMarkets@macmillan.com.

10 9 8 7 6 5 4 3 2

For all the girls who feel too much

Down Comes The Night

CHAPTER ONE

Wren had never seen a worse radial fracture.

She replayed the break over and over again, each moment frozen like hoarfrost on the backs of her eyes. The boy, desperate to escape, scrabbling up the side of a tree. His fingers catching on a branch. The *crack* of snapping wood. The *crack* of snapping bone. And then, worst of all—the flare of her magic, calling out to heal him as he screamed.

Wren perched on the knee of an upturned root, watching as Una bound the boy to the tree he'd fallen from. Shadows hung as heavy as fog in the copse, and what little sunlight leaked through the alders turned sallow, gleaming cold on the shard of bone. It jutted from his wrist like a splinter waiting to be pulled loose.

Volar apex angulation, Wren thought. *Dorsal displacement of the fragment. No doubt an accompanying break in the ulnar styloid process.* It was an easy diagnosis of an injury she could heal in minutes.

"Don't think I can't see what's on your mind." Una dropped the chains, and they struck the earth with a decisive *thud.* As always, she cut an imposing figure in her black military tunic, its stern rows of buttons shining like steel. "Enemy spies don't deserve your pity."

Maybe not. But they didn't deserve cruelty, either. Wren rested her chin on her fists, trying for nonchalance even as her stomach roiled with guilt. "I haven't the slightest idea what you mean."

"No? Then perhaps I imagined that misty look in your eye."

She bristled but held her tongue. Una had been so *ornery* all morning, and Wren was almost exhausted enough to oblige her with the fight she clearly wanted. *Only one more hour,* she reminded herself. Soon enough, the rest of their unit would arrive with the carriage, and from there they would drag their prisoner back to Knockaine for a proper interrogation.

Una snatched the boy's rucksack and stole out of the clearing. Silhouetted at the cliff's edge, she carved a gash in a sky reddened with sunset. Its light burned like embers in the darkness of her eyes and deepened every worried line on her face.

Wren sighed, her breath pluming in the winter air. Her best friend had always carried far too much responsibility on her shoulders. As much as she wanted to throttle Una right now, she empathized with her. Times like these demanded draconian measures.

Three of the Queen's Guard had vanished in the last four months while patrolling the border Danu shared with Cernos and Vesria, and Queen Isabel had tasked Una with finding out why. More accurately, with every rag in the city publishing invectives against her, the queen had demanded evidence that her greatest enemies— those so-called *Vesrian heathens*—were responsible. Although she'd brokered an armistice with Vesria a year ago, her subjects were still reeling and embittered from the surrender of a centuries-long holy war. Now that the fragile peace had splintered, the queen refused to appear ineffectual and passive any longer. No slight would go unpunished.

But after three weeks of searching, of bitter cold and sleepless nights, all Wren and Una had to offer Isabel was this boy, whose only crime so far was running from them. So much good it had done him.

Wren studied the grisly arc of his forearm, the unnatural angle of his thumb. The air had thickened with the too-familiar stench of old blood: saltwater and rust and sugar gone bad. Her magic bubbled up within her, eager to mend him, but she knew Una would never allow it. It was painfully predictable how it would all unfold, this moral debate on whether or not it was right to torture their prisoner. They'd known each other too long—five years now, after they met as recruits in the military academy. They'd trained together, taken their meals together, fought in the war together. And since then . . .

Well, things were complicated.

Una met her eyes, her braid falling over her shoulder like a spill of dark water. Wren turned away before she could decide what shimmered in her superior's eyes.

Still, all Una's bluster guaranteed was their prisoner's slow death by infection. A winning argument on medical grounds, if not on moral ones. She'd just have to build her case carefully.

Steeling herself, Wren sidled as close to Una as she dared, her footsteps crackling softly in the thin layer of snow. From here, Wren could see the shadows of the bare trees curling like vines over Una's wrists, deep violet against her ochre skin. She held a tattered notebook up to the light and pinned the fluttering pages down against the wind.

Wren gathered her cloak tighter and buried her nose into its fur-lined collar. They hadn't been truly alone in weeks, and now that she had Una cornered, she hardly knew what to say. In the end, she settled on what felt most honest. "Are you alright?"

Una snapped the notebook shut. "Why?"

"Permission to speak freely?" she asked dryly. When Una cut her an irritated look, she continued, "Oh, I don't know. It's just a hunch, considering you've been snappish and brooding all day, and now you've decided you don't care about a child—"

"A child," Una scoffed. "You're too soft on him. He's about as old as we were when we were recruited."

"Be that as it may, his arm is going to get horribly infected."

Sunlight glinted off the saber on Una's hip, and for one horrible moment, the hilt looked wet with blood. "Good. Maybe that'll loosen his tongue."

Wren let out a startled laugh at how infuriatingly *typical* Una was being. "Forget it. I don't care about him right now. I care about you. I wanted to check on you, since I know this mission has been . . . difficult."

"It's been long. I just want to get this over with."

Avoidance. The most effective tool in Una Dryden's armory to keep everyone at a carefully measured distance. Wren wanted to remind her it was only the two of them out here, but pushing a mountain would prove easier. They each dealt with their grief in their own way, and Wren would respect that—for now.

Because if she were being honest, she didn't know if she could bear to talk about it either. She wasn't ready to admit she had anything to grieve.

Last month, Sergeant Jacob Byers—her only friend besides Una—had gone missing. One day, they were bickering over normal things, like whose turn it was to buy dinner when they stayed late at work, or which of them would file Una's paperwork. The next, he left on a routine patrol of the border they shared with Vesria and Cernos. Thanks to the cease-fire, those missions were supposed to be formalities. He was supposed to come back within the week.

He never did.

In her darker moments, Wren wished she had been with him on that patrol. Maybe it would've been her instead. Maybe if she'd seen something—a shred of his uniform or his knife forgotten in the snow—she could mourn him properly. But she refused to believe he was dead. Until she had answers, she couldn't lay him to rest.

This prisoner—this *boy*—did nothing to assuage her. With his coltish limbs and streaming nose, he hardly looked capable of petty theft, much less kidnapping.

"Are *you* alright?" Una asked, jarring her from her thoughts.

No, she wanted to say. Instead, she said, "I am."

"Really?" Una drawled. "Just a minute ago, you looked like you wanted to strangle me with those chains."

"And why ever would I want to do that? You're always perfectly agreeable."

Una barked out a laugh. "Now I know you have an agenda. Out with it."

Wren considered changing the subject; it was so rare to get a smile out of Una these days. But she had to secure the boy's safety before she could let herself relax. "Let me heal his arm. At this rate, you'll have to interrogate his corpse. His wound is going to go necrotic before we reach Knockaine."

At first, Una did not react. She stood so still Wren almost believed she hadn't listened to anything she'd said. Then, without a word, Una extended the notebook into the empty space between them.

Wren gingerly took the edge of it. "What's this?"

"See for yourself."

Wren began to leaf through the book. Names and physical descriptions, written in a child's halting scrawl, filled page after water-stained page. With a sinking horror, she realized she knew all these people. Bold red marks slashed some of them out, but she couldn't exactly make sense of the pattern. Captured targets, maybe? But no—there was Byers's name, entirely unmarked. The letters shimmered through her tears.

"What *is* this?" she repeated, unable to keep the mounting dread out of her voice.

"A catalog of every soldier who's patrolled this section of the border for the past year. I found it in his bag. It looks like he's been documenting potential victims."

Every righteous protest crumbled to ash in her mouth. It chilled her to trace the shape of her own name. Then the decisive cut through Una's. No, this couldn't be right.

"Still think he's just an innocent child?" Una asked.

Hissing through her teeth, Wren thrust the notebook back at Una. The skin-crawling sensation of those cursed pages still lingered on her fingertips. "It doesn't matter what I think. It matters that he's wounded."

"It seems to matter plenty what you think. Every time you get an idea like this in your head, it goes poorly."

"That's not true."

"Then allow me to remind you of the time you insisted on stopping to heal a soldier during the march on Donn."

Wren didn't need a reminder. The thorough excoriation from her superiors, and later the queen, guaranteed she'd never forget that mistake.

"Or perhaps the time you wanted to save a stray dog caught in the cross fire?"

Now Una was being unfair. Heat climbed up Wren's neck. "That was different."

"It's no different," Una snapped. "If anything, you're painfully consistent. You're too easily distracted by your feelings and hell-bent on self-sabotage. I need you by my side, Wren, and the queen will discharge you for another offense. His suffering is a small price to pay, especially if he had a hand in capturing Byers. He's a worm, beneath your pity. Let it go."

But she couldn't. She wouldn't. "She wouldn't dare. Who would replace me?"

Una looked like she wanted to say something but refrained.

"She doesn't have another healer like me. How many lives did the antibiotic I developed save? How many surgeries did I help perform on the battlefield?"

"Talent isn't hard to come by. All the medical advancements in the world won't save you from the queen's impatience forever."

"But being the best healer in the Guard will." It was something she told herself every day, but right now, Wren wasn't sure if she believed it.

Isabel—or, as her illegitimate niece, should Wren say *Her Majesty*?—had made it painfully clear that one more mistake would land Wren back in the Order of the Maiden. She had been raised in the abbey, but it wasn't home. There, Wren had been nothing but a castaway: forgotten, unwanted, purposeless.

She never wanted to feel that way again.

Medicine and magic had provided her an escape, but to return would be to admit she truly was as worthless as the queen thought she was. Which meant she couldn't afford to slip up today. Even if treating their prisoner this way was cruel. Even if it was wrong.

"Lieutenant Southerland," Una said. Such a cheap trick, to invoke rank at a time like this. "As your commanding officer, I'm responsible for you. Your mistakes are on my head."

"Oh, spare me the speech."

"Enough." Righteousness rang like the clash of metal in Una's voice, every syllable as sharp as a blade. "Until the others get here, I won't give him a single opportunity to escape. I know you think I'm being cruel, but he's the only lead we have on Byers."

She *knew*, but her stomach still twisted in guilty knots.

"I'm going to sweep the area one more time, so don't do anything reckless while I'm gone," Una said. The word *reckless* struck Wren like a pebble between the eyes. She'd heard it enough over the years to know the real meaning of that word.

Emotional. *Weak.*

"Yes, Major," Wren muttered sourly.

With one last dissatisfied scowl at the boy, Una walked toward the dark, silent wood. Her black hair swung like an executioner's rope, and brittle twigs snapped like fingers beneath her boots. As Wren watched her leave, she sighed with exasperated longing.

Although military life offered her freedom from the cloister, Wren's oath to the Queen's Guard meant little in itself. Una, however, filled her with purpose. Despite her sharp edges, Una cared deeply about her country and her subordinates—about protecting them at any and all costs. Following her was a creed Wren chose, not one foisted on her.

I need you by my side.

And there Wren would stay, even if it she couldn't always

stomach what *at any and all costs* entailed. She cursed the empathy that flowed in her blood as surely as her healing magic did. If only she could filter it out, boil it down to something curable like a disease. Then everyone would know for certain she belonged in the Guard.

Wren slumped into the yellowing litter of pine needles and groaned at the tension headache blooming in her temples and the damp chill of the earth seeping into her skirts. Overhead, the trees dripped with melting icicles and glittered with a delicate crust of snow. Now that they were alone, she stole a sidelong glance at the boy. His white, freckled face was bloodless, as sickly pale as his exposed bone—and nobly but unconvincingly stoic. Even from a distance, the trembling of his shoulders revealed him for what he was, a scared child holding back tears.

Be detached, Wren reminded herself sharply. *Be strong.*

She would not be moved. Not by a Vesrian spy.

This close to the Vesrian border, it made perfect sense that his people had abducted their soldiers. While neither side had officially broken the armistice, Wren knew it was only a matter of time. She'd grown up alongside war, could smell it brewing like a storm on the horizon. And once it came . . .

Danubians lived by the core tenet of the Triplicate Goddess, the Threefold Law: *Whatever is done unto you, let it be repaid thrice over.* Wren had seen enough during her military service to know what happened next. Entire towns burned. Entire battalions slain. Blood repaid in blood until there would be none left to spill.

Neither country would survive it this time.

A muffled sob drew her out of her thoughts and twisted her traitorous heart with pity. She should have been desensitized to this by now, but her magic made it too easy to empathize, to *feel* the throb in his mangled arm. It hurt, all of it. It always had.

This is so wrong, she thought. If she let this boy suffer until they brought him before the queen to answer for his crimes, how much better was she than the Vesrians?

Una's backpack lay in the snow-dusted grass beside her, its front pocket enticingly open.

Better to ask forgiveness than permission, she decided.

Before she could change her mind, she took the key. In her hands it was a weapon, catching the sunlight like something sharp and deadly. As she approached the boy, he glared at her with an intensity that turned her stomach. It was a look as wild and vicious as an open flame—one she'd seen only on the front line.

Hatred.

"Stay away from me," he growled.

His accent stilled her. It wasn't Vesrian. It wasn't like *anything* she'd ever heard. Then again, she'd never listened to Vesrians speak much. Their language was a distant memory, its rhythms indistinct echoes in her nightmares. Shaking it off, she said, "I'm not going to hurt you. I'm a healer."

He pressed himself flat against the tree. "I don't believe you."

"Alright, then." Wren sighed impatiently as she tossed her medical bag on the ground. She rummaged for a painkiller. "Got a name?"

"Whatever you're going to do, do it already." His voice cracked. "I'm not afraid to die."

"Clearly not." Wren fished a vial of poppy tincture from her bag. "Although you may want a painkiller. Setting your arm may feel worse than death, at least for a minute."

"I'll be fine."

He still thought she was going to hurt him. It was almost precious.

"Suit yourself." In his unbroken stare, Wren saw Una, hard and defiant. It filled her with affection, of all things. "Look. Whether you're guilty or not, it's not right to leave you like this. So what's it going to be?"

In the silence, she marked time with the sound of his tight, shallow breathing. At last, the boy squeezed his eyes shut and turned his head away from her. "Alright. Do it."

Finally, an ounce of trust. She'd take it.

Wren unlocked the manacle from his injured wrist and held him fast. As she called on her magic, a second network of veins, the *fola,* ran silver and glimmering down the length of her arm. An aura radiated from beneath her skin, wrapping her hand in a glow like moonlight.

"Ready?"

He nodded, his features stark and hollow in the cold, flickering light.

Wren squeezed his wrist reassuringly, the only preparation she could offer. Then her magic poured into him, and he whimpered through the realignment of bone, the rapid division of cells. The healing took several minutes, and by the end of it, the boy was panting and clammy with sweat. He ran his fingers over the unbroken skin and the straight line of his forearm with a slack-jawed awe, as if Wren had performed a miracle. She beamed with satisfaction. Her healing was far from miraculous—only a biological wonder. Even so, she wasn't sure she would ever grow accustomed to her patients' wide-eyed gratitude.

"Thank you."

"You're welcome." She had a thousand questions, but his trust was a delicate thing, like a rabbit's spine. It would be easily broken if squeezed. "I can tell you're not a fighter."

The boy huffed. "What do you know?"

"Nothing, I guess."

After a pause, he spoke almost too quietly to hear. "You wouldn't understand. Where I come from, this is the only option. My family can't protect me anymore."

"I do understand." Wren smiled sadly through her exhaustion. War had made orphans of them all.

All at once, uncertainty prickled her skin. She shouldn't speak to him this way. She couldn't. No matter how pathetic he looked as he cradled his arm like a broken doll, he was connected to her comrades' disappearances.

He was her enemy. A spy. A Vesrian.

The boy must have seen her darkening expression. "Please. I swear I don't know anything."

Her magic still sung in his veins, forging a connection between them. Every one of his vital signs betrayed him. The stutter of his heart shouted, *liar, liar, liar.*

Before she could say another word, he slammed his fist into her solar plexus. Her breath fled her lungs in a whine, and as white burst behind her eyes, she watched her life unravel like this: the boy scrabbling for the key in the grass; her body surging forward to stop him; her skull cracking against the tree; the rattle of chains and cold metal clamping around her wrist.

He moved far too quickly to be a civilian, and the energy humming in her very bones whispered, *magic.* The world split like a cell in mitosis: two wavering keys fell from the boy's open hands and into the bloody slush. Step by swaying step, two boys backed away from her.

"I'm sorry," he whispered. Then he was gone.

It was over in a moment, quicker than her diaphragm could unseize.

He'd manipulated her. And she'd let him.

With a shout of frustration, Wren pulled against her restraint until it rubbed her wrist raw and red. No matter how hard she struggled, the key was just barely out of reach. Her stomach churned with a familiar dread, and her breathing was too heavy, too loud.

This wasn't real. It *couldn't* be real.

She had lost their only lead. Her only chance to learn what happened to Byers. Her only chance to ensure no one else went missing. The queen was going to kill her if Una didn't first.

No, death would be a blessing. She'd proven the queen right. Wren didn't deserve her approval, and she certainly didn't deserve her spot in the Guard if she let her emotions make her weak and gullible and—

Reckless, just like Una said. She was right, as always.

Talent couldn't protect her from the queen. As long this bleeding heart beat within her, she would never be good enough.

"I have half a mind to leave you there."

With one hand clamped over her face, Wren hid herself from Una's anger. Her other hand hung loosely behind her, still chained to the tree at her back. When she weighed her options, dying here sounded far preferable to facing Isabel. Both promised a slow, tortuous demise. But at least if she stayed here, she'd go to her grave with her pride mostly intact.

"It's for the best," Wren agreed.

Una growled her annoyance and plucked the abandoned key from the grass. Wren worried for one agonizing moment that Una would hurl it into the woods. Mercifully, she unshackled her—but kept Wren's wrist firmly manacled in her fist. Her pulse thrummed frantically against Una's leather gloves.

"I asked you not to do anything while I was gone. What were you thinking?"

"I wasn't thinking. He was suffering."

Una let out a strained sigh. "Your compassion is sorely misplaced. It's going to get you killed one day."

"Maybe it will!" she snapped. "But I'm a healer. I don't want to play Goddess and decide who lives and who dies."

"It's too late for that. If anyone else goes missing—"

"I *know*." Wren couldn't keep the quaver out of her voice. Thanks to her misguided compassion, their only lead had escaped. They were no closer to finding Byers, and if anyone else went missing—if *Una* went missing—that would be on her head, too. Softer now, she said, "I know. I'm sorry."

Fighting with Una always hurt. After so many years, they were too familiar with each other's wounds: how to reopen them, where to rub in salt, how to stitch them up again. Even still, Wren loved her. It was hard not to, with the starlight tangled in her black hair and the weight of an entire nation on her broad, unbent shoulders.

Especially when she looked at her like this, fury and exhaustion and relief crystallized in the amber of her eyes. Una's grip on her wrist slackened until Wren could almost mistake it for a comforting touch.

"How did he get away?" Wren dared to ask.

Whatever tenderness Una had shown was abruptly hidden behind her scowl. "He got a head start."

"What do you mean?"

"When I saw him running, I didn't hesitate. I came back here first."

It was so unlike Una, she was convinced she'd misheard. *"Why?"*

"Because." It was frustration distilled into two syllables. "I thought something happened to you."

"Are you saying you were worried about me?"

Una grimaced. "Don't push your luck."

Wren longed to hear her admit it, but Una would never be so plain, so vulnerable. She hadn't always been so hard, but war taught her never to bare her throat. Choosing Wren over their mission's success, however, came dangerously close to it. As much as she'd protest, not even Una was immune to fear. After Byers had vanished, Wren had watched a storm gather behind Una's eyes, dark and melancholy. It hadn't cleared since. Wren had known his disappearance wounded her, but now she knew it made Una softer than she could afford to be.

"It wasn't your fault, you know," Wren said softly.

"I was his commanding officer." Una offered her a thin, empty smile. "Of course it was my fault."

"Please don't say things like that."

"It's only the truth. His life—all of your lives—were entrusted to me. I ask you all to risk your lives for me every time we leave the city. What kind of leader would I be if I didn't owe you the same?"

"You don't have to ask. I would do it anyway."

"Good." Una pursed her lips. "Then don't make me give you orders next time."

"Yes, Major," Wren murmured.

Wren swallowed a surge of guilt. For Una, this mission wasn't only about justice or pleasing the queen. It was about redemption. Although Wren wanted to reach out to her, she remained still, as if any sudden movement would shatter the tentative truce between them.

Slowly, Una's face hardened into its usual mask, stern and impassive. "I'll need to draft the report for the queen tonight."

Wren wanted to mourn the lost moment, but the painful reminder of the queen bled her dry of any emotion but fear. She gathered up a fistful of grass and twisted it, desperate to ground herself in something solid. "You can't."

"I have to. My duty is to the queen above all else."

"But what's going to happen to us when she finds out? What about your promotion?" Una had been angling for the promotion to lieutenant colonel for months. A mistake like this would cost them both dearly. Una could face a reduction in rank—and Wren could be stripped of hers entirely.

Traced by the bruise-purple glow of dusk, Una's expression was unreadable. "I don't know."

They sat in silence and watched the sun thin into a brilliant orange ribbon behind the mountains. On a night like this, not even Una's warmth beside Wren felt much like comfort.

CHAPTER TWO

As they waited for their appointment with the queen, Wren's every nerve unbraided to the rhythm of *tick, tick, tick*. Hung from the sheer stone walls of the North Tower were hundreds of clocks. Carved and painted cuckoo clocks, clocks on glass mosaics, clocks with swinging pendulums and clocks with churning gears, clocks in glass cases, clocks wrought from metal. Far too many clocks for any one person to have and stay sane. It was said Isabel commissioned them to surround herself with things that ran smoothly, things that were easily fixed, unlike nations.

The hall of the North Tower stood empty, save for Wren and Una. Ribbed vaults laced the ceiling like a corset, and stained-glass panels loomed above them, caged by their leaded frames. Wren hated this place. Its echoing vastness, how the dust swirling through the fragmented light looked like wraiths in the darkest edges of her vision. It held nothing but books and icons and the suffocating gloom of her aunt's presence. The only thing bright and alive here was Una, limned in multicolored sunlight as it streamed through the glass.

Any other day, Wren's breath might have caught at how easily Una could be memorialized here, another stained-glass warrior queen. Beautiful and fierce. But today, it filled her with dread, not wonder. She could only think about how Una *belonged* here and she did not.

"You're staring," Una said.

"Just wondering if you have any grand plans to get us both out of this unscathed." It sounded more hopeful and pathetic than Wren intended.

When Una met her gaze, it was steady as stone. "I'll try."

Although *try* was far from reassuring, it was all Wren could ask for.

A cacophonous sound rent open the silence as every clock struck ten. As the chime of the largest clock echoed through the hall and vibrated in Wren's skull, Isabel's straight-backed attendant materialized in the threshold of a stairwell. "Her Majesty will see you now."

They followed the lacy train of the attendant's skirt up a spiraling staircase and into a stone antechamber. At one end loomed a massive set of doors carved with the royal seal: a full moon flanked by a waxing and waning crescent. That symbol alone was enough to send Wren's heart skittering off course.

Breathe. Wren squeezed her hands to flush blood into her deadened fingers. *Breathe.*

She still hadn't found her nerve when Una pushed open the doors to the queen's office. Cold air billowed into the hall and settled heavy on Wren's shoulders. In five shaky strides, she crossed the antechamber and entered the room, where the middle-aged queen sat behind a mahogany writing desk. Rigid and imperious as a stone-carved icon, Isabel did not deign to lift her head as Wren took her place beside Una.

Wren never failed to be struck by the queen's beauty, too sharp to look at straight on. No one would guess they were related, which was how Isabel preferred it. With her auburn hair and hazel eyes, Wren's royal blood had been effectively diluted by her father's common genes. Isabel, meanwhile, was a Southerland through and through: pale white skin, hair the color of a summer wine, eyes that gleamed like quartz. Myth had it that Danubian queens' blood flowed right from the Goddess's veins into theirs. Wren believed it. As beautiful and withholding as the moon, Isabel could be nothing less than the Goddess made mortal.

She was reading the notebook Una had confiscated from the boy. During the carriage ride to Knockaine, Wren had pored over it so many times, she'd burned Byers's name behind her eyelids. It made his absence—and her failure—seem more real. She couldn't bear losing anyone else. And Danu couldn't afford to lose any more soldiers. During the last years of the war, the military had been decimated. Only the greenest, youngest recruits—and those like Una, already war heroes at eighteen—remained.

If war broke out, what would happen to the rest of them?

Isabel scanned the rows of names as if each were another wrong to add to her carefully tallied scale. The queen ruled with cold, impersonal order, an endless stream of paperwork and reports and written law. After she signed the armistice, she shut down the royal palace and secluded herself within the North Tower. It rose far above the smog and squalor of Knockaine—far above the lives of the people she swore to serve. Her opponents called her the Paper Queen, too embittered to deal with anyone except in writing.

To her country, Isabel was something of a joke. A failure. It was, after all, the birthright of the Danubian queens to reclaim the land Vesria had stolen.

Three hundred years ago, Vesrian raiders had poured into the River Muri, wreathed in black smoke and carrying the banner of their death god. His people, eager to please him, built their empire on conquest. In the turn of a moon, they took Danu. Tore down the temples of the Goddess, ripped the royal family from the palace. Occupation lasted for nearly a decade, until the exiled

Queen Maeve rallied her armies and drove the Vesrians back over the mountains.

Whatever is done unto you, she'd said, a decree from the Goddess herself, *let it be repaid thrice over.* Blood for blood, sorrow for sorrow. And so she burned all the Vesrians' shrines. Banned their language. Forced everyone within Danu's newly established borders to convert or face execution.

Although war had ravaged their nations in fits and starts ever since, Vesria still held a quarter of what was once Danu's land. Parliament, fearful for the nation's draining coffers and declining birth rate, had forced Isabel to broker the armistice last year. But popular sentiment held that she was a weak queen, ready to abandon their land and strand generations of Danu-Vesrians who deserved to come home. If it would keep her from being remembered as a failure, Isabel would never rest until she'd exacted her threefold vengeance.

"Wren," Isabel said flatly. Then, with tenderness, "Una."

How many times had Wren longed to hear Isabel say her name like that? By now, swallowing her jealousy was automatic. Nothing she did would earn her aunt's affection. Isabel loved Una for her devotion and her ruthlessness about as much as she hated Wren for being a stain on the Southerland line. Once, Wren had dreamed of making her into the mother she'd never had. She wasn't so naïve anymore. Now, Isabel's approval mattered only insofar as it guaranteed the security of her position.

It didn't mean the rejection didn't still sting.

"So you let the boy escape." Isabel's voice was as quavering and soft as a wind chime. Wren had to lean in to hear and hang on her every word.

Una rested a fist over her heart in grim salute. "It was my fault, Your Majesty. I underestimated our target."

Wren kept her face blank, even as her knees threatened to buckle. Una did say she would try to help, but lying for her was not what she had expected. Wren tried to catch Una's eye, but she was an unmoving picture of obedience, even as her jaw was set in defiance.

"So you editorialized in your report. How strange that he removed his restraints, incapacitated two of my Guard, and evaded capture, all with a broken arm."

"As I said. I miscalculated."

"I have never known you to miscalculate when it comes to such an easy target. Beyond that, your reputation precedes you. Your men revere you for your commitment to justice. To *truth*." Isabel leveled her with an icy stare. "On what account did they misjudge you? Are you a liar, or are you incompetent?"

Una's fists tightened, the only sign of her anger. "I confess, I more than anyone am shocked to learn I'm not infallible."

"I took a risk letting you climb this high this young. It seems I've made a mistake."

Una flinched. The first crack in her resolve.

"It would be a shame to demote you, since you've otherwise shown such promise," Isabel pressed. "Are you sure you've not misremembered the details?"

"I—"

"I removed his restraints, Your Majesty," Wren cut in. "I healed him."

Una let out a sharp sigh, somewhere between relieved and frustrated. Despite the dread that flooded her, Wren didn't entirely regret her intervention. It was true she couldn't afford another mistake. But she couldn't let Una sacrifice her career like this, either.

Isabel's gaze fell on Wren like a guillotine. "Why?"

"Because it was the right thing to do."

"I see." Isabel opened a drawer and ran her fingers over the feathery tops of her folders. The chilling calm of her voice only made the anticipation worse. "You should consider yourself lucky the Goddess blessed you with such a strong manifestation of your gift."

Sometimes Wren could convince herself jealousy tinged her aunt's voice when she spoke of magic. Today she focused only on stifling her anger and her heresy. The Goddess had nothing to do with her skill. Mother Heloise's brutal training regimen, however . . . "Thank you, Your Majesty. I do."

Isabel tossed a file on the desk and began to read. "A history of impulsivity and disrespect in your lessons. A religious skepticism unfitting for one raised by the Order of the Maiden. I trust I needn't remind you of what happened the last time your pity was misplaced. This will be your third offense."

"It won't happen again."

"I'm afraid I don't believe that anymore." Isabel narrowed her eyes. "These abductions are blatant acts of war, and we are without allies. When I muster forces to retaliate, I need my Guard at its best. You're nothing but a liability. You have lost valuable information, and you have jeopardized lives. You may have my sister's blood, but you have yet again proven yourself unworthy of it."

Rage darkened the corners of Wren's vision. *Proven yourself unworthy.* She had proven nothing, when her unworthiness was a decree from Isabel herself since birth. Shortly after her mother died, Isabel banished Wren to the abbey. A monarch who'd inherited a losing war, after all, could spare no patience or pity for her sister's underfoot orphan. Barred from court and excluded from the line of succession, Wren knew very well that no matter how badly she craved acceptance, no matter how hard she tried or what she did, she could not scrub that stain off.

"Unworthy? And what of the rest of my file?" Wren asked. "Surely it documents more than my shortcomings. How many other surgeons do you have? Any two-bit medic can be a competent healer, but unless they have other skills—"

Una held out her hand, a clear command to stand down. "Please excuse her insolence, Your Majesty. Lieutenant Southerland is under my direct command. I accept full responsibility for her actions. Any punishment must be as much mine as hers."

"Very well, then, Major. It's clear to me now that Wren is a bad influence on you. Since your fondness for her is distracting you from your duty, I will remove her from your command. Wren is suspended from duty."

Suspended. How easily one word could shatter her.

"What?" Wren choked out.

"I thought what I said was clear. I will not have you impeding investigations. You're suspended until further notice."

The knot of anxiety in her stomach went taut and snapped. The room was suddenly too hot, the injustice too much to bear. Wren slammed her palms on the queen's desk. "No. This is absurd."

Isabel only regarded her impassively, her thin lips set in a challenge.

"You cannot punish me for doing what's right. Mistreating prisoners is not an example we should set for the world."

Una grabbed Wren's shoulder. It was a warning: *Calm down before you make it worse.* "Your Majesty, Wren and I have worked together from the beginning. I need her."

"There are equally qualified healers who don't let their feelings get in the way of their orders. War is coming. I need someone who is focused to support you in battle. Even one mistake will cost your life against someone like Hal Cavendish."

Hal Cavendish. The Reaper of Vesria.

His name alone sent a shiver up Wren's spine. In the silence of the room, she could hear Una pop her knuckles, her one nervous tell.

Every few generations, Vesria put forth a soldier more monster than human, and Hal Cavendish was the worst of them all. Wren had seen him only once, when she was fifteen and newly deployed. Her memories of the war often crumbled into fragments when she reached for them: the clash of metal and the burst of gunfire; the sickening pull of her magic to everyone, everything; the way the river swelled in the rain and spat bloated, muddy corpses onto its banks.

But she remembered the Reaper perfectly.

It was the Battle of the River Muri, and Wren had hidden herself in a thicket to tend a woman too wounded to leave the battlefield. And there, through a tangle of yarrow and birch, she saw him. Just as she snuffed out her magic, a man lunged at the Reaper, his blade wet with blood and sluggish sunlight. Then, as if every muscle in his body seized, he froze with his knife barely an inch from Hal's throat. Convulsions wracked his body, and he dropped in a heap, dead before he crumpled to the earth. Hal hadn't even flinched; his gaze killed anyone who met it.

Wren wasn't sure if she made a sound. Wasn't sure if she even moved. But the next moment, Hal turned his chin toward her. His *fola* still glowed silver at his temples, but his eyes consumed all the light, as black as the ravens who glided hungrily above him. Worse still, they were *empty*. Remorseless.

Most nights, Wren still jerked awake drenched in sweat and gasping. Her dreams were lit by raging fire, the stench of burning flesh coating her skin and screams ringing in her ears. But did someone steeped in so much death even feel the weight of it anymore?

She wasn't sure what possessed him to spare her that day. Maybe she'd only imagined his attention. Maybe someone had called out to him. All she knew for certain was that she never wanted to see him again.

"Hal Cavendish is as good as dead if I encounter him," Una said. "I fully intend to bring you his head on a silver platter."

"No." Isabel lifted her chin, obscuring half her face in shadow. Although she wore no crown today, it was impossible to mistake her for anything but what she was. A warrior queen, cold and calculating. "The day we march on Vesria, you will bring him to me alive. His life is mine to dispose of, and I intend to make a show of it."

"All the more reason why I need Wren to—"

"Enough." The clocks *tick, tick, tick*ed until Isabel broke the silence again. "You will leave tomorrow to pursue the boy. Without Wren. Do you understand?"

"Yes," Una said bitterly. "I understand."

"And you, Wren, will return to the abbey until I decide what to do with you."

"*No.*" Wren squeezed her hands into fists.

How could she sit back and watch another friend walk headfirst into danger? If Una disappeared, too, then Wren would truly be alone. Locked away in the abbey, she'd become that scared little girl again: unwanted and forgotten. Denied the chance to have some small say in how she lived her life. A failure.

"Please," Wren rasped. "I can't go back."

"Wren," Una whispered sharply, almost pleading.

"Since you've been relieved of your post, I'm afraid you don't have much choice in the matter."

All mages served the Goddess in one way or another. As her earthly representative, Isabel headed both the state and the church and could dispose of her subjects as she willed. With all mages subject to mandatory enlistment—a precautionary measure in this war-torn queendom—she'd be forced into contempt of the law. As a retired combat medic, Wren would live out her days in devotion to the Goddess, performing healing acts for the common people. To refuse was to surrender her magic.

Wren said nothing. She had forgotten how to speak.

Anger roiled in her stomach like a ship tossed on the sea. With the blood thrumming in her ears, she could think of nothing to do but turn on her heel and run for the door. Her vision swam, and she dragged the heels of her palms underneath her eyes to catch any tears that dared fall. She hated that she cried when she was angry. It was another weakness, another reason why she wasn't cut out to be a combat medic, another reason she was suspended. Her emotions, too uncontrollable to manage, would doom her every time.

CHAPTER THREE

It was several hours after their meeting with Isabel that a knock sounded on her door.

"Are you home?" Una pressed her face to the window, squinting into the darkness.

Wren's heart leapt into her throat. Una hadn't come to her flat since . . . No, she wouldn't think about it. They had agreed never to discuss it ever again.

Drawing in her breath, Wren rose and let her inside. As Una drank in the room, Wren collapsed onto her chaise and drew the blanket over her head. Almost immediately, she felt a tug—then cringed as the light flooded back in. Una had peeled back the edge of her makeshift cocoon and curled her lip, as if she had found something half-formed inside.

"Please don't cry," Una said. "It makes me uncomfortable."

"I'm not going to cry."

Una unstrapped the saber from her hip and gingerly perched beside Wren on the chaise. Comforting others was never exactly

t's my responsibility to keep my subordinates safe and out of
le." Although her face was as stark as ever, the strain in her
betrayed her. Wren didn't have to push to know Una was
king of Byers. "And I— Oh no. Don't. Don't do that."

orry. I can't help it." Wren scrubbed her face to hide any ev-
ce of her tears. When she looked up again, the world was still
and hazy. "I've got to cry enough for the both of us."

ave it. You've troubles enough of your own, and I can handle
."

I'm well aware." Wren pulled the blanket back over her head. "I
don't understand what I have to do to get her to respect me—or
ast not *despise* me."

You could try following orders for a start." Una paused, her
ession softening. "You know there's nothing you can do. The
n has high expectations, but she's never intended for you to
t them."

hat was true enough. When Isabel banished Wren to the ab-
she hadn't expected the military recruiter to come knocking
heir gates. With the war's body count rising, they needed every
ing and able healer they could find, young or old. And Wren
more than willing. Since then, the queen had found every way
naintain the distance between them. Wren would never fully
p why Isabel hated her so much, what unlovable thing lay at the
of her. She was a bastard, yes, a stain on the perfect Souther-
l line, but they had no other close family but each other. Rather
n accept her, Isabel would sooner let some distant cousin swoop
o take the throne when she died heirless.

"What am I supposed to do now?" Wren asked.

"You will wait patiently until I clean up this mess and convince
queen to reinstate you."

"I can't be patient doing *nothing*."

"Fortunately, you won't be doing nothing in the meantime.
aling works and prayer and general drudgery, if I recall? I've
ured your complaints enough to know that much."

"I'm not joking, Una."

her strong suit, but Wren would credit her for tryi
you turn a light on or something? This is depressi

Wren groaned, curling into a smaller ball. She
ing her, but then she saw her flat through Una's
stood at least some of her concern. She was always
or buried in her research, mapping out the pat
perfect her surgical techniques, or studying the
the apothecary down the street saved for her. She
quently that she'd never bothered to decorate the
herbs bound with twine hung from the ceiling, s
lavender, jagged bundles of nettle, and orange cale
chipped cornice was peeling floral wallpaper, stai
smoke and spattered with the exploded remnan
tincture.

Wide windows, although caked with dust, ove
her busy street, which glittered with fog-muffled
her desk, she could watch the woman across the st
to dry on the line in the mornings; and by night
men cart off reeking wicker baskets from the ces
she had the luxury of a military salary, she owned
made bed shoved close to the iron stove, on whic
kettle. Its sparseness made its disarray starker, n
least it would be easy to pack up tonight.

Una pulled a loose thread on the ratty chaise.
ning light sneaking past the blinds, Wren could
her facade and the exhaustion lurking underneath
make you feel worse. I thought you'd want some

She did. She always wanted Una's company, ev
a special brand of torture to have her *here,* on
taunting her with the memory of what they could

Wren pressed her knuckles into her stingin;
above, Una. What were you doing back there? Y
ined everything you've worked for."

"You're welcome."

"Why?"

"Neither am I." She kicked her feet up onto the armrest. "It's only a suspension. All things considered, yours is a mild punishment. You should be grateful."

"Yes, technically it's mild, but she knew it would hurt me the most. The helplessness is almost worse than the humiliation. I'll never forgive myself if you get taken, too."

Una flinched. "I won't be."

"How do you know that?"

Una thinned her lips into a grim line.

"Exactly. And in the meantime, what am I to do? Content myself with hours of contemplating the Goddess in her infinite mystery? Or wait for your letters to come like some lovesick housewife?" As Una's expression grew darker, more distant, Wren homed in on the single infuriating thing within her control. "Get your filthy boots off my chaise."

"It's *already* filthy."

"Just listen to me," Wren snapped. "Please."

Una slowly lowered her feet to the floor and watched Wren through narrowed eyes. "I'm listening."

"Not three weeks ago, Byers was sitting exactly where you are. We had tea. We chatted. We said goodbye. Everything was so . . . normal." She couldn't scrub the very last image of Jacob Byers from her mind: him, carelessly waving over his shoulder as he walked down the moon-silvered cobblestone street outside her flat. "I can't go through that again, Una. Especially not if it's you. I don't know if I'd survive it."

"You can't protect me." Una's hand ran along the sheathed blade of her saber. The filigree of the scabbard gleamed cold in the light. "It won't make a difference if you're there or not."

"That's the least reassuring thing you've ever said to me, and that's saying something." Una was completely missing the point. But how could Wren ever make her understand something so irrational? That if she stayed behind, the world might crash down. Inside the abbey's walls, she would be alone, unable to sweep up the pieces.

"The only reassurance I can offer is my word. I will come back for you. I *will* set this to right."

"Your word. What good is that?"

"You tell me."

It meant everything. But it still wasn't good enough.

Before Wren could respond, Una let out a long sigh, a rueful smile curling on her lips. "I told you I didn't come here to make it worse. So much for that."

"It's a good thing I don't keep you around to make me feel better." Wren nudged Una's knee with her own. "That's what tea's for anyhow."

"Is that a request?"

"Oh, never! You're my guest. But if you're offering . . ."

"Fine," she said gruffly. "I'll make you a cup. Black? Why are you staring at me like— Ah, too late for caffeine. Right. Chamomile, then."

Una moved through her kitchen as if she'd never been away. After almost a year, she still knew exactly where Wren kept the teas—alphabetized, by scientific name, in glass apothecary jars above her sink—and her favorite earthenware mug. The simple tenderness Una showed her in boiling water and measuring out tea leaves nearly destroyed her. It didn't help that she still wore her full regalia; every time she reached into the cabinets, the medals on her lapels merrily jangled.

Wren really was too soft. And try as she might to stifle it, she was still a little in love with her commanding officer. The worst, most foolish of her feelings. A romantic relationship between a soldier and her superior would get them both court-martialed.

Last year, when the ink was still drying on the armistice, Knockaine became a strange and hazy place at night. Everyone wandered the streets like sleepwalkers. One of those nights, Una appeared on Wren's doorstep, more fierce and hard-eyed than she'd ever been in the military academy. Sometimes, Wren convinced herself it was a dream: her back hitting the door, Una's mouth on hers. But she still remembered the exact iron-and-woodsmoke taste of her, the way the jagged scar on her shoulder felt beneath her lips.

Most of all, she would never forget the way Una looked at her the next morning. It still haunted her. Full of regret—maybe even fear. Of course she was afraid; fraternization was a dismissible offence. Beyond that, Una Dryden did not say the word *love*—not after the war took her family from her. And she most certainly did not talk about her feelings, so Wren was left alone with hers.

A mistake, they had agreed. *Seeking comfort in the wrong places.*

It would never happen again.

But sometimes, Wren still caught Una's lingering looks. Sometimes, she worried about the part of her that had turned corrosive. The part of her that hadn't forgiven Una, that still ached whenever she heard rumors about the civilian girls Una courted.

Una pressed the cup of tea into her hands, and Wren banished her dark mood with the sweet smell of chamomile.

"Thanks." Wren smiled wanly.

"You still look miserable. Do you want to . . . talk about it?"

"Uh, no. I think you might combust if I unload all my feelings onto you."

Una lifted an eyebrow. "Then at least this dump will burn with me."

Wren shoved her. "Shut up. I just . . ." *Just.* It was never so simple. Her throat tightened. "I miss him."

It was the first time she'd said it aloud, and the admission cracked open the wall she'd constructed around her grief. Memories of Byers fell through, scattered and sharp like the pieces of a dropped vase. His insufferable humming to himself while he worked. That obnoxious, boyish grin he wore whenever he thought he was being particularly clever. The way his eyes glowed with pride when he talked about his brother. Wren wanted their weekly pub nights back. She wanted to listen to him prattle on about the art of flower arranging, a family trade. She wanted him *back.*

Una cast her eyes to the rippled surface of her tea. "I miss him, too."

A smile tugged on the corner of Wren's mouth. "Do you remember that time he was late for morning drills?"

Una laughed, full and unguarded. The sound of it curled up, warm, in Wren's chest. "How could I not? I can still see Sergeant Huffman's face turning purple when she saw him try to climb through the window."

Wren grinned. "He was a complete disaster."

"You're *both* disasters. It's a true ragtag bunch military HQ assigned me."

"Lovable ones?"

"Don't get carried away," Una muttered. "You're a disaster, period. But mine."

Hers. How Wren longed for that to be true. She wanted to reach out to her—wanted to twine their fingers together in that uncomplicated way they used to *before*.

But Una had gone quiet again, the room somber in the gathering dark of night. "I think constantly about what I could have done differently."

"You couldn't have done anything differently. None of this is your fault."

"His capture may not have been. But I lost our one lead, and because of that, I failed him." Una had always put so much on herself—too much. More than anything, Wren wished she could take some of that burden from her. But part of what made Una a brilliant soldier and a commander worth following was this. Her unflinching dedication to her subordinates. Her sense of duty above all else.

"You didn't lose the boy. I did."

"I could have given you orders. I could have threatened you. I could have stood my ground and taken the queen's punishment. But I didn't." Her voice grew rougher, the notch between her brows deepening. "Now she's taken my healer."

"She wouldn't have if you left it out of the report in the first place." The words slipped out unbidden. She wished she could take them back, but Una only shook her head.

"I know you wanted more from me. This is all I have."

"Una . . ."

The wistful look in her eyes cooled. Once again, Una was her superior officer, imposing in her sharp-shouldered greatcoat and her silver epaulets. "I have orders for you in my absence."

"I'm not your subordinate anymore, remember?"

Una let out an impatient, almost pleading noise. "Then just promise me something."

"Anything."

"Until I regain her favor, stay *here*. You can't do anything—"

"Reckless." Wren knew this for what it was, a second chance she didn't deserve. But she couldn't help feeling like it was more like a wound reopened. "I know."

"Promise me."

"Fine. I promise." Wren tore her gaze away to hide the hurt prickling behind her eyes. "When do you leave on your mission?"

Una bowed her head, as if it had grown heavy with relief. "Tomorrow afternoon."

"Just come back to me in one piece."

"I will."

This, here, was how she wanted to hold Una in her mind if this was the last image she'd have of her. Loyal. Almost loving. Wren clung desperately to the small details: the inky spill of her hair over her shoulder, the fire crackling in her amber eyes, the devout solemnity of her voice.

But louder than anything were the words *I know you wanted more from me.*

She did, but if she could not have her, being at her side had to be enough. Una needed her healer, so Wren would earn her reinstatement. For now, she would prove she could be patient. And when Una came back to her, Wren would sharpen herself into the kind of girl deserving of Isabel's respect and Una's trust. The kind of girl who could bring Byers home.

CHAPTER FOUR

Knockaine was a foul, moody, stinking city. But it was home.
Wren had hoped to commit every detail to memory as she carried her two leather suitcases through the waking streets. But alas, it was winter. As it did every winter morning, a thick fog had rolled off the river and devoured everything in its path. By the end of the day, it would be blackened with soot and smoke from the factories, and the whole city would reek of sulfur. For now, it only reeked of sewage and—

No, it was best not to speculate.

Bare impressions of her surroundings emerged from the fog as she walked. Half-burnt buildings, still unrepaired from the last Vesrian raids a year ago, slumped like drunks in the alleys. Cracked windows leered at her from high above, grimed by the hydrogen sulfide wafting from the fetid wells. Far in the distance, the spires of the North Tower lanced the too-low sky, solid black against heavy gray. It was the only new and unblemished structure for miles.

Wren slipped through the secluded back streets until she crossed the River Muri. Most everyone hated it—for good reason, since its acidity was liable to dissolve nearly anything brave or foolish enough to set foot in it. But Wren harbored an odd affection for the sluggish black waters. It was said the Goddess rose up from the Muri, many lifetimes ago. That queens in the age of heroes found her washing her hair in its shallows. It seemed impossible that anything so foul and unimpressive had witnessed so many legends, but as she leaned over the bridge and found her reflection, Wren swore something stared back from beneath its surface.

With war's breath hot at her neck, that unfeeling black reminded her too much of Hal Cavendish's eyes.

Shuddering, she pressed onward, following miles of the Muri's oil-slick path through the city until it led her past the gates and into an open field. There, mist-veiled and crouched like a gargoyle in the shivering grass, was the abbey that housed the Order of the Maiden. The sight of it struck her as cold as the wind battering her face, stripped her down to a hopeless longing. When she was twelve years old, readying herself to leave for the military academy, she had gathered all her robes and sunk them in the river. Dramatic, admittedly. But it was as good as a promise to herself. She would never come back.

Now, facing down the enormity of it, Wren wondered how she'd ever believed she could escape the abbey's gravitational pull. Her fingers and shoulders ached from cold and the weight of her luggage. Only another mile to go before she reached the abbey's gates.

With every step, the Order of the Maiden loomed closer. Its bell towers and turrets scraped the clouds, and the tracery of its massive rose window shimmered like a spider's web in the gray sunlight. It depicted the face of the Maiden—the first face of the three-headed Goddess alongside the Mother and Crone—with her golden hair woven with wildflowers. Once Wren passed through these doors, nobody but the queen could free her.

I hope you're as persuasive as you think you are, Una.

She couldn't bring herself to take another step. These walls could not be her world; she had seen too much beyond them to be content here. Standing in the courtyard, the wind tugging at the hem of her traveling cloak, Wren swore this place remembered her. She could feel it like the chill of a lingering gaze.

Because someone was looking at her.

She snapped her attention to the west gallery, where a dark silhouette waited in a window. Wren staggered back a step—but then, as she let herself focus, she saw who it was.

Mother Heloise.

Dressed in her dark robes and wimple, she held a cracked leather belt loose in her hands. Wren had never felt its sting, although she likely deserved it. She'd never had the constitution for hours of adoration, for reading the borderline erotic devotional poetry of saints. She'd even tried to escape a few times in her first weeks there. But Heloise believed in implied threats. The promise of punishment controlled her students far more effectively than its execution. Lectures, however . . . Those, she did not hold back.

You have a gift, she would tell Wren in her stern, rattling voice. *No family. No faith. No prospects. Only your magic. Will you waste your life here, making mischief and wallowing in self-pity? Or will you make something of yourself?*

Heloise had given her an opportunity, a gift more precious than any gem. An education in medicine and magic. And with it, a chance to be valuable. Not a royal bastard hidden away behind the abbey's walls, but a healer of the Queen's Guard. Someone who could be useful if she couldn't be loved.

Now, Heloise stared down the slope of her nose with a look of palpable disappointment. Then she turned away from the window and slunk into the shadowed hallway. Wren flinched as if Mother Heloise had cracked the belt over her knuckles.

Drawing in a steadying breath, she approached the front gate. The stone tympanum perched above it, and all she could see in the weather-beaten carvings were anguished faces and blank eyes upturned to the Goddess. And higher still, the predawn sky was scattered with stars that glittered cold as shards of ice.

Wren rang the bell at the front gate and waited until the wooden doors creaked open. Tried to stand tall as their shadows stretched toward her, inevitable. On the other side was a woman—Sister Mel, who'd caught Wren weeping more times than she cared to admit during her first month there.

"By the Goddess! Is that you, Sister Wren?"

"Yes." Wren blinked away the sting of tears. She wouldn't be caught out again. "I'm back."

The sickbay of the Order of the Maiden echoed with consumptive coughs and groans. On a backless stool, Wren worked on her third patient of the day, a woman sporting a broken wrist. Truly, the universe had a twisted sense of humor—or a sense of cruel justice she had to admire. She'd spent all afternoon trying not to dissolve into hysterical laughter, which seemed to concern her patient some. Even now, her forehead was pleated with worry as Wren worked with her mouth screwed tight.

Awash with the glow of a hundred healing hands, the room seemed to swim with cold candlelight. Rows of beds stretched from wall to wall like pews in the nave. In too many ways, being among them felt like being a child again, the eternal discomfort of her hunched back, the tension in her hands, the infuriating rasp of rough-spun fabric. Her habit, as horrible and itchy as she remembered, was earthy brown. The color represented the symbol of the Goddess's fundamental mystery, the dirt in which things grew and were buried. Wren, however, simply thought it was ugly.

Acolytes of the Order of the Maiden believed healing to be a divine pursuit. A goodness done so that the Goddess's favor might magnify threefold. Although she hadn't lived here in years, memories of her lessons still plagued her: cold stone walls at her back, hard wooden benches beneath her, crumbling theological manuscripts in her hands.

The Goddess has bestowed the world with a gift most holy, the embodiment of her divinity, Saint Gia, the Order's founder, had written. *Immense knowledge—one that, without her light, grows cold. For every step toward understanding our impermanent forms, let us take three steps toward understanding her Mystery.*

But Wren had never found comfort in faith. Here, healing was nothing but a grim obligation. Over the past week, when she crawled into bed with her every joint aching from the overuse of her magic, Wren's older Sisters told her it wasn't always so awful, so busy.

In three hundred years of war, there had been quiet periods. But devout Queen Isabel had renewed military efforts with an unprecedented fervor, and those left behind still suffered. Honorably discharged soldiers, seeking management for chronic pain. War orphans, wallowing in illness after nights spent in the cold. Common people, injured on the job but unable to quit.

As she worked, Wren felt a familiar prickle on the back of her neck. Staring. Her Sisters' eyes burned, not always unkindly, with the same question. *Why are you here?*

The weight of their judgment piled on her shoulders. Maybe she was imagining it, but she swore it felt like pity. It wasn't exactly undeserved, when her failure would be circulating in every gossip column and tavern in the city by now. She could imagine the headlines now: *Paper Queen Isabel finally wearies of keeping her sister's bastard on the government payroll.*

Wren pushed away the bitterness and tried to settle into the familiar process of healing. Tried to find it in herself to feel satisfied, but it was mindless, grueling work. She would go mad with it, the repetition of her days, how the scope of her world coiled around itself smaller and smaller. Yes, she was helping people. But what was treating one man's gout, one woman's broken wrist, against countless dying in a war?

This was just so far from what she wanted. So far from where she belonged, tracking down whoever took Byers from her. Whoever might still take Una from her. Even if Una survived and traced the disappearances back to Vesria, war would come. Una would see combat again—without Wren to keep her alive.

No matter what, she thought, *I have to be reinstated.*

Wren forced a smile for her patient as the glow of the Healing Touch faded from her hands. A weary numbness washed over her in its wake. "Alright. You're healed."

"Thank you." The woman's eyes were round with wonder. "I can't ever repay you, Sister."

Before Wren could reply, gnarled fingers wrapped around her elbow. Wren turned to find Mother Heloise looming over her, a string of wooden prayer beads clanking around her neck. Exactly as Wren remembered, Heloise looked like an angry rook, although time had stolen more of the color from her hair and wrinkled her golden-brown skin. To see her again brought on an emotion Wren couldn't articulate. This was the woman who had raised her, who had trained her alongside the other apprentices. But there was no joy in this reunion. Only a cool recognition.

Wren could not forget the sight of her retreating back in the window.

As Heloise collected healing magic in her palm, Wren smothered her temper before it sparked. She hadn't seen Heloise all week, yet here she was, assessing her work as if she were a newly minted apprentice. Apparently satisfied, Heloise let go and rested her hand atop the other on her cane. "Perfect, as always, Sister Wren." To the woman, she said, "Go in peace."

As soon as Wren's patient scrambled out of bed and out of earshot, Wren rounded on the old woman. "Not perfect enough. I'm back here, after all."

"So you are." At first, it seemed she would leave it at that. She was as cryptic and frustrating as ever. Then Heloise reached into her robe's deep pocket. "A letter arrived for you this morning."

Although her swift pivot away from pleasantries stung, hope welled up inside Wren. Perhaps it was from Isabel, a message that she'd changed her mind. But shaking in Heloise's swollen hands was an envelope as red as an autumn leaf. The spark of excitement fizzled into embarrassment. She didn't need to look closely to know it did not bear the queen's seal. Red was far too garish a color for Isabel's preferred palette of white and only white.

Wren took the letter. Across the front, rendered in elaborate gold leaf, were stag's antlers, the mark of Cernosian nobility. The strangeness of *that* struck her like a freight train.

Cernos had the distinct misfortune of existing on the same peninsula as Danu and Vesria, but due to their hostile, mountainous terrain, they had successfully isolated themselves and remained neutral through three centuries of bloody conflict. As a rule, they did not engage with their larger neighbors at risk of provoking cries of favoritism. Rather, they looked beyond the sea for allies. Technology and trade afforded them riches enough to rise above the Danu-Vesrian wars. A necessity for a country that possessed no magic.

Danu had not had official contact with Cernos in . . . well, a long time. Yet here in Wren's hungry, shaking hands was her name written in elegant script.

"If you will accept counsel," Heloise said, "I would advise you to burn it."

On reflex, Wren clutched the envelope to her chest. "What? Why?"

"Cernos has ignored any request for aid for years. They've sat comfortable on their mountains of gold and watched our people bleed. They would not break their silence without a reason—and for them to come to you, a mere girl, disgraced and with no protection? What good could this bring?"

Every word struck true. And yet, this was her decision to make, hers to weigh. "Is that all you've come here to say, or are you confirming I haven't slipped during my time away?"

"I only came to deliver that." She glared at the letter as if it were cursed. "As for what you do with it, you can make your own judgments. You're not a child anymore."

Anger burned behind her eyes, and Wren willed herself not to cry with frustration. Not here. Not when the others were leaning closer to overhear them. Wren lowered her voice to a thin, pressurized whisper. "Am I not, Mother? You haven't met with me until today. I've had no say in what my duties are here. And now I have no say with whom I shall correspond?"

Heloise leveled her with an incredulous but patient frown, which made her feel childish for her outburst. "We all must pay the price for our mistakes."

Yes, and she was paying the price dearly. If she couldn't convince the queen to reverse her sentence, she would be trapped here forever while her friends died on the border. "I can't stay here."

"Perhaps it would be wise to consider this a new beginning. A blessing from the Maiden. Unless, of course, you would prefer the Severance."

Due to its risks, healing magic was forbidden outside the clergy or the military. A healer who hoped to live among civilians would face the Severance, a procedure mandated by the Danubian government. Although all healers took a vow of nonviolence, Wren always felt attracted and repulsed by her magic's gruesome edge. It could open an artery as easily as it could cauterize a wound. It could even impact the *fola,* veins that carried magical energy throughout the body. With a single snip to the central *fola* within the heart, the Severance cut a person's connection to their magic entirely. Wren had poured everything she had into mastering her magic. Without it, she'd be nothing.

"No, Mother," she said quietly. "I wouldn't."

"Good. It'd be a shame to waste your talent. You will find your path here, even if it is not the one you imagined." Heloise's eyes fell to the letter in her hands again. "Remember what I advised, Sister. Now, if you'll excuse me."

As Heloise shuffled out of the sickbay, whatever stifling power she held over the place lifted. Her Sisters returned to work as if they'd never been eavesdropping. The coughing resumed. Wren remembered to breathe again, all her muscles unwinding.

Heloise was right, of course. Now that word was out that Wren had no protection from the royal family, the opportunists, both within and outside Danu's borders, would come prowling. An heirless queen unnerved the monarchists, and any ambitious noble could use a puppet with a drop of royal blood. The barest shiver of temptation passed through her. Was it better to be locked away in an abbey or an aristocrat's house?

These are desperate thoughts, she chided herself. If she kept her promise to Una, everything would be fine. The safest thing for her to do was to stay here and toe the line.

Burn the letter. Obey the queen's orders. Rein in her feelings.

It was only a matter of time before she was reinstated, back on Byers's case, if not ready to fight a war alongside Una. But with dissatisfaction and fear threatening to consume her, Wren couldn't convince herself that any of that was true.

In her hands she held a bloodred letter and an ocean of doubt.

In the privacy of her room, Wren smoothed the letter out on her desk like a specimen ready for dissection. It was signed *Lord Alistair Lowry III,* and all at once, her mood soured. Of all the Cernosian nobility to write her, of course it would be the man whose name once appeared in every gossip column. His people might have refused all contact with Danu, but the rest of the world was all too eager to leak news from Cernos. Their latest inventions, their most extravagant fashions—which spawned cheap knockoffs that flooded Danubian ballrooms each season—and of course, their courtiers' latest scandals.

Alistair Lowry was widely, and perhaps rightly, considered to be something of a buffoon. The quintessential aristocrat, he wanted for nothing and had few ambitions beyond sleeping with beautiful people, writing middling poetry, and drinking fine spirits. In short, he was a useless dandy—or, at least, he had been. In the last year, speculations about his health and finances had replaced the accounts of his lavish parties. He'd simply vanished from the Cernosian social scene, as if he'd lost interest in it all overnight.

Strange, all of it. But nothing more so than this letter. Despite his waning stardom, he was still one of the biggest celebrities in Cernos, and Wren was nobody. What could someone like Alistair Lowry have to offer her? With curiosity overcoming her, she peeled open the envelope as if preparing to trigger a trap. Meticulous looping handwriting shone in dark ink on the page.

Dear Ms. Southerland,

I hope this letter finds you well. Let me begin by saying that I reach out to you with the greatest humility. Your reputation as a healer and a surgeon precedes you. But before I prattle on about my great admiration of your profession, let me first arrive at the point. I am in desperate need of your talents.

A sickness has decimated my staff, and just when I believed it had finished with me, my favorite servant fell gravely ill. I'd be absolutely gutted if he succumbed to it, and I'm already quite beside myself. While the local healers have done the best they can, they still have no idea how to cure him. Granted, this high in the mountains, it's quite isolated (and isolating!). I find myself wondering what good any of our advancements are if they can't save lives; all anyone seems to care about here is engineering. A horrible bore, believe me.

When I began inquiring about Danubian physicians, your name came up time and time again. I am not a man who believes in coincidences. Hence, this letter. What I propose is this: Come work for me. I will house you and entertain you when I can. You will treat his illness, and when he's well, I'll reward you however you please. While I am happy to send you on your way with wheelbarrows full of cash and my undying gratitude, I'll be candid. I've heard of your, shall we say, misfortune, and I believe I can help you.

It may come as a surprise to you that we Cernosians do care about the plight of our neighbors. I've watched Danubians and Vesrians tear each other apart for nearly three decades, and this armistice filled me with hope. However, it seems tensions are running high again with the disappearance of your soldiers. Matters of state have never much interested me, but wars have bloodied this continent long enough. Even I can see it is time we set aside our differences.

I want to broker an alliance between our nations, and I have reached out to you to discuss the matter with the queen. Writing to her directly was too risky, lest this letter be intercepted and misinterpreted.

While we can never hope to compete with your magic, we do have funds and weapons to lend to your cause. Our support will bolster Danu's military—and dissuade our Vesrian neighbors from any further acts of violence. Let us never forget who started this war to begin with, or whose god demands bloodshed. I fear unchecked, they will never stop.

Forgive me for being light on the details, but it is unsafe to discuss such sensitive matters over post. Please send a response to the enclosed address as soon as you can. If you accept, I'll send a carriage to escort you here. I await your answer with bated breath. I fear my servant has little time left.

Warmest regards,
Lord Alistair Lowry III

Wren reread the letter three times before she set it down.

This was her chance to redeem herself. Her chance to prove herself useful again.

If she secured Lowry's support, she could stop this war before it even began. Isabel would have no choice but to recognize that Wren deserved her place on the Guard. With her position restored, she could be with Una again—if not as her lover, then as her right hand. That, she told herself, was enough. It had always been enough. It still stung that Una chose her career over *them,* but whatever love Wren could get was better than none at all. She would show Una she deserved it.

It was so simple. Cure a man's illness, come home a hero.

And it was far, far too good to be true.

Heloise was right. Why would he write to *her*? Since the war had cleared out the Guard, Wren was among the more seasoned healers. And she possessed surgical skills and medical knowledge that surpassed most other medics, who focused most of their training on mastering the Touch. But his offer . . . It was too vague, too warm.

This was Lord Alistair Lowry III, whose fame came from his scandals, not his cunning. Even in Danu, everyone had heard about the time he had drunkenly vomited into the grand duchess's lap at a dinner party, or how a jilted lover once burned his effigy on the lawn and ruined the Duke of Matthonwy's birthday. She had her misgivings.

But if this was her one chance, she fully intended to take it. Then again, if she accepted Lowry's offer and left without permission, she'd be court-martialed for desertion.

A crime punishable by death, at best.

Which meant she would have to go to the queen first. The very thought of facing her again made Wren want to crumble into dust. But this time, at least, she had leverage. Tentative hope bloomed within her. Isabel didn't care a whit for her, but surely she'd set aside their grudge for the greater good. Lowry was offering them an alliance and military support, and Goddess knew Danu sorely needed both.

When I bring this letter to her, she'll be pleased with me.

Wren ought to have shaken herself for entertaining such a naïve thought. But was it truly so foolish to hope? Lowry had reached out to Danu because of *her*—because he recognized her talent in spite of her failures. Maybe his acknowledgment would finally convince Isabel to see her worth, too.

Wren pulled a sheet of parchment from the drawer and drafted a request for an audience with the Queen of Danu. By the end of the night, she received a response, stamped with the royal seal in glittering silver wax.

1000 hours. Do not be late.

CHAPTER FIVE

Although it had only been a week since she left Knockaine, Wren had nearly forgotten the *noise* in the heart of it, the suffocating press of the crowds. Crashing down over her was the chatter of pedestrians and the nicker of horses; the clatter of carriage wheels on cobblestones; the screech of brass bands; and cabbies' shouted conversations from across the road.

Wren followed the flow of traffic along the narrow streets, carried along in a sea of petticoats. She swore as she dodged out of the way of a carriage that nearly crushed her foot, earning a scandalized look from the woman in front of her.

She was already sweating beneath her itchy tunic and traveling cape. This city was always bustling—a gift, sometimes, to melt into a crowd as faceless and blank as fog—but this struck a new fever pitch. The air thrummed with an infectious, almost ecstatic energy. One she hadn't sensed in what seemed like years.

Danubians hadn't had much cause to celebrate lately.

It wasn't a holiday, as far as Wren could remember, and it couldn't be the snow, as rare as it was. Thick flakes fluttered down from the cracked slate of the sky, black with soot and acrid with pollution.

All along Sroth Street, brassy-voiced boys sold papers from overturned crates and the heavy bases of iron streetlamps. People thronged them, as hungry for today's news as they usually were for the mulled wine peddled in the market barrows farther downriver. As Wren craned her neck to catch a glimpse of the headline, someone hurrying by checked her shoulder. Her bag—red letter and all—landed with a wet *slap* in the slush. Wren readied an insult while she straightened her habit's coif, but the man dipped down to retrieve her bag for her.

"So sorry, Sister." He grinned at her from beneath his mustache. "Have a blessed day."

Wren stared incredulously at his retreating back. No one was ever that nice here.

Clutching her bag close, she continued toward the harbor, where the North Tower turned its watchful glass eyes over the sea. It was a monstrosity of a building, all jagged spires and imposing black stone. It was by far the tallest building in the city, reaching into the snow-laden clouds as if it meant to pull the Goddess herself to the earth. Wren understood why the queen had made it her home. From the window in her office, she could see all of Knockaine stretched out beneath her like a chess board. Isabel had fashioned herself into a goddess in her own right, removed and all-seeing.

Along with the stench of salt and sweat, the crowds only grew thicker as Wren drew nearer to the Tower. People lingered in intersections and filled alleyways. They buried their faces in the paper, jostling their neighbors and tripping over their own feet. They hugged. They wept openly. They stumbled out of bars with their slurred, singsong voices bouncing off the cobblestone streets.

Wren couldn't fathom what news had stirred everyone like this. For weeks, the headlines had all been the same: portents of war and heart-wrenching accounts from the families of the missing soldiers.

Maybe someone found them. Maybe Una could finally come home.

Her appointment with the queen was in twenty minutes, but she couldn't bear not knowing. Shoving her way through the crowd, she purchased a newspaper and ducked beneath an unoccupied awning to read.

Nestled among advertisements for gold-plated spoons and malt vinegar, gossip columns and theater announcements, was a portrait. It had been years since she last saw Hal Cavendish's face, but it was unmistakably him. Everything about him oozed imperiousness, from the downturn of his full lips to his bored, coal-black stare. On reflex, she tore her eyes away from his deadly gaze—and tripped over the headline.

"REAPER" HAL CAVENDISH FOURTH VESRIAN
THIS YEAR TO DISAPPEAR; TENSIONS RISE AS
VESRIA TURNS TO DANU FOR ANSWERS

Wren hadn't known Vesrian soldiers were vanishing, too. And while the news troubled her—confused her, really—she could not stop herself from grinning at the first part of the headline.

Hal Cavendish, missing. How could they get so lucky?

At nineteen years old, he was the favored candidate to become the next grand magistrate, and Wren shuddered to think what horrors would come of Hal's reign. To please their ravenous god, Vesrians held elections that were little more than blood sport. Every five years, each of the eight ruling families put forth a candidate whose worthiness to lead was tested in combat. This year, however, Hal would be the ninth mage—and the first Cavendish in two generations—to stake his life for power.

The magic in the Cavendish bloodline had run dry with Hal's grandfather, and true to Vesria's brutish customs, his family had been stripped of its title and barred from the magisterium. Now, Hal would slaughter and intimidate his way to glory among the aristocracy. A sordid redemption, indeed. Who, after all, would be fool enough to challenge the Reaper of Vesria? No one knew how many Danubians he'd killed. And even before joining the war, he'd committed atrocities. Rumor had it the Vesrian military academy graduated only half their recruits. The other half died, slain by their own classmates in a tournament.

Good riddance, she thought. *One less monster left in this world.*

"Anything interesting?" Una asked.

Wren whirled toward the sound of her voice. It took a moment to process that it was Una—really Una—standing there. She almost didn't recognize her in civilian clothes: a black tie and knee-length coat against a crisp white shirt. In the hazy light, her amber eyes had darkened to the warm, rich color of syrup, and her black hair shone starkly against the gathering snowfall. It dusted her eyelashes, melted into the wool of her jacket.

"Una." She surged forward and crushed her into a hug. Una, predictably, stiffened, but right now, Wren didn't care. She would hear no protests. "You're home. You're alive."

"Of course I am." Una extricated herself from Wren's arms. "I said I'd come back."

"You did, but—"

"It's only been a week."

"I was stricken with separation anxiety."

"Clearly."

Wren bit her lip. It was almost overwhelming to have her back. She wanted to extract every detail about the mission from her. She wanted to tell her to never leave her behind again. But she couldn't be late. "I have a meeting with the queen. Walk with me a while?"

"Lead the way."

Una fell into step beside her, and their conversation tapered into an uneasy silence. The major had always possessed the single-mindedness of a steam-engine train, but today, she wielded it like a weapon. Something about the upward cant of her chin, the rhythmic *clack* of her boots on the street, split the crowds in twain. Nothing broke her focus or her grimly disinterested expression. Not the workers hoisting protest signs outside factory gates. Not the merchants winding up wheezing clockwork trinkets, shouting, "A marvel all the way from Cernos, Sister!" Not the market stalls brimming with pears and glazed pastries.

She was avoiding something, and Wren would get it out of her one way or another. Nudging Una's shoulder with her own, she said, "So? Tell me everything."

Their surroundings must have become significantly more interesting. Una was staring determinedly at the Tower in the distance. Thick gray clouds had consumed it until only the barest hints of its intricate openwork spires pierced through, as lacy and intricate as the queen's gowns. By the looks of it, they'd be buried in snow soon.

"He got away."

Wren's heart sunk. How could the boy have escaped from Una *twice*? All she could say was, "Oh."

"We pursued the trail until it vanished near the Cernosian border. I expected the queen to be furious, but she wasn't." Una set her jaw. "She called off the investigation entirely."

A gust of wind off the river chilled Wren to the bone. She stopped dead in her tracks. "She's giving up on them?"

Una's face twisted with sorrow. "Yes."

If Wren let her eyes go hazy, she could still imagine Byers beside her with his ridiculous shock of blond hair, the cherry-red end of his cigarette. How could someone so vibrant just be gone? "But *you* can't."

"I don't have the luxury of following my heart. If you want your position back, I have to follow her orders."

Wren couldn't believe what she was hearing. Seven soldiers from Danu and Vesria altogether had vanished, including Hal Cavendish. And if each side was determined to blame the other . . . "Then it's only a matter of time before the armistice ends. We'll go to war over this, won't we?"

"It seems that way, yes." Una snatched the newspaper from her, curling her lip as she scanned the headline. "I find it all too convenient. Seven soldiers are missing. The grand magistrate accuses Danu, the queen accuses Vesria, and a war will break out because neither of them can see past the end of their own nose."

"You really believe that?" Wren asked. "You don't think they did it?"

"Absolutely not. I refuse to believe it's this simple," Una said sharply, but her anger was directed elsewhere. "I think it's more likely that we have a common enemy. But the queen won't admit her advisors, and she certainly won't listen to my counsel."

Wren detected the note of hurt in Una's voice. On paper, Una had no business offering her counsel. What was a mid-ranked military officer to a queen? But Isabel had taken a liking to her over the years. Sometimes, Wren felt blindsided by their similarities. Their ruthlessness, their righteousness, their uncompromising ideals. In many ways, Una was as close to a daughter as Isabel would ever have.

"You know as well as I do that she'll never rest until she defeats them," Wren said. "She wants a war."

"Then Parliament is spineless if they concede." Parliament had demanded the ceasefire for the well-being of the country, but an outraged populace and the papers' claim of an outright act of warfare would make it difficult to uphold. "I despise Vesria as much as anyone, but we're all doomed the moment we replace common sense with emotion. There's something else going on here."

The silence between them buzzed like tinnitus.

Wren didn't know what she believed. But if not Vesria, there were no other logical suspects. The entire world had distanced themselves from the Danu-Vesrian wars, and their nearest neighbor was Cernos. That boy with the broken arm possessed magic—she had felt it crackle in the air when he struck her—and Cernosians, as a rule, did not. Besides, just as Heloise said, Cernos kept to itself. Ruled by an oligarchy of dukes, it was a largely atheistic nation and refused to bloody its hands with religious squabbles and land disputes. When it came to magic, all the technology and wealth in the world could not guarantee a casualty-free intervention.

"Who else would it be?" Wren asked tentatively.

"I don't know." Wren couldn't ignore the doubt coloring her voice. Una was nothing if not unwavering, but before she could push, Una continued. "But my primary concern is my new assignment. Now that Cavendish has been reported missing, the queen hopes to find him alive and use him as leverage. If I'm the one to capture him, I'll get back into her good graces."

"A solid course of action." Wren's throat felt dry, but she managed to keep her tone positive. "And a dangerous one."

"Don't you start worrying about me again."

"How can I not when you clearly have a death wish?" She grabbed her by the sleeve and tugged her closer. "No one has faced Cavendish and lived."

"I don't need to look at him to strike him down."

Wren huffed in frustration. "Your pride isn't worth your life. You can't take this mission."

Una yanked her arm back. "I can, and I will."

"Una, *please.*" Desperation crept into her voice. "Do you know how hard this has been for me? Every day, I open the paper and pray I don't see your name. I worry enough about you going missing. Now you're telling me I have to worry about you getting killed by the Reaper?"

"Wren." Her voice was hard, unyielding. "I don't have a choice."

"Don't you?"

"No," Una said, so firmly she startled them both. "This isn't about my pride. It's about you."

"Me?"

"I told you before. I need you by my side."

Something aching and fearful and familiar flashed in her eyes, so faint Wren wondered if she'd imagined it. But no, she hadn't. She had never imagined that look. Not even on that one morning, when Una had told her *never again* as though the words were broken glass in her mouth. But then, as if realizing she'd slipped, Una blinked a cold edge back into her gaze.

Again the soldier. Again the girl with no weaknesses.

Wren knew Una loved her. Una's love was glimpses of vulnerability. It was raising her sword against anyone who dared threaten Wren. It was a cup of chamomile tea, and it was lying to the queen. But she also knew Una could only ever love her at a distance.

"I can't be with you if you don't come back," Wren said quietly.

Una heaved a weary sigh. "I'm not going to die. I know this has been hard for you, but be reasonable."

I know you want more from me.

Wren drew in a shaky breath. Deep down, she knew Una was right. Still, she ached for more: more support, more sympathy, more *anything*. Anything to let her know Una really cared, that she valued Wren's feelings. But asking Una to discuss things like *emotions* was as good as asking her to carve open her own chest.

"I don't want to fight with you right now," Wren said. "We can talk about this later."

Una looked incredibly relieved—and also incredibly tired. "Fine."

"Fine."

They walked until they arrived at the wrought-iron gates of the North Tower. Both of them lingered, clearly dwelling on the things left unsaid. Snow clumped thick in Una's hair now, a crown of sparkling white, and Wren thought she might not mind if they stayed frozen here forever.

Una broke the silence first. Wren half expected another harsh rebuke, but when she spoke, Una sounded tentative and almost gentle. "I'll visit you before I leave."

"I'd like that." Wren paused. "Don't wait too long. I missed you."

Una didn't respond immediately. Instead, she removed three gleaming black cuff links. As she rolled up her shirtsleeve, she revealed the long, muscled line of her forearm. And there, pale against her skin, was a scar. "I found the medic on my last mission lacking."

Gasping, Wren grabbed her arm and inspected the new shiny band of tissue. Not that it mattered cosmetically, but any healer worth their salt could close a wound without leaving a scar. "Why would you tell me that? Now I'll worry more!"

"I'm not trying to worry you. I'm trying to tell you you're missed."

Wren scoffed. "By whom?"

"Me." It was nearly inaudible.

"A confession! Extracted under duress, judging by that tone, but I'll take it." Wren checked her pocket watch. Five minutes until her meeting. "I have to go."

"What's your meeting about?"

Wren felt for the letter in her bag. "My reinstatement."

Una frowned. "Remember what you promised me."

"Nothing reckless. I know." Wren lowered her eyes. "And you?"

"I'll come back to you." Una gave her a wry salute. "Try not to worry so much. I leave in a few days. I'll stop by the abbey before then."

And with that, she was gone.

Today, Isabel's pale hair was ornately fashioned. It was braided around her head like a crown, woven with tiny white flowers and shiny silver ribbon. She looked divine and impossibly sleek, not a single strand out of place. Not a single imperfection, no matter how hard Wren looked.

She couldn't help noticing the details, for she'd been standing at attention for almost ten minutes while the queen read an interminably long document. Through it all, Isabel wore a faint, self-satisfied smile. The Paper Queen had consented to a rare meeting, but far more than punctuality, she appreciated torture. Every rustle of the pages sliced into Wren's patience, her pride. Every *tick* of the Tower's clocks rattled her bones.

Nose still buried in her report, Isabel said, "Sister Wren."

Wren startled, but recovered by dropping into her most obsequious curtsy. "Your Majesty."

"Your calling on me was timely. I have good news for you."

Wren tried to quell her stubborn glimmer of hope. There was no way Isabel would actually restore her position so soon after her suspension. Wren clenched and unclenched her fists to work the blood back into her fingers and braced herself for the worst. "Good news?"

"I've been thinking about what to do with you. You have been surprisingly patient."

Surprisingly. Wren's lips twitched in annoyance. "Thank you, Your Majesty."

"You show too much promise as a healer to be wasted." Isabel finally laid down her stack of papers and folded her hands. "As you well know, the miners' strike has vexed me for months. In recent negotiations, they've requested safer working conditions, and as a part of that, a medic to prevent avoidable casualties. I believe it will be a good placement for you."

Wren's knees almost buckled beneath her. This was a sentence far worse than dismissal. It wasn't hard labor, but it was no less deadly. Wren had heard horrific stories of workers crushed under rubble or suffering under a lifetime of lung disease. It was a future as long and dark and brutal as a mining shaft. Blood rushed in her ears, and everything sounded muted and garbled. Like she was underground. Already buried alive.

A sudden, horrible truth struck her. Isabel had never intended to reinstate her.

How could she be so naïve? Since her suspension, she'd struggled to do the right thing, the responsible thing. To do nothing reckless. And for what? No matter what Wren did, it would make no difference. With Isabel, there were no second chances. There was no mercy. Every path ended here: with Isabel disposing of her once and for all.

"That is very generous of you." Wren tried to speak calmly, but it came out surly and strange. As always, her emotions betrayed her.

"I understand it's not what you envisioned for yourself, but you will do well there."

"Your Majesty, if I may propose an alternative." Wren pulled the letter out of her bag. "I received this yesterday."

Wren watched Isabel take in the red coloration, the gold-leaf antlers. All the tendons in her neck strained against her papery skin. Wren didn't exactly expect happiness—maybe surprise, considering Cernos had never answered her requests for aid against the Vesrians. But the queen only glared at the envelope with a weary exasperation.

"What is that?" she said without inflection.

"It's a letter from Cernos."

"From whom?"

"Lord Alistair Lowry." Her face burned under her aunt's scrutiny. "He has a job for me. There is a disease in his household."

Isabel let out a harsh note of laughter, as high as shattering glass. "Lord Alistair Lowry? That fool?"

"But, Your Majesty—"

"He is mocking me. He and his people think themselves better than us, above our plight. This is clearly one of his games. One I don't intend to play."

"Forgive me for speaking out of turn, but this seems to be the opportunity you've been waiting for. Why would you turn down the first contact from Cernos in years? He's offering a political union in exchange for my help. His support could prevent a war. It could save lives."

"If I want your counsel, I will ask for it. You will not address me so informally."

"Your Majesty, I insist you reconsider! For the good of Danu, we cannot turn him away. We've already lost too many—"

"Allow me to be more blunt." Isabel rose from behind her desk. She dripped with clinking silver jewelry and venom. Even in ivory silk and a lacy muslin collar, she was terrifying. "Let us assume that Lowry requests your service in earnest. Let us assume that you would be the first person to establish contact with Cernos. With your track record, you're sooner to start a war than to end one."

"I know how to handle myself in—"

"You've done nothing but disappoint me." Isabel's voice grew sharp. "You're foolhardy. You're emotional. You're easily manipulated. You are the very last person I would consider sending on an assignment like this."

Every word was a needle, each one piercing deeper than the last. Wren forced herself to swallow her anger, and it burned all the way down. But the queen was not finished.

"And you are so very naïve. What did you believe you could do? You have no training in diplomacy or politics, no grace. You have nothing of my sister in you, and you tarnish her legacy." Her silver eyes flashed like steel. "She was a brilliant strategist, a fierce warrior—beloved by her people and feared by her enemies. Your no-name father was her one mistake. It was he who got her killed in the war. A descendant of the Goddess—a *queen*—throwing away her life to protect a man who grew up in a bar. I cannot fathom it."

Tears stung the backs of Wren's eyes—but *no*. No. She would not cry. She would not give Isabel the satisfaction, the power, of hurting her again.

Isabel only sighed as she opened a drawer on her desk and retrieved a silver case full of matches. She struck one, and the firelight gilded the sheer outer layer of her dress, glimmered on every silver ring and diamond on her throat.

"I see him when I look at you." Isabel lit a candelabra on her desk. As each flame sprang to life, the shadows deepened beneath her eyes. "His hair. His eyes. His insolence. And yet my sister gave you her name, and you carry it as if you deserve it. You dare to come before me as if you are fit to carry out the work of a princess. You are *not*."

Still, Wren said nothing.

"Now," Isabel said. She blew out the match, its heat still shimmering like a veil over her face. "Shall I arrange for your Severance or will you accept your new assignment?"

It wasn't an option to refuse the assignment. She only wanted to hear the admission of defeat. And even if Wren did refuse for the sake of her pride, she'd sentence herself to a life without magic, a life half lived and entirely wasted. Without it, she would never be anything. She would never be worthy of love.

"I accept."

"Good." Isabel stretched out her hand. "Give me the letter."

"No," Wren whispered.

"I will not ask again."

Wren slammed it onto the desk. Isabel dipped its edge into the flame of the candles flickering at her side. As the envelope withered and blackened, Isabel dropped it into a metal bowl. There went all Wren's hope, crumbled to ashes.

"That will be all." Isabel was barely audible, her words borne up and away in the writhing smoke.

"Thank you, Your Majesty." Wren managed to lift her chin and marched out with grim purpose. But in the main hall, the panic she had staved off pounced and crushed her under its weight.

Soon, Una would leave on a mission to pursue the Reaper of Vesria. If her new healer wasn't competent enough to not leave scars, for the Goddess's sake, what hope did they have of protecting her against Hal Cavendish's magic? Soon, Una could be another name on a headline. Another tragic story to fuel Isabel's war. Another blow Wren couldn't take.

She would never forgive herself if Una didn't come home.

And she would not let herself rot in that mine. She would not let Isabel win.

The steady *tick, tick, tick* of the clocks chipped away at her restraint. She had half a mind to tear them all from the walls and hurl them across the room. She took perverse satisfaction in imagining the shower of springs and gears, how Isabel and her attendants' mouths would gape in a collective, silent scream.

She needed to get outside. She needed to get out of this habit and away from its suffocating heat. Wren shoved her way through the door, and when she stumbled outside, she sucked in huge gulps of air. The sky pressed too close, but she wasn't afraid. She was furious.

Her anger brewed the entire walk back to the abbey, hardened by the whip of the snow and wind against her face. When she at last made it to her room, she cast her satchel aside, tore off her habit, and tossed them both on the ground. The fabric lay there like a skinned animal, alongside a slip of paper that fluttered from her bag.

The return address that had been enclosed in Lowry's letter.

Wren nearly threw herself on the floor and cradled the note against her chest like a newborn. Tears prickled the backs of her eyelids. She could still accept the offer. It wasn't too late. Once Wren secured the alliance, Isabel would come to understand the service she'd done the crown. She'd have no choice but to reinstate her.

It was the only hope she had left.

Wren sat at her desk, pulled out a sheet of parchment, and dipped her quill in ink. She hesitated for only a second before she reminded herself that she had been dismissed for insubordination. She was no stranger to disobedience and was well-known for acting recklessly.

With careful strokes, she composed a response:

Dear Lord Lowry,

Thank you for your letter. I am grateful for your kind words about my work and your condolences for my, as you say, misfortune. Mostly, however, I am sorry to hear of your servant's illness. To be brief, I would be honored to accept your gracious offer and am intrigued by your proposal. While I cannot be sure what ails your servant until I examine him myself, I am confident I can be of assistance. Please consider me at your service and thank you again for your trust.

Faithfully,
Wren Southerland

The wet ink on the page gleamed. It was a beautiful thing, dark and treasonous. She was not only disregarding the queen's orders but lying to her as well. When she failed to report for duty at the mines, Isabel would figure out soon enough where she was. But by the time she realized it, it would be too late.

This wasn't just about securing an alliance. It wasn't just about Una or Byers. This was about her. Running away might make her a coward, but at least she would be free.

CHAPTER SIX

On the third night, another red letter arrived by personal delivery. Wren slid a knife into the envelope's lip with trembling, overeager fingers. The note within was brief.

You're truly Goddess-sent. Be ready to leave tonight at 8. A carriage will be waiting for you a mile down the westbound road from the abbey.

—A

Excitement and terror struck her at once. Tonight was both far too late and far too soon to leave. She hadn't prepared. She hadn't packed. She hadn't figured out what to tell Una.

Una. She'd written to tell Wren she was coming to visiting hours tonight. How could Wren have forgotten?

All young healers were sent to the abbey for training before taking vows or enlisting in the military. The prospect of sitting in that stuffy reception room, surrounded by weepy apprentices begging their families to take them home, was enough to make her break out in hives. Besides, how was she supposed to face Una now? Striking a bargain with a foreign nobleman against the queen's orders was perhaps the very worst of Wren's bad, impulsive ideas. Una would take one look at her face and read the guilt there like a brand.

The shame of disappointing Una again might crush her. Wren couldn't say goodbye if she couldn't tell the truth. And she definitely couldn't tell the truth. Una had stood by her through a host of misdemeanors over the years—backtalking and disobeying her orders—but Wren had no doubt she'd draw the line at desertion.

As much as it hurt, her only option was to slip away unseen.

Before the bell tolled the start of visiting hours, Wren dressed in her civvies—a pleated gown, fur-lined traveling cape, and boots and gloves of bronze leather—and packed her bags full of medical supplies and warm clothes. When she'd finished, she crept through the darkened hallways and made her way to the courtyard, watched only by the waning moon and the gaunt silhouettes of trees bent-backed like crones. Walking out the front gate would draw too much attention, so she'd forge her own exit. She tossed her bags one by one over the courtyard wall, wincing at the wet thuds of her bags in the snow.

After a breathless count to ten, no one came running.

Like a runaway child, Wren climbed the rickety ivy trellis and heaved herself over the wall. She struck the earth on the other side, the shock reverberating up her knees. But she was too giddy with nerves and the taste of freedom to feel it much. No more suffocation by incense. No more waiting for someone else to fix her problems. No more exhortations for patience.

Her fate was hers.

Out here, nothing stirred. Snow-smothered fields sprawled for miles, silvered by wan moonlight and broken only by the hulking black shape of Knockaine in the distance. The wind whistled through the abbey's towers. Cold bit through her cloak, sunk its jaws down to the bone. It spread through her limbs, slow as rot, and if she stayed still too long, she feared she'd go brittle and crack.

It was the kind of night made for keeping warm—the kind Wren and Una might have spent at a pub, drunk on mulled wine and each other's company. She shoved the reverie away. No good could come of thinking on what she no longer had.

Gathering up her bags, she picked her way to the road and began to walk. Her breath wreathed her face with every shaky exhale, and as she struggled against the wet gusts of wind, it began to flurry. In the whorls of snow, Wren swore she saw faces, indistinct in the darkness. But there was nothing out there but the night, the whisper of the half-frozen grass in the wind. No one but her, traveling by the cold light of the moon—and the distant burn of a lantern bleeding orange onto the snow.

Her carriage.

Still, Wren couldn't shake the slithery feeling of being watched. *It's only paranoia,* she told herself. Not even the stars surveilled her tonight. But as she walked, she could hear the rhythmic crunch of footsteps in the snow, perfectly in time with hers.

No, it wasn't paranoia. Someone was tailing her.

"Wren?"

She would recognize Una's voice anywhere.

Wren willed the earth to open and swallow her whole. Of course Una intercepted her. Of course she would ruin everything.

Sharpening all her arguments into weapons, Wren turned to face her. But every harsh word melted on her tongue when she saw Una standing in the moon's white glow. There was the girl Wren cherished more than her own life, staring at her as if she'd done something awful. As if she'd hurt her on purpose. As if she could.

"Una."

"Shall we keep walking?" Una said neutrally. Wren had expected anger, maybe open hostility. But this frightened her far more.

Without waiting for a response, Una took one of her suitcases from her and continued down the road. The medals on Una's pristine black tunic twinkled cold as frost. "You weren't at visiting hours."

"I guess I forgot."

Una heaved a frustrated sigh. "What are you doing, Wren?"

Wren gestured helplessly to the empty field around them. "Going for a walk?"

"Right." Una's eyes flitted from Wren's suitcase to her civilian's cloak. As if speaking to a spooked horse, she said, "I heard what happened. We can talk about this."

"What did you hear?" Wren kept her voice breezy, her gaze fixed straight ahead.

"The queen shouldn't have moved you from the abbey. But as soon as I capture Cavendish, I will see that she listens to reason. She'll reinstate you and reauthorize our investigation. Together, we'll find out what happened to Byers."

"But what if you don't?"

"What do you mean, *what if I don't*?"

Wren stopped and dropped her suitcase into the snow. It fell heavier now, in thick flakes that clotted on her eyelashes. "What if you don't convince her? What if you don't find Cavendish at all? Or worse. What if you do and he kills you?"

A shadow passed over Una's face. "That won't happen."

"You can't guarantee that."

"You can't either," Una said sharply.

"So you expect me to go obediently to the mines and wait like a dog for you to come back for me?"

"You don't have any other choice. Just be—"

"I have been patient! I followed your orders this time, and look where it's gotten me." Wren drew in a deep, steadying breath. When she closed her eyes, all she could see was that scar on Una's arm, the only evidence she needed to prove that this was a risk worth taking. "The queen doesn't care about what happened to Byers and the others. War is coming. But if I leave now, I believe I can stop it."

"Are you listening to yourself?" Una hissed. "You sound delusional. I know you're grieving, but this—"

"Maybe I am delusional." Wren canted her chin. "Do you trust me?"

There was an unspoken plea in that question: *Choose me.*

The ensuing silence carried the weight of her every anxiety.

Why had she even asked? Why put herself through the agony of demanding an answer? In every painful beat of her heart was *I love you, I love you, I love you.* By now, Wren had hoped to be stronger, but she was shattering all over again. Una would never care for her the way Wren did for her. She would always choose her duty over Wren. No matter what, loyal soldiers like her delivered deserters to their queen.

"Just say what you came to say." Wren squared up to Una, but with her height disadvantage, she only felt small and foolish. "It's written all over your face."

"You're making a huge mistake."

"So let me make it."

"You're acting like a child." Una's every word dripped with acid. "Go back to the abbey. Now."

"You can't give me orders anymore, Major. I've been reassigned."

"You may not be under my command, but you're in contempt of the queen's orders." Una was nose to nose with her now. "If you take one more step down this road, I will arrest you."

The snowflakes seemed to hang suspended in the air, as if the whole world held its breath. Wren clutched the handle of her bag as if her grip could hold her together. "You're not serious."

"Of course I'm serious. If I have to choose between keeping you safe in jail or hunting you down as a criminal, I'll make the same decision every time." Una's eyes shone, as hard and black as jet in the dark. "Why are you doing this?"

"This is my last resort."

"No, it's not. How can I make you understand that this isn't an option at all? It's a death sentence."

So is going to the mines. So is losing you.

"If you ever cared about me, let me go and get out of my way."

"No. If you do this—if you desert—the queen will send me after you." Una was more undone than Wren had ever seen her. Her voice was raw, almost pleading. "That's my *job*. Do you think that's going to be easy for me?"

Wren couldn't do this. She couldn't do this if Una was breaking because of her. But if she pushed her away, maybe it would make this cleaner, easier. Wren squeezed her eyes shut and gave voice to those old, insidious fears inside her.

If you slip up, if you're not useful to her anymore, she'll abandon you just like Isabel did.

She doesn't love you because you're a burden.

"Honestly?" Wren asked. "Yes. I bet it'll be a relief for you."

It might have been a trick of the light or Wren's own helpless imagination. But for a moment, in her knee-high boots and black, war-decorated coat, Una looked less like a soldier in uniform and more like a child in costume. Then, like cooling steel, her expression hardened. "I see there's no reasoning with you like this."

No pleading, no appeal to her emotions, would move Una now. "Likewise."

Una rested her hand on the pommel of her saber. The metal guard flashed, and in it, Wren saw the reflection of the white emptiness around them. Wren's heart thrummed wildly with fear.

She's actually going to fight me.

"Wait. You're right. I haven't thought this through enough."

Una did not drop her guard. Her eyes burned with barely contained hurt. Wren had to *leave,* but how could she part with Una like this? She should have known she could never walk out of Knockaine unscathed. She'd built her life around Una, had loved her, had sworn to serve her. It bound them together at a cellular level. What would it take to sever a bond like that?

"I'll go back to the abbey." Wren's voice wavered. "I'll even go to the Tower if that's what you want."

A cold wind whipped across the field, lifting Una's hair. Snow swirled around them, glittering like crushed starlight. The distance between them was unnavigable.

Una let her arm drop to her side. "No. Just let me take you to the abbey."

"Thank you." Wren staggered forward a step, dropped her suitcase, and drew her into a tight hug. "I love you."

"Wren," Una said hoarsely. In the end, that was what did Wren in. The sound of her voice, so tender and strained. The tension in her muscles, somewhere between flinching back and pulling her close.

Wren cradled the back of Una's head in both shaking hands. The spinal cord was a tender thing, an ovoid hotbed of nerves and magical channels. The smallest energetic disruption could overwhelm the entire nervous system. It was forbidden to use the Healing Touch to harm another person. But to protect her friends—to stop this war—she needed to break a few rules.

Wren eased her magic into Una's cervical spine. Una jerked back, and Wren caught a glimpse of the terrifying spark in her eye. She'd seen it many times. In meetings with her superiors, ones who assumed their rank translated to competence. In basic training, when another healer once made Wren cry. In the war, when her comrades fell beside her in pools of their own blood.

Rage.

It was then Wren knew that Una would never forgive her for this. Someday, the Threefold Law would demand its recompense. As Una collapsed unconscious into Wren's arms, it felt like something vital ripped itself out of her. It *hurt,* but there was no wound. Nothing she could fix.

Wren secured Una's arm around her shoulders. She took one staggering step and almost crumpled to the ground. Goddess above, Una was heavier than she remembered, dense with muscle and weighted down by her all her regalia. Had they started manufacturing those medals out of lead?

Wren turned over her shoulder, shivering with nerves and cold. She'd only made it about a quarter mile from the abbey before Una intercepted her. Even from here, she saw the Maiden's disapproving stare from the rose window.

It took what felt like an eternity to drag Una to the gates, her breaths coming in ragged gasps. Someone would stumble upon her eventually, but she couldn't leave Una out here in the cold for long. Worrying her lip, she lowered her friend to the ground and propped her upright against the wall. Unconscious, with her lips parted and dark hair falling into her face, she looked young and frail. And so beautiful, her skin near lustrous in the silvery night.

"I'm sorry, Una." Tears made the world hazy. She tucked the loose strands of hair behind Una's ears. "I'm so sorry."

Wren rang the gate's bell. Then, she ran.

She nearly stumbled into the snowbanks as she paused to snatch up her suitcases, which lay abandoned beside Una's imprint in the snow. With every stride, her luggage bruised the backs of her legs. Her shoulders ached in protest and icicles seemed to cut into her lungs with every panicked breath, but she did not slow until she saw the carriage, an open-fronted glass coach lit by the flicker of a lantern.

It stood beside the black bend of the River Muri, a churning mirror that shattered the moon's pale light. The four white horses hitched to it snorted, their breath curling upward like smoke from a snuffed candle. A man in his fifties stood beside it, dressed in a worn brown coat and a tall hat.

"Ms. Southerland?" the driver asked, clearly flustered by her appearance. "I'd begun to worry you got lost."

"Not lost," she wheezed. "Just delayed. Sorry."

"Can I help you with anything?" he asked, bewildered, as she loaded her belongings into the open trunk. "I'm Basil, by the way."

"A pleasure." Wren opened the passenger door. "We have to go. Now."

He glanced over her shoulder, squinting at the abbey in the distance. "Right. I'll move us along as quickly as I can. There's a storm coming, and we won't make it to the estate if we delay."

Wren climbed into the carriage and slammed the door shut behind her. Basil took his place on the box seat, and with a snap of the reins, the horses galloped into the flurries and gloom. It would take a few hours for Una to awaken, and a few more still for the news of Wren's disappearance to hit.

By then, the storm would have gained force, and Wren would be long gone.

Wren pressed her face to the window. She hardly recognized her reflection in the glass. Although she had the same thick eyebrows and the same broad forehead, the harried girl staring back at her was a deserter.

Wren felt dead with exhaustion, but the rough shape of her breaths let her know, despite it all, she was alive. Without Una, without her job, she was still Wren. A Wren composed of all the worst, unlovable parts of herself. But still Wren.

CHAPTER SEVEN

After a restless sleep, Wren found her heart scabbed over in the daylight. It wasn't enough to feel entirely manageable, but it was enough to keep her from crumbling. To stave off the guilt, to keep herself from being torn apart, she'd have to keep herself busy. So she let her focus shift to her immediate needs. She let herself notice that she was cold and hungry and sore from hours of leaning against the door of the carriage. At least one of those she could fix. With a pulse of healing magic, she rubbed away the soreness in her muscles. It was a superfluous, careless use of magic, but the tingle of it on her fingertips filled her with relief. She still had it, all hers. She hadn't been Severed. She wasn't in a mine.

She was free.

The storm Basil promised hadn't arrived yet, although it clotted the sky thick and gray overhead. They wouldn't have another opportunity to rest, so they took a detour to a small Cernosian town just a few hours' ride from Lowry's estate. It was little more than a smattering of houses huddled together on the mountainside like shingles on a sloped roof.

They stopped at the only inn, the Guiding Light. Beneath its happily piping chimney hung a sign engraved with a comically beatific depiction of the Goddess. She cradled a misshapen little starburst that Wren assumed gave the inn its name. But the strangest thing was that it burned incandescently—not with gas lamps or firelight, but with a harsh glow like magic.

"How is it doing that?" Wren asked Basil as they walked the horses to the stable.

Basil squinted up at it. "It's electricity."

"Electricity," she repeated. "How does it work?"

He seemed puzzled. "Tubes and wires and generators. I'm afraid the science of it is beyond me."

Wren eyed the sign warily before he beckoned her onward. As Basil curried the horses, he said, "I just need some food and a wink of sleep, then we'll be on the road again. I don't want us to get caught in this weather. This time of year, a good snow won't thaw out until spring."

That was months from now. No one would be able to come after her anytime soon.

In her room, Wren entertained herself by flicking a switch on and off—light chasing darkness, over and over again. Then, when she'd quite perplexed herself with wondering how it worked, she warmed herself at the fireplace. Its blazing light bathed everything in a soft, hazy glow. After the brutal ride here, she longed to bask in the heat and relax.

Barely a minute passed before her stomach began twisting itself into anxious, guilty knots. She was restless by nature, as Heloise too often reminded her, and if she stayed still long enough, her grief would catch up to her. Since she had a few hours to kill, she might as well double-check her supplies. She retrieved her medical bag, a slim leather satchel, and knelt on the carpeted floor.

While most healers depended on their magic, Wren knew a truly great physician could not rely on magic alone. She liked to prepare for anything and everything, and took more of a scientific route, studying toxic plants and developing medications that could aid in the healing process. Faithful healers, meanwhile, believed themselves to be practitioners of a divine art. Psalms and scripture told of the first queen who had bound herself to the Goddess; moved by her devotion, the Goddess had blessed her with a piece of her divinity: the gift of regeneration.

The prayers of the good and righteous are powerful things, the Book of Morgane proclaimed. *Worship the Goddess, and she will take from you your sickness, your suffering.*

But magic, at its core, was nothing but a recessive trait that allowed for the manipulation of the energy that flowed through the *fola*—an energy that bound to receptors in the body's cells. Some theories posited that healing magic was the oldest kind, affording its practitioners the abilities to induce cellular regeneration and autolysis. Over time, it had evolved into more diverse, specialized branches of magic that varied from family to family. Magic like Byers's, which thickened his bones. And magic like Hal Cavendish's.

Vesrians' magic worked the same as Danubians', even though centuries of superstition had painted them as something otherworldly and wicked. Their magical bloodlines were old and powerful; in honor of their god, they arranged marriages to preserve them—as well as they could, anyway. The Cavendishes had nearly died out, and Hal was the first to manifest their magic in two generations. No one knew exactly how his abilities worked; autopsies of his victims showed little but ravaged brain chemistry, as if his gaze alone was neurotoxic. Wren shuddered at the memory of him, his eyes mirror black, the *fola* in his temples glowing silver like scars.

She put some vials back in her satchel and drank in the rest of the room. Her accommodations were plain but comfortable: solid wood floors, a downy mattress, a curtained window overlooking the jagged blue spine of the Dramlach Mountains. There was even a closet, stocked with a complete wardrobe for a young boy. Earlier, when her host had come by to bring her a pot of tea and a slice of spiced cake, Wren asked if he had a son.

At first, he'd looked utterly puzzled by the sound of Wren's accent. Then, after she repeated herself, he looked startled. "No. It's only me and my husband here."

The inn was indeed entirely empty. The silence unnerved her, as if the storm had frozen over the entire world. Earlier, she had wandered the hallway and paused outside each door. Nobody stirred within any of the rooms. Nobody made a sound. Still, she felt *watched*.

Even now.

When the crawling sensation became too much to bear, she rose from the armchair and descended into the lobby. Pulling her traveling cape tightly around herself, Wren slipped out the back door. White-barked maples and sturdy evergreens clung to the rock faces, and all around her were pale mountains as far as she could see.

A short walk through the grounds presented her with a fenced-in garden half buried in snow. The owners must have been ambitious gardeners, because it was stranger and more beautiful than any she had encountered, with colorful flowers growing in iron cages like captive finches. At the gate, a skull painted onto a wooden sign glared at her with peeling black sockets.

Its meaning was clear: *keep out, danger*. But Wren couldn't resist going in. Snooping in a Cernosian poison garden was far too good an opportunity for any healer to pass up. What Cernos lacked in magic, it made up for in harsh landscape and even harsher flora.

Wren pushed open the gate, the cold, unforgiving metal stinging her palms. She paced the neat garden rows, each marked with a plaque. There was deadly nightshade and autumn crocus, celandine and chinaberry, goldenseal and honeysuckle, hemlock and yew. And there, at the center, was a tangle of goddessblood pushing through a thin layer of snow. Wren crouched beside it and admired the membranous blue-violet petals bowing reverently over their stalks.

Goddessblood figured prominently in Danubian myths. It was said that the Goddess loved a man once. One night, he cut one of her three heads from her neck while she slept. What he did not know was that she could not die from a wound. Goddessblood sprouted from the pool of her blood, growing deadly in the succor of her bitterness and sorrow at the man's betrayal. In Cernos, however, this plant meant something else entirely. A warning to the rest of the world.

A few months ago, Wren had read a write-up of the world exhibition of arts and sciences in the paper. Cernos had showcased a gas laced with essence of goddessblood. While Cernos had never seen war due to its impassable mountains and carefully maintained neutrality, Wren could understand taking precautions. Her heart twisted when she remembered the account of the lab rats they'd tested it on, dead within seconds. On humans, it would likely only take a minute or two more. Unless someone developed an antidote.

Goddessblood grew only in harsh mountain air, so uncommon and strange in Danu that the thrill of studying it shut out Wren's scruples. Surely, no one would mind—or notice—if she took a specimen. She set her medical bag on the ground and pulled on gloves. She yanked the flower from the half-frozen dirt, and the tuber, like a fat vein, dripped clotted earth from its roots. Just as she stored the sample in her bag, a shadow fell over her.

Wren turned and squinted against the ruthlessly white sky. As her eyes adjusted to the light, the shape of the innkeeper came into focus. He was a round, kind-looking man, but the way he was looking at her now . . . He looked afraid.

"What are you doing in here?" he asked.

"Nothing! I was just . . ." Wren's face burned with embarrassment. While she hadn't expected to get caught, she should have asked first. She wasn't representing her homeland well at the moment. *So much for diplomacy.* "I'm a healer. I study poisons."

"You can't study these," he snapped. "This is my property, not a classroom."

"I'm sorry. I—" Wren fumbled for words. "I can pay you for it."

"No, no." The man pinched the bridge of his nose. "It's alright. You didn't know. Just go on inside before you catch your death out here."

Wren commanded her feet to move, but they were rooted to the spot. Why was he growing this? What use did common people have for the deadliest poison in the world? The questions died on her lips when she caught him looking past her, down at the patch of goddessblood.

"Please. Go inside." His voice was so quiet, Wren almost didn't hear him. His expression, however, would be burned into her mind. His eyes glassy, his skin ghostly pale, like he'd frozen to death in front of her. *"Go."*

Wren sprinted back to the inn, where it felt like a thousand eyes watched her from the shadows. As far as she was concerned, the sooner they got to Lowry's estate, the better.

CHAPTER EIGHT

B y midafternoon, they continued their winding way up the mountain. With nothing but darkness and flurries outside the window, Wren had little to do but wonder what kind of man her patient would be. She was used to dealing with difficult charges—soldiers had a hard time allowing anyone, especially healers, close. It was understandable, on some level. Everyone had heard of healers in high-pressure situations cauterizing the wrong artery. But her patient was a common man in the employment of a nobleman, not a soldier. Maybe he'd be pleasant.

As the day wore on and the temperatures dropped, they passed through a holloway, where skeletal trees bent over the road, their branches clasped like gnarled fingers and their knotholes watching her like crusted eyes. Everything looked the same as what had come before. They could be driving in circles for all she knew, and it was too easy to imagine getting lost in this world of endless, drifting white and gray. She trusted Basil, but after her time at the inn, anxiety dogged her every thought.

Wren unlatched her window and asked, "How can you possibly know the way?"

Basil cast her a knowing look over his shoulder. "There's only one viable way between Danu and Cernos this time of year, since they close down most of the mountain roads in winter. Don't let anyone tell you otherwise. How else do you think our borders held for the past thousand years?"

By nightfall, the tree cover broke, and the lights of a town glowed in the distance. Far above it, the jagged lines of an estate loomed. The spire atop its cupola jutted from the eddying snow like broken bone.

"Is that where we're headed?" Wren called to Basil over the wind.

"It is," he said, his voice much grimmer than before. "We've a bit farther to go now."

How could anything be lonelier and more isolated than this? Already, she longed for the smog and sprawl and noise of Knockaine. Wren wasn't a girl made to be alone; solitude armed her with too much to worry about.

She pressed her face to the window, and the cold glass bit into her forehead as she searched for any signs of life. But this late, everyone in town was likely holed up in their homes and holding their loved ones close. Tonight, Wren would be trapped with a dying man and his employer. She only prayed Lowry would be as entertaining a proprietor as his reputation promised.

"What's Lord Lowry like?"

Basil hesitated. "Eccentric."

"In a good way?"

"I like a more ordinary sort of folk." He cast his gaze to the snow-wreathed estate in the distance. "I think myself a sensible man, Ms. Southerland, but the stories one hears about that house . . ."

Wren frowned. "What kinds of stories?"

"No good ones," Basil said. "Some call it foul luck. Some folk would tell you it's haunted."

Haunted.

It was absurd. Wren hadn't believed in ghosts in years—hadn't

even thought of them since she was a child. Some of her Sisters believed a ghost lived in the abbey bell tower and would dare each other
to creep inside on interminable winter nights. Most of the time, they
only lasted a minute before they ran shrieking down the staircase.
They were nothing but games. Silly exercises of bored and overactive
imaginations, as Heloise often told them. *The Goddess gives new life
unto those who die,* she would say. *There is no such thing as ghosts.*

To Wren, it was all nonsense. She knew well enough by now that
no one ever came back from the dead.

"And what would you say as a sensible man?" Wren asked.

"I don't know. All I know is there's something not quite right
about Colwick Hall."

The carriage rattled its way onto a wooded road just as the snowfall grew thicker. Through the inky darkness, Wren looked up to
see the trees' limbs spread above her like the ever-branching vascu-
lar system of the lungs. Their trunks were bent at the waist, as if
recoiling from something buried beneath the snowbanks. Watched
by these grim mountains, Wren almost understood why people saw
spirits in these storms.

As much as she wanted to scoff at Basil, old folklore whispered
in the apprentice's quarters drifted into her thoughts. Just like that,
she was seven years old again, shivering beneath a duvet drawn up
to her ears. *To banish a ghost,* Sister Bernadette would say, candlelight flickering wildly in her eyes, *you tell it, "This place is of the
living and yours no longer."*

They traveled by dim, swaying lantern light until they reached
the end of the path. It was barred by a massive gate that stretched
between two stone pedestals linked by a wrought-iron arch. Across
it was a name punched out of metal: *Colwick Hall.*

Basil stopped to unlatch the gate. The hinge showered rust onto
the snow and stained it red. As they neared Colwick Hall, something about it called her in. Maybe it was the inevitable *size* of it,
or how at a distance, its silhouette was an absolute, perfect black.
Against the stark, snow-covered grounds, Alistair Lowry's estate
was another mountain peak.

When Basil parked the carriage in the driveway, Wren eased herself onto the ground, relishing the pop of her joints. She hardly had a chance to take in her surroundings before Basil removed her luggage from the trunk and shoved it toward her. For such a courteous coachman, he now was hurried and distant, already climbing back into the driver's seat.

"Do you want to come inside to warm up? Or to rest a little?" she asked.

"No." It was clearly sharper than he intended, because he forced a smile. "Thank you, Ms. Southerland. That's very kind, but I need to get home before the weather worsens."

Don't leave me here alone, she wanted to say. He was eyeing the house as if it were cursed. Even the horses swiveled their ears, pawing at the ground and kicking up plumes of snow.

Wren swallowed her reflexive, childish protest and instead waved limply. "Safe travels."

"Thank you," he said. "And good luck to you."

He snapped the reins, the horses took off, and Wren was left alone.

She stood in the ankle-deep snow covering the garden, if it could be called a garden at all. It was little but a snarl of leafless branches encased in ice like strange laboratory specimens. Wren turned toward her new home with its frowning pediments and eaves that dripped with wicked icicles. The house seemed to stare back at her from the belvedere squatting on its scaled roof. It raised the hairs on the back of her neck. Someone was *there,* watching her. She could feel it. But the empty windows all gleamed black as a beetle's wing in the moonlight.

How foolish, she scolded herself, *to be afraid of a house.* It was only the melted snow seeping into her boots. Nothing more than Basil's strange behavior worming its way under her skin.

As the snowfall intensified, blotting out her vision and tangling in her hair, Wren carried her bags to the porch. A vaulted arch made of iron hooded the entryway to the imposing double doors, and knotted up in the metalwork ivy were anguished faces and snarling gargoyles. Gathering her nerve, she grabbed the iron knocker. It burned her bare hand with the bitter chill of it. She lifted it and let it fall with a dull *bang* deadened by the thick snow. Here, no sound traveled. She could scream if she wanted.

No one would hear her.

After a minute, the doors opened to reveal a woman of about twenty, cast in the glow of a candelabra. Four columns of flame burned steadily, barely quivering in the wind that pulled at Wren's cloak. The woman's eyes were concealed by the shadows pouring off her brow bone, but her gaze seared, hot as the wax *drip, drip, drip*ping onto the worn floorboards in the rhythm of an intravenous infusion.

"Lord Lowry was expecting you hours ago."

Such hospitality. "My apologies. The weather delayed us."

The woman kept her gaze trained over Wren's shoulder. Without another word, she took Wren's bags from her hands and went inside. There was nothing to do but follow. Stepping over the threshold and into the fold of darkness felt something like being swallowed alive.

Inside, it was hardly warmer—or lighter. In the flickering orb of candlelight, Wren could make out the enormity of the hall, its startling emptiness. From where she stood, the ceiling towered three stories above her. If she craned her neck, the moon, as narrow and hooked as a suture needle, peered in through three bar-shaped windows lining the back wall. The grand staircase snaked its way along the somber blue walls, girded with a polished wood banister the color of wet soil. Everything outside the candelabra's unsteady reach swam indistinctly, as if the house itself breathed and stirred the shadows like wind over still water.

It was nothing like she imagined, so echoing and lonely. Where were the grand parties and gossiping courtiers? Where were the armies of servants carrying platters of cakes and pots of tea? There was no beauty here, no life.

Straight ahead, a fireplace burned red with low-banked coals. To the east, the mouth of a corridor was covered with a massive threadbare tapestry. The draft emanating from it was bitter cold, carrying with it drifts of snow that stole into the main hall like smoke. No wonder everyone here fell ill. The wisp of her breath curled in front of her nose.

"Follow me," the woman said. "I'll take you to him."

She led Wren up the staircase and veered into a hallway on the first floor. As they walked, candlelight traced the ragged edges of peeling floral wallpaper and rows of framed portraits. In the shifting light, the painted subjects' grins twisted into sneers and watchful eyes faded until they looked like the sunken orbital cavities of a skull. Shuddering, she focused her attention on her companion. The woman's unbound brown hair fell in loose, shining waves and was offset by the simple frock dress she wore. Firelight bathed her russet-brown skin in a glow like dawn. She seemed far too young to be the head of the household, but then again, Lowry had said most of his staff had perished from fever.

"I'm Wren Southerland, by the way. It's a pleasure to meet you."

"Hannah," was her only response. They stopped in front of a door. "Lord Lowry will receive you here. When you're finished, your room is upstairs. The last door on the right."

"And the sickroom?"

"Directly across from yours."

"Thank you. I—"

Hannah was already slipping away and rounding the corner. Her absence plunged Wren into near darkness, the corridor lit only by the frame of light around the door. Another time, Hannah's rudeness might have bothered her, but Wren couldn't feel much beyond her jittery nerves.

She knocked softly before entering. It was a library, but it had the closed-up, solemn air of a museum. Wall sconces burned with an eerie electrical glow, but the room was still dim, the air thick with dust. The ceiling had been dissected to expose the joists, its wooden beams veined with copper wire and studded with ceramic knobs. *Tubes and wires,* Basil had told her when she asked about how electricity worked. That must have been what fed the lights their strange power.

Heavy red curtains covered every window, and taxidermied specimens covered the back wall. Between stuffed and mounted rodents and birds were insects pinned by their wings like grim mosaic tiles. At the center, in the place of honor, was a twelve-point stag. It was unfinished; without its glass eyes, it watched her through gaping sockets.

The other two sides of the room were walled in by floor-to-ceiling bookcases, each shelf crammed with books about magic, medical textbooks, secular anthologies of essays, philosophical treatises, histories of ancient Danubian saints. Whatever she expected to find in a Cernosian library, it wasn't this. She could spend an eternity reading everything here. The abbey never had the funding to purchase expensive volumes like these. Her pleasant surprise, however, melted away to perplexity when she noticed *The Science of Magic: A Theory of Surgical Technique,* an early medical textbook, among the collection. What use would a socialite from a country with no magic have for something like this? Wren pulled the book out and brushed the dust from its spine.

"Goddess's tits! I didn't see you there. You scared me half to death."

Wren whirled around to find Lord Alistair Lowry leaning in the doorframe, his eyes widened and one hand pressed to his heart. The man was red, red, red from his sanguine cheeks to his garish waistcoat to the ruby-studded rings catching the light on his fingers. At the end of a chain around his neck was a gleaming golden key stamped with the symbol of Cernos: stag horns. No older than his late twenties, he had dark curling hair and a cleft in his square chin.

Wren bowed her head to hide the humiliated blush surely blooming across her nose. Not only had he caught her going through his things, but she was so . . . bedraggled. While she was still in her traveling clothes, he was fit for a royal audience. She stumbled over a curtsy. "I'm sorry for frightening you, my lord."

"No, no, don't apologize! It's not your fault. With all this *sickness* nonsense, my nerves are so frayed of late, I . . ." He cut himself off with a shake of his head. With more cheer, he said, "Enough of that, anyway. I'm not paying you nearly enough to burden you with my anxieties."

"It's quite alright. I don't mind."

"All the same, please allow me to offer you a warmer welcome." Lowry entered the room, pursued by the dramatic sweep of his cloak. As he approached her, she smelled warmth: coffee and rich spices. But it was the kind of late-summer warmth too quickly chased away. In its wake was something icy and almost floral, like sterilizing chemicals.

He towered above her, and if not for his wide-open expression, she might have found him overwhelming, almost intimidating. Still, she found herself flustered. He had a smile like an air pump. It sucked all the oxygen from the room. With a bow, he extended his hand to her. "Alistair Lowry, at your service."

Wren accepted his outstretched hand. "Wren Southerland. It's a pleasure to meet you."

"The pleasure is all mine. I can't begin to tell you how relieved I am you're here. Recently this has been such a lonely, eerie place."

"I can only imagine." Wren frowned. "This illness sounds quite serious."

"If I'm honest, I do my best not to think on it. The healers warned me I'd work myself up into a paranoid fever." After a beat, he glanced down at the book in her hand and said, "Ah. I see you're admiring the library."

Wren sheepishly replaced the book on the shelf. "Indeed. You have an impressive collection."

"It isn't mine to take credit for, I'm afraid." Lowry hopelessly gestured to the library, to all its dark corners and gawking taxidermy. "I dabble in the sciences here and there, but this is all my father's. Were he still alive, I know he'd demur and call it provincial."

No one could call this provincial. He had nearly the entirety of medical and mystical knowledge at his disposal. If she had free rein of this room during her stay, she'd die happy. "Your father was a scientist?"

"Ah, yes. He was quite the radical in his day, as a matter of fact. He was interested in the biology of magic. I could only understand his obsession as jealousy. He craved what he couldn't have. Such is life."

Wren could hardly envision a life without magic. To be born in a country without it seemed an awful fate. An unjust one. Cernosians' genetics equipped them with a fully functioning but inaccessible set of *fola*. The biological energy that produced magic coursed through them; they simply couldn't mold it into anything useful.

"Well." Wren cleared her throat, uncertain of what to say. "It's marvelous, in any case."

"You're welcome to browse any time you'd like." Lowry ran his hand absently along a shelf and sighed when his fingertips came away gray with dust. "It could use some attention, anyway. This room is just so . . . depressing. And rather grim and tacky. Although I do have a certain fondness for it, I myself being grim and tacky. Runs in the family, I suppose."

Wren let her eyes wander to the crimson gemstone swinging from his earlobe and the black cape pinned around his shoulders with a garnet brooch. "Oh, no. Not at all."

"You're darling—and far too obliging. I do mean it, though. Take whatever you'd like. I meant to clean out all his things years ago, but I couldn't bring myself to do it. Now I fear life has gotten away from me. When I had no energy to fulfill my social obligations, all but my dearest friend abandoned me. The house is falling apart around me. My servants are all dying." As he sank deeper into his fur-lined collar, he looked like a sad, fluffed-out bird. "And there I go again, unloading my anxieties onto you. I need a drink. Do you?"

"No, thank you."

With a shrug, Lowry walked to a bar cart beside a gold-trimmed writing desk and poured himself a glass of brandy from a crystal decanter. Although his tone was light and his words almost flippant,

Wren could see the despair that swallowed any of his former play-fulness. In profile, his eyes dulled to flat black. Perhaps there was more to him than his shallow reputation—maybe even some kind-ness, if he was eaten up about his servants enough to summon her.

"I imagine it's been difficult for you lately."

At that, he snapped back into himself, his smile chasing away the lingering gloom. "My apologies, Ms. Southerland! I'll be alright. You needn't let me talk your ear off. Come, sit. We have business to discuss."

Wren followed him to the writing desk and took a seat across from him. She caught a glimpse of her frazzled reflection in the desk's polished surface and tore her eyes away.

"Here is my proposal for you." He curled his hands neatly around his glass of brandy, all his rings glimmering in the dim light. "I've grown tired of being tired. Next month, I plan to make my grand return to society and host my annual Midwinter celebration. At the risk of sounding vain, it's among the most well-attended and well-documented events of the year. And I daresay it will be even more so this year. The people have missed me."

"Even in Danu, they miss you," Wren offered. "Last year, I read about nothing but your parties in the gossip columns. Now they have nothing new to talk about."

"*Did* you?" He seemed to perk up. "What did they say?"

"I . . . Well—"

"No, no. Ignore me. I'll carry us adrift." He swirled the liquid his glass. "Anyway. As I mentioned in my letter, there are serious debates among the Cernosian nobility about forging an alliance with the Danubian Crown. I intend to present you to my circle as Cernos's official liaison."

"Me?" Wren sputtered. "A liaison?"

"Yes, you. You'll be wonderful! It will hardly require any effort on your part. You'll wear a dress that will occupy every slavering paparazzo on the continent for weeks to come. We'll dance. We'll drink. We'll socialize. Once I take care of the tedious paperwork, all you need to do is deliver Cernos's messages to your queen. You'll be in court, and you'll be reinstated to your post, of course. What do you say?"

It sounded too good to be true.

Isabel's harsh words echoed in her mind: *You're foolhardy. You're emotional. You're easily manipulated. With your track record, you're sooner to start a war than to end one.*

"I don't have the constitution of a diplomat," she murmured.

"Nonsense." He winked at her. "I think you're perfect."

So much could go wrong. But Isabel would not be able to ignore her when Wren alone carried the privilege of delivering Cernos's diplomatic messages. Nor would she be able to ignore the slight of Cernos engaging with the royal bastard over her.

It *was* too good to be true, but it would be satisfying to see her aunt humbled. Wren couldn't help smiling. "I'll do it."

"That's what I like to hear." Fishing his pen from the inkwell, Lowry scribbled his signature on a sheet of parchment and slid the document across the desk to her. Wren recognized the same elegant script from his letter. "I've had my good friend, the Duke of Matthonwy, and his lawyer draw up a contract for you. I thought that might make you feel more secure about this whole arrangement. I understand your position is a precarious one."

Admittedly, a contract did reassure her. Since the world lately felt as if it were crumbling in her hands, she appreciated anything solid to hold onto. She accepted the pen from him and began to read. The preamble was little but stylized, overinflated jargon to her, but it covered the basics, his promise of asylum, provisions, and shelter. But the terms of her agreement gave her pause. They seemed . . . restrictive.

I, Wren Southerland, agree to the following stipulations:

1. I shall provide a detailed summary of the patient's progress each week, at a regular appointment to be mutually agreed upon

2. I shall uphold the curfew and retire to my bedroom
from midnight through six each morning
3. I shall not enter the east wing of the estate
4. I shall not leave the estate under any circumstances
without express permission

If I fail to uphold these terms, I understand that the
agreement is immediately terminated and accept all
consequences thereof.

Wren desperately hoped the puzzlement—and indignation—
that stilled her hand hadn't made its way onto her face. Curfews
and locked doors? Was she to be treated like a child here?

She snuck a glance at him. He was leaning back in his chair,
watching her with the tip of his tongue wedged into the corner of
his mouth. "Is something wrong, Ms. Southerland?"

A soft huff of laughter escaped her. "If you'll forgive me, Lord
Lowry, these terms are beginning to make me feel as if you're my
guardian rather than my employer."

Lowry looked appropriately mortified. "I understand your concern. Lawyers are exceedingly, maddeningly thorough. But please
don't let it alarm you. If you'll allow me to walk you through the
contract, perhaps you'll feel more comfortable with the arrangement."

Wren crossed her arms. "Very well."

"I assure you everything is entirely for your safety. As I mentioned
before, this house is ancient. Due to some, shall we say . . . structural
integrity issues, I cordoned off access to the entire east wing."

She remembered how cold it was on that side of the house.
"What happened?"

"A few months ago, I asked for some renovations. Many of the
walls are solid stone, which makes it difficult to install electrical
conduits, and . . ." He trailed off, waving a hand. "Well, I won't
bore you with the technicalities. While the engineers were working, a staircase collapsed and buried a few of them. Needless to say,

the east wing is too dangerous—and too dark, besides. Since that incident, I've put a moratorium on the project, so you may find some rooms still have gas lamps. Yours included, I'm afraid. Terribly sorry about that."

"Oh," Wren said quietly.

"As for remaining here . . . It's partly for quarantine, as I'd hate to see this disease spread beyond the walls of Colwick Hall. However, you are the professional, and should you need to leave, I will happily grant my permission. I merely want to know when to expect you home in case I need to send a search out for you. This time of year, you'll be dead of exposure before you can blink."

"Does that . . . happen often?"

"Oh, yes. Why, just a few years ago, we had a casualty at one of my parties. Wandered out into a blizzard, no shoes or anything. Goddess rest his soul, the poor bastard."

Lowry sounded so blasé about it all. How much tragedy had happened here? While it made sense to be cautious when he'd lost so much, Wren still couldn't help feeling uneasy about all these rules. "And the curfew?"

"Ah, that." Lowry offered a sheepish smile. "That one has no rational explanation, I'm afraid. I haven't been sleeping much since the illness broke out. Everything wakes me. I hope you'll allow me some unreasonableness. If it's any consolation, everyone abides by it, including myself."

"Of course." Wren swallowed thickly, racking her brain for anything else to quibble with. But she was a guest in his home. He was doing her an immense service. The very least she could do was swallow her pride and adhere to his ridiculous rules during her stay.

"Please, let me know if I can do anything else to put your mind at ease." A concerned furrow appeared between his brows. "I understand it can be cold and gloomy here. I want to make you feel as welcome as I can."

"No, no. You've addressed all my concerns." She managed a smile. "As for updates, I'll give you my initial assessment of the patient . . ."

"Henry," he supplied.

"Right. I'll give you my assessment of Henry tomorrow. I can meet you for tea?"

"Tea would be perfect." Lowry slumped lower in his chair, pushing his curls away from his forehead. Like this, even in his finery and polish, Wren could see the cracks. He looked utterly exhausted—and deeper still, something else burned. Something like iron, determined and unwavering. And something . . . almost frenetic. "I cannot begin to tell you what a relief it is to have you here. I don't think I can bear any more death."

Wren understood that sentiment painfully well. "I'll make sure you won't have to."

"Thank you," Lowry said hoarsely. "From the bottom of my black and shriveled heart, thank you."

"Of course." Her gaze fell on the contract again. Although her gut roiled in protest, what else could she do? She signed her name. The ink shone red in the lamplight.

When she looked up, the taxidermied deer head behind him leered eyelessly at her. Wren shivered. She wasn't superstitious, but to have so much death staring her down . . .

It boded ill for her patient's recovery.

The hallway outside Wren's room reeked of sickness: boiled herbs and stale air. Her body ached and her heavy eyes begged for sleep, but her healing magic pulled her toward her patient. The disease had settled over the house like a funeral pall, wedged itself into every woundlike crevice. She hated to admit that she was unsettled, but maybe the familiar rhythms of healing would soothe her.

It wasn't that she was afraid. She just couldn't shake the dread that had settled beneath her skin like a chill as soon as she'd signed away her freedom to the whims of Alistair Lowry. But it was an entirely unreasonable worry. Lowry was eccentric, as Basil warned her. Cautious, as anyone would be after witnessing so much death.

It wasn't as if she needed to go anywhere, especially in this storm.

It had begun in earnest now, wailing and rattling the windows like a ghost. Outside the hallway window, the view was solid, swirling white.

Wren slung her medical bag over her shoulder and crossed the hall to the sickroom. With every step, the sound of labored breathing grew louder. Her magic bristled again, tingling and hot in her fingertips. She'd never been able to resist its yearning to heal, but this was a new kind of hunger. Whatever illness the man had, it had raged for too long. Another few days untreated would likely kill him. The door creaked as she pushed it open inch by inch.

"Hello? Henry?" she called, hoping not to startle him. "I'm the healer Lord Lowry sent for."

There was no answer.

A single candle, melted down to a puddle, burned in the darkness, but shadows stubbornly clung in the corners like smoke stains. A four-poster bed took up nearly the entire room, its white canopy closed. It gave Wren the impression of a long-abandoned room, all the furniture cloaked and hidden. A wet, barking cough sounded from behind the canopy.

Wren sat in the chair beside the sickbed and drew back the curtain. A man lay tangled in the sheets and propped up by pillows. Although exhaustion made her sluggish, she collected magic in her palm and laid it on his chest to assess the damage. What could have decimated a household in weeks?

Her eyes adjusted to the darkness. Bit by bit, shadows gave shape to his face. Black hair and a fawn complexion. Long, imperious features. An almost pouting mouth. This was not the dignified butler she'd imagined. He was just a sullen boy. Just a—

Wren stifled a gasp and snatched her hand away.

This was no boy, no common servant.

Sleeping fitfully in the sickbed was Hal Cavendish.

CHAPTER NINE

lthough years had passed since their last encounter, he was
unmistakable. It was him. It was Hal. He was supposed to
be missing.

But here he was, laid low in a canopied bed. Wren stood
abruptly, and the scrape of the chair on the floorboards stirred him
awake. With a groan, his eyes peeled open. Wren's mind blackened in terror, the same color as his eyes. She fixed her gaze on his
chest to avoid meeting his. Even one second, one glance, would be
enough to stop her heart.

No, no, no. This couldn't be happening. Why, of all places, was
he *here*?

He was the Reaper of Vesria. He was a monster, above mortal
things like sickness. Yet he languished here the same as any flesh
and blood being with a fever. It was almost pathetic, the way he
shivered.

As fear solidified into rage, a thought slid effortlessly into her
head: *Kill him.*

The ink was already drying on a contract that required her to heal him, at risk of everything she'd taken such pains to secure. But this was a man with too much blood on his hands to wash away. It would be so easy, so right. She could sever his carotid artery right now and not spare a thought to the trifling consequences of breaking her contract.

Wren had never killed anyone before. Her oath as a healer forbade it. But she had watched her friends do it time and time again with the grace and remorselessness of a wolf snapping a rabbit's neck. Killing him now was as good as an act of mercy, as holy as healing. It was a far more honorable death than succumbing to fever like a feral dog.

Silver magic glowed in her palm. His every undeserved breath rasped.

If Una wanted her to be ruthless, she would be ruthless.

On the opposite wall, Wren caught a glimpse of herself in an old mirror, oxidized with dark spots like mold. With her tousled hair and hollow eyes, she looked haggard and desperate and afraid. She looked nothing like herself.

What was she *doing*? She was a healer, and besides . . .

A faint memory from her and Una's meeting with Isabel returned: *His life is mine to dispose of.* Wren's anger slowly cooled into realization. She couldn't kill him because Isabel wanted him alive.

She hated the sudden flood of relief. She hated that she wasn't strong enough to do this. But the opportunity Hal presented her with was almost too perfect. The queen had never wanted anything more than to make an example of the man who had turned the tide of war and tarnished her reign.

What if Wren was the one to deliver him to her? She could picture it now. The delicious, enraged shock on her aunt's face when she made her dramatic return. The shift into grudging respect. Everything she'd come here to gain—redemption, proof of her skill, the reauthorization of the investigation—she'd have it and more. She didn't have to waste her time here, sucking up to some dithering nobleman until the storm cleared. All she had to do was call a carriage to take her home and cure this disease so he didn't die before then. With an eerie, resolved calm, Wren settled back into the bedside chair. Her wavering shadow fell over him.

His eyes searched for hers, and she sucked in a startled breath and looked away. From the edge of her vision, she could see Hal staring at her so imploringly, it unnerved her. He said something in Vesrian that she couldn't understand, so quiet and raw, it sounded like he hadn't spoken in weeks. It frustrated her, the limits of her own knowledge.

"What did you say?" She shaped each word carefully, deliberately.

The corner of his mouth pulled into the barest smile. As if he hadn't registered the shift in language, he slurred in accented but perfect Danubian, "I know you."

Surely he didn't recognize her from the one time she'd seen him on the front line. Perhaps he'd seen her portrait before, but given she'd been excluded from the line of succession, she doubted he had reason to remember her name or face. Wren knew better than to humor people in the throes of delusion, but her curiosity won out. "Do you now?"

"You're here to end this." Wren was almost disappointed. Of course he didn't recognize her. He was delirious—he looked at her and saw the Crone.

"No." Carefully, she brushed his hair off his forehead, surprising herself with the tenderness of the gesture. It was strangely beautiful, even plastered to his face with sweat. Black and glossy as a raven's feather. Beneath her fingertips, his skin burned dangerously hot. "You won't get off so easy."

His expression was a snuffed candle, utterly defeated. Was he really so eager to die?

His eyes grew unfocused, heavier, as she watched him struggle for lucidity. Wren waited until his breathing evened out into shallow slumber. What a relief, not to have to speak to him anymore. And deep down, she didn't want to see the gleam of his eyes in the dark again.

Some said his power was unholy, unnatural—that he was no mortal but Vesria's god made flesh. Wren believed none of it. No matter how terrifying he was, it was only magic. Complex but explainable magic. Rationalization, however, did little to calm her churning stomach. He looked human enough, but if she cut him open, what would she find nestled in his rib cage? A beating heart or something burning black as coal?

"Are you awake?"

Mercifully, he remained still and silent.

This would be fine. Routine, even. He was like any other patient. First, she would record his vitals. Then, she would proceed to diagnostic tests. Drawing in a steadying breath, Wren unfastened his nightshirt from clavicle to sternum, efficiently as opening a surgical incision. As soon as she drank in the sight of him half bared, she felt disembodied and almost hysterical.

Goddess above, I'm undressing Hal Cavendish. Her eyes watered at the absurdity her life had taken on in the past twenty-four hours.

She laid her hands on his chest, warmed by the feverish heat. As she poured magic into his system, she closed her eyes and read the faint images of her energy mapping out his body. *Highly activated sodium channels, ventricular arrhythmias, hypotension.* Her mouth formed the shape of the words as she lost herself in the whispering of her magic.

Then fingers as cold and brutal as steel bands dug into her wrists. She couldn't choke back her gasp—equal parts startled and pained. What could have possibly set him off?

Then she realized. Her magic in his system, of course. Although "healers" existed in Vesria, they were more often assassins, trained to destroy their targets from within.

Wren jerked against his grasp. "Easy!"

Even like this, frail and faded, Hal was strong. *Strong enough to kill me.* But with skin-to-skin contact, her magic was a weapon as lethal as his eyes. The Healing Touch's silver light flickered wildly between them, blanching him white as bone.

"If you don't let go, I will sever every tendon in your hand before you even blink. Think careful—"

Before she finished her threat, he wrenched her forward.

He moved so fast, she couldn't track him, couldn't react. For one breathless moment, she was suspended and off-balance. The next, her face was shoved roughly against the mattress. Her teeth clacked together, the impact reverberating through her skull.

As he bore his weight into her, he twisted her arms behind her back and wedged his knee into the space between her scapulae. Over the sound of her short, panicked gasps, she could hear nothing. How could she be so stupid? She'd had the advantage, but Hal had been trained in combat since he was a child.

If he pulled, he'd dislocate both her shoulders.

"Wren Southerland." The sound of her name, so flat and disinterested, settled like a winter chill beneath her skin. Gooseflesh spread along her ensnared arms. Although roughened by disuse and illness, his voice was dark and rich as a woodwind. "It seems I do know you."

"Let go of me!"

She struggled, only for him to dig his knee harder into her spine. Her rotator cuff crackled in protest, desperately struggling to hold bone to socket. If she couldn't touch him, her magic was useless. *She* was useless. Death at his hands was said to come fast and silent, like an injection of barbiturate. But incapacitating her like this meant he intended to savor this. How much pain could she stand before she begged to look into his eyes?

The sound of wheezing cut through the haze of her fear. His breathing grew thicker, more faltering, until a hacking cough bent him double. All at once, his hold went slack.

This time, she did not hesitate. She grabbed his leg—the first thing she found—and sheared through muscle like fabric. Her traitorous heart lurched as he choked back a sound of pain. He rolled off her, and Wren scrabbled off the bed, hands raised and blazing with magic.

"Don't move." The sound of her own voice startled her. Such a sound, so wild and raw, couldn't have come from her. "Or I'll—"

"Wait." His chest heaved with every miserable breath. With her eyes locked onto his chin, she could see the blood dribbling from the corners of his mouth. Slowly, he drew his sleeve across his face. It was too intimate to see him so abject, so . . . ashamed. "Please."

"*Please?*" she snarled. "Are we using our manners now?"

"I acted too rashly. I'm more use to you alive."

Alive? No wonder he'd been so jumpy. He assumed she'd come to assassinate him. It was so ludicrous, she almost burst into laughter. Wren had devoted her life to her work. No matter how much she hated Hal, she was honor bound as a soldier and a healer to cure him. How she would relish the look on his face when she told him she'd been in the process of *saving* him. Then again, if he was so eager to bargain with her, he must be desperate. Hal wanted to live, and there were few things people wouldn't trade for their lives. If it meant forcing the Reaper of Vesria into her debt, she would bluff.

She would make him beg for her help.

"You think I'm here to kill you?" she asked incredulously. "I'm a doctor, not an assassin. Don't you know healers take an oath of nonviolence in Danu?"

Confusion pulled at the corners of his lips. "Then you were . . . ?"

"Examining you." The silver tracery of her activated *fola* faded as she crossed her arms.

"Why are you here?"

"I might ask you the same thing."

He did not respond. They glared at each other across the room, but Wren's resolve slipped as she watched him tremble with fever. Heat flushed his skin and clouded his eyes, and blood spattered his sheets. Yet he still carried himself like he might strike at any moment, watchful and intense.

Sighing, Wren broke first. "Lowry hired me to heal a patient. Imagine my surprise to find you. I considered leaving, but I couldn't resist seeing how far you've fallen." When he didn't respond, she pressed on. "It's a shame, really. A war hero dying like this. That disease should finish you off in a few days."

If it frightened him, he gave no discernible reaction.

Wren matched his blank expression. As long as he believed she could and would walk away from him, she'd won. She lifted one shoulder and turned toward the door. "Goodbye, Cavendish."

"Wait."

Wren allowed herself a self-satisfied smirk before composing herself and glancing back at him. "What?"

"I have information on your missing soldiers."

That, she did not expect.

All the air in her lungs left in a rush. "How would you know anything about that?"

He hesitated. "I've been involved with the case."

"Then Vesria *is* responsible."

"No, we aren't. But I have a lead."

Una's words flooded back to her. *Despite the fact it makes no sense, the queen believes Vesria is responsible. It can't be this simple.*

The air thickened like nitrogen, too heavy to breathe. If he was telling the truth, then their nations were indeed careening toward a pointless war. One Danu would not survive. Yet here he was, wasting away and hoarding information that could save them all.

"We had a lead, too," she snapped. "A boy with magic, watching patrols. If he wasn't your agent, then whose?"

His only response was blank-faced silence. Wren bristled.

"Fine," she said through gritted teeth. "Why did your government report you missing? Does Lowry know who you are?"

With unmoved serenity, he said, "If you offer me something in return, I'll answer your questions."

Wren wanted to scream in frustration, had to clench her fists to keep from shaking him. *Do you not want to find them? Does another war really mean nothing to you? Do you not still jolt awake from the nightmares? Have you ever cared about anyone at all?*

As satisfying as it would be, an outburst wouldn't help her. Wren willed herself to be calm. If she got his information, then hope wasn't lost. With a new lead, she could pursue the investigation again. She could still prevent a war. She could still have justice for Byers—and maybe even find him alive.

She raked her hands through her hair. It had come loose in their scuffle and hung in tangled waves down her back. As she knotted it back, she imagined speaking with all of Una's authority and condescension. "Alright, Cavendish. You have my attention. What's your price?"

"I want you to cure this disease."

Exactly as she predicted. Hoping she sounded suitably affronted, she said, "You realize you're asking me to commit treason."

"I know." He looked exhausted, defeat written into the slump of his shoulders. Blood still stained his lips, a red dark and vivid against his sickly pallor.

"How do I know you're not lying to me?"

"On my honor—"

"Your honor? What honor?"

Frustration edged into his voice. "I swear it on your Goddess. Please consider it."

His oath startled her. He'd said it before: *please.* But this time was different. It was so genuine, so vulnerable, something predatory shook loose within her and coiled tight in her gut like a viper. Wren wet her lips. "You'll truly answer *all* of my questions?"

"Yes. Anything."

Anything. Someone like him might never crack under interrogation, but here he was, offering himself up to her. Treason or not, only a fool would pass up the opportunity. "Don't get your hopes up. Until I know what the disease is, I can't promise you anything."

"Your effort's enough." He sounded so relieved. After a pause, Hal added, "Although if you'd allow me one more request, would you also fix what you did to me?"

"Why should I?" He deserved it, anyway. She couldn't be certain how much internal damage she'd done, but even a strained hamstring would take weeks to heal on its own. "It's my only guarantee you won't attack me again."

"I won't." Somehow, the weariness in his voice convinced her.

"Fine. I promise you a diagnosis for your illness and a functioning quadriceps femoris, for now. We renegotiate after that. Anything *else*?"

"That's all."

"Then it's a deal." Treason, sealed with four words.

While she'd always intended to cure him, saying it aloud made it all seem too real. Wren expected some rush of shame. An ominous parting of the storm clouds. But nothing happened. She supposed she should be more concerned with how easy betrayal was becoming.

"Just keep your hands to yourself this time," she added.

Wren approached him as if he were a caged animal: one creeping, measured step at a time. As she slid into the bedside chair and the last of her adrenaline faded, it set in how much everything *hurt*. She guessed that her pectoral muscles were strained, if not torn. Mottled bruises, a deep goddessblood purple, were already beginning to bloom on her swollen wrists and creep toward her elbows.

That brute. He'd have torn her limb from limb had his own body not shut down. Hatred burned steady as a flame in her chest. Right now, she wanted nothing more than to sink into a hot bath and soothe away the ache, but a deal was a deal. One way or another, she would have answers about her missing comrades. First, she had to—

"I'm sorry," he said.

Wren froze. "What?"

From the corner of her eye, she watched his gaze wander over her mangled arms. "I'm sorry for hurting you."

Laughter bubbled within her stomach, and her eyes nearly watered at the effort to contain it. He was *sorry*? After all he'd done to her people, *this* was what he chose to apologize for? He had to be mocking her. "Why?"

"I see no point to senseless violence, or in making enemies of those who're helping me."

"You see no point in senseless violence," she repeated slowly. With every word, her hatred sparked hotter. "Is that what you believed when you slaughtered my people in the Battle of the River Muri?"

Hal looked almost surprised.

"I saw you that day." She clenched her fists into her skirt so tight they trembled. "I stood ten feet away as you struck down my comrades without even lifting a finger. Or have you already forgotten?"

"No." He frowned, his eyes falling shut. If not for the eerie, distant tone of his voice, she might have mistaken him for remorseful. "I remember."

"Oh, do you? Then what a change of heart you've had over the past four years. And they say people never change."

"Perhaps they don't." He spoke quietly, but each word was as cold and hard as steel. It raised the hairs on the back of her neck. "Regardless, my apology stands."

"I don't forgive you. Words fix nothing."

Something flickered over his face, like a ripple in still water. She braced herself for a rebuttal—craved it. But he remained infuriatingly silent.

He was right, of course. People didn't change. Once a monster, always a monster.

She forced herself to ignore him as she rolled his pant leg above the knee. At least they matched. Bruises spread like decay along his thigh, with hideous black tendrils. It must have hurt terribly, which gave her a twinge of satisfaction. When she laid her hand on his skin, he flinched. Soldiers and their dramatics.

"Relax," she muttered.

He did not relax. But he remained, at least, as still as stone.

Repairing the muscle fibers and readhering them to the bone took only minutes, and Wren swore he did not breathe for the entirety of it. Few people *enjoyed* the sensation of healing; magic traveled through the body like the cold creep of an injection.

Once, after a sparring match with Una, Byers came away with a sprained ankle. As Wren healed him, he puffed away on his cigarette like a goddessdamned chimney. Despite her admonitions, he insisted it helped with stress.

I hate it, I hate it, I hate it, he'd said as she repaired his tendon. *I feel like you should've bought me dinner first.*

She pushed that memory far away, locked it deep behind the

mental wall that kept her grief at bay. As the last of Hal's contusions melted beneath her fingers, she sighed. "I'm going to examine you now. Prolonged healing can be uncomfortable, especially in the vital organs, but I can offer you a painkiller if you'd like."

"No." It was firm, the kind of tone that left no room for argument.

She couldn't help thinking of the boy with the broken arm and how proudly he'd refused the opiate. Hal's stubbornness suited her fine, as much as it exasperated her. She'd asked as a professional courtesy, but she had no qualms about making his experience a miserable one. "Very well then."

Wren slipped her hands underneath his shirt and pressed them against his chest. Sweat dampened his skin, and tension stiffened his entire body. Trying to keep himself from trembling as his body temperature climbed, most likely. So pathetic. So proud.

As her magic traversed his body, discomfort twitched his lips, but he did not squirm. It fanned out, tugging her gently toward the areas in need of her attention: his lungs, his heart, his eyes.

His eyes?

Curiosity won out. She pooled her magic in his skull and into the insertion of the optic nerve. The *fola* in his eyes were almost completely degenerated. So little of her energy could squeeze through the hyaloid canal, it was a wonder he could use his magic at all. Or maybe he couldn't.

She stifled her bitter laughter. No wonder he hadn't tried to force her to look at him. No wonder he wanted to bargain. He was powerless. Overuse injuries like this didn't happen overnight. The repetitive use of magic caused microtraumas to the *fola,* which, over time, swelled and tore like overstrained tendons. Hal's magic was effectively gone—and likely had been for some time. How long had Danu needlessly lived in dread of him? How long had he been lying to his own people? Without his magic, kidnapping him was going to be far easier than she anticipated. Assuming, of course, her hypothesis was correct.

Little by little, Wren probed deeper into his system, her magic catching on diseased tissue like debris in a river's sure course. Images came to her: damaged and weeping tissue, angry inflammation that ravaged capillaries, blood collecting in his lungs. The disease was an infection unlike any she had seen before. It had none of the typical signs of a transmissible disease. No bacteria or viruses that she could detect. Even his own cells seemed to be functioning normally—no autoimmune response, no cancer, no histamines. Nothing that could explain a sudden acute illness.

All her life, healing had been like breathing. Effortless. Natural. Necessary. Her magic opened the human body to her. It spoke to her, guided her. But this . . . This was like reaching into a void. As if her magic had turned away from her, left her blind and alone. It terrified her.

How could the etiology elude her so completely? If she couldn't diagnose him, she couldn't treat him systematically. She prided herself on her research, her ability to treat any disease, any injury. She couldn't be stumped by something as trifling as a servants' quarters illness.

"I need more time to come up with a diagnosis. In the meantime, I'll treat your symptoms so you don't drop dead before you're of any use to me." It was true enough. With his respiratory and immune systems as weakened as they were, he would die long before she could call a carriage to take them both to Danu.

"Thank you."

Wren tried not to visibly recoil. She did not want the burden of his gratitude. "Sure."

Bending over him, she began to heal him, sealing off leaking capillaries and soothing the inflammation in his bronchi. It was long, arduous work. The disease was aggressive and the damage profound. She feared she wouldn't have him stable before the journey home, but she would have to manage it.

Everything depended on his survival.

After an hour, Wren broke the connection between them, and Hal sighed heavily. There was no rattle in his lungs, no congestion damming his airways. Her hands tingled with exertion, the *fola* run raw.

"That's all for tonight," she said.

He eased himself into a seated position. His shirt still hung open, revealing a pale triangle of skin. In his prime, he must have been impressive. There was hardly a scar on him—a terrifying testament to how untouchable he was. Sickness had eroded some of his physique, but he was still in lean military shape.

Enough of that, she decided. Disgusted with herself for cataloging anything outside medical significance, she turned away and began to pack up her things.

His searching gaze singed her face like a brand. She tried to ignore it, but two impulses, *don't look* and *look,* warred for dominance. Fear drove the first, curiosity—and indignation—the second. He was staring at her so openly, so intently, she was certain he could see the exact center of her. Did he just go about gaping at everyone so brazenly? He was probably accustomed to getting away with such rudeness when no one dared to challenge him.

If only they knew how he'd deceived them.

I'll show him, she thought bitterly. *I'm not afraid.*

She dared to raise her eyes to his, and it felt like jumping from a cliff. Everyone said his eyes were black, but beneath the surface, there was indigo and cobalt, as clear and dark as glacial water. Wren waited for her heart to stop.

It didn't.

Her satisfaction melted when she took in his expression, lips parted, eyes wide. He looked like a man seeing sunlight for the first time. Starving. Almost . . . awed?

Before she could let the uneasiness of that settle, Hal spared her and glanced away. Just like that, whatever flicker of emotion Wren had seen was gone.

"What?" he said.

Such accusation condensed into one word. As if she held some power over him. "It's eye contact. Is no one permitted to look His Highness in the eye?"

"Permission is beside the point."

It was beside the point. Anyone else wouldn't dare take the risk.

"Your magic is gone," she said, quicker than she could think. "Isn't it?"

He was silent, but the air around him crackled with tension.

"I thought so." Wren leaned in closer. She wanted to see his fear. She wanted to see his shame. He gave her nothing, but his now bored, heavy-lidded gaze was a challenge. "Now I see why you're missing, Reaper. You don't stand a chance of winning your election like this. You ran away because you didn't want them to realize you're worthless. Didn't you?"

At the title, Hal flinched. His voice, however, was as flat and cold as ever. "And what of you? It's no secret what happened to you after your mother's death. Although you managed to escape your exile, you were born into shame and can't outrun that, no matter how desperately you try."

"You don't know anything about me," she spat.

She trembled at the inadequacy of her retort, but fury had left her near speechless. No one besides Isabel had ever so plainly twisted the knife in her greatest insecurity. No one besides Isabel had ever been so intentionally cruel. Without another word, she got up and left.

Across the hall, in the safety of her room, every feeling she'd avoided waited for her in the shadows. Her silent accusers: fear, stress, shame. They crowded in on her until she could see nothing beyond the haze of her own failure. As much as she wanted to be better, to be stronger, Hal had gotten to her.

She slid to the floor in a heap and wept.

CHAPTER TEN

In the cold light of morning, nothing made any more sense than it did the night before.

She'd spent sleepless hours struggling with what had happened last night and what it meant for her. All she had to show for her perseveration now were her bloodshot, swollen eyes. Wren stood before the mirror in the washroom, sighing at her harried reflection. She had a meeting with Lowry in thirty minutes and couldn't very well attend him looking like this.

It was a careful process, a work of illusion, to transform herself from the red-eyed girl in the mirror into a medical professional. She splashed her face with cold water, dusted her blotchy cheeks with talc, and neatly pinned up her hair. By the end of it, she was armored. Her smile, passably confident, would be enough to convince Lowry nothing was amiss.

She still looked desperate—a little wild in the eyes—but in light of how thoroughly her life had unraveled, Wren was beginning to suspect a little desperation had become a permanent fixture.

Wren turned on the faucet again and began to wash her hands. The hot water—another electrical marvel, apparently—soothed the ache in her joints, and steam coiled upward, silvering the mirror with condensation.

How could she be anything but desperate? Hal Cavendish was alive and *here,* and for the life of her she could not fathom why Alistair Lowry had summoned her to heal a man she despised. If she'd acted on her first impulse, all it would have taken was a single cut, one severed artery or neuron, and the Reaper of Vesria would have been no more. Lowry knew that, as surely as he knew tensions were rising between their countries. Concealing Hal's identity from her wasn't a minor omission—or a prudent one. Which meant the only logical explanation was that he'd thought her patient's name meaningless.

Maybe Lowry simply didn't know who Hal was.

No, not even Lowry could be dense enough to mistake the Reaper of Vesria for a common man. Then again, Cernos had maintained their neutrality for centuries, and the estate lurked deep in the isolated Dramlach Mountains. Lowry himself admitted he hadn't followed politics before now. Still, too many questions remained. How did Hal get here? And what was he *doing,* posing as a servant while his country mobilized for war?

Not that it mattered urgently when both she and Hal would be gone in two weeks. Earlier, Wren had dashed off a letter to the local carriage company, and when a servant boy dropped off her breakfast, she slipped the envelope into his hand along with two gold coins. He returned half frozen two hours later with a response:

W—

The weather is far too dangerous to leave today, but we should be able to get you down the mountain two weeks from now. Meet at 0500 sharp. Stay warm.

—Edward Collins,
Aldershot Sled & Carriage Company

All she had to do until then was maintain this house-doctor charade. From her examination last night, she could tell Hal's condition was critical. She'd need to treat his worst symptoms before she moved him into another room, much less across the country in a snowstorm.

Only fourteen days, she reminded herself. *You can do anything for fourteen days.* Even lying to the most influential man in Cernos and healing the most wanted man in Danu.

Wren winced at a sudden sting in her hands. The water gurgled as it circled the drain, stained pink with blood. The cold air last night had dried out her skin, and she'd been so absentminded as she scrubbed her hands, she must have chafed them raw. She turned off the tap. Blood ran slick off the end of her fingertip, then spattered in the bone-white basin with a dull *plop*.

Just then, a groan—distant, almost muffled—sent gooseflesh rippling up her arms. *What was that?* It sounded almost anguished.

After hastily healing the abrasions on her hands, Wren crept out of the washroom and into the hall. Nothing stirred save the painfully familiar *tick, tick, tick* of an old grandfather clock. The air seemed frozen, already splintering at the disturbance.

This place is of the living and yours no longer, she thought.

No, she would not indulge such nonsense. There was no such thing as ghosts. She'd heard only the groan of the house as it shifted in the wind, and sleeplessness wore at her already frayed nerves. Still, it couldn't hurt to explore her new home. For the sake of scientific inquiry, of course.

Beyond hers and Hal's rooms, doors stood watch like a line of soldiers. Each one she tried was locked, except the last. It resisted at first, but when she pushed her weight against it, the lock gave way with a whine, and the door eased open an inch. For a moment, Wren hesitated with her palm flat against the lacquered wood. She couldn't just invade her employer's privacy like this. But the door had opened for her, as if inviting her inside. She entered, the cold draft from within whispering over her skin like a sigh of relief.

Dust swirled through the milky wash of sunlight. It glittered on glass cases and dull metal, forcing her to blink until her eyes adjusted. When the spots cleared from her vision, Wren found herself in a veritable cabinet of curiosities. Wooden stands displayed a menagerie of objects: blades with elaborate pattern welding and elegant silver knots; bullets with engraved casings. In the corner was an old Danubian military uniform from the Marian era, nearly two centuries ago, a coat with long black sleeves with the moon phases embroidered in silver thread. The plaque beside it read: GENERAL AHEARN'S GREATCOAT, WORN AS SHE LED HER TROOPS TO VICTORY IN THE BATTLE OF GREINE (1663).

But strangest of all was the portrait hung on the back wall, framed by windows glimmering white as the sun refracted through the crackled layers of ice. She approached the heavy, gold-trimmed frame and squinted up at the familiar face of a boy.

It was a portrait of younger Lowry, dressed in a red wool coat and staring meaningfully into the middle distance. A shining aiguillette coiled around his shoulder like a serpent, and one hand clutched the hilt of a saber. Despite the twinkle in his eye and his dark curls catching the breeze, he looked . . .

Well, he looked like a soldier.

What was he doing with all this war memorabilia? The meticulousness and extensiveness of this collection indicated an obsession she'd only experienced when embroiled in her research. But as far as she knew, he had never served in the Cernosian military. Even if he had, she was almost certain they were little more than a team of munitions researchers.

"I see you've found my little museum."

Wren startled, turning around slowly to the tune of a soft chuckle. Lowry himself leaned in the doorway, wearing a gold brocade waistcoat and a maroon cravat. At the sight of the silk shining at his throat, she thought of her blood circling the drain. His eyes rested heavy on her, humorless and gleaming near-white in the shadows. That stare could cut clean through her.

"My lord," she stammered. "I wasn't expecting you."

"I finished my work earlier than anticipated, so I came to find you," Lowry said. "And here you are, in the graveyard of my childhood."

"Please forgive my intrusion. I'm . . . ashamed this has happened twice now."

"There's nothing at all to forgive." When he emerged from the darkness of the hallway, all his harshness burned away like an early morning mist. The brightness of the room softened his features into their usual, smiling placidity. "A curious mind is perhaps the most valuable trait in Cernos. I daresay you fit in perfectly."

He wove through the exhibits until he stood beside her, and Wren swore he'd be able to hear the pounding of her heart as she tipped her chin up at him. With the sunlight threading its fingers into his dark hair, he was as radiant as ever. Had she imagined his annoyance?

Clearing her throat, she fumbled to find the gentlest way to voice her confusion. "Are you a student of history?"

"A dilettante, really."

"I thought you weren't interested in politics."

"In politics? No." Lowry crossed his arms behind his back as he gazed up at his younger self in the painting. "In war, certainly—at least when I was a lad about your age. It all seemed rather romantic."

"Romantic?" she asked, unable to keep the bite out of her voice.

He laughed sheepishly, tilting his head toward her. "Well, I was sixteen. Full of ennui and eager to die for something bigger than myself. I'd hardly seen anything beyond these walls, much less past those damn mountains. I had everything I should have wanted. An education, fine food and wine, lavish balls, a staff who seemed to say nothing but *yes, milord*. My father kept me locked up while you lot were busy killing each other, and I was miserable."

"But . . . everyone loves you, my lord. How could you be unhappy?"

"Everyone is *amused* by me," he amended. "But no one respects me. I dreamed of commanding the respect—the admiration—of a military man. So I suppose suffering did seem romantic, young fool that I was."

Wren couldn't exactly sympathize with him, a lordling bored of his too-charmed life and hungry for admiration he'd never understand the price of. "So you . . . collected things?"

"Indeed." As he turned toward a wickedly sharp dagger, the slant of light struck his eyes pale as ice. He took it from its stand and turned it over in his hand. Wren couldn't look away from the pointed edge as he caressed the flat side of the blade. "And if I was lucky, sometimes my brother, Charles, would set aside his economics books to swordfight with me. Father was always *thrilled* to see us flailing about with all the expensive antiques he bought me."

"And when he didn't?"

"I found other ways to occupy myself." The knife in his hand flashed a reflection of his smile at her. "If Charles couldn't be bothered, there were servants or dogs or horses to torment into giving me attention. I've always had a persuasive streak, anyway."

When he replaced the dagger on its stand, she felt oddly relieved.

"But that's quite enough about me." Nervousness edged into Lowry's conversational tone. "How is our Henry faring?"

Dismally, she wanted to say.

However, Wren suspected Lowry wasn't the type who could handle the truth entirely unsweetened. "He's . . . sick. From my initial assessment last night, I would say his most concerning symptoms are lung damage and heart irregularities. I treated him with palliative care as best I could. It's an aggressive disease."

He swore under his breath. "Do you have any idea what it is?"

"No. Not yet." Admitting it aloud flooded her with shame. Even though the circumstances were . . . less than ideal, she'd never been so thrown by a disease. Wren turned away to absentmindedly inspect a flintlock pistol in its case. "It's not like anything I've seen before. You mentioned in your letter the doctors didn't know, either?"

"No." Lowry frowned. "None of their tests revealed anything conclusive."

"I see." Wren kept her tone as neutral as possible. Panicking him would do her no good. "Well, it's responding well enough to my magic for now. I'll have more concrete answers for you soon."

"I can only pray you do. If anyone else dies . . ."

"He won't," Wren said firmly. "I promise."

Not in this house, anyway.

"If only I had your confidence," Lowry said. "Or your abilities. I've absorbed enough of my father's ravings about biology over the years, but what good is knowledge if it cannot do anything to help people? I've felt so powerless."

Wren frowned. With any other patient or patron, she might have offered him more sympathy or reassurance about Hal's prognosis. But she was exhausted, still on edge, and she had an agenda far more important than preserving Lowry's feelings. She had to confirm whether he knew he was harboring a monster in his home.

"You've done everything you could." Wren paused, not wanting to ask him any leading questions. "I was wondering, Lord Lowry . . . Henry is not very lucid, so I haven't been able to speak with him much. Could you tell me, who is he exactly?"

Lowry looked puzzled. "He's my valet."

Wren pursed her lips to hold in an impatient sigh. "Do you know his full name?"

"Why, of course. It's . . . . Oh dear." Lowry grimaced. "I'm embarrassed to admit I don't know his surname. He only introduced himself to me as Henry."

The unsubtle ruse almost made her laugh. Hal, after all, was a nickname for Henry. But the earnestness on Lowry's face destabilized her, filled her with a self-doubt dark and swirling. There was no trace of deception. No caginess at her line of questioning.

So he really has no idea who Hal is.

It still didn't explain why Hal was here in the first place. And it certainly didn't explain why Lowry was so determined to save "Henry" if he truly believed him to be nothing but a valet. That needled at her, like reopening an old wound. To powerful people, soldiers and servants were expendable. She knew that well enough by experience.

"May I ask you a personal question?"

Lowry's eyebrows shot up. "Of course."

"You've gone through a great deal of trouble to bring me here. To some, I imagine it would seem to be more trouble than a servant is worth. Why?"

"To some, she says. A mysterious entity, that *some*. Have you been listening to rumors about me, Ms. Southerland?"

"Nothing like that." She frowned. "Just . . . a curious mind."

Lowry ran a hand through his hair. He looked preoccupied, distant, as he turned his gaze to the frost scoring the windows. "It's a fair question. I suppose I can't help but feel this is all my fault."

"Unless you're a pathogen, this is in no way your fault."

"*Some* would certainly argue the case," he said with a wry lilt, "but I digress. I know it's unreasonable, but I feel responsible for Henry in particular. I normally leave matters of household management to my staff, but I hired him myself. He appeared on my doorstep a few weeks ago, completely unannounced and looking for work."

Wren perked up at that. Why would Hal leave Vesria to come *here*? And if he truly only showed up a few weeks ago, how could he have ingratiated himself enough with Lowry to become his favorite?

"He had no references and hardly any belongings," Lowry said. "On any other day, I'd have turned him out, but there was the small matter of the estate being . . . understaffed. His arrival seemed a blessing, really."

"He just appeared? Did he say where he came from?"

"No. I know it sounds strange, but I didn't want to push him. I wish I could adequately describe how he looked. So determined and burdened. I felt sorry for him. He's so young, but his eyes . . ." Lowry paused. "They held secrets. I assumed he was running from a difficult past and looking for rest. How could I deny him that? A man is entitled to his silence. I figured he would tell me about himself in time, but Henry . . . Well, he's a humorless sort of fellow. Rather like a salted snail—withdraws into himself whenever you try to talk to him."

Wren wrinkled her nose at the too-fresh memory of their encounter, his surly silences and clipped retorts, the swaths of bruises still untended beneath her sleeves. "He is rather morose."

"I can't say I blame him. This whole house is *heavy*. Can you feel it, too?"

Wren hesitated. "Whatever do you mean?"

"I don't know. Sometimes, I feel as though I'm being haunted by death. First my father. Then the servants in the east wing. Now this." He laughed, but it was hollow, almost mournful. "I didn't call for healers quickly enough, and I paid the price. When Henry came, no one had fallen ill for weeks. I thought the worst had passed, but I was wrong. I should have turned him away."

"You couldn't have known it would come back." She had no energy to pity Alistair Lowry. Right now, she couldn't afford to pity anyone but herself. But as always, her traitorous heart compelled her. She placed a reassuring hand on his arm. "No matter how sinister this disease seems, I will get it under control. Try not to worry yourself."

"I shall certainly try," he said. "Worrying doesn't become me. Now shall we take that tea I promised?"

After escorting her out, Lowry lifted the key from around his neck. It spun on the end of its chain until he took it in hand and locked the door behind them. The *snick* of the lock was an unspoken but decisive message: *Keep out.*

But Lowry said nothing about it. Only slipped the chain beneath his collar again.

Unease settled over her, as thick as his despair. She had hoped Lowry would give her clarity, but instead, she felt even more lost than she had before. It left her with a single grim prospect. If she wanted answers, she'd have to get them from Hal himself.

CHAPTER ELEVEN

"Hello, Cavendish."

At the sound of his name, Hal turned toward her. Wren immediately dropped her gaze to the floor and cursed herself for her cowardice. *If you can see Cavendish,* the drill sergeants had told her time and time again, *you're already dead.* An old habit, she supposed. Although she no longer feared for her life, he still unsettled her with those eyes like a starless sky. Cold and completely unknowable.

"I brought you lunch." She lingered in the doorway, breathing in the rich smell of barley and herbs as it wafted from the bowl of soup in her hands.

"I'm not hungry."

"Try to eat anyway," she said irritably. "It'd mean the whole world to me."

As she met his hazy, dispassionate gaze, she couldn't decide whether to feel relieved by his semilucidity. On one hand, it minimized the chances of his reflexive paranoia injuring them both again. And on the other, it meant they had to *interact.*

"I'll try," he said at last.

How low had her expectations sunk that his concession pleased her? Wren settled into the chair at his bedside. Fragrant steam billowed from the bowl, weaving a partition between them. She counted five of his rasping breaths before she wanted to crawl out of her skin with discomfort.

"So. Are you docile today?" she asked as pleasantly as she could manage.

"Yes. Are you?" There was no wryness in it. Only a deep, wrung-out weariness that almost chastened her.

"As much as I ever am," she muttered. Wren dipped the spoon into the soup and tried not to feel self-conscious as she blew over the surface. Healing any soup-induced blisters would be a ridiculous waste of her magic. As soon as she extended it toward him, he angled his chin away from her like a petulant toddler.

"I can do it myself."

Hal and his goddessdamned pride. By the end of this ordeal, she swore she'd develop a twitch in her eye. "Be my guest."

She set the bowl down on the side table hard enough that the broth sloshed over the lip. As he reached for it, Wren watched a single moment unspool into eternity: Hal, uncoordinated from illness, swiping the spoon from its perch; the silver winking as it hung suspended in midair; his mouth twisting into a grimace. Then, in a rush, the spoon clattered to the floor, far too loud in the tense silence of the sickroom.

Hal frowned at the weathered hardwood as if it spanned the bottom of a chasm. She squinted at the reddening tips of his ears. *Frustration? Embarrassment?* It was such a strangely human thing. So achingly normal, she didn't care to interrogate it.

With a sigh, Wren bent over and fetched the spoon for him.

He must have moved at the same time because she nearly clocked him in the chin as she came upright. His nightshirt still hung open, the expanse of his chest and the elegant arch of his collarbones bared only inches from her nose. Close enough that her breath fanned softly against his skin—close enough that she detected the way he shivered. She jerked backward, heat zipping up her neck.

"Uh." The spoon dangled limply between them. "Here."

Hal took it from her with a peculiar expression. "Thank you."

After she passed him the bowl and ascertained he wouldn't give himself second-degree burns, she distracted herself from the unbearable awkwardness by scribbling notes. What was *wrong* with her? Where had her professionalism gone? Hal Cavendish was handsome, assuming one enjoyed the wasting sort of beauty of a dying rose. A completely neutral, observable statement of fact. There. Now she'd thought the unthinkable, she could purge it from her system. It would rise to bother her no longer.

Wren lifted her eyes back to him. "Let me know when you're ready."

"I'm ready."

She snorted at the pain in his voice. "It's healing, not torture. There's a small difference."

Hal gave her a doubtful look as he handed her his empty bowl. She set it aside; then, shifting forward in her seat, she placed her hands on his chest and let her magic flow into his body. While he didn't *say* anything about it, he didn't need to. His clenched jaw and rigid posture spoke volumes.

"It'll make it easier for both of us if you relax, you know," Wren said. "If I really wanted you dead, Lowry would already be promenading in his mourning colors. You wanted my help. I'm helping."

"Fine."

To her surprise, he did try. As his muscles slackened and his blood pressure lowered, her magic flowed more easily through his *fola*. Her awareness spread through his system within minutes, but what she found dismayed her. His condition had deteriorated overnight, as if she hadn't healed him at all.

It wasn't possible. No disease could be so aggressive.

She took even breaths to keep herself grounded. No good work arose from frustration, she reminded herself, even as she wanted to scream at the prospect of redoing everything from last night. Mother Heloise's admonitions still rattled in her head.

Patience, Sister Wren.

It was the refrain of her training, constant and relentless.

You must be patient. In the lab, where she would burn through supplies of herbs testing remedy after remedy. In the infirmary, where Heloise would tut with disapproval when Wren left a faint, ridged scar on one of her Sisters' arms. On the battlefield, where her outpourings of energy would leave grievous wounds healed but her hands numb for days. The human body could only withstand so much. Time was the greatest healer of them all.

Despite the familiar numbness creeping into her fingers, Wren didn't *have* time. She couldn't be patient. If she couldn't treat the worst of his symptoms in the next two weeks, he would die en route to Danu, and she would be tried for desertion.

When she finished healing him, she drew back and clenched her fists until the tendons crackled. Sweat beaded her forehead and the back of her neck, and as the chill of the room descended over her, she shivered against it. "Well. You're no worse, but you're certainly no better."

All the hope he'd managed to hold on to withered before her eyes. "So there's nothing you can do?"

"I never said that." Wren folded her hands in her lap. "It'd be wise not to insult me. You haven't exactly been the most pleasant patient to deal with so far."

"I meant no offense," he said, almost chastised.

"Good." At least he was being civil, if not curt. "Not everyone is as forgiving as I am, you know. Do you understand how lucky you are that I showed up?"

"I do." This time, he closed his eyes. The light elongated the shadows, the outline of his eyelashes scoring his cheekbones like scars. When he spoke again, irony and a strange kind of gratitude tangled together in his voice. "Perhaps it's divine providence."

That notion drifted too close to heresy, even for her. Their meeting here seemed a coincidence far more sinister, but she held her tongue on the matter. "Indeed. How strange that you have a lead on the very case I'm trying to solve."

Hal's expression shuttered again.

"I haven't stopped turning our predicament over," Wren pressed on. "A decorated soldier and future politician, throwing it all away to become a valet for a man who has no ambition other than to throw the most extravagant party of the season? I think not. It couldn't be your lead that brought you here, could it?"

Silence, as expected. It was wishful thinking to believe he'd feed her even crumbs of information. Wren crossed her arms. "Fine. Can you at least tell me more about this sickness? When it came on, how it felt?"

"Three weeks ago," he said. That seemed about right, judging by the atrophy of his muscles and the soft hollows beneath his cheekbones. "It was gradual at first. After about two days of running a fever, the cough started."

Wren frowned as she scratched a quick note to herself. "And was hemoptysis present initially, or is that a more recent development?"

Hal blinked at her.

"Coughing blood," she supplied. "Sorry."

"I see. That started immediately."

She lifted her pen as she registered the almost wry lilt to his voice. For the life of her, she could not tell if he was making fun of her or not. Shaking her head, she ignored it and jotted down another note. "Alright. Fever. Coughing blood. What next?"

"A worsening fatigue. By the third day, I couldn't get out of bed. It felt as if I were being torn apart from the inside." He paused. "I thought I was going to die."

"It's a miracle you haven't, frankly. And it's continued to worsen since then?"

"No. It leveled off fairly quickly."

"I see." Wren chewed on the end of her pen and considered everything she knew about this disease. A gradual onset of symptoms, followed by a sudden spike and plateaued progression. No infected people at the time of his arrival—not that it mattered, considering no viral or bacterial cells were present in his bloodstream.

So where had it come from? What *was* it?

If magic wouldn't work, she had to try something else. Although she had researched diseases thoroughly, she wasn't especially practiced in treating them. As a combat medic, she rarely dealt with things on a microscopic level, or things that systematically attacked the body. Soldiers' injuries were often dramatic but always contained, deep gashes and simple poisons, strangely angled limbs and torn ligaments. Hal's illness, meanwhile, was deep and invisible. It eluded her.

Wren opened her satchel—something Byers had always made fun of her for carrying around all the time. *That thing is a bottomless well of torture implements,* he'd told her when she'd once procured a scalpel to use as a makeshift letter opener. The memory panged like a knocked-against bruise, hitching her breath.

Not now, she thought. *Please, not now.*

Hal Cavendish would never see her wounded again. Shoving through the fresh wave of grief, she kept her eyes lowered until it settled around her as she rummaged through her bag for the supplies she needed. Out came a tourniquet, a bottle of alcohol, a syringe, and three glass vials.

"What're you doing?" Hal asked.

"It's clear that I'm missing something. Drawing blood will help me see what exactly it is."

He seemed to consider her response carefully. "Danubian healers don't usually practice medicine outside their magic."

A statement, she noted, although he waited on her response as if seeking confirmation.

"Not usually." Wren paused. "And?"

"You do." Hal tilted his head, as if it were obvious. "That's notable."

His tone was observational, his face blank, but she still felt a small spark of pride at his recognition. "Thank you?"

He seemed vaguely amused by her response. "It's only a state-ment of fact."

Wren resisted the urge to roll her eyes. "I didn't realize you were collecting information on me."

"Only some." He fixed her with an assessing stare, as if he hoped to glean more from her. "For example, you favor your left leg slightly, and you crack your knuckles after your magic fades. However, I don't need to look hard to find your tells. Your face telegraphs your moods so plainly."

Wren stared at him. "You do realize how unsettling that is, don't you?"

"Force of habit, I'm afraid," he replied. "Observation has allowed me to survive this long."

Definitely unsettling. In Vesria's ruthless court, she supposed it was useful to maintain a mental dossier on every person he met. "I get it. You're a perfect soldier and a perfect politician, even dying. Am I supposed to be impressed? Threatened?"

"I'm only making conversation. I'm . . . admittedly out of prac-tice."

Clearly. If this was his idea of friendly repartee, she doubted she would escape this place with her sanity intact. *Goddess, grant me patience.* As she affixed a vial to a syringe, she reminded herself how sweet it would be to deliver him to the queen.

"My face doesn't change that much," she muttered to herself. Then, to Hal, "Give me your arm."

He reluctantly obliged. She took hold of his wrist—and a cur-rent like electricity tore through her hand. They both flinched away from each other, but a warm sensation still crackled like fire in the space between them.

Hal's eyes locked on hers. "What was that?"

She heard the unspoken accusation in his question: *What did you do?* Wren threw up her hands. "Nothing."

"It felt like something."

Oh, it was something, alright. Healers rarely worked on the same patient for prolonged periods of time, lest *this* happen. But his tone rankled her too much to answer him straight. "Another astounding observation, Cavendish. Is it really so awful?"

He cut her an exasperated look. "It's uncomfortable, yes, to be so aware of you."

Good, she wanted to say. *Suffer with me.*

It *was* uncomfortable. This constant awareness of his energy all around her, the faint pressure of his heartbeat thudding against her eardrums. And when she touched him, that horrible crawling sensation beneath her skin. She couldn't wait to slice herself free of him. Only two weeks more.

Wren rested her hand on his forearm, shivering as her magic vibrated from within his body like a greeting. "The simplest way I can put it is that my magic is bound up in your cells, but it wants to come back to me. You're part of me, and I'm part of you. Eventually, as you recover, your body will flush it out. It's temporary—and completely unintentional, I might add. So if you would kindly stop glaring at me?"

His hostility gradually sagged into bitterness—then morphed into a stoic, pious sort of acceptance that annoyed her more than the alternatives. "I don't like it."

"I'm terribly sorry about that, but there's nothing I can do."

Wren swabbed the inside of Hal's elbow with alcohol and tied the tourniquet around his forearm a fraction too tight. He stared straight out the window while she smacked his arm, encouraging the veins to swell and rise. A dark, admittedly bored part of her enjoyed torturing him. It was so difficult to get a rise out of him, so if the knowledge that an enemy's magic lived inside him rattled him, she wouldn't let him forget it.

"You have good veins." She traced her finger along the thick median cubital vein in his elbow, relishing the way he stiffened with discomfort. "Very stabbable."

Hal ignored her.

"Get faint with needles?"

"No." His voice dripped with irritation. Hers, however, was as sickly sweet as an elderberry brew.

"No need to be tough. Just don't look." Without further warning, Wren slipped the needle into the crook of his arm. Taunting him would be a slow and petty vengeance.

She filled the vials with his blood, watching the clear tubes run a dark, living red. Tempting as it was to drain him, she took only enough to properly conduct her experiments. After she capped the last of the vials, she removed the needle from his arm and tapped the injection site with one finger. It sealed beneath her touch, leaving only a smear of blood behind. She pulled a handkerchief from her pocket and gently wiped it away.

Black spotted her vision, catching her off-balance for a moment. She desperately needed to sleep if the effort of healing that small wound had nearly drained her entirely.

"That would have healed on its own." Wren glanced up at him, surprised by the confusion that tinged his voice. "You're wasting your energy."

Wren primly folded the bloodied cloth over her arm. "I'm not. Your immune system is compromised enough as it is."

In truth, it'd been force of habit, almost ritualistic, to leave no trace. Even now, a world away from Knockaine, she couldn't dismiss that sneering voice in the back of her mind: *If you're not the best, if you make a mistake, what good are you?*

"But you're exhausted."

"Hardly."

"Even without this bond to betray you," said Hal, "you're a terrible liar."

Wren's face burned with humiliation, even as she willed it into blank composure. "I liked you better when you were less chatty."

Hal was almost being *nice* to her, and it made her feel small and childish for her earlier behavior. She doubted he was actually concerned about her—more that he was struggling to understand her. Through the tether, it was easy enough for him to sense her waning energy levels. When she tugged back, she could feel the truth of his condition, too. Sluggish vitals. High cortisol.

He was still in a lot of pain. Of course he hadn't told her.

Wren heaved a heavy sigh as she reached into her bag. She placed a bottle of painkiller on her nightstand. "Fine. I'm exhausted, and you're a martyr. Two drops. Take it or leave it."

Even after she closed the door behind her, she swore she could still feel Hal's gaze prickling the back of her neck.

As Wren settled herself behind her desk, everything else melted away. Here, surrounded by her equipment and faced with a problem to solve, she was in her element. This was what she was made to do. If her magic told her nothing, then surely his blood would.

Wren uncapped the first vial and dribbled a sample on a slide. It spread like a bruise across the glass, slow and creeping. What her nation would pay for this opportunity, to uncover the genetic secrets lurking in his cells. But underneath the microscope's lens, his blood looked the same as anyone else's. It would have been nice if it hadn't. How sweet it would be to see his wickedness twined into every strand of protein and spelled out in his platelets.

She adjusted the focus of the microscope and frowned. Well, maybe it didn't look exactly like everyone else's blood. As expected, his white blood cell count was too high. But among them swarmed something else.

Alkaloids.

"Goddess above," she whispered. In her search for viral or bacterial cells, she had overlooked something far more obvious—more sinister. Colwick Hall's mysterious illness didn't exist and never had. Hal had been poisoned.

Which meant someone was murdering Lowry's servants.

CHAPTER TWELVE

hat in the Goddess's name was she doing here?

Wren lowered her head onto the desk. Murder and sabotage lay far, far beyond her skill set. What if someone came back to finish the job? What if someone came for *her*? Her mind was an ever-tightening coil of *what if, what if, what if.*

She had to tell someone who was qualified to handle this. She had to tell Lowry. She had to take Hal and escape immediately. But she couldn't.

Her carriage wasn't ready; braving the mountain roads in this snowstorm would almost certainly promise death. And Lowry was already a frazzled mess over this illness, if that absurd contract was any indication. Telling him it was poison would send him into a nervous conniption.

Assuming, of course, he's not the one who did it.

But then why call for a healer? Why put on airs of mourning? If it wasn't him, there were only about five other servants on the estate besides Hannah. Her list of suspects was uncomfortably small.

She took slow, steadying breaths to keep herself grounded. Everything would be fine if she stuck to her plan. She couldn't panic. Fourteen more days. That was all she needed to endure. Fourteen more days to develop an antidote that would guarantee Hal's survival and her safety. Fourteen more days until she could go home. She didn't have to embroil herself in any of this. She just had to be quick and discreet. And focused.

So focus.

If she knew what the poison was, she could treat the root cause, but at least fifty different plants grew in this area that could cause his symptoms. She would have to visit the local herbalist to narrow down the options and acquire samples if she could. In cases like these, folk knowledge often surpassed scientific.

After pulling on every jacket she owned, Wren waddled into the hallway. Even in broad daylight, the house was impossibly dark, almost funereal. The only natural light filtered in through a round window at the end of the corridor that watched her like a half-shut eye. The snow accumulating on the windowsill would soon consume her view entirely. Wren wondered if this was how it felt to be buried alive, watching as the darkness swallowed a single point of light. After this ordeal, maybe she'd request a transfer to a coastal town.

Emerging into the grand hall, Wren clutched the banister and hurried down the staircase's three twisting flights. As she rounded the last corner, she smacked into something solid and red. She gasped, staggering backward, but gloved hands caught her and steadied her by the elbows. She twisted out of the grip, but stilled as a key swung hypnotically in front of her nose like a pendulum. Wren recognized it—Lowry's, of course—and looked up into his panicked blue eyes.

"Ms. Southerland?" As soon as he registered it was her, he wilted with relief and laughed breathlessly. He was dressed ostentatiously in red checkered trousers and a matching waistcoat. *A different outfit from this morning . . . ?* They'd met only a few hours ago, and it wasn't as if he'd entertained anyone or gone on a ride in this weather. "We really ought to stop meeting this way, scaring each other half to death."

"My apologies! My head is elsewhere, clearly."

His gaze lingered anxiously on the fur-trimmed collar of her coat. "Where are you off to in such a hurry? You're not leaving, are you?"

And what concern of his was it if she did? Then, she remembered—the contract.

I shall not leave the estate under any circumstances without express permission.

Forcing a smile, Wren said, "Would you give me leave to run an errand? I'm hoping to go to the apothecary. My supplies have run dangerously low, and I'm missing an ingredient for Henry's medication."

"I want to say yes, of course, but . . ." Lowry turned toward the window, his hands twisting together. The clouds beyond the glass were a solid gray wall. "That storm is nothing to trifle with. Once night falls, you'll never find your way back."

Wren tucked her bloodless hands into her pockets. Speaking slowly to edge the impatience out of her voice, she said, "In the military, I braved things far worse than a storm. I'm afraid I must insist. This is a matter of life and death."

Lowry's face paled, and she could see him wrestling with indecision. The choice was dire: risk his favorite servant, or risk the healer herself. "Perhaps I can order your ingredient for you? I understand it's not ideal, but—"

"He's getting worse."

"Please, Ms. Southerland, take pity on me. My nerves can't bear it."

Lowry laid an imploring hand on her arm. His grip was surprisingly firm—enough that she flinched back—and his eyes were too pleading, too wounded. This close, she noticed a burst blood vessel leaking red into the sclera. Against it, the milky blue of his irises shone like ice.

Frozen in the intensity of his stare, she had to wonder if he could have done it. If he could be lying to her.

"I simply cannot let you leave the house in good conscience," he continued. "I'll have nothing but terrible visions of the spring thaw. Just imagine it. Me, unearthing your frozen corpse from the garden like some sort of spud. It would be macabre!"

The wind wailed like a keening ghost, and the whole house groaned with strain. As Wren shivered, all of her fight went out, extinguished like a tapered flame. Alistair Lowry wanted her to believe he was a man concerned with the well-being of his servants, including her. And right now, with the genuine quaver in his voice, the artful fall of his hair across his furrowed brow . . . it worked.

He was right, after all. Night was creeping down from the mountains now, and wandering into a storm to find a town she only approximately knew the location of guaranteed death by hypothermia. Hal would do her no good if she was dead. Until the weather changed, she'd have to depend on her magic to keep him alive.

Her shoulders slumped. "You're right. I don't know what I was thinking."

"I appreciate your understanding. Truly." Lowry heaved a sigh of relief and let go of her arm.

Just like that, all of his urgency, all of his desperation, fell away. It was such a swift change, Wren was left reeling. Now that adrenaline couldn't keep her upright, she emptied of everything save for a haze of paranoia. Lowry was truly the most tempestuous and easy-to-reassure man she'd ever met, and she could not shake the queasy thought that she'd just been played for a fool. But after what she'd learned today, maybe she couldn't trust her own instincts. Even if Lowry was manipulating her, he certainly wasn't hiding anything sinister behind that self-assured smile. With no clear motive, he seemed an exceedingly unlikely murder suspect.

"Of course, my lord," she said quietly. "Thank you for watching out for me."

"Anytime, my dear. I'm all too sympathetic to the effect this house has on people in winter." He turned and leaned against the banister, a grim silhouette against the bar-shaped windows. The wan afterglow of dusk flickered in the shadow of the snowfall, and far below them, the darkness gathering on the ground floor churned like the rising sea. "It gets to be quite claustrophobic. The shortening days. The wind and snow and the insufferable creak of the old foundation. It's enough to drive anyone mad."

"Yet you've stayed," Wren said.

"For most of the year, I have plenty of company," he said. "For the rest . . . Well, I've come to find it peaceful, being so undisturbed. I have things to keep me busy."

"Like collecting?"

"Like collecting, yes." The amusement with which he spoke veered decidedly into the cryptic. Before she could press harder, he spun on his heel toward her and said, "And planning events, of course. Speaking of! I'm considering the color palette for the ball. What do you think? Black and silver, or navy and white?"

"Um." In all the chaos, the ball had slipped her mind entirely. Although she owed Lowry nothing, she couldn't help feeling another pang of guilt. All this planning, all this effort, would be for nothing. She would betray him soon enough. "Black and silver are Danu's colors."

"So they are," Lowry said. "So it shall be for my guest of honor. May I take your coat, my dear? I'll see to it that Hannah hangs it up for you."

A flash of movement past his shoulder drew Wren's attention. In the grand hall below, Hannah was dusting a lacquered table with such care, it may as well have been a work of art. Unsubtle eavesdropping if she ever did see it. Wren removed her overcoat and passed it to him. Lowry folded it over his arm like a butler's white serviette.

"Perhaps you'd like to assist me with the menu as well?" he said.

"That's very kind of you." Wren rubbed her temples. She could hardly remember why she'd come down here in the first place with how quickly he flitted from topic to topic. "But with the patient in the state he's in, I'm afraid I have no time."

Lowry frowned. "Of course. Do keep me posted on his progress."

"I will."

With that, he turned over his shoulder and snapped his fingers. "Hannah, darling?"

Hannah jumped, dropping her feather duster with a clatter that echoed through the hall. It dislodged a layer of dust from the east wing's tapestry.

Lowry pinched the bridge of his nose. "When you've quite surfeited yourself with scrubbing the varnish from that table, put this away for Ms. Southerland, will you?"

"Yes, milord."

"Splendid." Lowry descended the last flight of stairs and dumped Wren's coat into Hannah's waiting arms. She fumbled for only a moment before cradling it as reverently as a wedding dress. "I am going to calm my nerves, and you may do as you please. No one is to disturb me for the rest of the day."

"Yes, milord," she called after him as he rounded the corner. Somewhere in the depths of the house, his off-key whistling echoed off the walls before it was silenced by the slam of a door. Both Wren and Hannah flinched.

"Is he . . . always like that?" Wren dared to ask.

Hannah glanced her way, her mouth thinned to a wary line. "Like what?"

A tense silence washed over them. Although Wren wanted answers, she was painfully aware that she'd asked Hannah to speak against their employer. Hannah, who'd showed no signs of even tolerating her thus far. If she played her cards wrong, this could end badly for her. Considering her next move carefully, Wren said, "Erratic."

Hannah hesitated. Then, all the tension melted out of her. "Yes, milady. He's always like that."

Wren clutched the banister, her fingers whitening against the wood. If this behavior was common, was it evidence for or against his character?

Hannah stepped onto the staircase but stopped on the landing beside Wren. "He used to frighten me as well, but you mustn't let him get to you. Lord Lowry can be prone to dramatics when it suits him."

"I'm beginning to see that now." Wren paused. "Thanks."

Hannah nodded, then lowered her eyes. But Wren recognized the emotion sparkling in her eyes all too well. Relief. "If you'll excuse me."

CHAPTER THIRTEEN

As soon as Wren closed the door to her room, every coherent thought slipped through her fingers like water. Without anyone to talk to or keep her focused, exhaustion caught her out. She'd spent her magic, pushed herself physically and mentally past the brink. Her mind became a muddle of words like *murder* and *poison*—dragging her deeper and deeper.

Tomorrow, she thought as she crawled into bed. *Tomorrow I can . . .*

Wren startled awake to late afternoon sunlight. She groaned at the pounding in her head, the hunger twisting her stomach into knots. On her nightstand, cold tea and cold fish waited for her beside a note from Hannah, informing her she'd brought Hal his meals for today.

That news filled her with dread. She shouldn't let anyone tend to him until she determined whether his food was laced with poison. Just how long had she been asleep? She groped for the drawer and rummaged for her pocket watch.

Five o'clock.

She hadn't overexerted herself so thoroughly since her earliest days as an apprentice.

Wren dragged herself out of bed to get ready. She made quick work of it, devouring her lunch without relish and lacing herself into a warm flannel gown. Then, she staggered across the hall to find Hal reading in bed. He was clearly in the throes of a fever, judging by the sweat beading his temples and the covers cast halfway across the room. Still, he sat upright with grim determination.

"Good to see you're still alive," she said as she took her seat in the bedside chair.

Hal did not glance up from his book.

"You should lie down."

"Maybe."

"*Definitely.*"

He sighed through the fluid in his lungs, a rattling sound. "I've lain down for weeks. I'm bored."

She could understand that. Out of curiosity, she tilted her head to steal a look at the title. *A History of Warfare,* written by a Danubian scholar she vaguely recognized.

"*That's* your idea of fun?" she said skeptically.

"The selection here is admittedly limited, but Danu's history does interest me. I should know more of it than I do."

She waited for him to expound, but that was apparently all he had to say on the matter. "You say that as though it's an obligation."

"Isn't it?" This time, he fixed her with that eerily intent stare.

"Depends." Wren crossed her arms. "What, you feel like you need to know the bare minimum about the people you plan to govern by force? How cultured of you."

He looked a little slighted. "No, that's not my intention."

"Well, there's not much to it, anyway," she muttered. "War and suffering. Martyrdom. Perhaps some coal mining. Not that *you* need to be told about any of that."

"I suppose not." He flipped a page casually, as if he'd not registered her insult. "I just want to know your account of what was taken from you. Which cities, which resources, how many casualties."

To her surprise, there was no pleasure, no pride, in his voice. Only a pensive gravitas. What use could he have for figures like that, if not to gloat, or to see how easy it would be to eradicate them entirely? But she resented his confidence that he could boil loss down to numbers, that human life amounted to nothing but tally marks. That attitude had landed them here, blood repaid in blood thrice over, an infinite debt.

"You'll never know exactly what was taken from us. You'll never even know what *you* took personally. There's no quantifying something like that."

"I know," he said. "But perhaps someone should try."

Wren blinked at him. She was in no mood to untangle his evasive responses or discuss war today. "I guess I can't criticize you for your choice of reading material."

"What do you like to read?"

The corner of Wren's mouth lifted involuntarily into a smile. Apparently, he appreciated the change in topic as well. "Guess."

He considered it as he turned another page. "Theologians."

Wren snorted. "Goddess, no. I'm not so boring as you."

"Penny dreadfuls?"

"Suitably lurid," she said, "but no. Medical textbooks."

Hal's expression grew puzzled. "I see."

"Watch it, Cavendish. You haven't lived until you've read all the gruesome case studies of people living with parasites."

"Then I'll settle for my boring, half-lived life."

Wren pursed her lips to keep herself from grinning at him. When she let herself forget who he was and what he'd done, he was surprisingly easy to talk to despite his reserve. Or maybe she'd grown used to him already.

"And you?" she asked. "What would you be doing if you were home?"

"Much of my time lately has been consumed with reading policy and attending meetings." He returned his attention to his book. "To be honest, if I could do anything, I would be training."

Wren groaned. "Training? You can't be serious."

Out of the corner of her eye, she thought she caught a faint smile on his lips. But when he glanced up, he looked as expressionless as ever. "I'm always serious."

As the conversation dwindled into almost companionate silence, she turned her attention to healing him. Her fingers skimmed his chest as she unfastened his buttons, magic rippling over his skin like water. By some miracle, he didn't flinch. It seemed she wasn't the only one falling into the rhythm of their sessions.

Healing him had become a rote process by now, a matter of re-doing all her work yet again. After only two times, she'd obtained a morbid sort of familiarity with his body. The particular turns of his *fola,* the frail stutter of his heart. It no longer fought against her.

Although sleep had restored her supply of magical energy, she still felt listless. With no sample of the toxin and no guidance, Wren could give Hal no formal diagnosis and no effective treatment. And while he deserved to know the truth behind his illness, she couldn't bring herself to tell him just yet. Why worry him or give him more reason to doubt her? He was stable, and that was all that mattered.

At least until overuse ran her magic dry.

Despair, however, fixed nothing. She refused to give up until she's exhausted her every lead. The night she'd arrived, she'd no-ticed the extensive selection of medical books in Lowry's library. Perhaps that included a guide to medicinal—or poisonous—plants.

Wren's magic flickered out just as Hal heaved a long, unim-peded sigh. Night had unfurled over the mountains now, flooding through the window like the dark burble of a river. She lit the can-dles drooping in their waxy copper dishes.

A blade of fire danced on the end of the match, and of all things to sink her in grief, it was the smell of it. Here in the wavering dark of Colwick Hall, she could almost hear Byers: *Got a light, South-erland?*

The flame singed her finger, jolting her back into the present. She swore and shook out the match.

"Are you alright?" The light brushed gold over his features, as stark and shining as those of an icon of a saint. What threw her most, however, was the earnestness in his expression.

"I'm fine." Steadying herself, she said, "I think I'll have a diagnosis for you soon."

Hal glanced up at her, startled. "Really?"

"Yes." She hesitated. "If anyone other than me brings you anything to eat, don't take it, alright?"

Before he could ask any questions, she took one of the candles and slipped into the hallway.

Halfway down the staircase, a strange feeling bloomed cold at the base of her skull. Like the pressure of a thousand eyes boring into her—or the faint stirring of magic within her. Was someone hurt?

Wren glanced back up toward Hal's room. Surely he hadn't keeled over in the few seconds she'd been gone. It felt as if her magic urged her onward, downward. The shadows eddied around her skirts like a current: *go.*

She took one step. Another.

Then stopped dead.

Slowly at first, a moan welled up from below her.

"Hello?" she called, barely above a whisper. "Hannah? Lord Lowry?"

It crescendoed until it tore through her every nerve like shears. She *knew* that sound—the same one from yesterday morning. For a few seconds, she stood frozen, staring blearily into the whispering flicker of the candlelight.

Some folk would tell you it's haunted.

It was entirely, completely preposterous. And yet she trembled as if the temperature had plummeted around her. She hurried down the stairs. As soon as her boots touched the ground floor, her magic sighed across her skin. It tugged her, as if cinched around her wrist like rope, toward the forbidden east wing. But if Lowry found out she'd been inside . . .

What will he do? Send me away?

It seemed ridiculous, but fear forced her to skirt past it and into the waiting gloom of a corridor, past rows of closed doors illuminated by the orb of firelight. The force of her magic's pull faded—then intensified again as she turned a corner into what looked like a morning room, furnished with white couches and an elegant writing desk that overlooked a curtained window. The air swirled thick with darkness.

Here, her magic seemed to say, when she stood in the center of the room. *Here.*

Glancing over her shoulder to make sure no one was watching, she crouched and placed her palm flat on the cold floorboards. Magic shot up the length of her forearm urgently. But this room was empty and forgotten, as desolate as the rest of the house.

Wren sighed with impatience, crossing the room to the writing desk. While she was here, she might as well take more parchment and ink for her notetaking tonight. She slid open one of the drawers, letting candlelight pour inside. Inside was an oddity—what looked to be a bound sheaf of anatomical sketches.

A shiver tore down her spine, sudden and fierce as a hailstorm. Her breath caught high in her throat. Hairs on her arms and the back of her neck stood on end. She hadn't heard anyone in the hall, but without looking, she *knew.* Someone was standing behind her.

"This place is of the living and yours no longer," Wren whispered.

"*What* did you just say?"

Wren whipped around, throwing candlelight across the room like a spill of water. It sluiced over Hannah, who leaned in the doorway with one hand on her hip. More than anything, Wren wanted the darkness to swallow her whole. Anything to cut short this embarrassment.

"Oh, nothing!" Wren laughed a little too shrilly, hastily slamming the drawer shut. "Nothing at all."

"What are you doing in here? Are you looking for something?"

"Well, I was going to browse Lord Lowry's library," she said. "And then I . . . got lost?"

"Heavens," Hannah muttered. In her plain dress and hastily braided hair, she looked nothing like the specter who had greeted Wren on her first night here. She was all too mortal, clearly drawn away from her evening tea. After a moment's hesitation, Hannah asked, "Do you need me to show you?"

Wren hated she was relieved to have an escort. "Yes, please."

Hannah guided her across the grand hall and to Lowry's study, seemingly oblivious to the darkness that sharpened and lurched as they passed. From above the desk, the taxidermied stag's antlers cast long, stark shadows over the floor like a tangle of briars.

Hannah flipped a switch beside the door, and the wall sconces all sputtered weakly to life. Wren squeezed her eyes shut at the sudden flood of artificial light, but when she blinked them open, a gloom still hung heavy in the air. She'd never grow accustomed to this sickly, pus-yellow glow. She'd read by firelight for the rest of her life if she could.

"Do you need anything else?" Hannah asked.

"No, I can find what I need from here." Wren carried her candle to the shelves, letting the light spill over the gilt letters on the books' spines.

"Did you truly need to be shown to the library?" Wren turned to see Hannah standing in the doorway, her arms crossed.

"I did," Wren said, flustered. "Well, I suppose I wasn't exactly lost. But I *was* on my way here before I got sidetracked. I . . . heard a noise."

"A noise?" Hannah lifted her eyebrows. "We have our fair share of them here."

"It sounded like someone was hurt."

"I know the one, milady," Hannah said after a moment, her expression unreadable. "Don't be afraid. There are always sounds in the house; it's old. When I was a child, my mother told me ghosts roamed the corridors at night, hungry for little girls out past their bedtime. But they're nothing but stories, I promise."

"That's . . . reassuring," Wren said, still not entirely convinced. "Thank you."

Hannah nodded, her gaze dropping to the floor. "Don't thank me. Consider this my official welcome. And an apology for avoiding you since you arrived."

"Avoiding me? I hadn't noticed."

"Oh. I see." Hannah flushed. "That's good to hear. I'm still adjusting. Before . . . everything happened, I was third chambermaid. I never had to deal much with guests."

The sadness in her voice sobered Wren. "I'm sorry for taking you away from your evening tea. Consider us even."

"It's fine, really. I don't mind the company."

"Me neither." Wren offered her a smile. As much as she longed for a friend in this miserable place, she didn't exactly have time to make idle conversation. Hannah, however, presented her with an invaluable opportunity. A chance to talk to someone who knew just as much about this place as her employer. "So, you grew up here? What was that like?"

"Good enough. There were always lots of other children in the servants' quarters. Sometimes even Lord Lowry and his brother played with us."

Wren smiled, pausing to ease a few botany textbooks from the shelf. "Really?"

"Of course. There weren't exactly other noble children to play with." Hannah lowered herself into an armchair. "Lord Lowry liked attention, as you can imagine, and his brother preferred keeping to himself."

"If you don't mind my saying, you two don't seem terribly close for childhood playmates."

When Hannah went silent, Wren turned over her shoulder to find her expression darkened. Perhaps she'd pushed too far.

"Forgive me! I'm sometimes too nosy for my own good."

"No, no . . ." Hannah pulled her messy braid over her shoulder, twisting the end of it through her fingers. "There was no dramatic falling out. I didn't care for him much as a child, is all. He was a charming boy when he wanted to be, but his father indulged him too much. All it took was a smile, and the man was good as clay in his hands. It spoiled him—made him cruel sometimes for it."

"I can hardly imagine him as cruel," Wren said carefully.

"Men change." She laughed, an almost hollow sound. "It's funny now, really. I remember . . . I was perhaps six, and Lord Lowry eleven. Nelly—the cook—found a stray cat in town one day. And when she kittened, Nelly let me choose one to call mine, a black cat with white socks. I named her Midnight. When the young lords caught wind of it, they came to see the litter. Of course, Lord Lowry wanted Midnight for himself."

"What did you do?"

"I told him to piss off, and he looked me in the eye and told me . . ." Hannah trailed off, smiling sheepishly. "I suppose it's actually not that funny of a story."

"No, it's alright," Wren said. "Please go on."

"He told me if I didn't give her up, he'd cut her open. See what was inside, like his father did in his experiments."

"But . . . that's *awful*."

Hannah waved her off. "Nelly made a show of scolding me in front of him. Later, she told me it was only a name—I could still play with her all I liked. So I let him have her."

"What happened to her?"

She cringed. "A few months later, I found her on the edge of the woods."

Wren felt all the blood drain from her face. "Did he . . . ?"

"No," Hannah said quickly. "No, I don't think so, milady. The wolves got her."

The silence fell heavy between them.

Hannah rose from her chair. "Well, I believe I've said enough for tonight."

"Wait." No one else in this house spoke to her so candidly. If

Hannah could tell her anything about how this poison was administered, perhaps she'd have an easier time treating it. "Would you mind answering a few more of my questions?"

"About what?" she asked guardedly.

"About the sickness."

"Oh. That."

"There wasn't anything strange the patients were eating or drinking, was there?" When Hannah shook her head, Wren pressed, "And no one in particular who delivered all their meals to them?"

"Not anybody in particular, no. We changed up who brought their meals. Drew sticks on it, actually. No one wanted to go into the sickroom, considering, well . . ." A worried notch appeared between her eyebrows. "Why?"

"Standard healer questions." Wren pinned a smile in place. "And there was no one new in the house over the past few weeks who could have introduced the contagion?"

"The Duke of Matthonwy and a gentleman named Mr. Glyde— his lawyer, I believe—were here last."

The duke was widely reported to be friends with Lord Lowry, so he was an unlikely suspect. "What about anyone who dislikes him?"

"Standard healer questions indeed," she muttered. "Lord Lowry has a fair many people who dislike him. He can be . . . provocative. But he's harmless. I would say more people are worried about him. Nobody sees him much anymore. Last year, there was a party every week. And now . . . Well, he keeps to himself."

"And what of Henry?"

"Henry." She shook her head, as if exasperated. "He reminds me a bit of you. Always peppering me with questions. He wanted to know what guests Lord Lowry hosted, or if anyone we didn't know came through, but he was never pleased with the answers. I didn't know him well at all, to be honest. He wasn't unkind, but he wasn't friendly either. Before I could crack him, he fell ill."

"I see."

"Are you cold?"

Wren glanced down at the gooseflesh stippling her arms. "Oh, yes. I'm still getting used to the weather, is all."

She pulled at the edges of her sleeves like they were a stubborn knot. According to Lowry's account, Hal had left Vesria to come here and pose as a servant. If he was asking questions, it meant he was looking for something in Colwick Hall—something he never found before he fell "ill." Something, perhaps, regarding his lead on the missing soldiers.

The more the story unwound, the more of a tangled mess it became.

"I wanted to ask you something, too," Hannah said, drawing her from her thoughts.

"Anything."

"Do you really think you can cure him? Everyone who's gotten sick has lived longer than the person before, but . . ."

But no one survived.

Wren sagged under the weight of her books. The *truly* honest answer to her question was no. There wasn't a chance. With no sample of the original poison, she couldn't conjure a cure from nothing. But tentative hope shone in Hannah's eyes, and Wren could not bear to crush it. One of them needed to be optimistic, anyway.

"Of course I can."

"Good." Hannah offered a tight smile before a strangled sob slipped out. She turned away abruptly, dabbing at her eyes with the sleeve of her nightgown. "Oh, heavens. I'm so sorry. I just . . ."

It hurt, watching her smother herself. How many times had Wren done the same thing? Apologized for her own sadness, for daring to burden someone else with her feelings? Wren placed her books on a settee cushion and crossed the room to Hannah. "Please don't apologize. I can't imagine how hard this is for you. They were your friends and family."

"Thank you." Hannah drew deep breaths, blinking until the tears receded. "I was thinking it must be nice being a healer. I've always wanted to be one—never more than recently, when I felt so powerless. It's a noble profession."

"I wish I could claim to be noble. In Danu, all people with magic like mine become healers whether they want to or not." Wren let her magic collect on her palms, flickering between them. It illuminated the tears still beaded in Hannah's eyelashes. "But I got lucky. Even though I couldn't be anyone or anything I wanted, I don't know that I'd have chosen anything else. It's part of me. Maybe even all of me."

"I should hope not," Hannah said gently. "I don't care to believe that the sum of us is what we *do*."

Wren frowned, uncertain of what to say. If not healing, then what *was* the sum of her? And if she couldn't crack this poison and bring Hal back to Danu, how could she ever prove her worth? She had only thirteen days left before she could leave, a veritable mountain of books to read, not to mention the tedious process of mixing her antidotes . . .

"Anyway," Hannah said, "let me know if I can help you with anything else."

Then—an idea came to Wren.

"You know, I think you can," she said. "I'm working on developing a medication right now, and I could use some help taking measurements, recording failures, and the like. It's not the most exciting work, but if you truly wanted to learn to be a healer, it would be a start."

"So I'd be your assistant?"

"Exactly. What do you say?"

Her answering smile, as radiant as daybreak, shone brighter than anything Wren had seen in weeks. "I say yes. When do we start?"

CHAPTER FOURTEEN

Nine more days.

Wren had only nine more days to identify the poison and develop an antidote now that she'd wasted four of them researching. Skimming every botany book in Lowry's library had armed her with a frighteningly thorough knowledge of the language of flowers but had brought her no closer to an answer. Nearly every one of them had proven useless.

All that remained was a single tome, as thick as her fist and coated in dust, called *The Natural History of the Cernosian Highlands.* It was an account of the local flora, written sometime in the last century by a tourist from the mainland. Detailed botanical illustrations adorned each gold-leafed page, accompanied by dry annotations on each plant's properties.

She'd spent the morning browsing the table of contents, dismayed to find that the book contained a robust catalog of intoxicants and little else. But in the very back was a small section on poisons that looked promising. If she found nothing within . . .

No, she refused to entertain the possibility of failure. This book had to contain the answers she sought. But before she could begin reading in earnest, the grandfather clock tolled, announcing her evening session with Hal.

She crossed the hall and found the sickroom lit by warm candlelight. It lapped at the frost-rimed windows and pooled in the hollows of Hal's face. He was drowsing lightly, creases from the wrinkled sheets stamped onto his cheeks. Wren approached his bedside on silent feet and laid the back of her palm against his forehead. No fever, mercifully. The healing from this afternoon must have held up over the past few hours.

A stack of books lay abandoned on his nightstand. A quick glance at their titles confirmed he'd sent Hannah for military histories—and *philosophy*, of all things.

How pretentious.

It disturbed her, how familiarity birthed that insult. Almost as much as it disturbed her that her hand lingered on his forehead, her fingers itching to brush the hair back from his face. What was happening to her?

Every day stretched unbearably longer, and in the quiet moments, Hannah's words haunted her: *He reminds me a bit of you. Peppering me with questions.*

Hal was searching for something here, but until she provided him with a diagnosis and a cure, he wouldn't tell her what. What did he know about Lowry that she didn't? What was she *missing*?

Hal blinked open his eyes and startled, just barely.

Wren couldn't help smiling. "How're you feeling?"

"Well enough."

"Then you should be up for some walking." Hal cast her a baleful look, but by now, she had become adept at reading the meaning behind his silences. "I know. But you'll feel worse if you get bedsores or die of a blood clot. A truly embarrassing end to your legacy."

With great indignity, he accepted her outstretched hands. The warmth of her magic collected between their palms. A steady hum, a magnet's pull. Neither of them said anything.

Hal rose unsteadily, and Wren, now eye level with his chin, registered for the first time how tall he was. *This could end disastrously.* Tipping her head back, she watched worry light his eyes as he arrived at the same conclusion.

"Don't fall," she said. "I think you'll crush me."

Still, Hal said nothing.

A bad mood, she noted. Or maybe she'd grown far too comfortable teasing the Reaper of Vesria.

She slipped her arm around his waist and winced as he transferred some of his weight to her. He was surprisingly heavy, despite the time away from training. With every step, lean muscle rippled under her touch—a sensation she desperately tried to ignore.

"How far do you intend to take me?" he asked, his voice calculatedly casual.

A fair question. Hal's company was, if nothing else, an excellent cover for snooping. Since Wren had found those anatomical sketches hidden in the morning room's writing desk, she hadn't found another chance to look at them.

"More than five steps and fewer than five miles." At his despondent look, she added, "You know, if you were doing this every day as you *should,* it wouldn't be so onerous. For today, we'll go to the morning room."

"Very well." Although his voice remained affectless, his face was the most expressive she'd seen it. *Frustrated.* She supposed it would be humbling. In his prime, he was an elite soldier. Now, he was barely able to stand without aid from a girl meant to be his enemy.

They made it down the hallway, where the last of the light dragged its nails against the floorboards. His breaths already came thick and labored by the time they stopped at the top of the grand staircase. Sheer exhaustion dulled his eyes to gray.

"We'll take it slow," she said. "One step at a time, alright?"

"I can walk on my own."

This again? Wren thought he'd overcome the worst of his ego already. "Can you really? Frankly, you look like you're about to keel over."

"I don't need you to coddle me." Hal lifted her arm from around him and clung to the banister with a white-knuckled grip.

Wren bristled. She could have easily yanked him back to her side, or scolded him for being stubborn. But something else possessed her, rooted her in place as she watched him hobble downstairs, step by agonizing step. If he fell, she told herself she would take pleasure in it—that he'd deserve it. But through that goddessdamned tether, she sensed his struggle. His heart raced with exertion, pulling hers along with it. It nauseated her, filled her with a light-headed anxiety that deepened every time he faltered. Wren tailed him like a forlorn hound.

It wasn't until they alighted on the ground floor that she expelled the stale air from her lungs. He still walked determinedly ahead of her, through spears of wan sunlight that painted his black hair in shades of indigo. For all his wounded pride, Hal moved like a man made of glass, his every step rigid and delicate. He kept his face utterly blank, as if there were nothing at all wrong with him. *Typical soldier.* But Wren knew better. With his extensive organ damage, even this small exertion must have been excruciating.

She followed him into the morning room—and heard him trip before she saw it.

His foot scuffed the floor, as loud as a gunshot in the late evening gloom. Then he stumbled forward, tearing a gasp from Wren's throat. Before she could spring for him, Hal caught himself on the back of an armchair.

Wren approached him, uncertain whether to accost him with *are you alright?* or *what were you thinking?* first. He'd begun to trust her, so what had changed? Was it so terrible to need someone else? Was kindness such a horrible burden to endure?

"I hope you're pleased with yourself." Wren took him by the shoulders and all but shoved him into the chair. "Need I remind you that you asked for my help? I understand you're allergic to compassion, but you have to let me *try*."

Hal bowed his head, his bed-mussed hair falling over his eyes. "Alright."

Wren placed a hand on her hip. "Alright?"

"You're right. I do need your help." A concession, at last—not that he looked in any condition to resist her anymore.

"Good." Wren pinched the bridge of her nose, suddenly exhausted herself. "Rest for a few minutes, and then we'll go back."

But first, the sketches.

As soon as Hal let his eyes fall closed, Wren went to the writing desk and unlatched the drawer. It slid out with a squeal on its unoiled tracks.

"What're you doing?" Hal asked.

"Nothing that concerns you." Wren turned on her heel to face him. "Mind your business."

He blinked at her, clearly perplexed. "Pardon my intrusion."

Wren huffed. "I just . . . left something in the drawer. Sometimes I work down here. It's a nicer view than in my room."

While he didn't look at all convinced, he didn't ask her any more questions. Wren lifted the sheaf of papers out of the drawer and laid them on the desk. As soon as she spread them out, she was struck by their meticulous detail. Each page contained a sketch of a specific part of the body and included a map of the *fola,* composed in a tracery of black and silver ink.

She leafed through drawings of the heart, the femur, the hand— until she reached the last page, which depicted the bulbus oculi, the eyeballs. The *fola's* insertion points were marked in thick, decisive smears of lead. She bent closer, squinting at the cramped handwriting. This collection must have been part of Lowry's father's research, and based on what Lowry had told her about him, nothing about it struck her as unusual. Although the paper seemed too new, too preserved, to be more than a few years old.

She was almost disappointed.

"Well?" She replaced the papers in the drawer and turned back to Hal. "Shall we?"

"I need a few more minutes."

"Fine."

Wren sank onto the edge of a pink settee and stared past Hal, a solid black shape against the charcoal sky. Outside the window, snow continued to fall. The muffling silence of the estate would drive her mad soon.

Sometimes, she wondered if Hal would be easier to deal with were he as violent and tempestuous as the Vesrian stereotypes promised, or as cold as the war stories—and her own memory— described. In the Battle of the River Muri, she had seen a monster wearing his face. Remorseless. *Empty.* Even though he had spared her life, she could chalk it up to some kind of strange serendipity.

But the man sitting across from her was only pensive, sometimes even dryly amusing if she was being generous. Which one was the facade? What would she find if she pushed him hard enough?

"So, Cavendish. Are you always so taciturn, or is it only with me?"

"I don't believe in talking for its own sake," he said. "I grew up around people who enjoyed the sound of their own voice too much. It seems I can't escape them."

"What's *that* supposed to mean?"

He closed his eyes, as if bracing himself for a fight. "I don't mean you."

If not her, then . . . ? Oh. *Oh.* Lowry.

Wren choked back a laugh. "Then let's discuss something of import. Danubian history, perhaps? Or maybe the ever-engaging philosophical writings of Walsh?"

Wren watched emotion pass over his face like clouds over the moon, a slow bleed from defensive to confused to resigned. Hal sighed. "Have you read them? They're quite interesting."

"Alas, I haven't had the pleasure." Wren snapped her fingers. "But I can do one better. Let's discuss religion."

"You want to talk about religion," he repeated.

She'd meant it as a joke, but now that it hummed in the air between them . . . "Why not? If you're really interested in Danu's culture, I can tell you more than books can. Consider it a thought exercise. When have a Danubian and a Vesrian ever had the opportunity to discuss these things civilly?"

"I'm afraid you'll find me an inept conversation partner on the topic. You're clergy."

"Military," she corrected.

Hal cast her a sidelong look. "You were raised in an abbey."

"I'm not sure whether to be flattered or unnerved that you know that, but yes, I was. Case in point."

"Did you not study scripture?"

"I *did*. But I didn't do it because I wanted to. It's like you said. The queen wanted me out of the palace and out of her sight. She resented me for my mother's death. Said I reminded her too much of my father." Wren absently rubbed at the pilling fabric of the settee. "I think my magic awakening was the greatest thing that ever happened to her. It gave her the perfect excuse to disregard my mother's wishes to raise me in the palace.

"So, yes, I was raised in the abbey. But it wasn't a normal childhood or some training for my greater divine purpose. It was like . . . a prison, or a holding pen. Something to overcome. But the abbess taught me everything I know, and I was always so absorbed in my lessons, so focused on leaving, I never really made any attachments. I never truly felt like I belonged."

When she looked up again, he was watching her intently.

Her face heated at the realization she'd offered up some part of herself to Hal Cavendish of all people. But something odd stirred within her at his expression, a mixture of appreciation and shyness. He was actually listening.

"Sorry," she said. "That was more than you asked for, I'm sure."

"I don't mind." He replied more quickly than he usually did, startling her. Then, as if realizing his mistake, he paused to consider his next question. "So you don't believe in the Goddess?"

"Certainly not how most people think of her." She flexed her fingers. "How could a goddess of regeneration, who gave us this kind of magic, want so much destruction? I cannot believe the Threefold Law was meant to be applied this way. Your god, on the other hand . . ."

"It's true that the old books say death pleases God," he said curtly. "But just as yours have, it was politicians who warped that into what it means today."

Wren *hmph*ed her begrudging acknowledgement.

"Vesria's God is similar to your Crone. A being that eases the passage into death—a mercy killer. Whereas Danubians believe souls return to this Earth, reborn, Vesrians believe they remain untouched by suffering forever after." He seemed lost in thought. "All the same, neither demands violence for its own sake. Only for mercy, or protection. That's what war should be for."

"What do you mean he doesn't demand violence? How can that be true?" Wren asked impatiently. "You conquered Danu in his name. Violence shapes your whole society. The way you breed for magic. The way you train your mages . . ."

Hal, unruffled as ever, folded his hands across his stomach. "I don't presume to speak for God, if he even exists, or for my ancestors. Regardless, I imagine we train ours the same as yours."

"At least we don't kill our own recruits," she spat. "I've heard about the tournament in your academy. That only the strongest half survive."

The silence stretched uncomfortably between them.

At last, he said, "That would be very impractical."

Wren's righteous annoyance fizzled out. "So . . . that's not true?"

"No." Hal almost sounded amused through his confusion. "In my first days in the academy, we were told your healers could raise the dead. A profane magic."

"That's completely ridiculous."

"I've also heard all sorts of grisly ways you enforce the Threefold Law," he continued. "Taking three fingers from common thieves. Killing the children of adulterers."

"Ridiculous *and* insulting."

"Exactly." He tilted his head expectantly at her. "We've both grown up on lies."

Lies.

She'd never exactly questioned all the horrible things she'd heard about Vesria—about *him*. Her lack of knowledge made her feel small, foolish. But he'd sobered after his initial surprise; he did not seem to judge her for it. "So, what? Next you'll tell me it's a lie that your people emerged like demons from the Otherworld in a cloud of black smoke?"

"That one is true," he said solemnly.

"What?" she sputtered.

A ghost of a smile tugged on his lips.

Oh. He was . . . joking.

"Fine." Wren crossed her arms. "Mock the uneducated Danubian. As if necromancy isn't a preposterous notion."

"There are other rumors in Vesria, equally preposterous. That Danubian women have special favor from the Goddess and can cast spells on hapless men."

"I . . . I see."

"Discourse that circulated in the early period of occupation, I'm sure. Fuel for paranoia and forced conversions. But it's been revived lately in a curious trend of novels."

Wren arched an eyebrow. "What are they about?"

"Danubian priestesses who bewitch Vesrian men and sacrifice them to the Goddess."

Wren wanted to laugh, especially at the thought of *him* reading drivel like that. His eclectic reading habits were completely baffling. But a chill rushed through her as she thought about what she intended to do with him. Heal him. Earn his trust enough to subdue him. Bring him before the queen. Perhaps there was some truth to those rumors after all.

His eyes met hers, deep as a moonless night. Confusing warmth blossomed within her chest, unfurling into her fingertips. No one had ever looked at her like this—like she might be dangerous. She liked it. Especially coming from someone like him.

She rose from her chair and approached him slowly. "Sounds more like nonfiction to me."

Hal shifted in his chair, quiet and apparently fresh out of jokes for the day. She loomed over him, close enough to see the blue of his eyes.

"So, how does it go in these stories of yours? Have I bewitched you already?" she asked, dropping her eyelashes. "Or is there some sordid ritual that comes first?"

The tips of his ears reddened. "I'm afraid I don't know the details."

"A shame."

Was he actually flustered? It had to be her imagination. It couldn't be that she had any effect on him—that he wrestled with the same horrible impulses as her. To touch her carelessly, to talk to her as if they could be anything but enemies.

Nothing but the tether, she told herself. But as soon as she thought it, it rang hollow, as untrue as these ridiculous stereotypes. Although he was proud and sullen, Hal had surprised her. Despite herself, she'd come to enjoy his company, the way he'd begun to open up as if against his will. In this thin winter sunshine, she thought she recognized what he was hiding behind that breaking front. Hal Cavendish wasn't just desperate for her help.

He was lonely.

"Anything else you need dispelled?" he asked quietly.

"Your reputation."

His eyes narrowed. "What do you mean?"

"I've been surrounded by enough death to know that people reveal their trues selves at the end. And here you are, mooning about and reading your philosophy books. Looking miserable every time I say the word *Reaper*. Looking miserable in general, really. So which Hal Cavendish is real? The one I grew up fearing, or the one sitting here?"

Hal's shoulders went rigid. He tipped his face toward the window, obscuring half his features in shadow. "Neither. Both. Must we discuss this?"

"Oh, come on. What could you possibly be moping about?" She jabbed her finger into his chest. "There couldn't possibly be a heart under there. You've killed too many people for that."

Hal moved too quickly for her to react. In one motion, he pinned her hand to the armrest. His grip was firm enough to set her heart fluttering, but she wasn't afraid. "Do you have nothing better to do with your time?"

"No, indeed. I have all night. This is what Lowry is paying me for. To torment you."

He met her eyes: an accusation. "Everyone is afraid of me. But not you."

There was a strange brew of hope and frustration in his voice.

"Do you want me to be?"

"No." He removed his hand from hers. He spoke softly, almost achingly. "I don't."

It would be wise to fear him. No matter how he treated her, she had seen the truth. A part of him, however small, was capable of ruthlessness. Of committing atrocities with not a flicker of visible regret. No one could do such things and remain untouched by them. No one's goodness could survive it.

Yet he had given her this. Vulnerability. A good Danubian soldier would have exploited it, dissected it. But here she was, hopelessly enraptured by him. Maybe she was a little lonely, too.

"To be honest, you're not very scary," she said. "You're just kind of sad."

Reality crashed back onto her. Soon enough, she wouldn't be lonely anymore—because she'd betray his trust and make a prisoner of him. She couldn't feel sorry for him—couldn't feel *anything* for him. Would her heart always sabotage her? Would she always misplace her pity?

She had to kill her compassion before it became something far more problematic.

"And you're powerless. You're only acting this way because you need me. But I know what I saw in the war. They say you're the perfect soldier. That you feel nothing at all. That you're not even human." She lowered her eyes to avoid watching his confusion solidify into hurt. "I know that's all true."

"So it is." His voice was completely toneless when he said, "I'd like to go back upstairs now."

Shame burned in her cheeks, unbidden and fierce. "Then get up, Cavendish."

He did not speak to her the entire way back to his room, and as soon as she helped him into bed, he closed his eyes. It was as good as a door slammed in her face. As much as it stung, it was for the best to wedge distance between them.

Wren considered the philosophy book on his nightstand. Even if she'd effectively ruined any chance of getting him to be vulnerable again, curiosity about him burned strong. What was it that Hal Cavendish thought about during his lonely, torturous days? She pocketed it as she went.

In her room, she propped her feet up on her desk and flipped it open to where he'd ribbon-marked it. The title of the essay was "On Forgiveness."

Wren had never felt so wretched in her life.

"Nothing."

Wren tossed *The Natural History of the Cernosian Highlands* across the room. It struck the floor at the foot of her bed with a dull *thud*. Hannah startled, glancing with mild concern over her shoulder.

"I don't think throwing the book will make it tell you anything," she said, turning back to her work. She held a beaker full of golden liquid—another dose of Hal's blood fortifier—in her gloved hands, her hair piled high atop her head.

Wren pulled her hands through her hair. She needed patience, fortitude, *calm*. But how could she be unemotional when she was completely out of options? "I'm a failure."

"You're not a failure." Hannah poured off the medication into a smaller glass jar. As candlelight refracted through the glass, it burned like liquid amber.

"I *am*. If I can't do this one simple thing—"

"This is not a simple thing," Hannah said sternly. "It seems simple to you because you've been doing this your whole life. But this is complicated. We just haven't landed on the right solution yet."

"Maybe." Wren dug the heels of her hands into her eyes. "I don't know what else to try."

"You have a thousand of those little bottles in your bag. You're only using half of it to make these medications."

She did have a point. If no one or nothing could give her the answers she sought, maybe she could find it using what she had on hand. It would be wasteful of time and resources to combine things randomly, but what other choice did she have?

Wren opened her medical bag and emptied it onto the bed. Out tumbled the leather case that housed her surgical tools, a bag full of syringes, and a menagerie of glass bottles filled with tinctures and medications and herbs. One vial, filled to the brim with purple flowers, rolled toward her.

The goddessblood she'd taken from the Guiding Light Inn.

Wren stared at it for a long time. Symptoms of goddessblood poisoning included attacks on the heart, the kidneys, the lungs—symptoms that matched Hal's. The chances of matching the poison were laughably slim, but it was all she had. "Hannah?"

"Yes?"

"Can you do me a favor when you're finished with that?" She dug gloves out of the pile and snapped them on. "Can you bring me some boiling water?"

"Of course." Hannah worked as meticulously as ever, corking the tincture and pouring hot wax over it to seal it shut. After she placed it alongside the rest of the bottles she'd finished this evening, she slipped out of the room to fetch the water. A few minutes later, she returned with a kettle, still roiling.

Wren emptied the goddessblood and some water into a mortar, then ground the petals until they reduced to a liquid as dark as blood. Brewing a poison was as foreign as it was satisfying. It was all passion and imprecision, mixed with equal parts intention and rage. Her apprenticeship, meanwhile, had instilled in her a slavishness, a fastidiousness. She could close her eyes and feel Heloise there at her elbow, rapping a switch against the table while she measured out herbs by the gram.

Do you want to cure your patient or kill them? Heloise once hissed after Wren used far too much St. John's wort in a medicinal blend. *You must always consider the contraindications.*

But this excessiveness—it felt good. Almost natural.

Wren strained the poison into a vial. It swirled behind the glass, strikingly beautiful. The color of a winter night set ablaze with stars. Hannah leaned closer. "It's . . . pretty."

"Don't get too close." Wren held up a hand. "It's dangerous."

Her eyes grew round. "What is it?"

"It's, uh . . . a very experimental tincture. Unstable."

Wren pipetted one lethal drop onto a glass slide and studied it beneath the microscope. She twisted a knob to examine Hal's blood sample again.

An exact match.

Wren swore, nearly toppling over her chair in her hurry to stand.

"What?" Hannah asked. "What is it? What's wrong?"

Wren began to pace the room and bit the tip of her thumb. Of all poisons, it *had* to be this one. The one no healer had cracked. Logically, Hal should have been long dead—probably within minutes of the first dose. "You told me every person who's fallen ill has lived longer than the person before, right?"

"Yes," Hannah said slowly. "That's right."

If that was the case, what if the poisoner hadn't intended to kill Hal at all? What if they were experimenting with tiny doses and tracking the effects? Drop by drop, day by day. That was all it took to reduce the Reaper of Vesria to a shell of himself.

"This is bad," Wren whispered. "Really bad."

"Are you going to tell me what's going on?" Hannah's voice cut through her panic. "You're acting very strange."

She knew it. She knew, but she couldn't explain it. How could she possibly tell Hannah her friends had been *murdered*? Wren had no intention of uncovering the saboteur before she took Hal and never looked back. She couldn't live with herself if she abandoned Hannah with the burden of that.

"Do you trust me?" Wren asked.

Hannah heaved a vexed sigh, rolling her eyes heavenward. "Yes. I trust you."

"Then just trust that you don't need to know right now."

"But that's so cryptic! When exactly will I 'need to know'?"

"Soon," Wren said pleadingly. "I promise."

Hannah opened her mouth to protest but cut herself off as she glared down at the poison. "Alright. But you can't hide things from me forever."

"Thank you."

"Sure. I'll see you tomorrow."

As soon as the door clicked shut behind Hannah, Wren cradled her head in her hands and tried to breathe through her dread. Whatever this poisoner had planned for Hal, she intended to foil it. Assuming, of course, she could cure a supposedly incurable poison in the span of nine days.

It was a huge assumption.

For the first time in her life, she feared she had brushed against the limits of her skill. With a team, she could organize shifts. At home, she would have access to an entire apothecary, botanical libraries, and a host of other opinions. But here, she was only one girl.

If she couldn't bring Hal back alive, she needed a contingency plan.

It was time to renegotiate their deal.

CHAPTER FIFTEEN

al was sleeping.

Part of her was relieved to not have to face him immediately after their conversation earlier this afternoon. But more of her was annoyed, since she'd made herself perfectly clear that he was to walk—or at the very least sit upright—in the evenings. But in the low-burning candlelight he looked so delicate, she refrained from waking him immediately. His hair lay against his forehead like a spill of ink. Did he always wear it long, or had it grown unruly during his illness? If she wanted to, she could gather half of it into a tiny bun at the top of his head. The thought sent shivers of thrill and disgust through her.

Wren sat in the bedside chair, the wood creaking mournfully beneath her. His eyelashes were perfect black crescents against his wan skin. How tempting it was to touch him, simply because she could. How miserable would he be if he awoke to find his hair combed or his dark circles mended? Or perhaps he'd find her only inches from his face, healing his chapped lips as she traced the pouting line of his mouth . . .

His eyes snapped open, bleary but fierce on hers.

Wren jerked back but recovered, sitting straight-backed in her chair and planting her hands firmly in her lap. Heat crept from her collar like a rash. "You know very well you shouldn't be in bed."

Hal only let out a long, rasping sigh. He closed his eyes again, drawing the blanket over his nose.

"No, none of that now." She pulled the covers away from him and cast them onto the floor. "Thrombosis is the silent killer."

Wren helped him to his feet, her magic threading between their fingers, and held fast until he straightened to his full height. Then, she let him go finger by finger, as if worried a sudden wind would knock him over. "You need to make it to the parlor on your own, alright?"

"Yes," he said in a clipped, long-suffering tone. "I know."

Together, they trudged downstairs and to the parlor. It was a cramped, narrow den that someone with a greater appetite for melancholy might have called cozy. Velvet-upholstered chairs surrounded the fireplace in a semicircle, and on a pedestal in the corner was a wooden box that Hannah had called a zoopraxiscope.

When she'd cranked it, Wren nearly leapt out of her skin. An electrical light within it surged, throwing a moving image onto the wall. She had watched a stag gallop through a snow-covered wood, its every stride meticulously illustrated. *People's first reactions never disappoint,* Hannah had said with a poorly concealed smirk.

Hal dragged himself to the armchair by the window and let his head fall back against the cushion. Between the pained pinch of his eyebrows and the long, exposed line of his throat, he looked so vulnerable. Wren swallowed in tandem with the bob of his laryngeal prominence.

He was still upset with her, clearly. Wren knew she deserved it. He'd talked to her as an equal, patiently confronted her on her prejudices, and had begun to work on his own. Wren could not entirely make sense of her heart. She'd resolved to keep him at a distance, to hate him. And yet . . .

Goddess damn him for making it so hard.

She approached the coffee table, where she'd placed a tray before she'd woken him. Nelly, the cook, gave it to Wren only after she promised to report back how Henry liked her new frosting recipe. Wren wasn't entirely sure what he'd done to deserve doting, but she gave her solemn word nonetheless.

Nelly had truly outdone herself. Alongside a floral teapot were ceramic bowls filled with cream and sugar, as well as a two-tiered stand. Sandwiches with smoked fish and cucumbers nearly over-flowed from the first level. On the second were tiny cakes garnished with candied angelica. It was too indulgent for her tastes, but who was she to deny a dying man the comfort of dessert?

Carefully, she poured him a cup of tea and handed it to him. "So, Cavendish. I have your diagnosis."

Hal took a long sip of his tea. "Do you?"

"It's goddessblood." She turned another cup upright in its saucer and poured herself tea. The steam warmed her face with the smell of bergamot and lavender. "You're poisoned."

At first, he sat terribly still, his eyebrows drawn low. Then, as if she'd said nothing at all, he heaved himself forward and selected a cake from the display. She observed him incredulously as he popped it in his mouth and chewed solemnly. After what felt like an interminable wait, he swallowed. "I see."

Days ago, she might have been unsurprised to find him unre-sponsive, given he'd once displayed the emotional range of a boul-der. But today, she hated herself for it. He *had* to feel something. Where was that flash of hurt from earlier? She pined for that con-nection between them—that glimpse of his vulnerability before she ruined it. *Anything* but this.

For now, she had to content herself with watching him, grim as ever, choose petit fours like chess moves. She had half a mind to smack the second one out of his hand.

"I said I would make no promises until I diagnosed you." He wasn't looking at her, but rather at the last cake on the stand. As he reached for it, she snatched it and placed it on her tongue, where it dissolved with the flavors of orange zest and honey. This time, at least, he acknowledged her existence with a baleful look. "Goddessblood is the deadliest poison in the world, and I'm no specialist. There's no guarantee I can save you. I need your information up front if I'm going to sink my time into this."

"I can't."

Irritation sparked within her. "Why not?"

"I have no right to your kindness and no leverage. I can't die here."

"Oho, believe me. You very much can."

"You know what I mean."

"I *never* know what you mean," she said sourly. "You're the most deliberately opaque person I've ever met in my life."

A muscle feathered in his jaw. "Because I can't trust you."

"Meanwhile, *I'm* supposed to trust you're not lying to me?"

"You could always walk away from this," he said guardedly. "Whether my information is good or not, you lose nothing."

"Of course I lose!" Wren grabbed his collar, pulling him closer until she could see the flinty edge in his dark eyes. *Good. He has some fight in him yet.* "One of the people who disappeared was my friend. He was in my unit, and one day, he never came back from patrol. There was nothing left behind. No evidence. Nothing. Like he just stepped out of existence."

Hal appeared unmoved.

"If it's true that Vesria isn't behind this, then both of our countries are on the line. If I can't convince Isabel your people aren't responsible, she *will* go to war. Six people are already gone. Does that mean anything to you? If you die before you tell me what you know, how many more will we lose?"

"Up-front information will do you no good." Hal pried her fingers loose from his collar. "I deserted because no one would dispatch me. I pursued this lead alone. If you believe your queen will sanction an investigation here—or that Cernos will admit a unit of soldiers into their country—then you're more naïve than you seem."

They were locked together, his fingers still curled around her wrist. Her pulse beat wildly against his thumb. "What're you saying?"

"If you take this information to the queen, you will be laughed out of the North Tower. No one will believe you."

"Then what good is it? You misled me!"

"I promised you information, and you will have it. Whether it's useful to you or not is incidental."

"Oh, I see. Only *you* can solve this case. Everyone else in Danu and Vesria is too small-minded and corrupt to figure it out, and if I let you die, the solution to this case will perish with you. How convenient. How *trapped* you've left me."

"Yes," he said curtly, if not a little exasperatedly. "That's exactly correct."

How stubborn could he be? He was willing to risk everything, and it made her so . . . so *angry.* If he would not see reason, he would take Byers to the grave with him. It emptied her out of everything but a cold, mean core of desperation.

"I'm not the foolish girl you mistake me for. I will not be manipulated." She lowered her voice. "You're nothing but a coward. If you would place your own miserable life above your soldiers', then you're not fit to lead."

"Are you finished?"

"No. I'm not. You say you deserted because no one would dispatch you, but that's an excuse. You're running, aren't you?" Wren leaned closer. "I would run, too, if I had done the things you've done. But like you told me, there's no running from that no matter how desperately you try. You're not just a coward, Hal. You're a monster, and the world celebrated when it thought you died. You will *never* be forgiven."

Hal's breath caught. She'd drawn blood again.

When he met her eyes, it was not with the hurt she expected. It was with resignation. As if she'd delivered a sentence he'd long ago accepted. This was not the Reaper of Vesria. He was nineteen and painfully mortal. And so . . . *sad*. What had she done? She hadn't even meant half of that.

"I am a monster. I deserve your hatred." Hal was as quiet and cold as a winter night. "The things I have done are unforgivable. I'll face punishment for them, and someday, I'll gladly submit to whatever your queen sees fit. But not until I find them."

He let her hand drop, and with nothing holding her together, she trembled.

What was he suggesting? That he *wanted* to face trial for war crimes? That he *wanted* an end to their countries' war? That all his reading, every evasion of discussing who he was on the battlefield, belied guilt? It went against everything she'd believed true about him. All her life, Hal was the specter of an enemy who wanted to destroy everything she loved. This was the first time she considered he might not *want* be to Vesria's prized weapon. But hadn't he already told her the truth in the morning room? He did feel. He did regret.

"What does Lowry have to do with any of that?" Wren whispered.

"I said nothing about Alistair Lowry." Bitterness—maybe even hatred—twisted the sound of his name.

"No. I guess you didn't." But he had to be involved with this somehow if Hal was here. Wren crossed her arms as she studied the weariness seeping into his expression.

"I regret that I've been opaque with you. The plainest truth I can offer you is that I am afraid. I need you, but I can't allow myself to depend on you."

"I wouldn't depend on me, either," she said. Lately all she'd done was lie. All she'd done was betray her friends' trust and hurt them. "I gave you my word, though. I'll do my best to find an antidote."

Hal stared determinedly out the foggy window. "I'm sorry to hear about your friend."

Wren sucked in an audible breath. How could he give her compassion after everything she'd said to him tonight? "I'm sorry, too. I . . . don't know what came over me."

Hal glanced her way but said nothing. Forgiveness, she supposed, had to be earned. As Wren walked away from him, she replayed his words over and over again.

Not until I find them.

Were they really so different? Two weeks ago, Wren had thought she knew herself. A medic in the Queen's Guard. Reckless, yes, but good-hearted at her core. But with the weight of Hal's life and a war in her hands, she wasn't so sure anymore. Nothing was as simple as she wanted it to be.

CHAPTER SIXTEEN

Something about the thirty-third hour awake brought the world into sharp relief: a light-headed, transcendent clarity. If Wren was to have any chance of curing him, she couldn't waste time sleeping until she had a solid lead on the antidote.

As Heloise's apprentice, she'd welcomed the quiet comfort of the witching hour. Bone-weary after a long day of work, she often felt euphoric crawling into bed. Like she was the only person left in the world to watch the dawn sprawl out over the gray miles of hoar-frosted fields. Tonight's solitude, however, only made her feel small and unhinged. The wind rattled her windows, and with thick ice calcified on the glass, she could see nothing of the world outside. She existed now only within the wavering confines of a lantern's light.

A rat in a gilded cage.

Chipped white moonlight slipped through the latticework of cracks in the ice and illuminated her makeshift workstation. Crinkled papers littered the floor. Spilled tinctures stained her books and the heels of her palms. There were dirty pipettes and stirring sticks, overflowing beakers, and loose herbs dusting every surface like snowfall. Everything hurt. Everything. But she couldn't rest. Only five more days remained to develop an antidote for Hal, and all she could see in her own messy handwriting was

Failure
Failure
Failure

in a neat column down the page.

Not a single one of her experiments had worked.

Her anger had simmered itself dry hours ago. What remained was despair. She wanted to go home, far away from Hal and her guilt and fear. Home, where everything she loved waited for her. Una and her flat and the polluted River Muri and—

Her book's text warped and glimmered, and Wren squeezed her eyes shut to hold in tears. Self-pity wasn't productive right now, as much as she wanted to indulge it. She needed to prepare the next batch of antitoxin. She opened her pocket watch and set a timer. In five minutes, she could run another set of tests. And most likely collect another set of failures to add to her growing list.

"You have to go to sleep." Hannah's concerned voice came from the doorway. "You're going to run yourself ragged at this rate."

"I will. I just have to finish this one thing."

"You said that about the last five things, milady. Perhaps you should at least take a break. You're looking a little, uh . . ." She gestured vaguely to her eyes.

Wren could feel how swollen they were—could only guess at how bloodshot and crazed they looked. But if she tried to close her eyes, her thoughts and theories would torture her into wakefulness. Wasted time she couldn't afford.

Wren waved her pocket watch. "I'm on a five-minute break now."

"That hardly counts." Hannah sighed. "How about I draw a bath for you? Wouldn't that be nice? Or maybe—"

A low wail reverberated through the house. In the hallway, the single overhead light swelled brighter with a droning buzz—then flickered out. A chill, like an icicle dripping down Wren's collar, seized her spine. Magic rippled up her arms in time with the wave of gooseflesh. "What was that?"

Even Hannah paled, her eyes darting fretfully around the room. "A power outage. The wind will do that sometimes."

"As validated as I feel in my mistrust of those lights, I was talking about the sound."

"Also the wind?"

"That was absolutely *not* the wind." It sounded too human, too pained. Once, Wren would have ridiculed herself for being afraid. But sleeplessness shredded her composure and let her imagination unspool. What could be crawling in the darkness in Colwick Hall?

Or maybe someone was injured.

Or poisoned.

She was hardly prepared to heal anyone, halfway delirious and dressed for sleep. Her nightgown nearly drowned her in white fabric, frothing with ruffles at the collar and down her billowy sleeves. But if someone needed her, propriety be damned. She would sooner keel over than wrestle with corset laces right now.

"I'm going to investigate," Wren said. "Would you take that medication off the burner when it's time?"

"You're going to *investigate*? Why?"

Wren pulled a fur-lined cape on over her gown and snatched the candelabra from her desk. "Are you worried about me?"

"Of course not," Hannah huffed. "You're sleep-deprived, and it's showing. But it's almost midnight, and if you're not back before then . . ."

"If it's only the wind, I'll be back in just a minute. Lowry won't find out."

"But—"

"The forceps are on the desk next to the burner. Thanks!" Wren brushed past her and into the hallway, pursued by Hannah's groan of displeasure.

Outside her room, there was complete, esophageal darkness,

tight and swallowing. No one and nothing moved outside the sphere of candlelight, but with the wind outside, the house groaned deeply, wood straining against nails.

Somewhere below her, a door slammed.

She could hear herself breathing far too loudly. In her exhaustion, nothing looked distinct or real. The shadows outside the light were soft as mist but sharpened into long, severe lines as she walked. She stretched out her hand into the empty space to keep herself from bumping into anything—or anyone.

At last, her searching fingers gripped something solid and cold: the balustrades of the grand staircase. She sagged against it in relief. Past the banister, the long descent to the ground level seemed an endless chasm. The only light came from her candelabra, reflected dully in a tarnished mirror across the atrium. It looked as if another tired girl in a nightgown stared back at her.

Although she was loath to wander deeper into the dark, her curiosity got the best of her. She descended step by step until her bare feet touched the floor. The chill radiated from her soles to her crown. As she was about to call out, a noise—stone clattering against stone—rooted her in place. Then, the rustle of fabric.

Something was *moving* behind the tapestry.

Someone was in the forbidden east wing.

Wren extinguished the candles with a single breath and ducked behind a sofa. Slow, uneven footsteps marked every terrible second. From her vantage point, she saw the orange spill of lamplight on the swollen floorboards. She dared to flatten herself against the ground, shuddering at the cold raking across her belly. She caught a glimpse of black polished boots adorned with a neat row of silver buttons. Another shimmy forward brought the figure into full view.

Lowry. Despite the bitter cold, he wore no jacket and the sleeves of his stark white shirt were rolled up to the elbows and—

Was that blood?

It flowed in rivulets down his arm and beaded on his fingertips. He must have been the one who cried out. But what was he doing in the east wing? He'd told her it was dangerous—dangerous enough to get a wound like that.

Lowry held his arm up to the light. He flexed his fingers and scrutinized the way the tendons in his wrist corded against his skin. With every squeeze of his fist, blood seeped from his wound afresh. What was that look on his face? Assessment or admiration? She was obviously intruding on something she wasn't meant to see. And although it wasn't rational to be afraid, she didn't want to know what he'd do if he found her here. Nothing good could come of it.

As she shifted her weight backward, the floorboard whined beneath her.

The ensuing silence was resounding.

"Hello?"

His footsteps thudded menacingly on the floorboards. His lantern light glided toward her. Wren held her breath and cupped her hands over her mouth.

For a brittle eternity, Lowry did not move.

Then, with an indistinct mutter, he turned away. Darkness flowed back in like the tide.

Wren let out her breath shakily, pressing her head into the velvet back of the sofa. As her nerves settled, she felt a steady *tick, tick, tick* against her hip. Her pocket watch? She'd been so fixated on investigating that noise, she'd forgotten to leave the timer with Hannah. As soon as Lowry left, she'd have to hurry back upstairs. Her antidote would finish brewing in a minute, and she needed to make sure it was taken off the heat before it denatured.

Just as realization struck, her pocket watch rang as loud and bright as a whistle.

CHAPTER SEVENTEEN

ike a shock of cold water, fear doused Wren with an eerie numbness.

She expected Lowry to react, to scream, to startle. But he stood perfectly still, his expression slowly clouding with dread. "Who's there?"

She reached into the pocket of her nightdress and turned off the timer. With every churn of the second hand, it pulsed in her fingers like a beating heart. There was no use trying to hide. Wren stood on unsteady feet. "I'm sorry to disturb you."

"Oh, Ms. Southerland. What are you doing here?" He didn't exactly sound impatient, but there was an edge, an urgency, to his question. His lantern's flicker made the broken darkness swim on his tightly drawn face.

"I thought I heard a noise."

"What sort of noise?"

"A moan, I think." Her voice was surprisingly even. As she found her footing, she tried at a playfully stern tone. "And it seems I was right to check. You've hurt yourself."

Up close, through the steady trickle of blood, she could see his wound more clearly. It was already knotted shut with black thread, and his skin was puckered from the imperfect, hurried job. It looked like a railroad sewn into his flesh. Around it were other scars, shiny and ridged. Some were pockmarks, like strawberry seeds—others were wide and irregular like canyons.

"Oh, this? This is nothing." Lowry angled his arm away from her. "I wish you hadn't seen this. It makes me look quite hypocritical, doesn't it? That wing *is* a death trap, but it's . . . well, it's where the wine cellar is. I was going to fetch a bottle and took a spill in some debris."

Liar.

The explanation made little sense—the chronology even less so. She'd seen him emerge from the east wing just now, and the wound had already been treated, shoddily done as it was. Whatever he was doing in there, he had brought medical supplies with him. Not to mention, the cut was perfectly clean. No debris would leave such a deep, straight cut.

But a scalpel would.

He smiled, and although unease curdled within her, she smiled back. "Would you like me to take a look at it?"

"I couldn't impose on you. In fact, I hardly feel it." He smoothed back the limp mop of his curls. "You should be in bed."

Wren showed him her pocket watch. "Eleven fifty, my lord. I've ten minutes of freedom left."

"So you do." The key around his neck glinted as it caught the light. It was covered with fingerprints stamped in drying blood. "In that case, let me entreat you to join me for coffee. If you don't mind my saying, you look positively dreadful. Are you sleeping enough?"

A pocket of fear bubbled in her chest. Something was terribly wrong, and she didn't want to prolong this meeting any longer. She wanted nothing more than to lock herself in her bedroom and leave only when she could afford to never look back again. "No, thank you. I need to get back to work."

"Come now," he cajoled. "Don't tell me Henry is rubbing off on you with that attitude of his. Such seriousness will halve your life, Ms. Southerland."

He most certainly was not.

"Actually," she said sourly, "coffee sounds wonderful. I believe you're due for an update on Henry, anyway."

Wren followed him to the drawing room. He flicked on a switch and cursed under his breath when the lights remained dark. Only dim firelight from the hearth twinkled on a chandelier dripping with crystals and cobwebs.

"A power outage," Wren supplied.

"So it seems," he said, voice strained. "How charming."

Within a few minutes of ringing a bell, a bleary-eyed Nelly brought in a coffeepot piping out bittersweet steam. It smelled of roasted chocolate and jam and wealth. Wren swallowed her dread and chased it with coffee. It tasted burnt and astringent, thick as thrush on her tongue.

Lowry sprawled sideways in an armchair like an overgrown child, his legs spilling off one side. As he pulled down his sleeve and fastened the buttons at his wrists, blood seeped into the white fabric and spread like an unfurling petal. Wren lowered herself onto a chair as if settling into hot water. Now that her nerves had quieted, her magic alerted her to his pale complexion, his too-weak heartbeat, his too-shallow breathing. Even his energy was sluggish as tar.

"Are you feeling well?" she asked as innocently as she could.

Lowry's pupils were tiny specks in a sea of blue. "Why, of course. I feel amazing."

From her seat, she was struck by the stench that clung to him. Beneath the smell of coffee and cologne, something chemical burned the back of her throat and stirred hazy memories. What *was* it? If she closed her eyes, she could see the cold glint of scalpels.

Hollow cavities and pale, stringy tendons. Rubbery flesh beneath her gloves.

Formaldehyde?

No, it couldn't be. Perhaps laudanum? That would make sense of his jumpy, strange behavior and how he hardly felt the pain of his wound. But even if he had a drug habit, it didn't explain the stitches, or why he would bar access to an entire wing of the house. . . .

She focused more intently on stirring cream into her coffee.

"I fear I've been a poor host to you. I know it's hard to believe, but Colwick Hall used to be among the finest estates in the country. My friends have counseled me to sell it, but it's all I have left of my father." Lowry plucked a napkin from the silver coffee tray. His hands immediately bloodied the fabric. "Do you know what happened to him?"

"No." Wren dreaded this line of questioning. "I don't."

"He was a brilliant scientist but a terrible father, if I'm honest. He spent all of his time holed up in in this library." He dragged the napkin down each finger as deliberately as a whetstone over a blade. "But he had a single-minded pursuit. He so desperately wanted to know why Cernosians have no magic, whereas Danubians and Vesrians do. So one day, about five years ago, he wrote the University of Greine to inquire about conducting research in Vesria. Everyone suggested it was madness to walk into a war zone, but my father was a brave, somewhat reckless man. When he arrived on the border, the military asked him his business."

"What happened?"

"They told him they already knew the answer to his question." Lowry's gaze was level. "God had blessed Vesria, and that was all there was to it. To suggest anything more was heresy. Naturally, he asked what that suggested about Danu."

"What did they say?"

"Nothing. He was detained." Lowry sipped his coffee. "They didn't release him again."

"Oh. Lord Lowry, I . . . I don't know what to say. I'm so sorry."

"Don't be." He sighed. "After the funeral proceedings, my older brother inherited the dukedom and seaside view that comes with it. I, the courtesy title—and this." He swept an open palm across the library. "Colwick Hall, full of ghosts and memories. It's all I can do to keep it afloat."

With his tired smile, one crooked elbow pillowing his head, Lowry was the perfect image of grief. It was no surprise that artists across the continent flocked to capture even a glimmer of him on canvas.

"While your war has never touched my homeland, it took my father from me." Lowry's eyes grew wistful. "And I am so tired of death. Allying ourselves with Danu is the best chance we have to cow Vesria into stopping the atrocities they commit. Some might call it reckless to declare a side now, but what can I say? Someday, as the rest of the world catches up with our technology, we will be forced to choose. And I'm nothing if not pragmatic. When night falls, I won't be the one left alone in the dark."

It *was* a wise strategy to align himself against a common enemy. *And also wise*, she thought, *to capture and poison their future leader*.

"What're you thinking, my dear? You look as if you've seen a ghost."

"Pardon me, my lord. I was only thinking about Henry." Wren peered into her coffee, watching her pale reflection shatter again and again on its surface. "I haven't been sure exactly how to bring it up to you. I've uncovered the strangest thing about his illness."

When she looked up, Lowry had gone impossibly still. "Did you really?"

"It responds poorly to magic," she said, taking a sip from her cup. "If it were viral or bacterial, I could've encouraged his immune system to push it out by now."

For one moment, Lowry adopted his usual wide-eyed perplexity. But then, as if he thought better of it, he discarded it like a tired old coat. Laid bare like this, he radiated a jittery energy as he leaned across the table. "How unusual. What do you plan to do?"

No warmth. No humor. Only those eyes like ice, boring into

hers. She stood on the surface of a frozen lake, one misstep from slipping under.

"I'm currently experimenting with medications. His condition is still precarious, but I have him stable."

"I see." As he placed his cup down, candlelight thickened on the coffee's surface, painting it red as blood. "Then it sounds like you ought to tread very carefully indeed, Ms. Southerland."

"I'm always careful, my lord." Wren met his gaze evenly. "We have an agreement."

"That's what I like to hear. When this is all over," he said, each word deliberately and artificially pleasant, "I shall have to write to the queen about how well you've done."

Wren stilled. She knew a threat when she heard one.

But before she could stammer out a response, the grandfather clock gonged.

"Midnight already." Lowry clapped his hands, snapping back into his usual character. "My, how quickly time passes in good company."

Wren wished him good night and hurried into the corridor. Her path through the estate was lit only by the sputtering magic cupped in her hands like water. Through the tinny buzz of exhaustion in her skull, Wren almost believed that conversation was a dream. But as she replayed it again and again, Wren was becoming increasingly certain of two things.

One, Alistair Lowry knew who Hal Cavendish was and what plagued him.

Two, if she didn't cure this poison soon, *she* would be the one left out in the dark.

In the quiet of her room, everything fell away. Wren shed her suspicions along with her cape, casting them aside in a rumpled heap. At her desk, it was easy to pretend that this—the next batch of antidote—was the only thing that mattered. Right now, it *had* to be the only thing that mattered. She wanted nothing to do with sealed-off corridors and Lowry's veiled threats.

Hannah had taken the beaker off the burner for her and organized her desk—a gesture she appreciated. She prepared a slide with Hal's blood and dribbled in a few drops of the antidote.

Underneath the microscope, Wren watched as the serum's compounds enveloped the goddessblood toxin. Bit by bit, they broke down the poison until it was small enough to be engulfed by the immune system. Wren came untethered from her body and stared into the eyepiece with numb amazement.

It worked.

She could cure Hal. She could go home.

In a little over a week, she *would* be home.

To hell with the curfew. She'd administer the first dose to Hal at once. After gathering her supplies, Wren hurried down the hall, buoyed by the lacy trail of her nightgown and the light bounce of her hair. When she flung open his bedroom door, the air barely stirred.

The silence was eerie, unbroken even by the rasp of Hal's breathing. His heartbeat kept a halting rhythm, as faint as the flutter of moth's wings. As she approached his bed, the soft candlelight washed over him. He did not move beneath the blood-spattered sheets.

Cold terror seized her. He wasn't . . . He couldn't be . . .

Wren shook him by the shoulder. "Hal?"

His eyes cracked open, and in them was a glimmer that filled her with a rush of relief. *Salvation.* "You're here."

"Of course." She grabbed a fistful of the sheets and dabbed at the blood on his face. She could hardly dwell on the intimacy of it, how he let her fuss over him without any protests. How long had he been like this while Lowry detained her? She affixed the antitoxin to a syringe, squeezing the stopper until liquid oozed onto the tip of the needle like a pearl.

"Wren." He'd hadn't said her name since their first meeting.

Where that was all cold antagonism, this was . . . almost tender. *Delirious again*, she decided.

She pinched the skin of his upper arm and injected him. "Don't talk."

Given time, her cure would do its work. In the meantime, she had to repair the worst of his organ damage to ensure he would survive the night. Her *fola* wouldn't hold up long enough to mend him entirely, so she'd have to triage carefully. She called on her magic, and her veins ran silver. Although her hands tingled as if she'd plunged them into ice, she was too frantic to care right now.

Every button popped as she pulled apart his nightshirt. Placing her hands on his bare skin, she poured magic into him. How could he have taken a turn for the worse so quickly? Admittedly, ever since she'd begun research on the poison, she'd been distracted, but . . .

Her single-mindedness had almost killed him.

Be sorry later. Dead men can't forgive.

Time ceased to have meaning as she worked. Throughout the night, they spoke little, and by sunrise, Hal had fallen asleep. Wren, meanwhile, was ready to lay her head on his chest and succumb to exhaustion. Even after so many hours together, it still felt like a strange, unearned privilege to gaze upon Hal Cavendish without fearing for her life. In the hazy lavender dawn, he looked entirely untroubled.

I deserve your hatred, he'd said.

No you don't, she wanted to tell him.

His confession unsettled her more than she cared to admit. He had shown her patience, sometimes even kindness. And genuine remorse. Was he really so self-loathing as to overlook that? Could he truly not forgive *himself*?

Deep down, she knew Hal Cavendish was not what the world thought him to be. He had done horrible, unforgivable things. But so had her friends. Maybe the only difference between a monster and a hero was the color of a soldier's uniform.

As she smoothed the hair back from his face, Hal opened his eyes. Her heart skipped a beat. "Hi," she whispered. "The worst of it is over. You're going to live."

"Over?" he asked hesitantly.

"I found an antidote. You should be on the mend in a few days."

"Thank you." The space between them grew softer as relief swept over him. Gratitude still made her feel a little off-kilter. Especially when he was looking at her like *that*. Warm and golden, like sunlight on her face and honey in her tea.

"It's nothing." She stood abruptly, cursing the rising blush on her face. "Healing is my duty."

Unwelcome memories of a boy with a broken arm flickered behind her eyelids. Of Una, holding her wrists painfully tight as she growled, *Your compassion is sorely misplaced. It will get you killed someday.*

Healing was her duty, but performing it had once cost her everything. Wren closed the blinds with a decisive snap, unsure of what to do with this strange, fluttery sensation in her stomach. It was almost pride—and more troublingly, relief. What a wasted emotion, when she would soon deliver him to his executioner.

"I owe you answers," Hal said.

"Yes." Wren perched on the edge of his bed. "You do."

Hal shifted to the side. Giving her room or putting distance between them, she couldn't be sure. "What would you like to know?"

"Everything. Let's hear your wild theory."

Hal drew a deep, resigned breath. "I only noticed the pattern after my third subordinate went missing. They were always taken during patrols of our border with Cernos. It was so targeted, I couldn't help but feel it was a summons. When I approached the magistrate with my concerns, he dismissed me. Between war preparations and the upcoming election, he was unwilling to waste resources on speculation. He claimed Cernos had neither the means nor the motive to do such a thing."

"But Danu did."

"Yes."

Of course the magistrate believed that, just as Isabel believed it was Vesria. After so many years of antagonism, it was the only logical explanation. "He claimed we were trying to weaken your army before war broke out. Didn't he?"

Hal thinned his lips. "Yes."

How foolish they all were. How blinded by their hatred. Someone was kidnapping soldiers, but even if it made little sense, they were so eager to blame it on each other.

"And why didn't that satisfy you?" Wren asked.

"Because it was improbable. Because I don't want another war."

"You keep saying that." The harshness of her voice faltered. "And I believe you. I almost want to believe what they say about you is a lie, but I *saw* it. How could you have changed so much?"

"What's done is done. I can't change that. But I can do everything in my power to ensure no one like me exists again." Hal lowered his eyes. "I've come to hate what I can do. I remember all of them—every person I have killed. I don't know how much more death I can hold in my mind."

His conviction filled her with a strange longing—almost admiration. It took strength to confront your mistakes, and even more to change. After so many infractions, she'd only continued on, reckless as ever. She'd run away from her latest failure.

"So what'd you do next?" she rasped.

"After some research, I discovered that Lowry owned the borderland territory and had recently acquired a property called the Guiding Light from the Duke of Matthonwy. I also learned his father was detained by a group of military police." Hal frowned. "It wasn't much, but it was the only lead I had. So, I left to pursue my suspicion."

Wren still couldn't fathom that he had simply *left*. According to the newspapers, his life was perfect. He was the shoo-in candidate for grand magistrate. Wren had seen the few photos of him and his father on the front page, fuzzy and indistinct in the glare of the Vesrian sun. Hal, haughtily frowning at the camera. His father, hand on his shoulder, beaming with pride.

He had everything she'd ever wanted—a family, respect, adoration. Yet he had walked away from all of it.

"I found little at the Guiding Light. Shipment records to Colwick Hall—but nothing that identified the contents." He paused. "And here, only rumors. Everyone has a tragic story about a friend succumbing to disease. They also told me of Lowry's increasingly strange behavior."

"Like what?"

"Disappearing at odd hours and taking copies of the keys from the housekeeper. Barring off access to the east wing. Declining visits from friends. Strange stains on his clothes."

"Did you hear why he closed down the east wing?"

"Apparently, several servants were summoned there and never returned. The staff was informed it was due to an accident. I believe he said a staircase collapsed."

Lowry had told her the same thing. How could she have been so naïve, so desperate, as to believe him on that first night? "And did you go in?"

"No. Before I could, I fell ill. Given the circumstances, I have to believe I was close to an answer."

"And what's that?" Dread gripped her, as cold as liquid helium. "What do you suspect?"

For the first time in days, Hal held her gaze. "I suspect Alistair Lowry is responsible for the abduction and murder of six people."

CHAPTER EIGHTEEN

Wren couldn't breathe. She couldn't focus. The room swam with hazy light as if she looked at it from the bottom of a lake. *I suspect Alistair Lowry is responsible for the abduction and murder of six people.* After something like that, how could the world continue to spin neatly on its axis? Everything in her railed against the theory, even though she'd come to suspect it herself.

In no universe did it make sense that Lowry would poison Hal and then request her services. It would be nothing but wasted, pointless effort.

And yet, here they were.

Maybe Lowry never wanted her to cure Hal at all. Maybe it was a ruse to lure her here—and an incentive to detain her. *But if he just needed me to fritter away my time, why not use someone less recognizable than Hal as a fake patient?* And if it were purely for revenge against Vesria, why not kill him immediately? She could not piece together a motive.

All the same, Hal's accusation was a strange relief. It was confirmation at last that she hadn't gone mad or succumbed to paranoia. Something was undeniably rotten in Colwick Hall.

Whatever Lowry wanted with her and Hal, whether he'd been behind the poisonings or not, he clearly wanted them both alive—and here in Colwick Hall. But for what? What did he *want* from her? While Hal's theory was inconclusive about the abductions and Lowry's motives, she couldn't convince herself not to worry about what might happen to them if they stayed here.

Wren realized she must have gone quiet. Even recovering in what was nearly his deathbed, Hal cut an imposing figure. His gaze was unbroken and intense as he awaited her response. The early sunlight revealed the impossibly dark glimmer of blue in his eyes. How many people knew they weren't really black?

Tentatively, she said, "And now that you're well, you intend to go after him."

"What I intend is to find proof." He spoke with an eerie, cold composure. "Once I do, I intend to see him hang."

She should have let it lie at that. With his disease cured, she'd fulfilled her obligation to him. She could finally fall into a dark and heavy slumber. She could finally dream of Danu, of Una, of reclaiming her old life.

But she stayed.

Maybe it was because of Hal's cool, collected certainty—a magnetic steadiness when her life swirled in indistinct chaos. Or maybe it was because her conscience had always been stronger than her self-preservation.

"I saw Lowry coming from behind that tapestry last night." It came out before she could stop it, like a spurt of arterial blood. "He was wounded and stitched up like he'd come prepared with medical supplies, but he fed me that nonsense excuse about structural damages. And then when I hinted the disease wasn't exactly natural, he didn't seem surprised at all. I keep . . . *hearing* things in the house. Sometimes I think it sounds like screaming."

As the story poured out of her, a possibility she hadn't

considered—but one she'd desperately hoped for—leapt out. What if they were all still alive?

Hal's lips parted. Then he arranged his face into a mask made of broken slate, imperfectly blank. She could see his incredulity peering out through the cracks. "Are you offering to help me?"

Was she? *Could* she? Her carriage would arrive in four days, but Wren wasn't sure she had it in her to carry out her plan anymore. Capturing Hal would restore her reputation, but before desperation twisted her into the girl she was now, she'd wanted nothing more than answers. Justice for Byers and the other missing soldiers.

She'd called Hal a coward, but if she turned her back on a potential lead—if she gave up on a chance to save Byers—then what was she? She wouldn't deserve to wear her uniform. She wouldn't deserve Una's forgiveness. Whatever was going on here, it wasn't an option to ignore it anymore.

"Yes." Wren clenched her hands into loose fists. Her joints were swollen and her fingers numb from healing. "Lowry lured both of us here, and I want to find out why."

"Working with me is treason."

"Healing you was, too. What's another betrayal for my growing list?" Wren drew her legs onto the bed and tucked them beneath her. "Besides, this isn't about you or me. It's about Danu and Vesria."

"And suppose I don't want your help." It was entirely unconvincing when she could practically hear his hopefulness in every word.

"You're not exactly in a position to deny me, Cavendish. Physically speaking, you're useless." His expression soured into indignation. "And I can't do it myself. I have no investigative training. And no combat skills should anything go wrong."

Conflict tightened his jaw. "Why're you doing this?"

Because I'm not sure I'm strong enough to go through with my plan. Because Byers still might be here. Because if you're right, maybe I can finally prove myself to Isabel and Una.

"Because we want the same things."

"Do we?"

"Justice for our comrades," she said. "Peace for our countries."

The look Hal gave her was lingering, searching. Wren still worried that he could see right to the heart of her anxieties, her disgrace. But if he saw anything there, all he said was, "Very well."

"Her relief was immediate. "Then we should go to the east wing now."

"Now?"

Wren bristled at the surprise on his face. "Yes, now. If what I sensed was real, our friends still might be alive. If there's any chance we can save them, we can't let it slip away. We can't just sit here and do nothing!"

"Even if we do find them alive, what then? We've no plan and no escape from this place. Neither of us is in any state to run—or fight, should the need arise. I doubt they will be, either."

Wren wanted to argue, but as exhaustion and the cool evenness of his voice settled over her, she couldn't deny that he was right. Again. They couldn't exactly flee into a blizzard. Hal wouldn't survive it in his condition. Worse, that damnable contract she'd signed forbade her from going into the east wing. There was no telling what Lowry would do if he found her there, and the prospect of facing him alone—and confronting whatever horrors lurked in that cold, crumbling place—terrified her more than she cared to admit.

All she could think about was the sinister curve of Lowry's smile when he said, *Then it sounds like you ought to tread very carefully indeed.*

"If you're right and they've survived this long already, surely the danger isn't imminent," Hal added gently. "We'll be of no use to anyone right now."

"You're right. Waiting a few days until you've recovered surely won't make a difference." It felt like a feeble, impotent wish, but what other choice did they have? Her magic and her intuition had misled her too many times before; she couldn't risk both their lives on a hunch. "Besides, Lowry hasn't harmed us yet. Whatever he has in store for us, he must be planning to act at this party he's hosting.

He's waiting for something, or else hoping to make a spectacle of it. But we'll stop him before that happens."

She extended her hand into the tense, crackling space between them. After a moment's hesitation, he accepted it. With that, it was done. For the first time in centuries, a Danubian and a Vesrian would work together. As much as it should have terrified her, the strength of his grip was a small comfort in the chaos she'd created for herself. Like the rest of him, his hand was smooth and unscarred and warm.

Untouchable, except to her.

Absently, Wren ran her thumb along the back of his palm. It wasn't until she noticed his elevated heart rate and the distinct *absence* of his breath through the tether that she realized she'd even done it. Hal did not withdraw from her even when she raised her gaze to his. How terrible was it, she thought, to wonder how much closer he'd let her get?

Her mouth dried as his eyes drifted lower, and she dropped his hand. They had no time for whatever *this* was between them. Not when their mission had only two possible outcomes. Success meant preventing a war. It meant securing her position and finally knowing what happened to Byers—and why. Failure meant they might end up the fourth from each country to disappear.

Two more scraps of kindling for the war already sparking.

As late afternoon sun filtered through the window, Wren jolted awake to find herself curled up on an armchair she didn't recognize. Her eyes were nearly welded shut with sleep and the collar of her nightgown was soaked with saliva. She'd clearly needed the rest, to have slept so soundly here of all places. With a contented sigh, she unfolded herself to the satisfying crackle of synovial fluid.

A ripple of unease spread from between her shoulder blades and settled, cold and buzzing, at the base of her skull. *Someone else is here.*

She turned over her shoulder and huffed in relief. Of course someone else was here. This was Hal's room. He sat upright in bed with a peculiar, almost chastised, expression.

He averted his eyes and instead took great interest in the frost blooming like lichen across the windowpane. Had he been staring at her? Self-consciously adjusting her nightdress, she felt her ears began to burn.

"Good morning," she muttered.

"Evening, I believe."

Technicalities, really.

Wren went to his bedside and placed the back of her palm against his forehead. Beneath the hum of her magic, he wasn't hot or clammy. His vitals were stable. He was *alive,* and she was so giddy, she almost embraced him. Although she mortified herself with that unwelcome impulse, imagining his horrified reaction delighted her enough to excuse herself for it. "How're you feeling tonight?"

"Better."

"Good." She cleared her throat. "Well enough to conduct an investigation?"

"Well enough to walk, at least."

Wren took his hands to help him stand. Even uncertain on his feet, even with the exhaustion painted in gray beneath his eyes, he was striking—and so endearingly ordinary with his ruffled hair and the patchy stubble along his jawline. *Not even the Reaper of Vesria can grow a beard,* she thought with petty amusement.

"I can walk on my own. Thank you." He pulled his hands out of hers. "If you don't mind, I'm going to shower."

"No, not at all."

He teetered to the door without her assistance. As much as she wanted to ensure he didn't crack his head open on the tub, she suspected he'd glower—or worse—if she tried to follow him into the bathroom. *He'll be fine,* she told herself, waving away the image of him drowning in an inch of water. In the meantime, she would purge this place of his sickness.

She left the room and rummaged through the hallway closets until she found clean linens tucked away on a shelf she had to stand on her toes to reach. Then, she tore the sheets off his bed and managed to loosen the ice enough to pry open every window.

With the cold light pouring in, the room already felt less heavy, less miserable. The winter chill dulled the rank stench of disease. As she shoved the blood- and sweat-stained linens into a laundry basket, the door opened again. Hal stood in the threshold, water dripping from the ends of his hair. The dampness seeped into his collar, and although he'd left the first few buttons of his shirt undone, it was startling to see him looking so presentable.

Her eyes skirted over his exposed collarbones. She'd seen him undressed before. She'd touched his bare skin. Her magic lived inside him. But now, outside the pretense of medical attention, it was as if she'd caught him out, unaware and naked. He must have noticed it, too, judging by how he slowly fastened his buttons. As if he knew she liked what she saw and meant to exploit it. He made it all the more intimate. All the more humiliating.

Allies or not, he still managed to infuriate her.

She aggressively tugged the sheet over the mattress as Hal made his way to the armchair by the window. He sat silhouetted by the pale sun, struggling to close the buttons on his sleeves. She considered letting him suffer, if only to maintain a healthy distance between them. But if she were completely honest with herself, she didn't exactly want to keep away from him anymore—emotionally or physically. Approaching him now felt like toeing the edge of a cliffside. How close could she get before she fell?

With an exaggeratedly exasperated sigh, she dragged another chair next to his and sat. Her knees nearly brushed his, the flutter of her gown's lace hem bridging the gap between them. "Allow me."

Hal looked as if he were about to brush her off but then extended his arm to her wordlessly. His concession surprised her, but she said nothing as she threaded each button through its hole, as deliberate as suturing a wound. Heat began to spread through her cheeks at their warm, almost familiar proximity and the sensation of his eyes intently on her hands.

The last button went through the eyelet a little too forcibly, leaving an aching indent in the pad of her thumb. "There."

They both sighed, relieved, when she straightened up. But the discomfort lingered, as unwieldy as the weight of their truce. It settled lopsided over her shoulders. Hal was still something of a mystery. If she was going to trust him, she had to know *something* about him—something true. If they were going to work together—if she could truly move past everything he'd done—she needed to know more about him.

"Last night, you said I could ask you anything I wanted."

"I did," he said warily.

"First of all, I haven't meant to be so . . ." She cut herself off with a frustrated sigh. Tucking her hair behind her ears, she tried again. "I've said things that were perhaps unfair to you. I'm sorry."

Clearly sensing the hesitation in her voice, he remained silent.

"But I still can't forget who you are. If we're going to work together, I need to understand you. You told me you don't believe in God. So why? Why did you . . . ?"

Mercifully, he spared her from having to finish that sentence. "I don't believe in God, no. But God is many things to many people. All of us have something we believe in enough to kill for."

"What's it for you?"

Hal drew a deep breath, and for a moment, Wren feared he'd refuse to answer. "My family. My country. I was the first to manifest my bloodline's magic in two generations. I believed I had a gift—a duty. Not only to make my father proud, but to protect the defenseless. To be useful."

To be useful. Wren shivered at the familiarity of that sentiment. "And is that still what you believe in?"

"No. Not anymore." Hal lowered his eyes. "Some gods are false."

She stayed quiet, waiting for him to continue. But he only sighed.

"I'm tired." She believed him. He sounded like he'd aged ten years in minutes. "Perhaps we can talk about this another time."

"You have terrible coping mechanisms."

"Yes." He offered her a thin smile, the barest upward tug of his lips. "I know."

Their silence was almost companionate.

Wren was certain about few things in her life. But she'd always known, as certainly as she knew the cycles of the moon, that Vesria was the enemy and Hal was the worst of them. If he wasn't what she thought, what did that mean? What else was she wrong about? Trust and understanding—compassion—had forged this alliance between them. But after everything she'd lost, how could she let herself believe that *kindness,* not ruthlessness, was the way forward?

For now, Wren could only acknowledge that she was tired. So, so tired of arguing with Hal Cavendish. So she let herself surrender to this new order. Tentatively, she reached out and placed a hand on his knee. "Thank you. I know it's not easy to talk about the war."

Hal did not take his gaze from her hand. "Of course."

"I don't know if there's anything I'd kill for. I thought about killing you once—that moment when we first met. But I couldn't do it. Not for my country or my friends. Not even for myself. I thought I was so weak."

"That doesn't make you weak. Mercy is the most difficult thing."

But it wasn't mercy that'd spared him. It was pure selfishness. Her throat tightened. "Thanks."

"Maybe I'm wrong," he said pensively. "I still have things I would kill for. But perhaps the most important things—what truly drives us—are the things we would die for."

Wren stilled and let her hand drop back to her side. It felt oddly empty without his body heat and the warm buzz of her magic between them. Could that be true? She always knew she was reckless—acted in ways that Una said could get her killed. But she'd never acted thoughtlessly. Only on conviction.

"I'm not much of a philosopher, but I hope that's true."

"Regardless," Hal said. "I'm glad you didn't kill me."

She was, too.

Wren hesitated, searching within herself for levity. But nothing clever materialized. No barbs. She could only think about the way he had looked on the day she first saw him all those years ago, cold and unfeeling. The confusion that haunted her even now. Why had he left her alive?

Mercy is the most difficult thing.

"I've been wanting to ask you something," she said.

"What is it?"

"I mentioned I saw you at the Battle of the River Muri," she said hesitantly. "Did you see me?"

His expression was entirely unreadable. "I don't think so."

She didn't expect the sudden pang of disappointment. "Oh."

He did not press her any further. After a few moments, he said, "I should feel well enough in a few days to continue the investigation."

Right. The investigation. Wren cleared her throat. "Good. I have a plan. Lowry claims to abide by the curfew, so our best bet is waiting until midnight. I'll confirm he's in his quarters, and we'll go from there."

It occurred to her that Hal significantly outranked her. She had no business giving him orders. After the war, he'd been promoted to colonel. However, he only said, "As you command."

She carried out her confused feelings with the laundry.

CHAPTER NINETEEN

After the grandfather clock tolled midnight, Wren alighted on the ground floor of the grand hall and waited for Hal. She leaned against the wall opposite the massive tapestry covering the east wing, and in the darkness, it looked like a curtain of ink. The draft escaped past the bottom like a knife slipped between ribs, filling the entire hall with bitter cold.

Tonight, Wren had dressed practically in leather boots—the only part of her military uniform she'd kept—and a black wool coat lined at the collar with gray fur. Although her hands were warm tucked inside her thick sleeves, the glimpses of the east wing she caught beneath the tapestry's fluttering edge chilled her.

Something brushed against her shoulder.

Wren gasped, whirling around to face Hal. He stood beside her in a dark jacket. She noticed he'd trimmed his hair since she'd last seen him, but it still nearly fell into his eyes and over the tops of his ears. "Don't scare me like that," she hissed.

"Sorry. I can manage this alone if you're afraid."

"I'm not *afraid*." Over the past two days, under a steady regimen of healing and antitoxin, he had recovered considerably. He likely could manage it alone, but they'd agreed to do this together. "Besides, you can't get rid of me so easily. I'm the one with the light."

With a flourish, Wren pulled a metal vesta case from her pocket and struck a match. It sputtered and showered sparks onto the floor. As she lit the candelabra and shook the flame out, the air filled with the smell of sulfur.

The candles burned steadily, illuminating the tapestry before them. Wren had hardly paid it any mind the few times she'd passed it in the daylight. For the first time, she *saw* it. It was a scene from Danubian folklore. Queen Maeve, her golden hair unbound, stood before a Vesrian man kneeling at her feet, her red-tipped fingers pressed against his brow bone. It was pure anticipation captured in thread.

In the story, Maeve pulled out the man's eyes.

Hal regarded it grimly. "A charming piece."

"Indeed."

Side by side, they approached the tapestry. Hal pulled it back, allowing Wren to squeeze through with the light. As she stepped into a corridor as dark as sin, the temperature dropped—a gradual slither across her body, like sinking into cold water. Her breath unfurled in white, uneven bursts.

Here was a place people went and never returned.

There was nothing here but furniture covered in white tarps, but a sensation settled beneath her skin like a too-deep splinter, and her magic buzzed, tinny and frantic, from her eardrums to her fingertips. It was a familiar, unnerving pressure. A whisper against the back of her neck. All her life, she'd been attuned to suffering, to the sour smell of fear and rot. This feeling, this undeniable empathy, had once compelled her to heal that boy with the broken arm. And now, it compelled her so strongly, she was paralyzed with fear. *What happened here?*

It felt like being on a battlefield all over again. Her throat constricted with panic.

"Do you feel that?" she whispered. "It feels like . . . someone else is here. Someone hurting."

Hal appeared beside her, his voice almost soothing. "No. I only feel you."

"Right." Maybe it was nothing but stubborn hope, another trick of her addled mind. She couldn't trust herself anymore. Wren rubbed her arms as if the friction could warm her. "We should keep going."

To their left, an avalanche of loose brick blocked off what was once a narrow, spiraling staircase leading to the turret. So Lowry wasn't lying about *everything*. Overhead, she could see an uneven slice of night sky and the snow whirling against it. No wonder it was so freezing.

There was nowhere to go but forward.

In a matter of strides, she hit a dead end. Her candelabra flooded the grout with wicked orange light. The so-called east wing was little more than an antechamber with no outlet. But it couldn't be. She'd seen Lowry emerging with a sewn-up wound on his arm herself. They didn't have time to waste, didn't have time to search. While she'd confirmed Lowry was in his quarters, the possibility of him walking in made her edgy and anxious. Hal, meanwhile, calmly paced the length of the room. He placed his feet carefully onto each square tile on the floor.

"What're you doing?"

He ignored her, and Wren glared at his back. During their earlier healing sessions, he sometimes avoided talking to her by pretending to be asleep or looking puzzled by her accent.

Under her breath, she muttered, "I know you understand me, Cavendish."

He stopped dead in the center of the room. Kneeling down, he wedged his fingers beneath a stone tile, which slid away with a rasping grind. It looked as if he'd opened a portal into the Otherworld.

"How . . . did you find that?"

"There're no rooms adjacent to this one, and the only way up has been destroyed. And this tile sounded hollow."

"Of course it did." She approached him and peered down at the chasm, barely wide enough to fit her shoulders through. When she bent down, the candlelight illuminated the shape of a ladder, rough and flaky with corrosion. Her magic churned even more restlessly within her.

"I'll go first," he said.

Although she wouldn't admit it, she appreciated the gesture. The darkness beneath her felt hungry and endless past the reach of the flames. When Hal finished climbing down, she passed the candelabra to him and lowered herself onto the first step of the ladder. Her sweat-slick skin clung to the frigid metal, and she hissed in pain as she peeled it free. Rung by rung, she descended into the earth.

When Wren reached the bottom, she smelled wet rock and sweet ether, both dulled by the chill. They stood at the beginning of a tunnel that sloped deeper into the ground. Copper wires shone in the candlelight, and when Wren placed her hand against the wall, she found a switch. The lights strung overhead stuttered and buzzed, illuminating a path forward in flickering bursts. With every step, her heart rate accelerated. What waited for them at the end? Wren often thought the war had shown her the worst of the world, but now she couldn't be certain. Was it worse for a murderer to hide behind the uniform of a soldier or a gentleman?

At the end of the passage was a locked door, reinforced with an iron frame. As the unsteady lights plunged them into darkness again, Wren held up the candles. Orange firelight flooded into the keyhole. "Damn it."

They were so *close*. They couldn't fail now.

She threw her shoulder against it, but it did not yield. The force rattled her bones. She surged forward again, but Hal caught her by the arm before she made contact with the wall.

"You're going to hurt yourself." Although his grip was firm, his voice was surprisingly gentle. "We'll have to come back with the key."

"There's no way we'll get another chance! How are we going to find the exact key in this enormous house before he's onto us?"

"We will. As long as we leave everything untouched, he won't notice anything amiss. There's always another chance."

How she yearned for that to be true. Judging by the quiet determination in his voice, Wren supposed he did, too. But in this
dark place, she couldn't force optimism. Not when Byers might
be suffering just beyond this door. Not when so much counted on
finding concrete, damning evidence.

They trudged back to the ladder in silence. Wren handed Hal
the candelabra and began to climb.

Halfway up, she paused. The wind keened as it swept through
the room, but if she strained to hear over it, there were muffled
voices filtering in from the grand hall. Like a horse kicked to a can-
ter, her heartbeat quickened until she felt woozy with dread. If they
were discovered here, everything would be undone.

"Don't move," she whispered to Hal. "I think I hear something."

Before he could protest, she heaved herself aboveground and
crept closer to the tapestry. Hannah was shouting over the wind
at someone on the front porch. Not Lowry, then. But who would
come unannounced at this hour? Who would brave this weather?

Wren pressed her face to the window and peered through the
thick layer of ice. Although she couldn't see the guest at the door,
she could make out a carriage parked in the driveway.

"No," she whispered. "No, no, no."

Nearly feathering into the snowstorm, the carriage was white
and elegant. She would have missed it if not for an all-too-familiar
crest emblazoned in black. It was a full moon flanked by a waxing
and waning crescent.

The Queen's Guard was here.

CHAPTER TWENTY

Wren couldn't move. She could hardly think; her mind was nothing but a muddle of expletives and panic and bloody images. Why had she been so foolish to believe that Isabel would help her? Why had she been so careless and let Una see her leave? It was no surprise Isabel had sent a team to track her down, but Wren hadn't expected them to arrive so *soon*. The storm should have bought her more time.

A door groaned on its hinges. Then the steady *click, click, click* of heels striking stone reverberated through the house and beat against Wren's skull. They were inside. The Queen's Guard was *here*, only feet away, and she was rooted in place with terror.

Move, she told herself. *You have to move.*

"You've some nerve demanding an audience with his lordship at this hour," Hannah complained. "He doesn't like to be disturbed, and we've a sick man who needs his rest."

"So we've heard," said a Guardswoman whose voice Wren didn't recognize. "We only want to ask Lord Lowry a few questions."

At last coming to her senses, Wren hurried back to the ladder. A sliver of Hal peered up at her, appearing and disappearing in the flickering light. He looked lost somewhere between befuddlement and concern. "What is it?"

She dropped to her knees so she could whisper. "The Queen's Guard is here."

Hal's expression hardened into wariness.

"No, don't look at me like that! They're after me, not you. Please, Hal. I know this sounds bad, but you have to trust me. I'm not in contact with the Guard. No one in Danu has any idea where you are."

It would be easy enough for him to seal the entrance and abandon her to her fate. But he didn't. Wren could have cried with relief when he turned out the lights and stepped away from the ladder. "Quickly," he said.

The sound of voices suddenly quieted.

"What was that?" another voice asked. Suddenly, Wren was thrown fifty feet above her body, tears burning in her eyes. She would know that voice anywhere.

Una.

"What?" said Hannah. "I didn't hear a thing."

"That's an interesting design choice," Una said dryly. "I'd like to take a look behind it."

"It's not safe to enter."

"I suspect I'll be fine."

"Wren." Hal sounded strained.

Wren snapped back to reality and slid onto the first rung of the ladder. It would make a noise if she covered the entryway again, but what choice did she have? As carefully as she could, she pulled the stone tile over their heads, wincing as it rumbled against the floor. She nearly lost her balance in her haste to clamber down the ladder, and Hal reached out to steady her. The brush of his hand against her waist caused the magical bond between them to flare like a live wire. They flinched simultaneously, and if she didn't know better, she'd say Hal looked flustered.

She mouthed *sorry* while he blew out the candles.

They were plunged into darkness just as the sound of footsteps echoed above them. Una was only feet above her, and the pain of that nearly knocked her breathless. She hadn't realized how much she missed her until now. How unmoored she'd been without her lead. More than anything, Wren wanted to go home. But home had never been a place for her. It had always been her team. That warm glow of belonging.

The way Byers snorted if she made him laugh too hard, or how he could provoke her into a yelling match over complete *nonsense*. How she could get Una to crack if she imitated their old drill sergeant's droning voice. The tender look Una reserved only for Wren when they were truly alone.

But after Byers had disappeared and Wren had left Una in the snow that night, any home she'd ever had was gone. She would never get it back. She could hear it now, the glued-together pieces of her heart coming undone. Hal clamped a hand over her mouth, and Wren nearly gagged on the effort of not snapping at him. Then she realized—she'd let out a whimper. When she whirled around to face him, his eyes pinned her in place.

Steady, they said.

In this cramped entryway, Hal was too close for comfort. Over the clinical, cold smell of the tunnel, he smelled earthy, like strong-steeped tea and petrichor.

"Charming." Una sounded disappointed—and unconvinced, as if she knew there was more to find. "Let me be clear with you. I'm well aware that Wren Southerland is here. She broadcasted that information to the queen herself before she left. These things tend to go smoother with cooperation."

"And I'm completely certain she's not here."

The sounds of their argument and their footsteps passed overhead and toward the grand hall. All at once, relief surged through her. She bonelessly leaned against Hal, her head tucked into the space between his neck and shoulder. He tensed, a shiver running through him.

And then, after a breathless moment, he sneezed.

Even smothered, it reverberated through the tunnel—through her very bones. As she jerked back, his eyes were wide and apologetic, and it was the most innocent he'd ever looked while awake.

The world above grew deathly still, deathly silent.

They were both going to be arrested because Hal *sneezed*.

Una let out a humorless laugh. "I'll be back with a warrant. I'd strongly advise you to wrack your memory before then."

"But—"

"Ready the horses," Una said to her companion. "I've seen enough."

"Yes, Captain."

Captain? More had changed in Wren's absence than she'd thought.

The front doors slammed shut. Wren stayed in the comfort of the darkness until sensation came back to her fingers. Until her heart promised to remain encased in her ribs. Until her fear bled gradually into despair. Una had moved on—had been promoted without her. And if she couldn't open that door or prove Lowry was responsible for the disappearances before Una returned, both she and Hal would be carted back to Danu to face trial.

Wren slowly climbed the ladder. With every step, her dread mounted. It wasn't kind, and it wasn't fair, but if there was anyone easy to blame, it was Hal. As they passed through the tapestry and into the grand hall, she rounded on him. Framed by the window, Hal stood before a stretch of navy sky. Snowfall dappled the dim moonlight streaming in behind him. As lovely as ever, she thought bitterly—especially with that suppliant expression.

"What was that?" she hissed. "You could've gotten us both killed."

"Your hair," he said helplessly.

It was so completely *ridiculous,* her anger felt overblown. She deflated. "Great. Just *great.* Now the Queen's Guard knows we're here."

His eyes sparked with frustration, but his voice remained as cool and smooth as glass. "All they know for certain is that someone was in the basement. It'll take time to process the warrant. By then, we'll have discovered how to open the door."

"How *much* time? If they're staying in town, we'll have a few days. Maybe a week at most. We still have nothing."

"Tomorrow—"

Before he could finish that sentence, Hannah, who had been seething by the front door, hurtled toward them like a runaway train. Wren had half a mind to crawl back into the tunnel.

"Care to explain what the hell is going on?" Hannah thrust a creased paper toward her. Printed in bold capital letters across the top was WANTED: WREN SOUTHERLAND. Beneath it, a sketch of her face stared back at her. Fear struck first, hard and sudden as a slap to the face.

"You've been sneaking around the house and breaking curfew," Hannah continued. "And the other day, when you went downstairs to investigate that sound, you left all your books open. I didn't mean to look, but . . ."

Wren rested her face in her hands.

"That medicine . . . It was antitoxin, wasn't it? I didn't want mention it because you promised to tell me, and I trusted you. Now I don't know what to think. What does this mean? That all my staff—they were *murdered*?" All the fury in her voice suddenly shattered. What remained was despair.

"I'm so sorry." Wren hated that she was too much of a coward to meet Hannah's eye. "I didn't know how to tell you."

"So you were just going to, what? Avoid it forever and let me live my whole life in the dark? Cross your fingers and hope it didn't happen to me, too?"

"It wouldn't have happened to you. I *promise*. If there was any risk of you—"

"How can you be sure?"

"Ms. Southerland and I have been investigating this case undercover," Hal cut in. "We have reason to believe the murderer was targeting soldiers. It seems every civilian who fell ill before me was . . ."

"A test case?"

He nodded, his mouth a thin line.

Hannah slumped against the wall, laughing weakly. "I already grieved them once. I don't know that I can do it again."

"I'm sorry." Hal's voice was so gentle, it nearly gutted Wren. There was no pity there, only understanding. "I can't imagine how difficult this is."

"Just tell me what I can do to help." At first, Wren mistook the flatness in Hannah's voice as defeat. But when she looked into her eyes, she saw steel and fire. Raw determination.

"I want to know who did it," Hannah said.

Wren and Hal exchanged a look.

"For now, I need you to help cover for my mistake," Wren said. "The Queen's Guard is after me because of a misunderstanding. I know I can set this right. If Lord Lowry asks, tell him I've left for a few days and brought Henry with me. He probably won't even notice we're gone."

Panic flickered in her eyes. "And what will I tell him if he does?"

"We went to the next town over. Henry's condition worsened overnight, and I had to leave at once to find an herb for the remedy. I need you to tell him that."

She made no immediate reply. Then, quietly, "How do I know you'll come back?"

"I promised you I would cure this disease. I promised no one else would get sick. I kept those promises, didn't I?" Wren met her eyes steadily. "I know it's hard to trust me right now, but I swear I'll be back, and I swear no one will hurt you while I'm gone."

She hated to prey on Hannah's trust and her hope, but what else could she do? She and Hal couldn't stay here.

After a beat of silence, Hannah lowered her head and sighed. "Fine. I'll do it."

The resignation in her voice might haunt Wren forever.

Hal followed her back to her room, no doubt eager to hear her grand plan. In front of Hannah, she'd sounded confident. As if it were simple to slip out of this house without Lowry knowing and bide their time until they were prepared to strike. But really, she had no idea what to do, no idea where to go. Wren was no investigator. She was only a frightened girl who'd wandered too far out of her depth.

Tossing the wanted poster on the ground, Wren collapsed into her bed and pulled a pillow over her head. It smelled of her lavender soap and the indelible must of this place. Although she wanted to shut out the world—shut out *herself*—the sound of rustling paper caught her attention. Wren lifted the pillow from her head to see Hal smoothing the wrinkles out of the poster.

He scanned it with a raptness befitting some newly unearthed apocryphal text. "You're wanted for assault and desertion?"

"It was hardly *assault*."

Together, they listened to the groan and hiss of the house in the wind. "Did you know that girl?"

Sighing, she said, "Yes. I know her. She's my commanding officer and my best friend. Former on both counts, I suppose."

Hal sat beside her on the edge of the bed, his features washed in shadow. "What are you really doing here?"

"I never lied about that. Lord Lowry hired me to heal you. I just didn't know it was *you* when I said yes." She rolled onto her stomach. "The problem is, the queen never gave me clearance to take this job. So I kind of . . . left."

"But she knew where you were going," Hal said slowly.

"I know, I know, I *know*. I don't need your criticism right now, Cavendish." She buried her face in her pillow again. "I had my reasons, alright? Lowry made a lot of promises."

"I understand." Mercifully, he didn't push her, although she almost wanted him to. He more than anyone would understand how it felt to be one of the most hated people in Danu. "What now?"

"First," she said, "you need another dose of antitoxin."

That, at least, was something she could accomplish. Without waiting for his response, she rolled off the bed and went to her desk to prepare a syringe. Behind her, fabric rustled. Buttons popped on his shirt. Heat curled within her belly as she listened to the slide of starched cotton against his skin. Imagined the candlelight pooling in his collarbones. Wren drew in a deep breath as she flicked the air bubbles out of the vial. Her confinement in Colwick Hall had begun to reduce her to depravity.

"You think leaving is the best option?" he asked.

"For now, yes. In a few days, when Una finds no trace of us, we come back and deal with Lowry. While that may make it harder to investigate, I'm less afraid of him."

As soon as she'd said it, she wasn't entirely sure she believed it. If they stayed, Una would arrest them. And if they left, who knew what Lowry would do when they returned? There were no good options, but thinking about it too hard made her feel nauseous with dread.

"Una Dryden is not a forgiving person," Wren said. "She'll arrest me on sight—and you . . . I don't want to find out what she'd do to you."

When she turned around, he sat on her bed, traced in golden light. His jacket lay beside him, and he'd unbuttoned his shirtsleeve to roll it above his elbow. Wren fought to keep the dumbstruck look off her face as she took his elbow in her hand.

"Would she truly?" he asked. "If you were best friends?"

Wren hesitated, his skin and her magic warm in her palm. "She would, and I'd deserve it. She tried to stop me from leaving. Hence, the assault charges." She busied herself with injecting the serum into the crook of his elbow. Hal hardly flinched. "It's funny. I deserted because I was reassigned. Because I wanted to stay with Una. But now she hates me, and I'm completely alone."

"Why were you reassigned?"

Wren sighed, watching the vial drain gradually into his arm. "Because I healed somebody I wasn't supposed to. We had a prisoner with a compound fracture. Una thought it was *misplaced pity*. She tried to stand up for me when the queen dismissed me, but she's always thought I was too soft anyway."

"Then why are you friends?"

He asked it so plainly, it startled her. "What do you mean 'why are we friends'? We went through the academy together. We survived the war together. We've done *everything* together. I love her."

"While you made a tactical error," he said, "compassion for its own sake isn't something worth punishing."

Wren withdrew the needle from his arm. "What are you getting at?"

"I don't know that I would've given you the same order." He paused, as if considering his next words carefully. "Do you see what you did as wrong? Do you see compassion as a weakness?"

Always *questions* with him. Wren absently healed the puncture on his arm and let her fingers trail lower, along the ridge of his palmaris longus tendon. Her entire life, everyone had told her that her emotions would be her downfall. They made her too irrational, too impulsive, too sensitive. That much was true, but compassion . . . She didn't know if it was wrong.

"If I could change it, I would. It would make my life easier."

"Yes, it would. It's easier to feel nothing." He hesitated. "If she's worth your loyalty, she'll forgive you. In the meantime, you're not completely alone."

Wren looked up, her heart fluttering at the tentatively warm glow in his eyes. "No. I guess not."

Her hand still lingered on his forearm, and here, in the comfort of her bedroom, she realized just how close they were. How easy it would be to bridge the last of the space between them. Her focus narrowed to the whisper of candles around them; to the shape of his mouth, soft and serious; to his bared skin and that goddessdamned jacket beside them, so casually rumpled. She wanted to lay her hand flat against his beating heart, beneath the fine black embroidery of his waistcoat. She wanted to—

Oh no.

Pulling her hand back, she said, "You mentioned that you went to an inn called the Guiding Light?"

The tension between them shattered.

"I did." He righted his sleeve and began to fasten his buttons. Regret chased each deft movement of his fingers. "Why?"

"Something's been bothering me since you mentioned it." Wren worried her lip. "I've been there before, too. I found goddessblood growing in its garden. You said Lowry owned it. That can't be a coincidence."

"No," he said quietly. "It doesn't seem like it is."

"Since we need to lie low, why don't we go there? See if we can turn up anything?"

"It's a good idea, but dangerous. The weather might not hold until we get there."

"What? Hal Cavendish, scared of a little snow?"

His eyes narrowed. Only Hal could look so irritated with the slightest change of his expression. "I'm only trying to consider the potential risks."

As practical as ever. "Fair enough. We'll leave for town early tomorrow morning before sunrise. Maybe someone can get us there before the storm blows in. Then we'll stay in town for a little while."

"Understood." His eyes searched her face and, although it looked like he wanted to say something else, he settled on, "I'll let you rest."

"Yeah. Thanks. Good night."

As soon as the door latched behind him, Wren raked her hands through her hair and tried desperately to dissect these bothersome feelings. He left her with something bubbling bright within her chest. And beneath it, something sour and strange. What she felt for Hal was more than attraction—far more than the familiar pull of the tether between them.

She admired him for his dedication to his cause. She liked the way he listened and the way he looked at her, like she was the first breach of sunlight on the horizon. He made her feel important. Like she mattered. Like she wasn't entirely broken.

Goddess above, she was such a *mess*. Even if she chose to indulge herself, they could never be together. Besides, what good did this distraction do when their investigation was about to crumble around them? Staying here promised certain discovery. Leaving— and so blatantly breaking Lowry's rules—promised something worse in its mystery. How much would he curtail their freedom? What horrific plan did he have in store for them?

With poison, Lowry had taken down six elite soldiers and kept them imprisoned here. In his prime, Hal might have stood a chance, but he had no magic now. They had no defense and no evidence. They didn't even know where the key to that door was.

They had *nothing* but the hope they'd uncover something at the Guiding Light. And only a week and a half before the ball, presumably when Lowry would act against them. If they failed before then, a war would break out, and they would be dead.

Panic knifed through her. Desperate for a distraction, Wren returned to her desk to rummage for disinfectant. Shoved in the depths of the drawer was a slip of paper that crinkled under her touch. She pulled out a letter and scanned the messy handwriting.

The weather is far too dangerous to leave today, but we should be able to get you down the mountain two weeks from now. Meet at 0500 sharp. Stay warm.

She sucked in a sharp breath. Since she'd begun working with Hal, she'd nearly forgotten about the carriage she ordered. As if from the shadows, a voice whispered, *It's not too late.*

It *was* too late. She couldn't take Hal prisoner—not anymore.

Or could she? What was Hal Cavendish against everything she held dear? What was guilt against the certainty of survival, of redemption? She liked him, yes. Far, far more than she should. But she could not trust her own heart; she had wrecked herself in the storms of its desires time and time again.

You have to be rational, she told herself. *Ruthless.*

Her choices were simple. Stay and be arrested. Hide and become Lowry's next victim. Or leave and reap the rewards of Hal's capture.

She wouldn't be abandoning her comrades, even if they were still alive. With the queen's trust and a full unit, she could easily return to Colwick Hall and find Byers. Danu could use Hal to bargain Vesria into submission. And she'd prove at last to Isabel and Una that she was worthy. All of it was within reach, and it would be too easy now that Hal trusted her. Maybe even cared for her. The very thought of exploiting that made her feel despicable.

If I can quash just one feeling in my life, she thought, *let it be this one.*

She would have to kidnap Hal tomorrow.

CHAPTER TWENTY-ONE

The next morning, Wren stirred sugar into Hal's sedative-infused tea and carried it into the parlor. Hal stood with his nose nearly pressed to the window, a blade of predawn light slicing through the parted curtains.

Past the glass, rimed with frost and the ghost of Hal's breath, the world had darkened to an eerie slate gray. Wren saw only unbroken miles of snow and the restless churn of storm clouds over the mountains. Cold drummed its fingers against the windowpanes, impatiently waiting for her.

Dread weighed her down, like stones in her pockets. She didn't know if she could do this, but for now, treachery was as simple as placing the teacup into Hal's hands. "Will three teaspoons of sugar suffice, or shall we hasten your death by sweetener even more?"

"I've survived worse." Hal took a sip of tea and furrowed his brow.

Wren went rigid with panic. He couldn't know, could he? It only smelled of bitter, long-steeped leaves and lavender.

She forced a laugh. "What? Not enough? Too much?"

"No." Hal drank again. She watched the bob of his throat as he swallowed his tea and wasn't certain if she wilted with relief or regret. "It's perfect. Thank you."

"Sure." She leaned against the wall beside him. "Do you mind if I check how you're doing before we go?"

Hal shook his head.

Wren lifted her hand to his temple, trying to ignore the way her face heated under his scrutiny. When they first met, Hal had been sallow and frail. Beautiful in that stark, wasting way impermanent things were: the sunlit drip of icicles in early spring, the flush of trees in late autumn. Now, he looked almost solid—present, with his height and the shrewd glint in his eye.

Her initial sweep of his system turned up mercifully clear of goddessblood toxin. He wasn't completely recovered, but his body would begin to repair itself without her magic.

Everything but his eyes, of course.

The swollen and leaking *fola* behind his eyes made her shiver. She let the magic flicker from her hand, sighing at the way it hummed between them. "You must have terrible headaches."

"How do you know that?" he asked guardedly.

Wren tapped his forehead. "You've got a lot of pressure behind your eyes. Ever considered that's why you're so miserable and tired all the time?"

Hal flinched back as if she'd burned him. "I didn't realize that was part of your assessment."

"Forgive me for being holistic," she grumbled. "You've allowed your *fola* to degenerate, which could've been prevented if you'd had someone competent looking after you. If you don't get it under control, it could blind you someday."

"I appreciate your concern."

"Must you refuse any and all kindness? Honestly. It seems exhausting."

"I don't know what to do with yours. It so often feels like an attack," he said wearily. "Regardless, I allowed my magic to degen-erate because I wanted to. It's for the best."

"That's all well and good for your self-flagellation campaign, but as your doctor—" Wren cut herself off with a quiet sigh. It didn't matter much now how he dealt with his magic, did it? "Shall we head to town before the storm picks up again?"

Hal shrugged on his coat, and when she foisted a scarf on him, he squirmed away from her like a child from an overbearing parent. Although he'd gotten better, he still accepted charity like an insult. Today, she wouldn't compromise. He would need all the warmth he could get.

"If you catch a cold, I'll be so cross with you." She tugged a hat over his ears. "Cooperate."

With that, they were ready.

They slipped out through the servants' quarters and into the snow. Those first, tentative steps allowed her to walk on the thick, glittering crust before she sank to nearly her knees. She squinted through the drifts at the town some mile and a half in the distance. An ocean of snowfall and pine separated them from civilization, the surface rippled by wind. As it gusted past her, the trees shook loose showers of snow and ice from their fine green needles.

Hal matched her stride, but Wren slowed down when she real-ized that he was struggling to keep up. His breaths were long and deliberate, but she could hear the rattle in his lungs over the snow crunching beneath their boots. Even though he was faring well, he was still a way off from a complete recovery. And judging by his vital signs, sensed dimly through their tether, he didn't have much more than an hour before the sedative took effect.

It took them nearly forty-five minutes to push through the worst of it, to where carriages and footprints had packed and worn a glassy road into the town square. Compared to the fog-thick gloom of Colwick Hall, it was quaint—even cheerful.

Incandescent lightbulbs burned in the streetlamps, and the smoke curling from the chimneys filled the air with scents of woodsmoke and baking pastries. Still-sleeping taverns leaned against inventors' shops. Wren paused to gawk in a storefront window. A plaque beneath a prototype, apparently called a telephone, claimed you could use it to talk to someone miles away. Impossible, yet sorely needed in a place like this. Her fingers had gone numb in her gloves.

Hal's reflection appeared beside hers in the glass. "I like this place."

Wren turned to face him. "Oh?"

"It reminds me of where I grew up."

"There are snowy hellscapes in Vesria as well, then?"

Hal shook his head at her. "It's a feeling. The quiet and the cold. The smell of bread and storms."

Wren lifted her eyebrows in surprise. "A small town then?"

"Yes." The curve of his lips was wistful. "My father was a fisherman. My family moved out of the city when the bloodline ran dry two generations ago."

It stung a little, imagining what kind of life he could've had. Sun-browned and rough-handed, briny winds tangling in his hair and a ship by the harbor. Still serious, still dedicated—but unhaunted.

Happy.

"I left home to enlist when I was eight." At her horrified expression, he frowned. "They recruited us young—and my father was eager to see me go. I haven't been back since and don't expect I ever will be."

They both looked up as the snow began to fall. It gathered in her eyelashes, the world going pale and sparkling. In spite of herself, she wanted more from him. More personal things to keep safe. "Do you miss it?"

"I do." Hal tucked his hands into his pockets. "But I can't make a difference from there."

Too many follow-up questions arose. Too many thoughts, all unhelpful and masochistic, flooded her with unwelcome dread. If she did this, Hal would never see Vesria again.

"I don't feel well," he said.

Her heart twisted sharply. "Let's get you inside then."

They continued down the quiet, lamp-lit street, the cobble-stones slick and shining. This early, still before full light, none of the townspeople had stirred yet. All the better for her. No witnesses. Wren counted the slowing beats of Hal's heart, observed his move-ments as they became looser, less precise. Any moment now, he'd be out.

Give up already.

In front of the carriage company, Wren saw eight dogs, tails wagging, hitched to a sled. The snowflakes danced madly against the gas lamp, reminding her of a swarm of flies around a carcass. Hal stopped in his tracks, his eyes hard as he turned toward her.

Three things happened at once.

Hal pitched forward, Wren caught him by the shoulders, and a knife pressed into her jacket, directly between her third and fourth ribs. Aiming for her liver, she noted. He was good. That would make for a slow and painful death. The kind she deserved.

They were close enough that Wren could inhale the cloud of breath curling from his parted lips. One sudden movement would draw blood.

"You drugged me." His voice was colder than the air and firmer than she'd ever heard it. But as terrifying as that flinty glare was, the sedative would claim him at any moment.

Wren grabbed his lapels harder. "Yes. I did."

"Let me go."

"You first."

Hurt—betrayal—sparkled in his dark eyes.

Before she could process it, he went limp. Her knees buckled under his weight when she caught him. He was all limbs, tall and lean, and made even more unwieldy by his winter jacket. It took considerable effort to drag him through the snow and lay him on the sled. His head lolled to the side, his mouth still open in an unspoken accusation. The wind whipped by her, tugging her back toward the estate. But it was too late to turn back.

She was going home.

Snow squalls blotted out everything. Although it was nearly mid-day by her estimation, Wren could see no sunlight, no life. Only the dim shape of the driver, Collins, stood out in the storm. He leaned over the front of the sled, as sturdy and guiding as a ship's figurehead.

They'd been traveling for hours, but Wren could not shake a crawling feeling of unease. The valley stretched out to her right, the cliff's edge serrated by snow cornices. She could feel the hunger of that chasm, darkness swirled through with gray.

As if someone had whispered it into her ear, she thought, *We're going the wrong way.*

Granted, the way up had been winding and dark, and she had slept half the time, but . . . No, no, she could not doubt herself. This couldn't be right.

There's only one viable way between Danu and Cernos this time of year. She remembered Basil grinning at her over his shoulder. *Don't let anyone tell you otherwise.*

"Excuse me," she shouted over the howl of the wind. "Where're we going?"

"The normal route is too dangerous in these conditions." In pro-file, Collins looked like something that had crawled out from be-neath the ice. Frost whitened his eyebrows. "I know a better way."

Bullshit, Wren thought.

Her eyes fell on Collins's bag, lying on its side in the footwell. Maybe something inside would provide her with some insight. She reached for it but with Hal weighing her down, her fingers curled into open air.

Hal, still unconscious, had proven more unwieldy than she'd hoped. He lay sprawled out with his head in her lap, his thick, snow-matted hair whipping into his face. Carefully, Wren disentangled herself from him and rolled him onto his side. As she adjusted the hood tighter around him, his arm fell limply off the edge of the seat.

She unbuckled Collins's bag. Whining hinges opened to reveal clothes folded in neat, crisp piles and a thin folder tucked into the side. She leafed through it, pinning the papers with her thumb as the wind tried to tear them away from her.

And there, she found it.

Shoved in alongside his passport, his bills, and a few letters was a poster. In bold, black letters was the word WANTED. That son of a bitch. It figured he'd betray her. The bounty was at least triple what she could offer him.

Replacing everything exactly as she found it, Wren called, "Can you stop?"

"What?" Collins turned halfway over his shoulder again. "Didn't you say this was urgent?"

Wren gestured to Hal, lying deathly still. "I'll double your pay if you stop in the next town. My friend isn't holding up well."

"No can do, miss," Collins said. "Like I said, this is the only way that's safe."

"I'm afraid I must insist."

With an edge to his voice, he said, "Sit down."

"Not until you tell me where we're going!" Wren shoved his shoulder—and immediately regretted it. She'd meant it as more of a warning than an attack, but it was enough to provoke him.

He reeled on her, slackening his hold on the reins. The dogs overcorrected the sled's course, and it lurched, skidding sideways along a patch of ice. Wren stumbled backward, clinging to the edge of her seat to steady herself.

"Are you insane?" he yelled. "We're going to Danu, just like you asked."

The dogs barreled ahead, howling. Fear, cold and stiff as icicles, pierced her heart. Her options raced by, quick and ungraspable as the screaming winds. She could try to take over the sled, but the thought of hurting Collins by mistake made her hands tremble.

She was paralyzed.

If she did nothing, they'd both be arrested. She would be Severed. Or worse.

Do something, she told herself. *Move.*

Before she could talk herself out of it, Wren slipped off her glove and dug her fingers into the back of Collins's neck. "Sorry!"

Her magic flooded into his nervous system, and Wren felt the moment his consciousness flickered out. He slumped forward, the reins slipping from his deadened hands. Bent over the front seat, Wren fumbled for them, her eyes stinging in the wind. The dogs veered off course, their paws scrabbling in the wet snow as the sled teetered dangerously close to the precipice. She whispered frantic prayers as they strained against their harnesses.

Another lurch, and the sled crested an embankment, up to safety. Wren's relieved sob misted the air—just as the tracks hit an icy outcropping. The sled jolted, and her boots left the floor.

On reflex, she grabbed the back of Hal's collar, and together, they tumbled off the side of the open-backed sled. For one moment, there was nothing but wind and darkness wailing around her. Then, a sickening *crack*, a stupefying burst of agony, as her head struck the ice. Hal's dead weight crushed her as they landed in a heap, forcing the air from her lungs.

Far ahead of her, the dogs faded into the veil of the blizzard. Her vision swam with snow and stars as she shoved Hal off her, her breaths coming in long wheezes. As the pain pulsed in her skull, she heaved herself onto her knees and vomited.

Not good, she thought hazily. A concussion, most likely.

Exhaustion and nausea pulled her back down. As the cold seeped into her coat, she turned to look at Hal. The last thing she saw was a pair of black eyes regarding her through the flurries.

Then, darkness.

CHAPTER TWENTY-TWO

The world howled as Wren blinked into consciousness.

She turned onto her side, already numb from cold, and looked for Hal. But as the white and black tendrils of the storm twisted and knotted around her, she realized that his imprint in the snow was all that remained of him. He'd left her.

And he'd taken her stuff, that bastard.

At least the grogginess blunted some of the terror. The blow to her head had thickened her thoughts to molasses and attenuated her focus. But she knew, deep down, that if she didn't get it together, this would be bad. She didn't know how long she'd been out, and while her extremities were numb, they weren't frostbitten. Not yet, anyway.

The longer she stayed curled up here, the more heat she would lose and the quicker she would die. Once her core temperature dropped enough, her control over her magic would falter. Then her mental faculties would slow—followed soon enough by her heart.

No, she couldn't die here. Not after she'd come so far.

Wren rubbed her temples and pushed as much magic as she could spare into her head to ease the concussion. Her fingers came away caked with blood. The wind had already covered Hal's tracks, but he couldn't have gotten far in weather like this.

She dragged herself to her feet and began to walk.

It felt like hours that she wandered in the dark, alternately stumbling and clawing her way forward when it took too much effort to keep upright. Ice slipped into the nailbeds of her ungloved hand. Her eyes and nose streamed from the bitter air, which froze the water on her skin in seconds. And with every step, she sank deeper and deeper into the drifts until she feared she'd be entombed.

Everything that lay behind her was as white and featureless as what lay ahead. The world was insubstantial, little but wind and cold water slipping through the gaps in her bone-white fingers. No matter how she looked at it, it was hopeless. It would be so easy to lie down.

Wren sank to her knees. Everything hurt, every part of her fragile. Ice wound its way through her blood until she couldn't even remember her own name, much less what she had set out to do in the first place.

No rush, then, she decided. She deserved to rest.

And then she felt a tug at the center of her chest, like a rope gone taut. Somewhere over the wind, a voice called to her.

"Wren."

Right. *That* was her name. She imagined responding, but her whole body was so heavy. Her lungs would not expand. Her mouth would not open.

"Wren!"

I'm here, she thought. *Right here.*

In the distance, a shadow emerged from the solid white of the blizzard, blooming like ink dripped onto parchment. It came closer, morphing until it became a man blink by blink. He crouched beside her, and Wren squinted up at him. Raven-dark hair and eyes the color of a lightless lake. Snow dusted the sharp lines of his jacket, clung to his eyelashes. He looked star-scattered. Beautiful.

Wren wanted to touch his face. She wanted to knot her hands in his hair and kiss him, even though she knew she shouldn't for reasons she couldn't exactly recall.

His arm slipped around her waist and he hoisted her to her feet. Her thoughts twinkled like ice crystals catching the sunlight, and she let herself lay her palm flat against his cheek. No warmth radiated from his skin, and he recoiled with a look of singular concern.

"I know you," she said.

"Yes. It's me." His voice was rough as he pulled her to his side. "Can you walk?"

"Mm-hm."

The world was still spinning. At the center of it was *him*.

"Hal," she found herself saying. His name unlocked something in her. Tears burned her dry eyes. "Oh, Hal. I messed up."

"We'll discuss it later." Discomfort clipped each word short. "Walk."

They stumbled over each other, dragging and clinging, as they waded through the snow. Hal's rasping breaths were a metronome that kept her on course, and as movement flushed blood through her, she regained her wits enough to push magic into her head. With every pulse, her thoughts cleared enough for her to quit worrying about her skull. She needed to save her strength to treat their imminent hypothermia.

Wren couldn't be sure how long they walked before she saw the glow of a town in the valley below. They slid and staggered down the mountainside, and with the last of her energy, Wren urged them onward until they reached the inn at the heart of town. The sign above it read THE GUIDING LIGHT INN. That beatific depiction of the Goddess glowed like a remote star, lit by her eerie electrical light.

How ridiculous, she thought, that they should end up here all the same.

But as they passed through the door, all she could focus on was the roaring fire in the lobby. It stung her skin with heat. She sobbed noiselessly, gasping in her first lungful of warm air. *Alive.* Somehow, they were alive.

"You made it back?" The innkeeper whistled admiringly at Hal. "I was about to send someone to look for you."

Of all the self-loathing, foolish things he could do.

He came back for her.

Upstairs, Wren stripped off her wet clothes and tugged on the spare tunic the innkeeper had left for her. She was too far gone to care about propriety as she helped Hal undress. None of their limbs worked quite right, and she fumbled with every button until his clothes lay in a sopping pile on the floor. The flow of her magic had abated some of her symptoms, but Hal still shivered violently.

She guided him onto the floor beside the fireplace and threw a blanket over him. His lips were tinted blue, and he was so pale, it was as if frost crept like lace beneath his skin. Wren laid her hands on his chest. He was *freezing,* his heartbeat weak. Nearly dead because he had saved her miserable life.

"This is all my fault," she whispered. "I'm such an idiot. A selfish, reckless idiot."

His eyelids drooped. "I understand."

He *understood*? There were so many things to say, to ask, to scold him for, but right now, she needed him alive. "You're clearly not of sound mind. You need to stay awake."

"I am awake," he protested.

Then his eyes fell shut.

Wren swore and set to work immediately, pouring what little magic she had left into him to speed his metabolism. Once he was stable and flushed, she collapsed beside him, her magic entirely spent. Although she wanted to stay awake, wanted to make sure he'd last the night without her, the comforting heat of the fire and the reassuring warmth of his body put her to sleep in seconds.

When her eyes peeled open again, the first thing Wren saw was fire. Behind the mesh curtaining the hearth, orange veins glimmered beneath the crackled, ashy skin of the logs. The fire exhaled a plume of sparks, warming her face.

Alive, the heat seemed to remind her. *You're alive.*

She groaned softly at the unpleasant reality of that. A dull pain still throbbed in the back of her skull, and all her joints were swollen from overexertion. As she rubbed at her eyes and readjusted to consciousness, she realized she was nestled in a blanket. Deep exhaustion had crystallized in her bones, and she swore she would never be able to scrape the chill out from beneath her skin.

Or the guilt.

She rolled over and found Hal already awake, propped up by a few pillows he'd pulled off the bed. In the glow of the flames, he looked like an oil painting, achingly pretty and textured. Wren reached out to touch him, to check his vitals, but Hal shifted away from her.

"Don't." He sounded tired but sure.

As much as it stung, she deserved his distrust. "You should have left me there and saved yourself."

"Perhaps." Firelight danced in his eyes. "Am I still your prisoner?"

"Yes. So answer me this. Why'd you do it? Why'd you save me?"

"My life for yours." He sounded so formal, as if there'd never been anything at all between them. "My debt to you is paid."

"There's no debt you owe me." She couldn't keep the irritation out of her voice. "If anything, I'm still in yours. You spared me once already."

"What're you talking about?"

"You said you don't remember, but I do. That day at the Battle of the River Muri, you saw me. I was healing a woman in a birch thicket when someone attacked you. You killed him, and I thought you would come for me next. But you didn't. You just walked away." Wren drew her knees up to her chin. "I've wondered about it ever since."

"I'd given up by then," he said gently. "I wouldn't have attacked you first."

Wren wrapped her arms tighter around herself. "Maybe you should've. I only healed you so you would survive when I kidnapped you. That's the full truth. So there. Now you know I'm selfish and cruel. You surely regret saving me now."

"I've seen cruelty. You're not cruel. You're only afraid."

"What would you know?"

He didn't answer her. *How typical.* Were they truly back to this? Back to strained silences and fighting? And yet even now, Hal Cavendish was kinder to her than she deserved. Kinder than she was to herself—and far kinder than she was to him.

Her satchel filled with all her supplies lay within reach. She grabbed it, appreciative of the warmed leather in her cold hands, and rummaged until she found a flask filled to its stopper with brandy. She wasn't sure if she craved it for its throat-burning heat or for distraction, but she drank and passed it to Hal.

He sniffed it cautiously and made a face.

"It's not drugged," she said bitterly. "Just drink it. It'll help."

They both rose on unsteady feet. While she pulled her stiff, wet hair out of its chignon, he took a swig of brandy and leaned against the wall. Seeing him here, watching her as he always did, set her aflame with indignation that she didn't entirely understand.

"What have I done to upset you now?" he asked.

Wren closed the gap between them and shoved him. He hardly budged, which only made her burn hotter with annoyance. Because *of course* she couldn't move him, even now when she'd nearly killed him.

"You saved me." With every word, she beat her fists against his chest. "I'm your enemy. I tried to kidnap you. You're Hal Cavendish, the most calculating and logical person I've ever met. This is illogical. This was the wrong decision—so obviously! How could you be so self-destructive, so—"

"Emotional?" Hal grabbed her wrists, only hard enough to remind her to stop hitting him. His hands were wind-chapped and callus-rough. And so, so cold. He smiled, but it was an unkind one. "Is that still what you believe? That I feel nothing at all?"

Emotional.

The word singed. Made her want to cry for reasons she couldn't exactly place. It was confusion and longing and hope all snared up. *Your compassion will get you killed,* Una had told her. For so long, everyone had drilled it into her. Kindness and compassion had no place in the Queen's Guard. But Hal's kindness had saved her tonight, and Wren didn't know how to make sense of it.

"Yes," she said breathlessly. "Emotional."

Hal let her go. Her skin stung from the sudden loss of him. While the glow of the hearth still stained his eyes orange, the fire in them had gone out. The flickering shadows sharpened the dark circles beneath his eyes, the edges of his cheekbones.

"You must be tired," she said.

He nodded.

"Then let's get some sleep and—" Wren peered over his shoulder and at last noticed the single bed squatting like a toad in the center of the room. Dread and desire both pooled in her stomach.

As if sensing her discomfort, Hal cleared his throat. "It's yours."

Wren walked across the room as if it were scattered with coals, then perched on the edge of the bed. Silence, unbroken save for the popping of sap in the grate, stretched out. She swaddled herself in the blanket while Hal remained statuelike in front of the fire.

"Are you just going to stand there?"

"I don't sleep often," he said, as if that explained anything.

"I won't be able to either with you looming over me like that."

Obligingly, he took a seat in an armchair. Even at rest, he was elegant, ankles hooked together, hands folded at his ribs. Wren rolled over and tried to ignore him. His presence was like breath on the back of her neck, not entirely unpleasant but entirely disconcerting. Wren flipped over to face him again. "That's no better. It still feels like you're watching me."

"Shall I go outside, then?" he asked, his voice flattened with annoyance.

"Why don't you lie down?"

Conflict burned in his eyes, like he couldn't decide if he was repulsed or fascinated by her. For the first time, he looked like the nineteen-year-old boy he was. "With you?"

"Goddess above," she groaned. "Don't say it like that. Come here."

Wren tried to settle the pounding of her heart as he came closer. He drew back the covers, admitting only a whisper of cold air that made her skin prickle, and lay beside her. They'd been close before, but something about this felt more intimate than healing. From here, she drank in this rarity. Him, unarmored, even as he refused to look at her.

"How'd you find me, anyway?"

"It wasn't difficult. I could sense you through the healing bond."

Never had she been so grateful for it. "You could've easily let me die. Why did you come back for me?"

"To settle a debt."

"Ugh. You're such a liar."

"I'm tired of people dying because of me," Hal told the ceiling. "I'm tired."

"I'm sorry," she whispered. "I'm so sorry."

Hal turned so that they were almost nose to nose in the semi-darkness. "You're confusing."

"So are you."

"I can't figure out what you want from me." He sounded almost anguished, but his eyes still held accusation. "If I keep my distance, you needle me. If I'm vulnerable, you burn me. I let you in because you're the first person in years who isn't afraid of me—who actually seemed to care more for *me* than my magic."

Wren winced.

"This is what trusting you has earned me. And yet, after everything else I've done, I couldn't leave you to die. How can I be so pathetic?"

"You're not pathetic," she said softly. "Once, you told me mercy was the most difficult thing."

Hal's expression softened.

"I don't know if I can ever tell you how sorry I am. I understand if you can never trust me again. But I swear to you, I'm done. I don't want to hurt you anymore. I don't want my position back if you're the price of it."

"Why does it matter so much to you?"

Even if it would never make her actions right, she wanted to give him this. "I don't care about the military, really. But it was an escape for me. I told you I never felt like I belonged at the abbey, but it was more than that. Being there . . . it was letting the queen win. Admitting I was worthless. Disposable. Like I wasn't her niece but a piece of trash. I knew she would never love me, but I could make her acknowledge me. So I made sure I would never be disposable again."

Wren clenched her fist, absently watching her magic flicker. "Healing is the only thing I'm good at. The only thing that makes me useful. I had to be the best, or I'd be sent back."

"That isn't true," Hal said. "You're worth more than what you can do."

"I guess," she murmured. "But that was the fire that kept me going through my training and the recruitment process. And then I met Una."

She still remembered seeing Una for the first time. They'd locked eyes across the field. Una had tossed her hair over her shoulder and given her a look of pure disdain. Wren had been helpless against it. Love at first sight, she supposed.

"The first weeks of basic training were hell. Rumors circulate fast, so everybody knew who I was. Most of them kept their distance, but a few other recruits were *awful* to me." She understood it. Her aunt hadn't done anything for anyone since she took the throne, and Wren had become an easy outlet for the frustration her peers inherited from their parents. "Una caught wind of it one day. She's always had this sense of black-and-white justice and no patience for nonsense. I'll never forget the look on this girl's face when Una pulled a sword on her."

Wren still shivered when she remembered the ring of Una's saber loosed from its sheath. The flutter of her tormentor's pulse as the blade quivered a bare inch from her throat. The righteous anger gleaming in Una's golden eyes when she said, *If you'd like a* real *fight, I'll happily oblige.*

Of course, Una had shrugged off her thanks. Back then, she had wielded her confidence like a blade, painfully aware of her lack of magic. But she had always been dedicated to protecting those weaker than her. People like Wren.

"Ever since that, we were best friends." She closed her eyes. To be loved by Una was all she'd ever needed, her company like a warm and golden light. "She was my new purpose. I would've done anything for her, followed her anywhere, because I loved her. I believed in her. And I guess I was *in* love with her, too, until just recently, when . . ."

She glanced up at him and flushed. What *had* changed, exactly?

It wasn't only Hal—not the fact of him, here and warm beside her. But now, as she turned over their conversations, Wren began to wonder why she'd always thought she needed Una so desperately. She had grown so used to Una saving her from herself, she'd come to believe she needed it. But did her feelings truly make her weak? Could someone love her because of them, not in spite of them?

"Until recently," Wren concluded. "That's why my position matters to me so much."

Wren watched him process what she'd said, carefully turning over each word as if it were delicate. Then, once he'd slotted everything into place, he said, "I understand."

It felt like an absolution.

"Will you finish telling me what you brought up the other day?" she asked quietly. "You said you didn't believe in the military's cause anymore. What did you mean?"

As he lay unmoving beside her, Wren thought he might curl back into himself. Pretend to sleep, or conveniently lose his grasp on the Danubian language again. "The Vesrian army was a haven for people who hid their true intentions behind the banner of patriotism. They twisted good intentions into monstrosity and encouraged the cruelest among us.

"I didn't always want to be a soldier. But when my magic awakened, I was . . ." He trailed off, searching for the words. "It was an accident, that first time. I can hardly describe what it feels like when it happens. There's a moment when the connection snaps into place and neither of us can look away. Cold, and then all I know is fear—not my own. It's horrible."

"Who . . . ?" She hadn't meant to let it slip, but she couldn't take it back now.

"A friend." Bitterness crept into his voice. There were no words for that kind of horror. Wren could picture it too clearly. Hal, still innocent in boyhood—confusion melting into terror. Had anyone witnessed it? Did anyone help him? "I was devastated. But my father was so proud."

"What?"

"I was the first Cavendish mage in two generations. He told me there was no shame in what I'd done. That it was a blessing from God. That I was destined to restore our family's lost honor. It was then I realized I had a duty to the world. If I made a name for myself in the war effort, I could regain my family's title and its position in the magisterium—and only kill those who deserved it. I was so determined to be useful, I think part of me lies buried with my first victim."

And what remained was the Reaper of Vesria.

"Immediately, my superiors noticed me. I worked hard. I formed no attachments. I was single-minded. Exactly the monster you believed me to be, fed by the promotions, their praise, the promise of political power." He paused. "But my victims haunted me. I had to look into their eyes to kill them. I can't forget a single one of them."

She shivered, despite the warmth beneath the covers.

"Over time, I could not shake the growing suspicion that this war was wrong. That *I* was wrong. They told us we were defending our way of life. They told us we were saving you from yourselves." Shame clouded his expression. "You saw me at my blackest moment. By then, I had realized everything I stood for was a lie, even if my superiors believed what they were saying was true. If the war were truly about protecting Vesria, why did they order me to kill healers and civilians? Even some of your soldiers were hardly older than twelve. What harm could they have done us?"

Wren reached for his hand. This time, he did not pull away.

Hal stared somewhere far beyond her, his eyes as black as the deepest water. "That war protected no one. It was a massacre."

"All of us followed orders. Our superiors told us the same things about you." Wren's voice came out wrong, weak. "What else were we supposed to do? We were too young to know better. We all saw what happened to deserters."

"Don't absolve me." He drew an unsteady breath. "My life has been a series of regrets. But before I die, before I accept punishment for what I've done, I'll make restitution to Danu. I'll end this war. And I'll rebuild Vesria into the kind of place where children grow up happy, not as soldiers. The only way I can do that is by becoming the grand magistrate—and by solving this case."

"Hal . . ."

She did not know what to say. What he told her excused nothing, but Wren could see so clearly the circumstances that had shaped him: loneliness, desperation, trauma. Just like her, Hal had believed his magic was all he had to offer. Her compassion frightened her. He was still a war criminal. The people he killed were never coming back.

But it was so *unfair*.

Their countries forced them to dull their emotions, to fight before they knew any better. War demanded sacrifices they were not prepared to give, the cost of which they could not understand. People like Hal shouldn't have existed. Both Danu and Vesria created monsters the moment they stooped to recruiting children.

She'd never forget those months of deployment, the countless hours she spent bent over bodies too small for their issued uniforms, in tents so crowded she gagged on the cloying stench of putrescine. She'd never forget how she helped dig graves until her hands blistered and her shovel dulled. She'd never forget the hot nights spent curled tight against Una's side, so close it left no space for dreams.

"Why are you crying?" he rasped.

She was crying for Hal Cavendish. For herself. For the broken people they were and the children they should have been. For her lost comrades. For all the people who would end up like them—or dead—if their nations went to war over Lowry's crimes. All she could manage to say was, "Goddess knows you won't do it yourself."

Hal didn't speak. He looked as if he might break.

"Give me another chance to help you." She smeared away the tears on her cheeks. "Please. I won't rest until I see Lowry behind bars, and you as Vesria's grand magistrate. We can stop this war together."

Her words tugged something loose in both of them. He reached out to her, as if to swipe away a tear, but let his hand drop before he touched her. Wren had never felt such disappointment at something so small. She had never wanted anyone to touch her so badly.

"You can," she said, lower and more breathily than she intended.

His eyes darkened, surprise melting into hunger. Wren tried not to panic. Tried to dismiss the churning heat within her as a natural, hormonal response: a flood of oxytocin from their conversation and nothing more. But it was far too late to theorize this attraction away.

Hal, tentatively, slowly, raised himself up onto one elbow. The springs of the mattress groaned under his weight, and his heat rolled over her like the flow of the tide. As he bent closer, the ends of his hair tickled her face. His lips nearly brushed against hers, his breath sweet as brandy and honeyed tea.

The space between them was a question.

It would be so easy to wrap her arms around him and pull him against her. But it would never be simple. He was Vesrian, and she was Danubian. Even if they forged peace between their nations, they would have to go their separate ways. It would hurt too much. She'd lost too many people she cared about lately.

She turned her face away from him. "It's late."

"So it is." Hal settled back down beside her, disappointment and relief tangled in his voice.

The spell shattered. Her senses returned to her, and it felt like surfacing for air—painful but needed. Her vision shimmered, and when she dared to look at him again, he was sleeping lightly, the rise and fall of his chest reassuring her that he would survive the night. As she watched his peaceful expression, the knot of yearning in her stomach tightened again. This time, it was homesickness.

Hopelessness.

No matter what, things would never be the same. How could she slip back into her life as if nothing were different, when her perceptions of the world—when she—had changed? But she could worry about her feelings tomorrow. Her soul-deep exhaustion dragged her into the fold of sleep.

CHAPTER TWENTY-THREE

The world came to her gently, the sun still slumbering beneath the horizon. With her limbs heavy, Wren almost believed she'd dreamt the last month, that she'd open her eyes to her own flat. But as she eased into consciousness, she found herself entwined with Hal.

No such luck for dreaming.

Although her first impulse was to shove him away, she let herself remain still in the languorous warmth of his embrace. His arm was draped heavily across her waist, and his breathing flowed soft and even over her skin. With her forehead tucked against his neck, she listened to the steady beat of his heart.

He was alive, and it was almost a miracle.

Wren wanted to preserve him this way: peaceful and boyish, sleeping with his jaw slack and his forehead smooth. As carefully as she could, she slipped his arm from around her and pried her knee loose from where it was wedged between his. No sooner had she extricated herself than he jerked awake, so surprised and bleary-eyed, she had to stifle a laugh.

"Good morning," he mumbled.

Although Wren yearned to stay pressed against him a little longer, warm and safe, restlessness had already crept into her bones. Byers still might be in Colwick Hall, but they couldn't return without a guarantee they could find the key to that hidden door—or evidence convincing enough to indict Lowry.

This inn, however . . . Hal had told her Lowry had purchased it. She'd taken the goddessblood sample from its garden herself. Maybe it held the answers she sought.

"Rest a little longer. I'm going to take a look around."

Hal looked like he might protest, but when she pulled aside the blanket and let the cold air in, he retreated deeper under the covers like a snail into its shell. "Alright."

Wren crawled out of bed, retrieved her coat from beside the banked fire, and pulled it on as she made her way downstairs. The floorboards in the lobby creaked under her weight, the only sound apart from the faint crackle of logs in the fireplace. It was early, but there should have been more activity. Perhaps the smell of rendering fat from the kitchen, or the tread of footsteps overhead as the other guests awoke. Just as she remembered it two weeks ago, the place was too silent, as if it were hardly meant to operate as an inn at all.

Wren approached the window and pressed her hand to the glass. Outside, past the fog of her breath, she could see the pinkening sky uncovered by clouds, the breathtakingly blue peaks of the Dramlach Mountains. At last, the storm had broken. The town slept—all but the innkeeper. In the distance, at the end of a trench in the snow, the glow of a lantern illuminated him as he split logs with an echoing *thunk* of his ax.

Perfect.

Hal mentioned he'd found shipment records from here to Colwick Hall, but she wanted to confirm it herself. Taking a last surreptitious look around the room, Wren ducked behind the reception desk. At her back was a locked door, which likely led to an office or the innkeeper's living space, and a wooden board from which they hung the room keys. For now, she'd try the drawers.

She opened one, and as she began to rifle through the papers, an oddly familiar voice sent her stomach plummeting with fear. "Miss? What're you doing?"

Stay calm, she told herself. *Lie.*

But when she lifted her head, she froze. Carrying an armful of firewood was a boy, no older than twelve, with sandy blond hair and a smattering of freckles. His apprehension snapped into recognition. Then she saw her own terror reflected in his eyes.

The boy with the broken arm. The boy who had cost her *everything.* The missing evidence that connected Lowry to her comrades' disappearances.

"It's *you.*" It tore out of her, violent and unrestrained.

His hands went slack, and the wood clattered to the ground, loud as a roll of thunder. She hardly had a chance to blink before he bolted toward the door.

Not this time. She wouldn't lose him again.

He stumbled over the firewood, buying her precious time. Wren slid out from beneath the counter and tore after him as he scrambled to his feet—and ran smack into Hal. They both staggered back from the force.

"Excuse me," Hal said.

He glanced back and forth between them. As he registered the boy's terror and her anger, his confusion became apparent. Wren seized the boy by the back of his collar before he could wriggle free. He opened his mouth to scream.

"Make a sound. I dare you. I'll make that broken arm look like a joke." It was an empty threat, but he went deathly still. She jerked her chin at Hal. "Do you know who that is?"

He glanced up at Hal—then gasped and dropped his gaze to the floor. "Y-yes."

So this is what he endures, she thought. *So much fear.*

The boy was trembling, and Wren tried not to draw a vicious satisfaction from it. She understood now why Una had left him to suffer. Byers was gone, and the only guarantee at justice she had was this. Hurt for hurt, blood for blood.

"Do you care to explain why you're threatening children?" Hal was looking down at the cowering boy, his features softening with weariness.

"This child," she said, "is the cause of my disgrace. Una and I caught him documenting patrol routes in Danu. And here he is, hiding away in a property owned by Alistair Lowry."

Hal's expression darkened.

"I can explain! Please!" As if he'd remembered her order not to make a sound, he slapped his hands over his mouth.

"I hope it's a good one. If I find out you're lying—"

Hal cut her a sharp look that soured her stomach with shame. "You're frightening him."

He crouched beside the boy, who shrank away from him with his eyes screwed shut. In this heavy, predawn silence, all Wren could hear was the anxious chatter of his teeth.

"I won't hurt you." Hal's voice was mild, almost paternal. "I only want to talk."

"And why should I trust you?"

"There's no good reason to." Hal reached out and retrieved a piece of firewood. "But you may find me surprisingly reasonable."

The boy did not answer at first. Wren felt her patience come undone to the *clack* of wood as Hal gathered it into his arms. This boy held valuable information. In himself, he was enough to damn Lowry. But Hal was treating him so *tenderly,* it was almost frustrating. When he'd retrieved the last of the firewood, he pressed it into the boy's hands. Slowly, hesitantly, the boy dared to meet Hal's gaze. His lip quivered, but after the first experimental second, all the tension flooded out of him with a whimper.

"Alright?" Hal asked gently.

The boy nodded.

"Let's sit."

Wren gaped at Hal in astonishment as the boy headed glumly toward the fireplace; he only met her with a faintly self-satisfied smile. Checking his shoulder, she brushed past him and sank miserably into an armchair. The boy knelt beside the fireplace, meticulously stacking the wood in its iron rack. The concentric whorls of the cut ends watched her like widened eyes.

Hal took his own seat. "What's your name?"

"Will."

"Will," he repeated. "Can you tell me what you were doing in Danu?"

Will cast a furtive look at the window. His father was still chopping logs to the steady beat of *thunk, thunk, thunk.* "Lord Lowry owns this inn, and it's all my family has. If we don't do what he says, he could take it away."

Wren's hands clenched into white-knuckled fists. She knew that feeling all too well.

"He won't find out," Hal said.

"He wanted information about Danubian patrols," Will said in a rush. "My dad is from Danu, so I know the border well. And, well . . . Lord Lowry doesn't know I have magic. Pa just told him I'm fast. I am."

"What kind of information did he want?"

"Times and routes. But most important, he wanted to know what kinds of magic they used."

"Wait, *what?*" Wren's blood ran cold as she remembered the notebook they confiscated from Will. Una's name had a dark slash through it. Wren cycled through the names of the missing soldiers. Byers. Williams. Turner.

All of them had magic.

"Hal . . . ? How many of your missing subordinates had magic?"

He shot her a wary look. "All of them."

"That son of a bitch," Wren whispered. "It doesn't account for his servants, but Lowry is only targeting soldiers who're mages."

For one moment, Hal became someone she didn't recognize anymore, his face eerily blank, his voice low and chilling. "Why?"

"I swear, that's all I know! He never told me anything." Will's voice was pleading. "I didn't even know about anybody disappearing. Honest!"

As much as she didn't want to, Wren believed him. "What about the goddessblood in your garden? Was that something Lowry wanted as well?"

"I . . . I don't know."

"Will," Hal said softly. "I understand you're worried for your family, but we're investigating the cases of six missing people. If you help us indict Lowry, you won't need to depend on him anymore. You won't need to be afraid."

Will gazed up at the water-stained ceiling imploringly, as if the Goddess herself might still intercede. "You promise you won't tell Pa I showed you?"

"We promise," Wren said hastily.

"Alright. Follow me."

Wren and Hal exchanged a glance before obeying.

After Will fetched the key from a drawer in the counter, they slipped behind the counter and through the locked door. It opened into a room, dimly lit by what little sunlight lanced through the shutters. On all sides were wooden shipping crates stacked and looming like a crooked toy box version of Knockaine. When they reached the back, Will stood on his toes and pulled a heavy box from a rack. He lowered it to the ground and swiped the thin layer of sawdust from its lid. Beneath his smeared handprint, the label bore the address of Colwick Hall.

Wren wanted to feel triumphant. She wanted to feel vindicated. She was another step closer to answers. Another step closer to finding out what had happened to Byers. But all she felt was dread. Maybe oblivion was better, safer. But it was too late to turn back now. Dust swirled around them like smoke.

"Open it," she said.

Will took the crowbar mounted on the wall and wedged it carefully beneath the lid of the box.

"There," he said sullenly, once it was open. "Is that what you're looking for?"

Drawing in a deep breath, she lifted the lid. Inside were petals in every blinding shade of deep purple and blue, swirled like a winter sky. Goddessblood. In that one crate, there was more than enough to sicken six soldiers and Colwick Hall's entire staff.

"It's not enough to make a case."

Hal tossed the shipment records onto the low coffee table, startling her enough that she dropped her knife—Hal's knife, really, that she'd borrowed without his permission. She was kneeling on the floor of their room next to the cast-iron radiator—an invention she'd wished she'd known about last night—basking in the heat and slicing apples to keep herself busy.

After escorting them out of the shipment room, Will had begged them again not to tell his parents. He had even pilfered some apples from the kitchen to secure their silence. It was a small, simple thing—but it delighted her. After eating nothing but rich food and gamey meats for two weeks in Colwick Hall, she'd desperately missed fruit.

Wren picked up the knife again. Juice dripped from its edge, warm as nectar in the firelight. Hal sat in an armchair beside her, his legs stretched long and crossed at the ankles. Limned in the golden glow of the hearth, he was the picture of contemplation, and Wren wanted to slice him in two with frustration.

"What do you mean it's not enough? That"—she gestured to the files with the blade—"is concrete proof. Will's existence proves there's a connection between Lowry and the Danubian soldiers. And these records prove he had poison delivered to his door!"

"Since we can't bring Will with us, we have no story but a nobleman with a taste for the macabre. There's evidence enough already to corroborate that." He took a sip from his mug of tea. "We need a victim. Or a witness."

"I have you, don't I?"

"You do." The significant look he gave her sent her heart racing. "While Vesria may accept my testimony, Danu certainly won't. We need a Danubian to present a compelling case to the queen."

As much as she hated to admit it, Hal was right. They needed Byers. She'd sensed *something* in the east wing the other night, but even if she could trust that feeling for certain, would he still be alive by the time they returned?

No. She couldn't give up on him just yet. Whether it was a live victim or a body to autopsy, she could easily draw the connection between all these disparate pieces if she found signs of goddessblood poisoning in someone's system. But even with her and Hal's testimony and all the scientific evidence she could unearth, they were missing the most fundamental piece of the case: a motive.

Wren took another apple in hand, as thick and red as a heart. She sliced carefully into the skin until the knife struck the table with a dull sound. "That means we have to go back."

"We do."

"But we still don't have any idea where the key is, and I don't know how Lowry will react when he finds out we left. He made me sign an agreement that I wouldn't leave without his permission, lest I face some horrible, undisclosed penalty."

"Concerning," Hal said neutrally. Then, ever helpful, he added, "That was unwise to sign."

"Well." She punctuated it with another decisive cut into the apple. "I didn't exactly have many options at the time. I hadn't met you yet."

He seemed ready to deliver some retort. But then, finally realizing what she was doing, he blanched. "Where did you get that?"

"Oh, this?" She turned the knife over in her hands. "I took it from your coat while you were making tea."

"That's not what it's for."

"Oh, is it not?" Wren waved the point loosely in his direction. "I had no idea. Silly healers and our oaths of nonviolence! It makes a very good kitchen knife, all the same. Nice and sharp."

He held out his hand expectantly, and she reluctantly gave it back to him. Absently, he wiped it clean with his coat sleeve, then inspected the edge as if concerned she'd dulled it. "You should know how to use one. It would make me feel better."

"I don't need to know how to use a knife. I know how to kill someone if I really want to."

"Yes. I suppose that's true."

Hal set his mug down and slid off the chair to sit on the floor beside her. He took her wrist, turning it over carefully to bare the delicate skin underneath. Could he see her pulse thrumming under his touch? He placed the knife's hilt in the center of her palm and adjusted her fingers into the correct grip. When she looked up, their mouths were only inches apart. This close, she could nearly taste the tea he'd been drinking on his breath. Bergamot and honey. He didn't withdraw his hand. It settled warm over hers.

"Keep it," he said. "Just in case."

"This is absurd," she whispered. "I can't kill somebody. I'd freeze."

"You'd be surprised at how easy it is."

Wren imagined herself plunging a blade into Lowry's heart. Imagined the blood staining her hands, red, red, red, and impossible to scrub clean. She shuddered. "No. Absolutely not."

But if things went south, if they were outnumbered . . .

"We need your eyes."

His calluses scraped softly over her skin when he pulled back. While he'd largely mastered the art of a blank expression, she'd begun to learn his tells. Conflict thinned his lips and weighed down his eyelids. "I'm afraid of going back to who I was."

"I know it's complicated for you. But this time, it would be different. You're different."

"How can you be so certain? I hardly know who I am."

"Someone trying to do good. I'm certain of that much. You'd be protecting yourself and your comrades and—"

Me. The word caught in her throat, but she couldn't say it.

Hal still watched her uncertainly.

"From what I saw of the damage to the *fola* in your eyes, your case is far along. But I think I can do it. You don't need to make a decision now, but consider it."

"I will." He said it like an oath, solemn and binding.

But she was so tired of solemnity. Just for one day, she didn't want to think about shadows or death or Colwick Hall. "Maybe consider it later. In fact, let's not consider anything dark or terrible until we're back at the estate. This is like . . . a holiday."

"A holiday."

"Since we don't have the key to the east wing passage, we might very well die tomorrow." Both of them shifted uneasily under that grim reality. Wren pressed on. "Come on. When's the last time you didn't think about anything dark?"

"And what do you suggest we do?"

Immediately, her eyes fell to his lips. Memories of last night, sweet and seductive, drifted like smoke across her mind. How desperately she wanted him to kiss her.

Oh, no. Not this again.

With the heat rising in her face, Wren frantically cast her gaze about for something, *anything*. She smiled brightly and took a slice of apple still lying on the table. "Um . . . I cut a lot of these?"

Lifting a skeptical eyebrow, he took one. They ate their apples in silence. The brightness flooded Wren's mouth, and here, hunkered down against the cold, she thought of long winter nights in the abbey. On the worst of them, Heloise brewed cider. If Wren closed her eyes, she could taste the tartness of it, the warm, earthy spice of cinnamon. That was among the few things that held real magic in her childhood.

"Makes me think of being a kid," she said almost dreamily. "Sometimes, we got cider. Everyone would line up for what seemed like *hours* to get a little portion, but if I'd been good that day, Heloise would let me help make it, and I'd get the first helping."

"Did you usually misbehave?"

"What do *you* think? I've always been a terror."

"I'm shocked."

She knocked his shoulder with hers. "And I imagine you were a perfect child. Some kind of prodigy."

"Not always." Hal leaned his head back against the armrest, smiling faintly. "As a child, I was quite eager to please and impress, and my friend James was an instigator. He wrangled me into all sorts of schemes. The worst of them was sneaking onto a boat headed for the mainland while it was docked in the harbor."

"You ruffians! How far did you make it?"

"The sailors found us before they set sail, of course. When my father came, I was terrified—far more terrified than I was at the prospect of actually seeing our journey through. He never lifted a hand to me. Never even raised his voice. But I'll never forget that look of disappointment." After a moment, he said, "That was his name. James."

She didn't need to ask to know who he meant. She reached over and squeezed his knee. "Byers. Jacob Byers."

It felt right, somehow, to trust Hal with his name. They sat in companionate silence for a moment before he said, "If only I had warmer memories to share. I've had enough cold to last a lifetime."

Wren gave him a wicked look. "So you're saying you don't want to play in the snow? That was my next idea."

"You may go outside if it pleases you. I'm content by the fire."

"We don't need to go outside."

Wren clambered to her feet and approached the window. It peered out above the icy eaves, giving her a view of the sleeping village below. When she tried to unlatch it, the frame rattled. Frozen shut. But another jostle, and the casement swung open. Cold air kissed her face, bracing but invigorating. Standing on her tiptoes, she leaned out to scrape a layer of snow from the roof.

"What're you doing?"

Wren grinned, her fingers aching with cold. Then, she packed the snow into her palms, turned—"Think fast!"—and lobbed it at him. It struck him on the chest with a wet thud.

Hal looked at her as if she were the most insufferable person he'd ever met.

It filled her with an indescribable delight, fizzy and bright, like sunshine marbling the ocean. As she watched him dust snow off his jacket, it occurred to her that they could stay here. They didn't have to go back to Colwick Hall, which almost certainly promised failure.

It would be so easy to simply . . . quit. There was too much at stake for so little chance at success. Without that key, they had no case. Without the case, neither of them could find redemption and go home. Somewhere in these mountains, the Guard lurked, waiting to collect on her bounty. At the estate, Lowry awaited with a sinister plan. If they wanted, she and Hal could find a future somewhere beyond this nightmare.

Before she realized she was speaking, she said, "We could run away."

"Run away?"

"Think about it. Right now, no one knows where we are. Not even Lowry. We could take the nearest train off this Goddess-forsaken peninsula and go somewhere else. Anywhere else. We could start over where no one knows us."

"Wren . . ." Her name on his lips, full of yearning, shattered the dream.

It was impossible. If they ran, war would break out. They'd let Lowry get away with his crimes. They'd never see home again. It was a foolish idea, as tempting as it was.

They weren't children. They were soldiers.

For them, there could be no ordinary life, and no matter how far they ran, they could never outstrip their mistakes or their duty. Yesterday, Wren had almost lost every chance they had at finding Byers and the others. She wouldn't turn her back on her comrades again.

"In another life, maybe." She closed the window, and suddenly the room felt suffocating. "Or maybe when there's peace."

"Peace," he echoed. "I've never allowed myself to think much of what comes after peace."

"You'd better start thinking, Cavendish," she said. "It'll take a long time to undo three hundred years of war, and you can't work *all* the time."

Past their window, pristine snow glittered like diamonds beneath the first break of daylight. To give the next generation a chance—no, to give *themselves* a chance to truly live—they had to go back. They had to stop Lowry, or die trying.

CHAPTER TWENTY-FOUR

They returned to a Colwick Hall in chaos. Nothing could have prepared Wren for seeing it, the vision of her naïve imaginings, the house she had expected when she'd first arrived nearly three weeks ago.

Throngs of bustling servants carried long strips of black silk and tablecloths, shining silver platters and glinting silverware, long coils of wire and boxes full of lightbulbs. As Wren and Hal wandered into the grand hall, they dodged between people wearing the livery of the major Cernosian noble families—no doubt they had been lent as a favor to Lowry after his staff had been so *tragically* decimated. The main staircase was polished to a syrupy gleam, and the balustrades that gated each landing were woven with copper wire and fragrant juniper and holly and crowned with metal lamps in the shape of a stag's antlers. A blue electrical light blazed on each point. From her vantage point, she could look up and see the second-floor landing bedecked with silk and dotted with cocktail tables boasting centerpieces of evergreen and white catkin.

Once it was filled with music and guests, it would be spectacular.

As Wren made her way through the crowd, she bumped into Hannah. The other girl reeled back, nearly dropping her comically long to-do list. But as she realized it was them, all her startled exhaustion melted into relief.

"Hannah," Wren breathed. "I'm so glad to—"

"I don't have much time to talk. Follow me."

Hannah led them into the drawing room and shut them inside, muffling the chatter from outside. The heavy curtains were drawn, letting in the late-afternoon sun. It washed over the parquet floor and suffused the room with a peculiar, sterile light.

"Is the Guard here?" Wren asked.

"No. They left yesterday." She lowered herself into a chair, her expression nearly euphoric. She must have been on her feet all day. "I'm fine, by the way. Not at all harried. Not at all overwhelmed. I don't suppose I could convince you reprise your role in the staff, Henry?"

"Unfortunately not."

"Alas. We've another day until the ball, but we're still barely going to be ready." Hannah sighed, restlessly folding her list into smaller and smaller squares. "I tried to cover for you both. I truly did. But Lord Lowry came looking for you. He's . . . displeased."

Of course he was. Wren hated that she was afraid. Since he needed them for something, Lowry wouldn't hurt them. But that was exactly the problem. Over the past few weeks, Wren had learned there were things far worse than death.

"You did all you could." Wren leaned against the wall and crossed her arms. "I guess I owe you an explanation now."

"Yes," Hannah said quietly. "I believe you do."

It all poured out. Lowry's initial offer, her discovery of the poison, its connection to the missing soldiers in Danu and Vesria, the tunnel in the east wing. Hannah sat ramrod straight in her chair, listening as her folded hands grew paler, her eyes grew duller.

"Alistair Lowry was never a good man, but I never thought . . ." Tangled up in her voice was grief and rage. "Some of them raised him. Some of them *loved* him."

"You will have justice," Hal said, "if it's the last thing I do."

"Good." Hannah rose from her seat, dusting off her apron. She wore her prim expression, brows arched and lips pursed, like armor. "Then I suppose I should let you both get back to work."

With that, the three of them slipped back into the grand hall. A new wave of servants seemed to have arrived in the few minutes they'd been gone, transforming the house yet again. They'd hoisted chandeliers, twinkling with red gemstones and red lights, above banquet tables draped in dark fabrics. Wren breathed in the delicate smell of flowers; bouquets of deep purple calla lilies and black roses spilled from a nearly waist-high vase. She paused to admire the scene, but before she could say a word, a voice cut through the buzz of the room. Wren's heart plummeted like a stone to the bottom of a lake.

"Out of my way! Begone, all of you."

A group of servants clustered on the second-story landing scattered like billiards to the edges of the staircase. Lowry emerged from the middle of them, descending the stairs so quickly he seemed to glide. The sight of him snatched her breath away.

He stood at the landing above them, clutching an overfull glass of dark wine, which lapped hungrily at the rim. He had forgone his usual jaunty red in favor of solid black, from his polished boots to his billowing tailcoat to his ribbon-wrapped top hat. The only bright contrast was his ever-present key, winking gold at his throat.

A bolt of realization struck her. Of course. How could she have overlooked something so obvious? The bloody fingerprints coating it on the night she'd caught him in the east wing.

"Hal," Wren whispered. *"Look."*

His eyes flashed with recognition, just as Lowry noticed her. She caught Hal's wrist. His forearm tightened; then, his fingers went slack. With the pads of her fingers, she painted the grooves between his knuckles. He took her hand in his. They needed each other to survive this, as they always had.

Lowry's even stride faltered as he drank them in, hand in hand. Something strange flickered across his face: fear. Then, in an instant, it vanished, as if she'd imagined it altogether.

Today, all his warmth was gone. In its place was cold fury. Wren nearly staggered back at the force of it. He alighted on the ground floor and stalked toward them with such purpose and malice radiating from him, she feared he would lunge. Hal placed himself between her and Lowry.

"Where have you two *been*?" His voice was icy and quiet, but every servant in the room seemed to hold their breath to listen. Even the house itself sagged like a bellows, as if every wall buckled under the effort of overhearing.

Wren stammered. "I asked Hannah to tell you—"

"Yes, indeed. Hannah told me your inane rationale," he snapped.

"Lord Lowry," Hal began, but Wren was in no mood for his politicking. "This was—"

"Inane?" she cut in. "He would have died!"

With one violent arc of his arm, Lowry dashed the glass he was holding against the floor. It shattered with a high, ringing sound. Glass shards skittered across the floor. Wine spattered Wren's skirts. The silence that followed was broken only by her shaky exhale when she remembered how to relax her diaphragm. She did not recognize this man. There was nothing of the nervous, gracious host she had first met. Nothing of his easy charm or sugary promises.

There was no more pretense. He was a stranger, and he *terrified* her.

"I was . . . beside myself." Lowry's voice was quiet. "You didn't tell me where you were going, and I didn't know what to do."

Wren tore her eyes away from his distressed face. At her feet, the wine stain spread across the floor like a pool of blood.

"Look at me. What a fool I am, already in mourning for you both. And worst of all, I've wasted a perfectly good vintage." He glanced, dismayed, at the glittering mess of wine and broken glass. He placed a foot over the intact stem. It split in twain with the same neat *pop* of a tearing ligament. "I quite liked that one. It was the last bottle I had. Alas."

"I'm sorry for worrying you," Wren said placatingly.

"Worrying me?" He rounded on her again. "You nearly killed

me with fright. I feared the storm had taken you. What would I have told my guests? Or your aunt for that matter? I *need* you, Ms. Southerland. Do you understand?"

"No," she said shakily. "I don't. I've already done what you've asked of me."

"Not yet," he said, almost to himself.

Then he noticed Hal bristling beside her. Lowry's emotions cycled too quickly for her to process them, but he settled on excitement. He clapped Hal on the shoulder. "Would you believe it? Henry, you're alive and well. I'm positively thrilled."

It made Wren's skin crawl to hear such a blatant lie. *You did this to him,* she wanted to scream. *So why did you send for me?* Countless servants were dead. Their comrades were gone. But she and Hal were still here, still alive. For what dubious honor? For what scheme?

"I am," Hal said tersely. "By the grace of Wren Southerland."

"And we shall drink and compose epics in her name tomorrow," he said. "We've somehow fared this long without you, and I've so much extra help for the ball already. How about you take the night off tomorrow? Consider it a celebration of your health."

"How generous of you, my lord."

Lowry turned back to Wren and clasped her hands beseechingly. His rings, glinting clinical and cold as stainless steel, dug into her skin. He was unrecognizable from even a few moments ago. As if his outburst had exerted him, he wilted like an underfed plant. "My dear, I've frightened you. Please forgive me. I fear I'm not myself. There's been a tragedy in your absence."

"A tragedy?"

"Yes." He held her tighter, bleeding the heat from her skin. "The Duke of Matthonwy—Fitzwilliam Barrett, my dearest and oldest friend—was kind enough to help me put together a search party. They went looking for you last night, but something terrible befell them. We've only recovered two of them. One man is dead, and the other is barely holding on. We found them only hours ago. Barrett is distraught."

"What happened?"

"It's far beyond me to know exactly." His breath smelled of rich red wine: sharp with alcohol and warm with black pepper. And beneath it all, that cloying, repulsive stench of formaldehyde. "Although when I last checked on him, he seemed to be experiencing early symptoms of renal failure. It's passing strange."

Wren squeezed her eyes shut to fight back the hot prickle of tears. There was no way he'd know that. Not unless he'd done something to induce it himself. Once, Lowry had told her he was no scientist—that had no interest in his father's arcane medical texts. Wren did not know if she would ever strike the bottom of his lies.

"I see."

Lowry straightened to his full height, again the picture of flustered anguish. "I hate to demand more of you than I already have, but . . ."

"Take me to him at once."

"As you wish." Lowry ascended the stairs, trailed by his long tailcoats.

Wren tentatively placed one hand on the banister. Before she could take another step forward, Hal reached out to her, his face drawn with concern. "Don't. This can bring no good."

"I know."

But she couldn't let someone die on her watch. And until they had the evidence they needed, what other choice did she have but to play Lowry's games? She rested a reassuring hand on Hal's shoulder before following Lowry upstairs.

It was far, far worse than she expected.

The library looked like Lowry had disemboweled it. Wren saw both sides of him laid out in the arrangement of the room. His rage, in the overturned side table, the papers and books littering the room, the crystal decanter leaking brandy into the carpet. His cold calculation, in the way he'd already prepared the room with a bucket of water and a few surgical basins. As soon as he'd showed her to the door, he'd left her alone with nothing but a sly murmur of "Good luck."

One servant—his body, anyway—was sprawled across a velvet chaise lounge. At a glance, he seemed to be sleeping, curled on his side with his arm pillowing his cheek. His body was split like the horizon with bruises. The entire left side of his face was marbled grisly black and purple with stagnant blood. The living man, barely alive as he was, lay sedated and shallowly breathing on the makeshift operating table of Lowry's desk.

Above it, the taxidermied stag's twelve-point antlers impaled the milky light. Wren removed her coat and tossed it over the stag, where it hung from the antlers like a torso gored and gone limp. It was better than the alternative. She couldn't have it judging her work with those empty sockets. Trepidation melted away as she unfastened her medical bag and began sterilizing her instruments. Once she snapped on her gloves and arranged her tools, she began examining her patient and the corpse, letting her magic flow through their bodies. Protocol and procedure mechanized her, shielded her from the full brunt of her horror. She was saving a life, nothing more or less. She could fall apart later.

Because based on their wounds, Wren was quite certain this was murder.

They were far too practiced, far too intentional. The first man had died quickly, likely from the blunt trauma at the base of his skull. Her living patient's injuries, however, assured Wren that Lowry was either more foolish or far cockier than she gave him credit for. They were bombastic, almost mocking. As Lowry suggested, the man's kidney was necrotic from a poison she vaguely recognized but had no time to treat. He would need a transplant in order to survive.

This wasn't just a punishment. This was a test of her skill.

Wren dragged the dead man, cold to the touch, from his seat with a mumbled apology. As quickly as she could manage, she sliced his kidney free from its nest of tissue and placed it in a waiting bowl. Then, her magic white and sharp, she opened an incision in her patient's abdominal cavity. Skin and muscle and fat peeled back like a zipper beneath the Touch.

The procedure demanded all of her focus, all of her magic. And in the haze of desperation and fear, her control over her magic slipped, grew looser. She couldn't afford inefficiency or the way her energy bled out of her, but she couldn't help it. Magic burned like cold flame, leaping higher and higher and casting the room in a pale light.

This man's life was in her hands. She would not—*could* not—let Lowry kill again on her watch. Transplants were especially difficult. Partly because they were rarely required and thus rarely taught. Partly because organs were tangled in a net of blood vessels and *fola*, fine and gleaming and too easy to slice. A single mistake could be fatal. Few medics, especially combat medics, had the skill or practice to perform transplant surgery. But Heloise had ensured that she did.

If you cannot be loved, she'd said, *you must be indispensable.*

The months before Wren's acceptance to the Guard were among the most grueling of her short life. She dared not to think of how many lab rats lay buried from her failed attempts at transplant surgery: leaking arteries, rejected tissue, complicated infections. Then, one day, as if by a miracle, both donors lived. Two mice, whiskers twitching, each with the other's heart. Wren sometimes wondered how she'd ever thought herself kind.

It was a steady rhythm of cut and ablate, cut and ablate. She sliced and mended flesh like she was hemming fabric, and when it was done, she implanted the kidney and encouraged it to take root like a sapling. As she sealed the incision, a single thought tormented her. *What is the point of all this?* Wren could not imagine. Did not *want* to imagine.

These men were no soldiers, no mages. Had they been wrong about how Lowry chose his victims? Was this all just some sick game, entirely meaningless? The very thought made her want to retch.

The damaged kidney lay discarded in a bloody dish. The dead man looked like a slaughtered goat: slit open hastily, his abdomen gaping like a maw. Blood trickled slowly from the wound like sap from a splintered tree.

After peeling off her gloves, she dunked her hands in the bucket of water and scrubbed with a poultice of herbs until her skin was raw. She stopped only when she was bleeding, soothed when her own magic closed the abrasion. A buzz in her joints followed. Then, a familiar numbness in the tips of her fingers.

Overuse. The bitterest irony of healing magic.

She'd known she was pushing herself, but she'd *always* pushed herself. She always teetered on the brink of too much. This time, she feared she was dangerously close to toppling over the edge completely.

She needed to rest. Her *fola* needed to recover from what she'd put them through, or else she'd risk permanent damage. Experimentally, she pushed magic into her palms. Its silver light guttered like a candle. Still there, still hers, as faint as it was.

Hers.

Her magic was the one thing she had left in this world. How crushing—and how unsurprising—to learn not even that little was guaranteed.

Wren found Lowry in the drawing room, speaking with a man in a hushed voice. She couldn't make out what they were saying but observed the small nonverbal details. The man resolutely angled himself away from Lowry and white-knuckled his snifter.

So it was an argument.

This must have been Fitzwilliam Barrett, the Duke of Matthonwy. She knew little of him other than his long-standing friendship with Lowry—and his Danu-Cernosian heritage. He was chief among the Cernosian nobility lobbying for an alliance with the Danubian Crown. Beyond that, the slim dossier the Guard had on him only included notes on his collection of antique Danubian-made swords and his rumored enthusiasm for military strategy and history.

Wren cleared her throat to announce her presence. Both men startled. "I'm sorry to interrupt. He's resting now, but he'll survive."

When Barrett looked up, he fixed her with a sad but earnest smile. It was out of place with his sanguine complexion and thick beard. Unlike most politicians, he had a face like undisturbed water, transparent to anyone who looked into it. His money gave him his influence, but it was easy to see why he'd earned his reputation as gregarious. "I've heard so much about you over the years. It's a pleasure to finally meet you, Ms. Southerland."

Wren grimaced. If he'd heard of her, it was likely only for what little publicity she got as the queen's castaway. "The pleasure is all mine, Your Grace."

"How unfortunate that making your acquaintance is overshadowed by such a horrific accident."

This was far from an accident, she thought bitterly. *How could you be so blind?* All she said was, "Horrific indeed."

Lounging with one ankle hooked over his knee in a figure four, Lowry watched her from above the rim of his glass. His eyes were alight with interest and self-satisfaction. Like he'd proven something to himself—or won big on a wager.

"I hope to make your acquaintance properly soon," she said, "but I'm exhausted."

"Of course, of course. It's been a long evening for you, I'm sure."

"Although I would like a word with you before I retire, Lord Lowry."

"As you wish." Lowry's smile didn't falter as he turned to Barrett. "Would you leave us a moment?"

Barrett excused himself gallantly, with only a murmur of "good night" before he vanished through the doorway. Wren came inside the room and gingerly took his place.

Lowry tipped so far back in his chair, Wren prayed he would fall backward into the fire. "What do you think of the décor?"

It seemed he intended to toy with her. "It's lovely."

"Lovely, yes. It's remarkable, too. While you were gone, I finally finished wiring the grand hall. For the first time, this estate will be lit by hundreds and hundreds of incandescent lightbulbs." Lowry looked almost longing. "Soon enough, you'll never need to waste candles again. All across the country, marvels like these are becoming a reality. A device that will let you communicate verbally over long distances. Carriages powered not by horses, but by combustion engines."

Wren did not have it in her to look impressed.

"Where's your sense of wonder tonight?" He clucked his tongue. "It will be *spectacular*—a showcase suited for the star-studded company we shall have. We Cernosians are always eager to share our knowledge. We are always looking forward, progressing, evolving. See, the evolution of species is such a fascinating, frustrating concept. I—you are familiar, yes?"

She would endure his prattling, but she would not abide condescension. "Of course I am."

"Ah, excellent. Then stop me if I'm wrong. From my understanding, it claims that the fittest survive—that mutation drives genetic variation. It stands to reason that you mages are the more evolved of us humans." His voice grew darker, more fervent. "Yet Cernos has immense wealth, expansive trading routes, and technology that you could not dream of achieving for decades. We are superior by all accounts, and yet we have never been taken seriously as a global power. Why do you think that is?"

Wren let out a thin breath through her teeth. "Magic."

"Magic." Lowry snapped his fingers. "Exactly. In this war-torn world, all anyone cares about is magic. But for hundreds of years, Danu and Vesria have sent your mages to die like dogs in the street. You've squandered this genetic gift. Used it for your squabbles over nonsense like *religion*. Just imagine if every healer applied themselves to research as you do. What diseases could be cured? How long would your people live?"

Wren remained silent.

"Oh, very well. Shall we reframe the discussion?" He leaned forward. "You're a woman of the Goddess. Tell me, why do you suppose your people were blessed with magic, while mine were left to wallow in our ordinariness? Why has the Goddess abandoned us, when *we* are the civilized ones?"

"I thought you weren't interested in your father's work," she said bitterly.

Lowry laughed softly. "I've a curious mind, Ms. Southerland. His death has left me with so many questions."

There were countless answers she could give, theological and scientific alike. Wren, however, knew that magic was little but a genetic anomaly. Fewer than 10 percent of the global population possessed it. But she was in no mood to debate or play games. Besides, she knew the answer, as plainly as she knew the answer to why Isabel hated her. It was the kind that would never satisfy or heal. Knowing did not bring understanding, and it would never bring his father back.

He had no magic because nature had coldly decreed it. No more, no less.

"You already know the answer, my lord. A common trait of Cernosian people is the suppression of genes that produce usable magic. It's inert within you, like an engine with no fuel. It always will be."

"Come now. That's a politician's answer if I've ever heard one."

"What do you want, Lowry?" Wren growled.

"Your professional opinion." He rose from his chair, crossing his arms behind his back and turning to the window. Frost bloomed like mold across the glass, and beyond, a row of dripping icicles hung like incisors. "With science, is there hope for us to compete with the likes of you?"

Horrible understanding began to dawn on her. More than anything, she wanted to say *no*. No, no, no. Most mages possessed broad-reaching abilities: the ability to change their bone density, the ability to thicken the collagen in their body, or to affect the regeneration and death of cells. Without an innate ability to manipulate the energetics of the body, there was no means to manipulate cells, the scientific explanation for what they called magic. Unless Lowry intended to replace every bone, every tendon, every *cell* in his body, it was impossible.

"It's something you're born with. It's not something you can build like one of your machines."

"You didn't answer my question."

Was it overuse or anger or fear making her hands tremble? She didn't want to answer. She didn't want to consider the ethical and ontological implications of such a thing. "Theoretically? Maybe."

"Maybe?" When he turned toward her, the firelight peeled back his face. For a moment, she saw him as he was in that strange, soldierly portrait. His eyes looked black and depthless and *hungry*. "Well, thank you for indulging my fancy."

"The ball is tomorrow," she said lowly. "I am no fool. You don't plan to reward me for healing him."

"While you've disobeyed me, I *do* plan to present you as my liaison, exactly as I promised. I've even secured the queen's support of your new position."

Wren's breath hitched. No, that couldn't be true. He was only manipulating her again. The queen would never reinstate her—not for anything. "You're lying."

"On the contrary." He pulled a cream-colored envelope from his breast pocket, on which the official royal seal, although broken, was stamped in silver wax: a full moon flanked by a waxing and waning crescent. Lowry extended the envelope to her. When she didn't take it, he smiled like the slow bleed of a wound. "Ah, you silly, paranoid girl. You think there's a catch. I'm a man of my word. All I ask is you attend the festivities, as there's someone I'd like you to meet. After that, you're free to go home. You and I will be in touch, of course, about political affairs."

Lowry always honeyed his promises. Even if Isabel had approved her position, even if it was *real,* it was nothing but a gilded fetter. Marionette strings to dangle her from. She'd depend on Lowry and his mercurial favor for the rest of her life. What other horrors would he force her to endure to keep it? "And if I refuse this new position?"

"I withdraw my support of you," he said simply, almost pleasantly. "I've been very patient, Ms. Southerland, even as you've broken my trust. Don't push me any farther."

A surge of heat tore through her. It darkened the corners of her vision, set her every nerve ablaze. Never had she felt something so powerful, so poisonous.

Hatred.

Wren took the envelope from him. "I understand."

"Good." He straightened his lapels. "Now, if you'll excuse me. That corpse is going to cause quite a stir if I don't move it."

"I thought you liked scandal," she muttered.

He looked affronted. "I *do*. But this, I'm afraid, requires a bit more subtlety than I'd otherwise like."

He absently wound his golden key on its chain, tighter and tighter. As it spun, its surface reflected the light again and again. It would be so easy to reach out and take it.

But then what? Her magic lay still and quiet within her, and although Hal's knife pressed cold against her thigh, she still was too much of a coward to use it. Her hands trembled with restraint, and when she lifted her eyes back to his face, he was studying her like she was a creature that might bite if he turned away.

"Until tomorrow," she gritted out.

"Rest up," he drawled. "You'll need it."

CHAPTER TWENTY-FIVE

Wren made it to Hal's room before she fell apart.

She slammed the door shut behind her and leaned against it, her breaths coming hard and uneven. It was dark. It was always so *dark* in here. No amount of laughter echoing through the halls could lighten it. Between the heavy spill of the draperies, the moon was a gray disc outlined with thread-thin silver. The mountains had never felt more like a cage, solid black shadows against a solid black sky.

Rest up, Lowry had told her. *You'll need it.*

They had to get the key before the ball ended. What was he planning?

She twisted the lock shut as Hal rose to meet her. Veiled in the blue light, he looked painfully soft. As she lifted her chin to him, she saw concern and relief plain on his face. He raised an uncertain hand between them, as if he would brush the side of her face or tuck a strand of hair behind her ear. *Please,* she wanted to say. *You can.*

Just once, she wanted someone to hold her.

He let his hand drop to his side, slid it into his pocket. "Are you alright?"

Despite herself, Wren let out a soft laugh. "Mostly."

"What happened?"

"Sick games. Threats. What else?" She wrapped her arms around herself. "But I didn't get the key while I had the chance. We won't get him alone again."

"We don't need him alone. This event will provide far more cover and distraction than we could orchestrate on our own."

He had a point. At the ball, it would be nearly impossible to keep track of them in a crowd. No one would miss them if they disappeared. "That's all well and good, but how're we going to get it off him?"

He gave her a pointed look. "Do you have any of what you gave me left?"

Wren snorted out a laugh, half to conceal her panic. "You want me to drug him?"

"It'll be easy for his guests to brush off. He likes to drink."

"He does," she said miserably. "But he's going to be swarmed with people. I'll have to administer it in plain sight, with the eyes of every Cernosian courtier on me."

"Yes. You will."

A heavy silence filled the room. Wren could hear the wind rattling the windows and the distant, warm sound of conversation from the floors below. "I guess we don't have any other options. Unless you've got a trick up your sleeve."

"No tricks." He hesitated. "Just my magic."

His magic. Wren shook her head. "You don't have to—"

"It's the practical decision," he said with a steely resolve.

She laid a hand on his arm. "Forget practicality. Is it what you *want*? I know you don't want to kill anyone."

"It's far too late for me to have compunctions about that." He gazed down at her hand, small and white against the solid black wool of his coat. When he spoke again, it was distant and wistful, almost as if it'd slipped out against his will. "It's as you said. It would be different this time. It would be worth it."

It filled her with an inexplicable sadness. Thanks to her quick temper, Wren had never exactly been tactful. Her feelings were often so intense, so sudden, they were alien to her. How could she respond to him properly? How could she express this feeling that welled up when she hardly understood it herself? No one had prepared her for this. He was her nation's greatest enemy, and he had saved her life. On the surface of her muddled feelings about Hal Cavendish, however, was something simple and something true. Something impossible.

Before she could think it through, she was opening her mouth. "It's as *you* said. You're worth more than what you can do. I don't care about that Goddess-forsaken magic of yours. I care about *you*."

Hal stared at her as if she'd struck him across the face. Her cheeks heated uncomfortably. "You care about me."

"Yes." She wanted to lie down and die of humiliation, but she managed to stand up straighter. "What of it?"

Hal glanced away. "I'm not sure that's wise."

"When have I ever pretended to be *wise*?"

Slowly, the wounded shock on his face melted into an emotion she couldn't quite place. "Then heal my eyes if you can. I need to ensure you're . . ."

Her heart fluttered in anticipation. "I'm what?"

"You're . . . sufficiently covered," he offered. "So our mission remains uncompromised."

"Oh. Of course." She tucked an errant strand of hair behind her ear, wincing at the disappointment in her voice. "Your magic is a last resort. Only if I fail, and only if we're attacked."

"Only as a last resort," he agreed.

She cleared her throat when she couldn't think of anything else to say. "Well, then. We should do it now."

Hal nodded. She was still leaning against the door, painfully aware of the scant inches between them. "Where would you like me?"

Right now? Far, far away. She waved a hand in the direction of an armchair. "Sit. Get comfortable."

He picked his way across the room, frustratingly slow, and chose an armchair by the window. As she came closer, every creak of the floorboards reminded her of this painfully significant silence. Or maybe the thickening of the air was only in her imagination.

Moonlight traced his features, and with his eyes half-closed, he was unreadable. Wren settled on the windowsill beside him. They'd been exactly here only last week. Him, struggling to button his shirt. Her, struggling to figure him out. Shoving aside the memory, Wren reached forward and rested her too-cold fingers against his temples. "Ready?"

"Yes."

Her *fola* glowed softly, and as she eased her magic into him, the numb, tingling sensation spread from her forearms into her wrists and fingers. It wasn't wise to push through the discomfort, but they were running out of time. Although she'd nearly let her nerves get the best of her during the transplant surgery, this time, she *had* to maintain her focus. For Hal's sake, she had to be perfect.

How different this was from their first session, when he'd nearly gutted her for coming this close. Even a few days ago, the magical link between them had made them both crawl with discomfort. Now, it felt like coming home, a settling in, a yielding. As if her energy belonged in him. All her life, healing had been an obligation, a means of proving herself. And with Hal, it had been a punishment. Now, this was about protecting them.

Something else, too. Something almost tender.

She worked in concentrated silence. Although the glass was cold at her back, sweat beaded on her forehead. The eye was among the most delicate and complex structures to heal. His leaking, frayed *fola* twined around ophthalmic blood vessels that could kill him if cut; embedded themselves into the muscles anastomosing the sclera and optic nerve; spanned across the conjunctiva like hairline fractures in bone. One wrong move and Hal would lose his eyes. It took all of her energy to knit together the pathways, to soothe the inflamed tissues.

After what felt like hours, the tension that always pinched his brows together and locked his jaw began to ebb away. She repaired the damage until her fingers trembled too hard to safely continue. The energy from her hands surged, then sputtered like a flame on a wick. There was still so much work to do to restore his eyes completely, and the pain of wanting to do more almost outweighed the pain of her own degenerated *fola*.

Her fingertips still rested on his temples, right against the gentle thrum of his temporal pulse. Hal opened his eyes and reached up and wrapped his hand, warm and rough, around her wrist. Could he feel her heartbeat, too—how it leapt at his touch?

His thumb slid upward, caressing her palm. "I can tell you're exhausted."

The silver glow of her magic flickered once more and died. Darkness washed over them.

"I'm sorry." Her face burned hot with shame. "I think this is all I can do for now. You'll have one use, maybe two."

"Then once will have to be enough." Hal didn't release her hand. He was studying every detail of her face from beneath his eyelashes as if she were a work of art. She couldn't remember the last time someone had looked at her like that.

Like she was beautiful.

Nerves twisted her stomach into knots, but her longing emboldened her. Would he let her do this? Slowly, uncertainly, she guided his hand upward and laid his palm flat against her cheek. When he didn't move, when he let her turn to press her lips to the heel of his palm, she gathered up her skirts and slid her knee onto the chair beside his hip.

"Wren." His voice was exquisite agony, even as he rested his hand on her thigh. "We can't."

It would be more self-destructive, more selfish than anything she'd done before. Logic and centuries of bloody Danu-Vesrian wars forbade this. Tomorrow night, the fate of their nations depended on their success. If they succeeded, they'd have peace. And if they failed . . . Either way, there was no world imaginable that could hold space for them. Wanting him would lead to nothing but ruin in the end. They both knew it. But his expression was darkening, and Wren was powerless against those eyes of his. Even with so little magic, they were weapons.

She and Hal could never be together, and if they might fail tomorrow, why not have this moment? Maybe for tonight, they could forget they were soldiers on opposite sides of a battlefield. For a night, they could set aside everything and just be Hal and Wren. Nothing more or less.

Words snarled up on her tongue, and although she felt small and childish, she managed to whisper, "I know. But I want to. Just this once."

Hal bowed his head until his nose could rest in the crook of her neck. His sigh was a surrender. "Just once."

Her body reacted immediately to the sensation of his lips against her skin. A rush of fear that came with letting go—and heat that throbbed within her. Just this once, she wanted to run toward the things that frightened her. She settled into his lap. Neither of them so much as breathed. There was no space between them now, heart to frantically beating heart. There was nothing else to say. So she cradled his jaw in both hands and brushed her lips against his.

The sound he made was one of a man either absolved or damned. His mouth was surprisingly soft against hers—not at all what she expected—but his stubble scraped her chin with every kiss. The newness of the sensation made her shiver. He tasted deep red, like wine. Like the first wild strawberries in spring.

His hands burned a trail from her hips to her waist, up the curves of her rib cage. He touched her like he wanted to savor it, meltingly, maddeningly slowly. Every kiss, every touch snared her thoughts into a tangle of pure need. She was equal parts lost and certain as she fumbled with his cravat until it came loose, as she knotted her fingers into his hair.

It *hurt,* how good this felt. His mouth against hers. The solid press of his body against her. Surrendering to the storm of her emotions instead of fighting. Staying, instead of running, always running.

She'd known it for a while now. Hal Cavendish, who held her against him like he'd die if she slipped away, was no monster. She wanted to cling to this version of him—*hers*—and never let him go.

But now he was drawing back, dragging a humiliating low whine from her throat. He leaned his forehead against hers, and when she opened her eyes, she saw his pupils blown wide, ringed like the full moon in cobalt blue. Everything went still as a winter night. She tried to find the meaning in that look, in what he wouldn't say to her aloud. Her head was still spinning, her body wound tight. So she settled into the stillness. Nose to nose in the dark, inhaling every ragged breath he let out.

She could have cried at the sight of him, so perfect, so ruined. She'd ruffled his hair and reddened his lips. Without realizing it, she must have unbuttoned his shirt, and now, she let her fingers trace the line of his bare collarbones. Hal twisted a lock of her hair around his finger and watched the strands separate with such raptness, it was as though they were spun from gold. It was an unfamiliar bliss to casually touch and be touched.

One that she couldn't cherish for long.

Wren worried one of his loose buttons between the pads of her fingers, then laid her palm flat against his bare chest to feel the warmth. "I'm so afraid of what'll happen."

He didn't respond at first. The sounds of distant conversations and the wind as it rocked the house filled the silence. Finally, his voice vibrated against her palm. "I am, too."

"Are you? I'm still getting used to the idea of you being scared of anything."

"Once, I feared nothing." Hal traced absentminded patterns on the small of her back. "In Vesria, they say death is a blessing—that we return to nothing, our suffering ended. That it's an honor to die for your country. Once, I believed that."

"But now?"

"Now, I believe death is not so light a thing. I haven't stopped thinking about what you asked. What will we do after there's peace? Until coming here, I don't know if I ever made a single decision for myself. I became a soldier because it was expected of me. I'll become the grand magistrate because that is my duty to our people. That's the end point of my path, and I've never looked back. It does me no good to dream of what could've been. But to choose something, truly, for myself? To hope? That terrifies me."

"And what do you want?" she whispered.

"I don't know." Hal closed his eyes. "If I could be selfish? Right now, all I want is this."

Wren tried to ignore the painful squeeze of longing in her chest. She buried her nose in the underside of his jaw so she wouldn't have to see his face when she said, "Then can I stay with you tonight? Please. I don't want to be alone."

This time, he didn't hesitate. "Of course."

"You understand you've made a serious commitment, yes?" She wound her arms around his neck. "I might not let you go."

"A terrible fate, indeed, to be your prisoner."

When he kissed her again, she couldn't help smiling against his mouth. This feeling—too close to belonging, to *happiness*—was dangerous. It could heal her, or it could break her. With so much at risk, she couldn't be sure which it was.

CHAPTER TWENTY-SIX

No one could ever accuse Alistair Lowry of lacking a sense of humor.

On the dressing table was a mask with a long, hooked beak carved from whitewood. It looked like it had been imported straight from last century. Unlike the masks healers wore in the plague outbreak, however, the beak was delicate and tapered, leaving the bottom half of her face exposed. Suppressing a shudder, she replaced it on the table. In her opinion, the mask ruined the beauty of the dress Hannah was currently lacing her into.

Although she was smirking now, Hannah still wouldn't make eye contact. Early this morning, a knock on the door had startled Wren and Hal awake. Before she had managed a plaintive, "Wait!," Hannah had already barged in.

"Good morning! I didn't find you in your room, so I thought you'd be . . ." She'd trailed off when she caught a glimpse of Hal, hair mussed, trying to disappear beneath the rumpled covers. Her face flushed. "Oh. Come find me when you're ready."

Wren still wanted to melt into the floor with embarrassment, but she was yanked from the memory as Hannah pulled the bodice laces taut.

"Goddess above," she muttered. She took shallow breaths as her ribs acclimated to the pressure of the corset boning. No one had taken her measurements for the gown, and Lowry's tailor had over-estimated how narrow she could make herself.

"You look lovely." Hannah stepped back to admire her sadistic handiwork, hands planted on her hips. "And stiff!"

"What else could I aspire to?"

As was customary for the winter social season, the gown was black and flowed neatly to the floor with a train like an oil slick. The sleeves, however, were an absurd, impractical nightmare. They swelled at the shoulders, then tapered in and poured off her elbows in a tumble of chiffon and lace. If she stretched out her arms, she looked like a well-groomed bat.

Hannah gave her an approving nod. Then, her satisfaction fizzled until grim silence settled over the room. "Good luck to-night."

Wren would need it, although the plan was theoretically simple. After Wren took the key from Lowry, she and Hal would go to the east wing, find their evidence, and slip out of Colwick Hall un-noticed. Tonight, they'd get as much distance as they could from this infernal place. Come morning, they'd part ways. Hal would go to Vesria, Wren to Danu. But she tried not to think about that part. Instead, she imagined the relief of knowing Hal was safe at home—and the triumph when she presented their findings to the queen.

"Thank you." Wren met Hannah's gaze in the mirror. "If I don't make it out—"

"Don't." Hannah retrieved the mask from the dressing table and considered it thoughtfully. "You will. Besides, you're not doing this alone. You never were."

Wren swallowed down the knot of emotion in her throat. "True."

"And if you're nervous," Hannah continued, "there'll be no

shortage of liquid courage tonight. I've seen the cellars, and they've nearly been emptied."

"Oh," Wren said with forced cheer. "How reassuring."

Hannah placed the mask against her nose and knotted the ribbons at the back of her head. Once it was in place, she clapped her hands together. "*Now* you're ready. You look terrifying."

Wren did. The mask was positively ghastly. In the mirror, the deep set of the eyeholes made it look as if she had no eyes at all. Round empty sockets stared back at her. Hannah pinned a black feathered headdress to the back of her ironed curls.

"All done." Wren turned away from her reflection and stared down at Hannah. After a tense moment, Hannah took her hands. "Be careful, won't you?"

"I will. I promise we'll set this right." Wren squeezed her hands. "I'll write to you after it's all over."

Hannah left her alone with dread clawing its way up her throat. Wren collapsed onto the seat by the vanity and retrieved a vial from the drawer. It was filled with a thick, clear liquid. This dose of chloral hydrate would knock Lowry unconscious within thirty minutes. All she had to do was doctor his drink in front of hundreds of potential witnesses. She'd faced worse odds. Even so, her stomach twisted itself into slick, anxious knots. Wren closed her fingers over the vial to steady herself.

Three sharp knocks on the door startled her.

"Come in."

Hal's reflection appeared in the mirror. Dressed in a short black coat and a white cravat, he leaned in the doorframe, dangling his mask by its ribbons. Wren did not expect the answering stutter of her heart. Last night still felt unreal, like a hazy, half-remembered dream. Once they'd curled up beside each other, they'd fallen asleep, and come morning, she could almost believe their kiss had never happened. It was better that way.

Her own words echoed like an admonition: *Only once.*

As she approached, she didn't miss the lingering of his eyes on the curve of her waist or the bare slope of her neck. Goddess bless this heinous mask for hiding her surely beet-red face. "Do you have something you'd like to say?" she said tartly.

Hal offered his arm, and when she took it, he bent close enough to speak against the shell of her ear. "No. I've no words."

"You never do, Cavendish." She closed her eyes against the pleasant shiver that ran down her spine. Through their tether, she could feel the uneven beat of his pulse. "Now put on your mask."

They stepped into the grand hall at the stroke of eight. They only had until midnight—the end of the ball—to uncover Lowry's secrets and expose him.

Over the sound of the orchestra, the din of one hundred conversations echoed through all three stories of Colwick Hall. Below and above them milled dignitaries and courtiers, all spectacularly dressed in black, all in masks, each more twisted and grotesque than the last.

In Danu, Midwinter festivities lacked fanfare. It was little more than the longest night of the year. At the abbey, they had spent hours praying until the sun broke on the horizon. *For rebirth,* Heloise would say in those black hours before dawn, *there must first be death.* In those bleary, delirious moments, Wren had come close to believing there was something divine out there.

But in Cernos, it was a festival of dramatics—a show of light. Past the holly-twined banister, the darkness was a cold night sky. Hundreds on hundreds of lights dangled from fine strings, seeming to hover in midair. They sparkled in twisting, antler-shaped sconces. They rained like hail from delicate chandeliers. Just as spectacular as Lowry promised, a thousand man-made stars, the heavens dragged down to earth.

Tightening her grip on Hal's arm, she descended the staircase, the fabric of her dress whispering with every step. They slipped into the crowd. Everyone looked the same. The same dark colors, the same leering masks, the same indistinguishable drone of their voices. On her every side was another sharp point of an elbow, a towering body, a too-loud laugh.

The gossip had already begun. Lowry planned to host a seance. Lowry had imported one hundred cases of Danubian wine. Lowry intended to propose marriage, by her estimation, to at least five different people tonight. She could even hear her own name in the sibilant peaks of whispered conversation.

Pretender. Illegitimate. Disgraced. Traitor.

If she failed tonight, was that all she'd be for the rest of her life? The voices spiraled closer, tighter. Her corset was starving her of oxygen. The smells of wintergreen and roasted game and perfume suffocated her. It was too much—too stimulating.

"I need air."

"Come on," Hal said.

As soon as he glowered, a path cleared for them. He guided her through until they broke out into a pocket of empty space in the corner. Only a few solemn-faced, assessing courtiers coquettishly fluttering bone-girded fans hovered by the windows. The glass was scabbed over with frost and overlooked a spread opulent enough to put a royal feast to shame. There were cheeses sliced as fine as paper and rolled up like roses; gamey meats roasted in a crust of fragrant spices, their juices soaking into plump root vegetables; fruits of every color, drizzled with honey and tucked into flaky pastries; and there were tiny cakes lined up like gleaming white battalions, iced with buttercream and garnished with mint. Hal was gazing at them hungrily.

"Focus." Wren snapped open her own fan. "Do you see Lowry anywhere?"

No sooner had she spoken than an excited hush fell over the crowd.

He'd arrived.

Wren stood on her toes. There, high above the clusters of top hats and towering headdresses, was Lowry. He and Barrett descended the grand staircase to the pop and flare of tripod cameras. While Barrett wore a sensible, well-tailored jacket, Lowry wore a long, jet-studded cloak. Here, in his element, Lowry exerted his own gravitational pull. As they walked, the crowds parted for them like oil dropped into water. Some sneered their disdain, and others gazed on in open adoration. All of them were rapt and unblinking.

Lowry turned his head to smile roguishly at a camera, revealing the mask fastened to the side of his head. A wolf snarled at Wren, so lifelike, she paled. She thought of its fangs sinking into her, bleeding her onto the marble ballroom floor.

Breathe, she reminded herself. *You can do this.*

A servant passed, balancing a tray filled with flutes full of sparkling golden wine. Wren reached out and plucked one off the platter by its stem. For good measure, she took a sip, and while it tasted crisp and more expensive than her life was worth, it settled like grease in her churning stomach.

Wren turned back to Hal. "Guard the cake while I'm gone. And save me a dance, will you?"

"If I must. I'll dread your return."

Wren grinned at him and turned to leave. Before she could take a single step, Hal reached out and caught her by the hand. She understood the unspoken message in the warm pressure of his fingers, the worry in his eyes. *Be careful.*

"I'll be right back," she said, more tenderly than she'd intended. "I promise."

Hal let her go.

It took her a few minutes to wade through the masses, but the motion of the crowd eventually swept her into the parlor. Here, muffled by a set of heavy doors, the strains of the music were fainter. Roughly thirty people hugged the edges of the room, elbows planted on cocktail tables, backs turned to the crackling fire in the hearth. At the center of it all, Lowry luxuriated on a velvet lounge as if it were a throne. Barrett and two women she didn't recognize basked in the twinkling light of the gems on his hands and jacket. Even Wren stilled.

He was laughing. The eye-crinkling, doubled-over kind. Among his friends, he looked almost . . . happy. Then her gaze landed on the golden key glinting at his throat like an exposed artery. Wren squeezed the vial of chloral hydrate in her palm.

Now or never.

As she approached the group, Lowry looked up and met her gaze. Surprise flickered across his face before he concealed it behind a wide, welcoming smile. It matched his mask: all fangs. Ignoring the prying stares of his other guests, Wren edged herself into the circle. "My apologies for interrupting. You seemed to be having such fun."

"Oh, we are." Lowry wiped the heel of his palm across the bottom of each eye, brushing away tears.

"At last, someone to put a barrier between us." Barrett pulled out a chair beside him. "Join us. Please."

Wren sat. Two carafes of deep red wine rested on the end of the table, one already drained to the dregs. But what chilled her was the centerpiece. Five skulls arranged in a circle, each of their parietal bones lopped clean off. Red and golden petals, all from deadly varietals, spilled from their empty eye sockets and open craniums.

One skull for each missing soldier—all but one.

Wren raised a hand to her lips to conceal at least half her horror. For so long, she'd yearned to find answers. She'd yearned to find *them*. Now, she wished she could take it all back. Some horrors were best unknown.

"Looks like she's seen your new décor, Alistair." Barrett grimaced. "It's downright sacrilegious to exhume relatives, if you ask me. Gaudy at best. Honestly, five of them?"

"It's their debut, so they needed to make a lasting impression. They're most striking as a collection," Lowry protested. His eyes sparkled with curious, hungry delight as he watched her expression morph. "Although I'm still missing one."

If he was so flippant, so open, Alistair Lowry was even more of a monster than she imagined. Was he *mocking* her?

"Surely as a healer, Ms. Southerland, you can appreciate the beauty of anatomy laid bare," Lowry continued. "Be honest with me. I can take it."

"It's dreadful," she breathed. "I've never seen anything so macabre."

When Lowry's face fell, Barrett slammed his fist delightedly on the table. Wine shuddered in the carafes. "At least there's someone else with some taste in this place."

Lowry picked up a skull and chuckled to himself when the jaw, bolted at the temporomandibular joint, hinged open as if it had seen something scandalous. "I daresay I'm the only one here who has any fun."

Wren had never hated him more. But she managed to plaster a smile onto her face and gesture to his empty glass. "How right you are. I'm being so dour, when tonight is for celebration. Another drink?"

"Very well." Lowry replaced the skull on the table, shaking his head as if recovering from a particularly rich joke. "I do believe I promised Henry a drink to your talents."

"That's what I like to hear!" Barrett leaned across the table to fill Lowry's glass with the last of the wine.

Wren watched Lowry absentmindedly twirl his glass. Wine rolled down the sides like tears. This was her opportunity. All she had to do was distract him long enough to pour the drug in. The vial in her hands was as hot as a lit coal.

But all around her were hungry eyes hidden behind whitewood masks. They raked down her spine. If she hesitated, she would miss her chance. But if she was discovered, it was all too easy to imagine how everything would crash down around her. There would be no justice for her or Hannah or Hal. There would be no peace for Danu.

And she would hang for sabotage.

Wren opened her mouth to get Lowry's attention, but when Barrett's booming voice interrupted her, her jaw clacked shut. "Ms. Southerland, I'm so glad you came by tonight. We still haven't properly met."

He was too loud for how close they were, and his breath was ripe with alcohol. As friendly as he was, she didn't have time to engage in idle conversation. "Oh, Your Grace, you're too kind. I'm afraid I lead a boring life compared to the rest of our sparkling company."

"On the contrary, I've been dying to speak with you since I arrived. I consider myself something of a military scholar." He puffed out his chest proudly. "I hope you won't find this prying, but I must ask. You served in the Danu-Vesrian War, correct?"

"In the medical unit, yes."

"What an honor you've done your country." Barrett spoke with grim admiration. "I've done much reading, but I've never heard a firsthand account. You must tell me what it was like to serve under General Flynn. She demonstrated some of the finest displays of military tactics in history."

Wren had only seen General Flynn once in her life. "Uh . . . thanks?"

"Fitzy, please." Lowry groaned. "And you call *me* macabre. Don't subject my guest of honor to your raving."

"To the devil with you," Barrett said. "This, Alistair, is why the alliance is crucial. The leadership in the Queen's Guard is unparalleled. Why, in the famous Battle of Donn—"

Never had Wren known someone to discuss flanking maneuvers and scorched-earth tactics with the same soaring fervor of a besotted schoolboy. Wren did not believe Barrett had ever seen combat, but she doubted even General Flynn herself could muster such gusto.

Lowry let out a long-suffering sigh and whispered something to a fair-haired woman whose lips were toxin-bright beneath her mask. Whatever he said must have been funny, for she tossed back her head and burst into a peal of laughter. Her glittering necklace highlighted the elegant arches of her collarbones. Lowry's eyes traced them as he slung an arm over the back of her chair. Although every eye in the room was on him, he was the image of perfect ease.

Tonight, she realized, *was* a celebration for him.

He thought he'd bested her. Ensnared her.

And now his guard was down. He'd left his glass unattended.

Suddenly, Wren felt as if she'd been plunged underwater. Every sound in the room—even Barrett's incessant prattling—was muffled and faraway. She uncapped the vial in her sleeve. Would anyone else be able to smell that telltale aroma, like biting into a pear? Lowry was still shamelessly flirting, his hand scandalously high on his companion's leg. Barrett was regaling the woman beside him with tales of Danu's military victories.

With her heart pounding too loudly in her ears, Wren tipped the vial into Lowry's glass. It struck the surface with a *plop* as loud and startling as a gunshot.

"What is that?"

Wren snatched her hand away before she could finish measuring out the full dose—but not soon enough. The woman beside Lowry was staring balefully in her direction.

She saw.

Wren was so cold. She swore all her blood had evaporated. "I—"

Lowry turned around, but his gaze landed past Wren's shoulder. Amusement danced in his eyes. Her breath fled her lungs, leaving her wrung out in her seat. Behind her was a man promenading across the floor with the skirts of his iridescent tailcoat trailing nearly ten feet behind him.

"Can you believe it?" The woman sneered. When she tossed her hair, the crystals studding her braids glimmered in the candlelight. "How gauche."

Lowry laughed and picked up his glass. It cast a shimmering red aura on the white tablecloth, as dark as a bloodstain. "A toast," he said to the table. "To us, the most gauche and macabre of them all."

"To new friendships," Barrett interjected.

To Danu. To Vesria. To everyone we couldn't save and everyone we will.

Their glasses clinked. Drunk on his own hubris, Lowry swilled his wine in one audible gulp. Wren hoped it burned all the way down.

CHAPTER TWENTY-SEVEN

Thirty minutes had never passed so slowly.

After the toast, Wren floated somewhere above her body, numb and uncomprehending, as Barrett explained to her the finer points of a military-issued flintlock—of which, he assured her, he had many. Wine and conversation flowed so readily, she feared she'd administered the drug incorrectly. But then Lowry began to sag, unable to bear the weight of his own skull. She watched him eagerly over the brim of her glass.

It was only when he hauled himself upright and muttered something about fresh air that Barrett stopped yammering. "You look awful, Alistair. Are you alright?"

"I *feel* awful," Lowry said crossly.

He took one lurching step forward and stumbled. He threw one hand out to catch himself on the back of Barrett's chair. Wren swore the air pressure changed from the room's collective stifled gasp.

"You're unwell." She disgusted herself with her own fake wide-eyed concern. "Let me take a look at you."

Wren rose and slid an arm around his waist to steady him. His body tensed at her touch, and although he was too weak to shove her off, she felt the fight kindling within him. If he accused her of foul play now, he might sink her. Their gazes met, and Wren's breath caught.

He looked furious.

Then, as if she'd imagined it altogether, he heaved an over-wrought sigh and promptly dumped all his weight onto her. Wren grunted as she tried to get a handle on him. He was nearly a full head taller than her—and it certainly didn't help that he'd gone completely limp.

"Help me a little, would you?" she grumbled.

"I fear I cannot." Annoyance punctuated his every word. "I'm in pain."

Their every uneven step jingled merrily as the gemstones on his coattails bumped into each other. It added insult to injury as she dragged Lowry into the drawing room, pursued by the gawking stares of the peerage. She didn't want to imagine what tomorrow's gossip columns would say. Kicking the door shut behind them, she dropped him onto a chaise and backed away. Lowry sprawled out, still managing to look both elegant and absurd in his glittering suit.

"What did you give me?" he groaned. "My stomach is going to turn itself inside out."

"I didn't give you anything," she said icily. "You're drunk."

"Indeed," he snapped. "Drunk *and* my healer has drugged me at my own party. My suffering never ends."

The grandfather clock *tick, tick, tick*ed in time with the sway of its pendulum until at last, it tolled. In minutes, the drug would drag him under.

It could not come fast enough.

"It's chloral hydrate, if you must know. If you try to make a scene, my magic can render you unconscious far faster."

"Me? Make a scene?" Lowry laughed ruefully, his eyelids droop-ing. Against his damp black curls, his skin was ashen. "I wouldn't dream of it. In fact, I'm glad we have this moment alone. Tell me, how did it feel to be among the aristocracy? You looked quite at home tonight."

Wren was in no mood to indulge him or endure his mockery. "I hated it."

"It shouldn't be that way. You were made to be among them." There was a quiet, desperate edge to his voice. "You should've grown up in the palace, but the queen tossed you out as if you were no better than a stray dog."

"I'm no noble. I belong in the Guard."

"*Do* you, though? You've dedicated your life to serving her, and you still haven't earned her recognition, her acceptance. Doesn't that embitter you?"

Wren turned away from his imploring gaze. Of course it did. But she'd never give him the satisfaction of admitting it.

"I can see it in your eyes," he said. "I was once so much like you."

"You and I—"

"Are nothing alike," he finished with a wave of his hand. "Protest all you like, but we are. Both cast aside. Both hungry for peace. Both longing to be taken seriously, to make real change in the world. I, however, have learned to *act*."

"You're reaching," she snapped. "Your games won't work."

"You're so ungenerous with me." Lowry laid his head against the armrest. "Everything I've done has been for your own good. Can't you see that I'm on your side?"

"It's only been for *your* own good. You only care about yourself."

"There you go again. So dismissive." He curled his lip. "Think! You're too clever a girl to be fooled by Hal Cavendish's pretty face."

She *knew*, yet hearing him say Hal's name with such raw hatred . . .

"What?" she whispered.

"Aren't you tired of this charade? Yes, I know very well who he is." His eyes locked on hers, burning with cold fire. "He killed countless of your countrymen. His people took our parents, left us alone in this world. But I can make them pay. *We* can. If you'd let me help you, we'll both get what we're owed. If you trust me, I can give you everything you want."

"How?" she spat. "Even if I become your puppet liaison and the queen reinstates me, it means nothing. It's not acceptance, and it's certainly not love."

His expression darkened. "You're so determined to make things painful for yourself."

"No. In case it's not obvious to you, this is over." Wren reached out and grabbed the key around his neck, pulling the chain taut. "I know what you've done. I know you're the one who kidnapped those soldiers. As soon as I find what you're hiding in that passage, as soon as I know *why,* I will see you pay for it."

Wren wanted to savor his dread, but the man was like quicksilver, deadly and changeful. His fear was gone before she could blink. In its place was smug resignation. "You still haven't met my guest of honor." He carefully enunciated each word as they began to slur together.

"What guest?" she hissed. "What do you mean?"

Before she could demand any other answers of him, Lowry slumped over.

Wren swore. It didn't matter. He was only trying to daunt her.

From beneath his eyelashes, she could see the whites of his eyes like slick, wet moons. In another life, one where Vesria hadn't killed his father, what would he be like? He could have used all that charm and intelligence for something good. But the world only had a part in shaping him. All of them had suffered from this war. It was *his* choice to succumb to the pain it had caused. *His* choice to meet hatred with hatred. If she didn't prevent the war, it would only create more monsters like him.

Wren lifted the key from around his neck. Clenched in her fist, it felt like a weapon.

She found Hal where she left him, arms crossed uncomfortably, lurking by the buffet table. With the adrenaline coursing wild

within her, it was a challenge not to abandon her poise and run to
him.

Look at ease, she reminded herself.

After Lowry's mysterious bout of illness, attention would already
be on her. They needed to act discreetly. No small feat when a clus-
ter of people lingered by the east wing, the tapestry billowing in
the draft. Wren worried her lip. Anything unusual or unexplainable
was cause for talk. So how were they going to sneak in without
drawing suspicion?

And then, the perfect plan came to her.

Hal didn't notice her until she slid her arm into his. She warmed
under the relieved, heavy weight of his gaze on her. "Will you honor
me with the next dance?"

He recoiled. "Why?"

"Because if we're going to sneak into a cold, empty room hidden
behind a tapestry without looking incredibly suspicious . . ." No
recognition lit his eyes. His mouth remained a hard, unconvinced
line. Was he really so *oblivious*? Wren felt her face heating beneath
her mask. "Do you want me to spell it out for you?"

"No, I understand." With a bow she thought was a bit *too* gracious to be earnest, he took her hand. "I accept."

When they took their place on the floor, Hal slid an arm around
her waist, pulling her close until their bodies were nearly flush. He
dipped his head to the junction of her neck and shoulder, his lips
barely brushing her skin. Suddenly, his hand was burning hot on
the small of her back. Her world constricted to the scratchy wool of
his jacket against her palm, to his breath tracing an electric path up
to her ear. She dug her fingers into his shoulder and let herself melt
against him. "What are you doing?"

"It needs to look as if we're trysting. Was that not what you were
suggesting?"

"Yes." She hated the nervous, breathless tremor in her laugh.
"That's the idea."

He played his role a little too convincingly.

The music at last picked up, a dulcet swell of strings that softened into the steady sway of a waltz. Wren nearly groaned. Of *course* it would be a waltz when she was trying to ignore this . . . *feeling.* The dread that fluttered in her gut, however, met no reflection in Hal. Rather, he focused intently on guiding them into position, taking her hand in his and raising their arms into an elegant *V.* Last night, she'd sworn to surrender to this attraction between them only once. She was beginning to regret her noble restraint. It was far too easy to relax into him, especially when he was surprisingly skilled. He led them across the floor in slow turns.

"You implied you didn't dance!"

"I implied I didn't *like* to dance."

"Must you be good at everything?" she asked sourly. "It's annoying."

"You think I'm good at everything?" He said it so plainly, she wouldn't have caught his meaning if not for the playful glint in his eye.

"Ha! No, actually." How she prayed he couldn't see her hopeless yearning behind the mask. "Since you and your ego have made such an impressive recovery, I've no need to coddle you anymore."

Hal actually laughed, barely a rumble against her ear. What she wouldn't give to hear that more often. "I'm not good at everything."

"Name one thing."

"Conversation," he said. "You, on the other hand, are vibrant. You have an ease with people, and you express your feelings so openly. I admire it."

"Oh," she mumbled. "That's kind of you to say."

"Where did you learn to dance?" he asked after a moment of silence.

"Victoria Hebert taught me at a military formal." The memory made her smile. Victoria had so gallantly led as Wren bumbled her way through the steps. Una had had no patience for her ineptitude after Wren had scuffed her boots the year before. "You?"

"Here and there," he said. "It's useful for political events."

"So it is."

When he spoke again, this fragile romantic illusion shattered. "Do you have the key?"

"Yes. But we'll need to move quickly and very carefully. I don't think anyone saw what I did, but they know he's sick." She paused as he extended his arm. She spun before snapping back into position. "And Lowry mentioned something about a guest of honor. I have no idea what he meant, but he said it very . . . threateningly."

"He's cornered and bluffing."

"I hope so. As soon as this song is over, we move."

"Understood."

He navigated them through the other dancers and toward the east wing. As she let herself succumb to the steady *one*-two-three of the music, a small, naïve part of her longed to cling to this moment. She liked the way he held her like something to cherish. This was supposed to be an act, but there was something real there, too. She knew it by the way he kept absently stroking her waist, his warmth sinking into her. By the way his eyes lingered on her mouth when she spoke.

It was torture, denying him. Denying herself. But this had always been temporary. If they succeeded tonight, they'd never see each other again. Wren sucked in a breath, surprised at how much that realization stung. Why did she always want people she could never truly have?

As the last of the music faded, he drew back, and there was a battle in his eyes. "Wren . . ."

He lifted his hand to her face, but just as it grazed her cheek, a terrible feeling slithered down her spine. Someone was staring at them.

It felt like a blade at the back of her neck.

A shadow fell over them, and Una's voice was as cold and sharp as the ring of metal. "Mind if I cut in?"

CHAPTER TWENTY-EIGHT

As always, Una was beauty drawn in stark, severe lines. Her knee-length greatcoat gleamed with heavy buttons and rows of battle-won medals, and the silver fringe of her epaulettes flowed from her shoulders. At her neck was a black bow tie framed by silver collar stays and the night-dark spill of her hair. The sword at her hip, although sheathed in an intricate jeweled scabbard, was not purely ceremonial.

"Una," Wren breathed. Her heart lurched, ready to tear itself in half as it warred between joy and fear. Her best friend—and her undoing. "Wh-what're you doing here?"

"I was invited."

"I mean *here,* talking to me. I don't have time for this right now."

"I see." Una glared over her shoulder at Hal. "Am I interrupting something?"

Wren wedged herself between them. While Lowry had arranged Isabel's tenuous forgiveness, it was all over if Una saw underneath

Hal's mask. Una's gaze slid back to Wren, hard and searching. "Surely you can find time to spare me one dance."

Before she could say anything, Hal bowed his head deferentially. In a clumsy approximation of a Cernosian accent—so he was right; he wasn't good at everything—he said, "She's all yours."

The key to the hidden passage hung heavy in her dress pocket, which meant he must have some vague plan to free her from Una.

Una smiled, mirthless and fit to cut to the bone. "Well, then. Shall we?"

Wren accepted Una's gloved hand and followed her onto the floor. In the close press of the crowd, the air reeked of cut-onion sweat and cloying gardenia perfume. Despite the tension and hurt between them, it still felt like comfort to have her near. Everything about her was painfully familiar. The judgment in her eyes, the impassive set of her jaw, even the pressure of her gloved hand on her waist. And although Wren's heart still ached in her presence, something was undeniably different.

One year ago, her love for Una had changed for the worse. Sparked in desperation and kept alive, secret and stifled. It was a hungry, selfish kind of love, never fully satisfied. A love that kept score. Something that flared painfully now and again, like a bone that had never set quite right. Looking at Una now, Wren felt oddly free of it.

She loved Una, she realized, no less fiercely—but with her eyes fully open. She didn't long for what they could have had: kisses stolen in the dark and whispered promises they'd never be able to keep. She longed for the girl she'd talk with for hours as the rain beat down on their standard-issue tent. The girl who'd throw herself in danger again and again if only it meant her subordinates were safe.

She wanted her friend back.

"So," Una said, all icy distance. "The queen intends to reinstate you tonight."

"Tonight?"

"You didn't know?" Una spun Wren to face the grand staircase and gestured toward a high, secluded balcony. It was lit by twinkling lights and shrouded in shimmery, gossamer-thin fabrics. It was hard to see from this distance, but the woman watching them all from her wingback chair was unmistakable.

Isabel.

Her blond hair tumbled straight to the floor. Her lips were painted plum. Atop her head was the ceremonial crown, twisting into three branchlike points that were sharp enough to impale. It was preposterous. It was impossible. Isabel had never left Danu. Even though Wren could not see her clearly, she felt the exact moment the queen noticed her. All her blood turned to ice in her veins.

"We arrived earlier this evening," Una said. "Our future liaison, however, failed to greet us."

"Lowry neglected to inform me you were coming."

"I see," she said skeptically. "Who's your friend?" Wren didn't like the way she said *friend*. Like a curse, dripping with scorn.

Una guided her in harsh, sudden angles through the crowd, clearing space with the forcefulness of her footwork, the whip of her long hair. While Una was graceful and fierce, she was not a dancer. She was a soldier through and through. They moved to the rhythm of the music, but this was no dance. This was a fight.

"No one you'd know," Wren said quickly.

"Of course not. Does he have a name?"

"Yes. It's Henry."

"Henry what?"

"Henry . . ." Every single surname she'd ever known slipped through her fingers like water. "Ca . . . wart . . . bark?"

"Henry Cwartbark." Una looked entirely unamused.

"They're no family of note, the Cwartbarks. Very minor Cernosian nobles," Wren said quickly. "So when, exactly, does Her Majesty intend to do me the honor of reinstatement?"

"She's given me no details. Only that she expects you and Lord Lowry to meet with her and come to an agreement on some matter. Although I've heard rumors he's taken ill." Her eyes narrowed. "How strange."

This was bad. Whatever Lowry had planned would come to fruition in the queen's presence tonight. While the chloral hydrate had bought her time, it wouldn't last all night. But now that she had the key, she didn't need to prove anything to Una. She could *show* her.

This nightmare would end here and now.

Wren leaned closer so she could speak softly into Una's ear. "I'm about to tell you something that may sound mad."

"And why should I listen to a word you say?"

"Because I've solved the case of our missing soldiers."

Hope softened her features. "Go on."

Thank the Goddess, she was listening. She was actually *listening*. If there was anything Wren could count on, it was Una's ability to set aside her feelings for the sake of her country. "Alistair Lowry is responsible. For months, he's been targeting mages on border patrols. As soon as he isolates them, he poisons them with goddess-blood to kidnap them. I don't yet know why, but—"

Una let out a pressurized sigh.

Wren fought to keep the hurt out of her voice. "You don't believe me."

"Look around you. Lowry is nothing but a fop with an unhealthy obsession with the color black. He's brokering an alliance with Danu, after *centuries* of inaction. Why would he target us? Why risk retaliation?"

"You know it's not just us. It's Vesria, too." Wren ignored the glares of the couple who knocked into her as they danced by. "I took a made-up job for the promise of a made-up alliance. It was all just a ruse designed to lure me here."

"But why?" Una said impatiently. "I don't see a motive."

"Can't you just trust me?"

"I *did*," she snapped.

"I know I've wronged you. I wish I could tell you how sorry I am." She tried not to be deterred by Una's unimpressed silence. "I don't know his motive yet, but if you come with me now, I believe we can find the answers. There's a secret passage in the east wing, and— Quit looking at me like I'm insane! What harm will it do to just humor me and *check*?"

"I've indulged you for far too long already," she said slowly. "You expect me to believe someone like you solved this case? Do you have evidence?"

Someone like you.

Emotional. Reckless. Weak.

Anger sparked within her. "There's goddessblood being shipped here. I can prove that."

"And do you have any concrete proof people were being poisoned here?"

She had Hal. But if she told Una about him, he wouldn't make it out of this estate unscathed. "Not yet. But I saw that boy we captured at an inn where they're growing it. He can confirm everything I've told you."

"And can you prove that he's there? Right now? Can you guarantee he'll still be there?"

Wren clenched her teeth. "No. I can't."

"Then why would you expect me to insult our host and jeopardize this alliance by sneaking around the house like a common thief?"

"Because we're friends!" Her voice seemed to shatter the air around them. Dozens of curious stares skewered her as she stood humiliated and paralyzed in a whirl of black fabric.

"Are we really?" Una asked lowly. "Time and time again, I covered for you. I tolerated your emotional outbursts. I risked my job for you. You repaid me by lying to me and leaving me alone in the cold."

"Why would I lie about this?" Her voice thickened with tears. Her vision swam until she saw nothing but watery light and Una's wavering form. "Lord Lowry is the one who convinced the queen to reinstate me. Why would I sabotage that if I didn't have a good reason?"

"I don't think you're lying. You truly believe this theory of yours."

"It's not a *theory*!"

"Look at you, crying like a child even now." She sneered. "You're still weak because I was too soft on you."

Wren heard her own sharp intake of breath. Heard the exact moment her heart cracked down the middle.

Una closed her eyes. When she opened them again, they were as flat and cold as a sheet of ice. "My orders are to keep you in this ballroom. I'll not choose you over my duty again."

So this was it. If she couldn't convince Una to join her, she had no other options. She would have to push her away.

Wren reached deep into the well of hurt that had opened with her, and what she found was acid. "You think you can punish me so you don't have to punish yourself. But I can see through it, Una. You lost Byers. You lost the boy. And then you lost me. You're not as perfect as you think you are, are you?"

A flush spread across Una's cheeks. Shock turned to anger turned to *shame*. Exhilaration still hummed in Wren's veins at loosing some of the bitterness she kept locked inside, but there was nothing satisfying about this. As the last, wavering violin ceased to play, Una wrenched her hand free and packed away every emotion until her face revealed nothing at all. "You're pathetic, Wren."

Hurt begat hurt, over and over again. Wren didn't know how to stop it. More than anything, she wished things could go back to how they once were. But everything they had, everything she had hoped for, lay in ashes at her feet. Gathering her skirts into a mocking curtsy, Wren said, "Thank you for the dance."

"Don't move. You're not leaving my sight until your business with the queen is finished."

Just then, Wren caught a glimpse of Hal, her medical bag slung over his shoulder, skirting the edge of the room. At his side was the Duke of Matthonwy. As the two men approached, Barrett gazed at Una in a way that could only be described as reverential. He removed his mask and clasped it in front of his heart.

"Please forgive my intrusion, Captain Dryden," Hal said mildly, "but I wanted to make an introduction. The Duke of Matthonwy has an immense appreciation for Danubian military strategy—and an impressive collection of sabers."

Barrett bowed deep enough to scrape the floor with his beard. "It's truly an honor to meet you, Captain."

Una gaped at the two of them in vague disgust and palpable confusion. "A pleasure."

"The pleasure is all mine. I've heard so much about your leadership in the war."

"Yes!" Wren interjected. "Captain Dryden was my commanding officer in the war. She is not only a fearsome soldier but also a brilliant storyteller. You must tell the duke of your exploits during the Second Battle of the River Muri." Turning to Barrett again, she clasped her hands together. "She renders it *achingly*. There's never a dry eye in the room."

Una seared her with a warning glare.

"I'd love nothing more than to hear your account." The duke's eyes grew round and exultant. Then they fell on the sword on her hip. "What a beauty! That's true Danubian steel if I ever did see it."

Perfect. Una would never be free of him now.

Wren grabbed Hal's hand and squeezed. The last thing she saw before they melted into the crowd was Una's face contorted with pure, agonized hatred.

Down the ladder and beyond the locked door, Wren struggled to keep herself steady. It wasn't the darkness that unsettled her, or the cold seeping into the thin fabric of her gown like bog water. It was the way her magic went completely silent.

When she and Hal snuck into the east wing last week, it had nearly screamed at her. It had pulled her to whatever lay behind this door, to the heart of the rot in Colwick Hall. Now, as she and Hal descended an echoing stone staircase, she couldn't help feeling abandoned, bereft. Whatever had been here before was gone.

What had happened here since they left?

The staircase beyond the door eventually opened into what felt like a cellar, as open and wet as a fresh wound. Hal flipped a switch, and electric sconces surged, buzzing in protest, until the room came into view orb by wavering orb. Although the gloom still hung as thick as low-hanging fog, pale unnatural light shone on the glass vials and gilt book spines that lined the shelves.

The worn red carpet muffled the sound of their footsteps. As she passed a tidy writing desk, Wren trailed her fingers over the page of a book propped open. An empty cup lay beside it, old coffee staining the silver spoon laid out on the saucer. The quiet ordinariness of this place unsettled her. It was too lived in, too frequented.

"There's another door over here," Hal said, startling her.

"I really don't want to go in there." But Wren knew their answers lay on the other side. She just didn't know if she was ready to face them. She forced herself away from the solidity of the desk and into the cold, empty air. *One step at a time.*

Her fingers curled around the doorknob.

Hal gave her a reassuring nod.

She pulled open the door and immediately gagged.

It reeked of death. That sickly sweet, old-meat stench dragged her back to the war, to memories of tents filled with dying soldiers, of bodies bursting open and rotting on the riverbank.

You're here, she reminded herself. *Stay here.*

Wren turned on the dim overhead lights, and sparks burst in one bulb before dying. As she broke out in a cold sweat, she cataloged the room to ground herself. In one corner was a table draped in a rust-spotted towel. On it was a tray full of steel surgical instruments arranged in precise rows. Her eyes skirted over a wickedly long bone marrow needle and mallet. Deeper in the room, hunkered in the fold of shadows, was a bed. Someone lay underneath the sheets.

Wren opened her bag and snapped on gloves and a mask. "You don't have to stay for this. It's not the same kind of death as on the battlefield."

"I know. I want to."

Wren frowned but handed him a mask. "Alright."

When she felt steady enough, she approached the bed. Every step felt wooden, sent her drifting farther and farther above herself. In the folds of sheet and shadow, she could make out the faint outlines of a face. Goddess above, she did not want to do this. But someone had to bear witness to what had been done here.

With a trembling hand, she peeled back the sheet to reveal a young man. He had dull, half-open eyes, blond hair like a shock of goldenrod, and a mouth missing a cigarette. Wren took a deep, steadying breath against the tide of her horror, her grief. At long last, she'd found the proof she was looking for.

This was Jacob Byers's body.

Focus. Fall apart later.

She could do this. For just a few minutes, she could be objective and cold. As she forced her eyes back to his pallid face, she noted he was in the earlier stages of autolysis. No bloating. No liquefaction of the organs or fluid oozing from the orifices. Only a faint yellow discoloration and blistering of the flesh. If she had to estimate, he'd been dead for fewer than twenty-four hours. Which meant they'd been here when he died.

She could have saved him. But she was too late.

A soft sob escaped her. Deep down, she'd *known* none of Lowry's victims had survived. Until now, she'd still been clinging to hope. She'd still believed that maybe Byers would shuffle back into the office one day, reeking of tobacco and asking about what he'd missed. Just a few weeks ago, they'd been holed up together, filing Una's paperwork and laughing at each other's jokes. He slacked off and burnt the coffee. She needled him and did the work. That was her life. It was *routine.*

Her hands were trembling. Her throat burned from the sting of bile and the strain of holding back a scream. She wanted to push magic into him. To expand his lungs and contract his heart. To light up his nervous system. Anything to give his spent body life, movement. How many times had she seen a corpse on the battlefield and lamented the insufficiency of her magic? How many times had she yearned to undo death?

Fall apart later, she told herself with a new ferocity. This was bigger than her grief—bigger than even Byers. *All* of them were dead, Vesrians and Danubians alike.

"Did you know him?" Hal asked quietly.

"Yes. I knew him."

"Byers."

"Yes." She bowed her head and sucked in steadying breaths to keep the tears at bay. If it was the last thing she did, Lowry would pay.

"Wren," he said hoarsely. "I'm so sorry."

"Don't. I need to finish my examination."

Understanding lit his eyes, and she turned back to Byers. With the sheer force of her will, she summoned enough magic to perform an examination. The pain that radiated up her arms was sharp and immediate, the silver light of her magic sputtering. *No,* it couldn't fail her now. Gritting her teeth, Wren pushed until her *fola* burned with protest. A quick assessment showed her the same damage patterns as Hal: goddessblood poisoning. And a series of stubborn, unhealed wounds.

Wren drew back the sheet to reveal a series of thick puncture wounds on his forearm, some scabbed over, some fresh. As she plumbed them with her magic, she realized they drilled straight into his bone, into the very marrow. Likely biopsies—but *why*? On the other, a long, unhealed gash stretched from elbow to wrist.

Hal sucked in a sharp breath and turned away.

"You should wait in the other room," she said gently. "I've got this."

He nodded and withdrew, leaving Wren to her work. She retrieved a syringe from her bag and began to draw samples of blood and tissue from the corpse. As soon as she ran forensic tests, she could confirm that his cause of death was goddessblood poisoning. That, along with the shipping records from the Guiding Light Inn, would present a compelling case to the queen.

And now, with a body, she could finally let Byers go.

Wren wasn't sure how to do this. How could she grieve something so unspeakable? How could she leave him alone in a place like this? He deserved a hero's funeral. He deserved to be buried in Danubian soil. He deserved so much more than *this,* dying alone and afraid. One of her Sisters might have said a prayer over him. Wren, however, had seen too much suffering to believe that the Goddess, if she existed at all, cared for them. She had no prayers left.

"You were strong," she told him, her voice thick with tears. "I'm so sorry."

In the end, he would save her, even if she couldn't save him.

Wren finally allowed herself to crumble.

When she finished storing the evidence and composing herself, Wren stepped out into Lowry's macabre study. As soon as the door clicked shut behind her, Hal rose to his feet. A question burned in his eyes, and Wren drew in a deep breath before shaking her head. *Not yet.*

Not until they were out of this place. Not until they were safe.

Books lay scattered on the desk, some so old and worn their pages spilled out like entrails. They were all the same kinds of tomes as in the library: philosophy, anatomy, biology.

"I see you rearranged the place," Wren said weakly.

"I was looking for something."

"And did you find anything useful?"

"Perhaps you should take a look."

Slowly, Wren approached him and took a seat behind the writing desk. A notebook lay open to a spread of pages filled by long columns of numbers. Her eyes, still burning with tears, ached as she read. Dates long before the first of the soldiers was taken. Ratios of kilograms and milliliters, all but one marked *fatal.*

Wren knew exactly what this was. Documentation of Lowry's early experiments with goddessblood. It explained Hal's survival—and why Lowry had targeted mages only after he'd finished killing off his servants. Before he started abducting soldiers and drilling holes in them, he'd needed to determine what a nonlethal dose of poison was. Just enough to keep someone subdued. And what better lab rats than the people living in his house? They'd been powerless against him.

Disgusted, Wren flipped through the notebook until she came across a detailed illustration of the humerus, shimmering *fola* threading through the spongy tissue within. On the next adjacent side, a simplified drawing marked incision points along the length of the bone, a cross-section of a cylindrical core of marrow labeled with the word *hemopoietic.* Page after page was filled with frantically scrawled clinical notes, each one in Lowry's familiar looping handwriting.

> Day 8: Today, the side effects worsen. Nausea, fatigue, sores. And despair, the worst of them all. I fear the marrow transplant has not taken, although briefly, as I lay half-dreaming this morning, I swore I felt something like magic burning cold within me.
>
> Day 12: Nothing, nothing, nothing. Again, it is nothing but failure. I allowed myself to truly hope with this one—to believe this marrow could breathe new life within these inert cells of mine. There is still, however, one thing yet to try.

The log ended there.

"What was there left to try?" Hal asked, jolting her from his thoughts.

If she let herself look at Lowry straight on—all the things he'd said, all the things she'd witnessed and endured—didn't she already know the answer to that question? When she closed her eyes, she saw blood beading on the tips of his fingers. How it flowed freely from the wound in his arm as he had emerged from behind that tapestry. Maybe he'd failed that night. What person, after all, had the skill and the bravery to perform a complex surgery on themselves?

That was why he had summoned her here. *That* was why he had tested her with that brutal transplant last night. To serve as assistant in his sick experimentation on mages.

"A full organ transplant," she said absently. "Jacob Byers had the ability to manipulate his bone density. That's why Lowry was taking his marrow."

Hal lifted his eyes to hers, and she did not miss the flicker of fear within them.

Wren drove her fist against the wall. Her knuckles popped, but she ignored the ache of it, the way her skin split. Her breaths came hard and ragged. "How could I have missed it? How did I not *know*?"

Because she'd always assumed it was impossible. Even in skilled hands, an experimental surgery on people like Byers, whose abilities were diffuse and broad-reaching, would kill both the donor and the recipient. To have full use of magic like Byers's, Lowry would need to replace every bone in his body. But a more localized magic—one that lived only, say, in the eyeball . . .

It was possible.

All she could see were those detailed drawings in the morning room desk's drawer. Every line drawn in silver ink on the drawing of the bulbus oculi. Every insertion point marked with fervent certainty. All she could hear was Lowry's hatred as he uttered the name *Hal Cavendish*.

Lowry wanted magic. He wanted revenge.

"That's why we're here," Wren said slowly. "That's why he's kept us alive so long."

"What're you saying?"

"He wants your eyes."

Hal swore, a sudden, sharp burst of a Vesrian word—one of the few she understood. He paced the room, all the color draining from his face. All his disgust, all his horror, came out in a single word. "Why?"

"Because he thinks he deserves it," she said. "Because it'll hurt Vesria."

"Whatever he hopes to gain from them will bring him far more suffering," he muttered. "A fitting curse."

"*Don't.* Don't even joke like that." The grief she'd tried so hard to stifle surged anew. It churned around her, rising higher and higher until she feared she'd choke on it. "I failed him. He'd only been dead a day. If I'd had the courage to stay . . . If I hadn't run away when I was afraid, he'd still be alive. I know it."

"You can't know that." Hal crossed the space between them and cradled her jaw in one hand. As he lifted her chin to meet his gaze, she saw only tenderness there. "What's done is done. What-ifs will only tear you apart."

"So what am I supposed to do?" she whispered. "How do you do it? How do you live with that kind of regret?"

Hal didn't respond immediately. When he did, his voice was weary. "You keep walking forward. You're strong enough to carry the weight of it."

"No one is as strong as you, then."

"That's not true." In the dim light, she could see tears glimmering in his eyes. He squeezed them shut, turning his face away from her. "Forgive me. I'm too weak to stay composed. I can't even take my own advice."

Wren took his hands. They were ice-cold in hers. "You are *not* weak for grieving. For feeling anything."

Hal looked startled by her sudden ferocity. Saying it wrenched something in her free. Could that be true? After everything she'd endured because of her emotions, after everything Isabel and Una had told her, could she really believe that?

Yes, some buried part of her said. *Isn't that what makes us strong?*

Her sensitivity had always forced her to look straight at the darkness in the world—and allowed her to imagine how she might fix it. Empathy brought her and Hal together. It carried them here. If they could work together, if they could learn to care for each other, then there was still hope for their people.

She wasn't weak for feeling, either. Hardened hearts were

breakable. But hers had endured again and again. As much as it terrified her, Wren wanted more than anything to believe herself. But right now, she only needed to convince Hal.

All she'd ever wanted was someone to help hold her together. Maybe Hal did, too. Wren took a tentative step forward and wrapped her arms around his middle. He smelled like comfort: like black tea and sugar on a long winter night.

"I know it's not enough," she said against his collarbone, "but I'm so sorry, and I'm here for you."

Hal stiffened in her embrace. Then, slowly, he relaxed and rested his chin on top of her head. Although he said nothing, she heard his response in the stuttering beat of his heart. *Me-too, me-too, me-too.*

CHAPTER TWENTY-NINE

As they emerged from the hidden staircase, Wren strained to listen over the mournful cry of the wind. The faint sounds of dwindling conversation and music reached her. The snow poured in from the broken staircase and swirled across the floor like freshly swept dust. In the cold and quiet, the room felt peaceful. Undisturbed, as if they'd stepped back into a world that never knew they'd left. Twelve distant gongs of a clock announced the arrival of midnight.

Somehow, they'd done it. Now all she had to do was find the queen.

"Have you discovered the dark and terrible secrets of Colwick Hall?" a voice said.

Wren turned sharply to see a shape in the darkest reaches of the room. Candlelight glimmered on a fine cloak encrusted with jet like mussels on a dock.

Lowry.

He strode forward, carrying a candelabra. Painted all in stark

orange and black, he looked like a thing half-made in fire. Chills
erupted over the back of her neck. She'd known the dosage was
smaller than usual, especially with alcohol in play, but he still
shouldn't be conscious.

He shouldn't be *here.*

"How?" was all she managed to spit out.

"Chloral hydrate," he drawled. As he took another step toward
her, the firelight snagged on a flash of metal. In his other hand, he
held a knife loosely at his side. "Potent stuff—or at least it used to
be. I began taking it years ago for insomnia."

Hal nudged Wren behind him. "Find the queen. I'll handle
him."

Lowry clucked his tongue, setting his candelabra on the floor.
"You'd not be so hasty if you realized how thoroughly ensnared you
are. How easily I could sink you both."

Every logical part of her begged her to listen to Hal, to run. But
the hateful sight of Lowry, so smug . . . Just once, she wanted to see
genuine fear light his eyes. Just once, she wanted him to know he'd
lost. She wanted to punish him for what he'd done to Byers.

Wren shoved past Hal. "No. You're the one who's sunk. You
murdered my friend, and now you're going to pay."

"Am I?" Lowry raised his hands and drew the knife across the
heel of his palm in one fluid motion. Wren sucked in a sympathetic
breath through her teeth, but Lowry's face remained entirely un-
changed. Blood pattered on the stone floor, splashed his boots.

"Imagine, if you will, the Queen's Guard stumbling onto this
tableau. Poor, bumbling me cornered by the girl who betrayed
her country and Hal Cavendish." Lowry closed the gap between
them and grabbed her elbow with his injured hand. "What kind
of conclusion would they jump to if they found you covered in my
blood?"

Wren tore herself away from him, recoiling at the smirk spreading across his face. When she looked down, her hands were trembling. Dark, hot red streaked her right arm from elbow to fingertips.

"It's entirely plausible," he continued. "You drugged me and attacked me. Once I give myself a wound far worse than this, it'll seem a wonder that I was able to escape with my life."

"Is *that* your plan? Still attempting to force my hand? You've gotten desperate."

"Yes, theoretically, I suppose those would be the actions of a desperate man." Lowry absently twirled the wet blade through his fingers. "But, alas, no. That's not my plan, as riveting as it would've been. The scandal of the century: Alistair Lowry nearly assassinated at his own party by the royal bastard and the Reaper of Vesria."

"You have to go," Hal said, more urgently this time. "He's only trying to distract you."

"You wound me, Cavendish." Lowry lifted his hands in supplication. "Well, perhaps I am stalling until my guests clear out. It's so much easier to conduct business when there aren't ears everywhere. But I come to you in earnest with a gesture of goodwill, my final offer. Although you've attempted to thwart me at every turn, I am nothing if not generous."

Wren could only stare at him, reeling. "You're in no position to be negotiating anything. As soon as the evidence—"

"Whatever you think you discovered, my dear, it means nothing."

Wren searched his eyes for the lie. "You're . . . you're bluffing."

"Oh, to believe that justice has any place in this world." Lowry sighed wistfully. "Your naïveté almost touches me. It'll be a shame to see your Paper Queen crush it once and for all."

Wren froze. What did he mean by that?

"You've both played the game admirably, but I'm afraid it was always a losing one. Aren't you tired, Cavendish? You *look* tired."

Hal said nothing, only glared at him with open hatred.

"You know as well as I do that you won't get far in this weather," he said, undeterred. "If you don't kill me—which would leave your ladylove here in an awkward position—I will tell the Guard you're here. But if you help me, we can come to another arrangement. Your eyes for your life. What do you say?"

"Whatever vengeance you think you're enacting will sorely

disappoint you," Hal said lowly. "As soon as I am powerless, my people will care nothing for me."

Lowry sputtered out a laugh—a delighted, fraying sound. "Do you truly believe this is about something as petty as *revenge*?"

Hal faltered.

"No, this is bigger than me and my father. This is about Cernos. Since recorded history, we've lived in fear of the likes of you. Never taken seriously, even though we are superior in every way. We have electricity, while you still fumble in the dark. Soon we will have carriages with no need for horses. Fully automatic firearms. Meanwhile, you still cling to the superstition of your gods. You rely on magic as power.

"However, my countrymen are shortsighted in their isolationist tendencies. Had your armistice held, peacetime would have allowed you to develop better technology, more sophisticated warfare. You may have hoped to catch up to us in a few decades. But if Cernosians were to seize magic for ourselves, we could secure our place on the global stage. We could *spread* our greatness instead of hoarding it. We could save countries like you from yourselves, give you the proper guidance."

Lowry tipped his chin toward Wren again, his eyes blazing with righteous fervor. "All I need is your help to demonstrate the procedure can be done. That a magic as detestable as his can be harnessed. Once Cernosians have magic, the world will finally know peace. Under our reign, no one will suffer again."

"No. Never," Wren spat. "You're even more delusional than I thought if you think you can save the world by conquering it."

Anger colored his cheeks for only a moment. He drew in a calming breath, and when he spoke again, his voice was cold and measured. "Your loyalty is misplaced. Nothing but this alliance can stop the war I've set in motion. As for *him,* he'll leave in the end. Do you really expect him to sacrifice his reputation to be with you? His family? His home? Would you be so cruel to ask him to?"

"Stop talking." Wren allowed her voice to go entirely flat. "You can't manipulate me anymore. No matter what you do, no matter what I lose, I will never help you. I would sooner die."

"I *tried* to be generous with you." Lowry raised the knife again, pointing it directly at Wren. Its tip still shone crimson with blood. "Talk sense to her, Cavendish, or I will—"

But he never finished his sentence. Lowry broke into tremors, his eyes flung wide.

It was a look of pure terror.

Wren slowly turned to see Hal, the *fola* around his eyes lit silver, his gaze locked on Lowry's. Lowry began to scream, and Hal winced. Every time Wren had seen his magic at work, his victims had perished silently. She knew she'd healed him incompletely, but she hadn't anticipated this.

It only took a few seconds before Lowry collapsed, saliva dribbling from the corner of his mouth. He wasn't dead, judging by his heaving sides and panicked breathing. His eyes were glassy and somewhere far away.

A trickle of blood welled up from Hal's right eye and carved a crimson line down his face. He sucked in a pained breath through his teeth and applied pressure to his eye with the heel of his palm.

"That was our last resort," Wren said. "Our very last resort."

Hal stooped down to retrieve the blade Lowry had dropped, his eyebrows drawn together. "I know. I didn't know what he was going to do. I thought he might hurt you. I just . . . reacted."

The sound of Lowry's anguished scream still seemed to reverberate through the silence of the estate. Wren cradled her face in her hands. The only thing she could think to say was, "This is bad. This is *so* bad."

Lowry was right. If the Guard found him this way, if they saw her and Hal together . . .

No, she couldn't fall for his lies. The evidence would be enough.

Distantly, through the sound of her own teeth chattering, she heard the rustle of fabric. Felt the weight of Hal's jacket settling over her shoulders. When she looked up at him, angry red lines fissured his sclera, and blood still smeared his cheek. She ached to reach out and soothe the pain with her magic.

"You need to go before the Guard finds you," she whispered. Somewhere, she heard the pounding of boots on the grand staircase, the muffled barking of orders.

Hal shook his head, just barely. "And go where?"

"Home. Anywhere."

"I'll never make it. I've no magic left. I have to surrender."

"No." The force behind it startled them both. "I won't let you. What about making Vesria better? What about *you*?"

"I have no choice," he said, his voice strained. "If what Lowry said is true . . . If the evidence truly means nothing—"

"Of course it's not true!"

"I can't risk it." There was a confession in his eyes. It was bright as a golden coin shimmering at the bottom of dark well water. Its intensity—its finality—frightened her. "I can't risk you. It's exactly as he said. If you can't indict him for murder, you and I will be tried for conspiracy against the crown."

"But if you surrender now, you'll die regardless. The queen will execute you for war crimes."

With the droop of his shoulders and the deep crease in his forehead, he aged years before her eyes. "I know. But if both of us take the fall here, there is no hope for peace."

"There has to be a better way."

His silence was answer enough. He'd given up.

But the look on his face didn't shatter her. It angered her. Maybe he was right. Maybe his surrender would give them the only chance they had at taking Lowry down. But Wren refused to let him sink into despair. No matter how miserably the odds were stacked against them, no matter what she had to do, she would fight for him. For *them*.

She took him by the shoulders. "Listen to me, Hal. You're not dying—not as long as I draw breath. As soon as the Guard comes, I'll demand to be taken to the queen. I'll tell her everything, and if the evidence doesn't convince her, I'll go to Parliament. And if they aren't appalled or afraid of Vesria retaliating against us, I'll . . ."

She'd find a way to appeal to the Goddess herself if she had to. She'd do anything if it meant he'd live.

"I'll get you home. I swear it on my life," she said. Maybe every promise she made him was naïve and reckless. But for once, even as tears stung her eyes, she was not ashamed of it. "Tell me you believe me."

"I believe you."

"Good."

Wren couldn't be sure which of them moved first. He crooked his finger under her chin, tipping her face toward his. She lifted onto her toes. His fingers were cold against her face, but the whisper of his breath against her lips set her ablaze. She had never wanted anything more than this last inch of space between them to disappear. She wanted to bottle that look in his eyes, so longing and desperate—for more time, for *her*.

"Check the east wing!" someone shouted.

They jumped apart, and Wren felt as if she'd plunged beneath the surface of an iced-over lake. The world flooded back, cold and dark. There was no more time.

The tapestry was rent from the stone archway with the *shush* of heavy fabric and clattered to the ground like a felled fortress wall. Light from the grand hall blinded her, and when the spots in her vision cleared, she saw Una, flanked by two Guardsmen, one hand on the pommel of her sword. Wren watched them absorb the scene piece by piece.

Lowry, unconscious on the ground.

Hal, his hands raised, Lowry's bloodied knife dangling from his fingers.

Her, standing bare inches from him.

A hush fell like an executioner's blade.

"Hal Cavendish," someone hissed, drawing his sword with a high ringing sound.

"Stand down," Una snapped. "Silence."

Her subordinates shifted restlessly, awaiting their next orders. Una, however, regarded Wren coldly before her focus locked onto Hal. Her hand did not drift from her blade. "Talk. Now."

"I wish to confess," Hal said quietly, "to the attempted assassination of Alistair Lowry. I surrender myself into your custody."

She jerked her chin at Wren. "And her?"

"I was about to dispose of her before you came," he said in a voice that chilled Wren to the bone. "It is because of her that he still lives."

"Don't listen to him, Captain," one of her men shouted. "Let me—"

"I said *silence*," Una barked. Wren knew that tension in her shoulders. It was the stress of a leader deciding what to do for the safety of her squad, for the good of her home. "Drop your weapon, Reaper."

Hal let it fall with a clatter onto the stones.

Una's eyes slid from the knife to the blood still drying on Wren's arm, as if trying to make sense of what had happened. "I've been waiting for this day for a long time. I'd only hoped you would put up more of a fight."

When he made no reply, she curled her lip with distaste. "Lieutenant Southerland."

Wren snapped into attention, startled. "Captain . . . ?"

"Blindfold him."

Una's subordinates exchanged anxious looks. Even though he'd surrendered, it was an immense risk to approach someone like Hal while he was unrestrained. But Una's expression was cold and assessing—nearly unreadable. *A test,* Wren decided. But of what?

If she let herself think on how disastrously this could go, she would crack. So she forced herself to shove her doubt deep inside herself, into the same locked chamber of her heart where she kept her war nightmares and her grief. She could do this.

I will have the queen release him, she vowed. *He will live.*

She reached into her bag, her fingers brushing the knife he'd given her. It was a beautiful weapon, the hilt carved and solid wood.

Hal remained completely motionless, his head bowed so that his hair concealed his expression. Unsheathing the knife, Wren bent down and cut away a long strip of her gown's train. With shaking hands, she stretched it taut and stood on her toes so she could fasten it around his head. The fabric hissed as she pulled the knot, shining like a serpent's scales. Wren ached to see the strip of bare skin above the stark white line of his collar, right where his pulse faintly beat.

A girl at Una's side tentatively asked, "Your orders, Captain?"

"Call a medic for the nobleman," Una said without missing a beat. "Restrain Cavendish and load him up. I don't want to see a scratch on him until I've gotten my hands on him."

"And Lieutenant Southerland?"

Wren stood tall, her shoulders drawn back. Deep within herself, she found an authoritative tone, cold enough to match Una herself. "Take me to the queen. Now."

The candlelight washed Una's eyes a hungry, wolfish gold. "Very well then."

CHAPTER THIRTY

Dull moonlight streamed through the window of Isabel's make-shift office, tucked away in the belvedere of Colwick Hall's highest turret. The queen gazed out over the wicked snow-caps in the distance, backlit by starlight and moon-painted snowfall. As always, she was terrifying in her beauty. She wore a dress as frothy white as Knockaine's fog, and her wine-white hair was braided tightly within a circlet carved from jet and charred bone.

She did not face them. Every *tick, tick, tick* of the grandfather clock in the corner drove a wedge deeper into Wren's skull. When Isabel finally turned around, it took all of Wren's strength to remain upright.

Isabel was *smiling*. Wren had to squint to see it, but it was there in the soft curve of her mouth and the warm glow in her pale eyes. "My niece."

Wren could not hide her astonishment. Even Una drew back in surprise. *My niece.* Each syllable was a hook beneath Wren's skin, tugging, tugging. How desperately she'd once yearned to hear those words.

Isabel crossed the room and placed one cold, delicate hand beneath Wren's chin. "You've done me an immense service. I've never been so pleased."

"Really?" It came out small and childish—barely a squeak.

Isabel was pleased.

Isabel was pleased with *her*.

That rush was enough to drown out any voice of caution. Suddenly, Wren was that newly orphaned girl in the abbey again, confronted by all of her fantasies made real. How many nights had she lain awake, praying that Isabel would change her mind and come to get her? How many missions had she returned from, certain—so certain—that this time Isabel would recognize her talent?

After so long, it was finally happening.

"Not only did you save Lowry's life, but you've given me a gift of immense value," Isabel said, her voice windchime soft. "You must tell me how you ensnared the Reaper."

Una stiffened, and all the crisp edges of her pressed uniform went jagged. The glare she cast at Wren was enough to make her shrink. Over the course of the evening, Wren had grown accustomed to that look, almost inoculated herself to its sting. But now, something new shone through Una's anger, dark and aching as a bruise.

Jealousy?

"She slipped beneath his guard," Una said. "I saw him at the ball, although I didn't recognize him beneath the mask. Wren's sway over him was obvious. The way he looked at her, I'd say he was besotted."

"Besotted." The queen's voice oozed disgust—and admiration. "Is it true?"

Was it? Guilt raked through her, and Wren lowered her eyes. "I've earned his trust over the past couple weeks, but—"

"Remarkable." Isabel's eyes flashed with a hunger Wren had never seen before. They were as silver as knives. "And you stabbed him in the back. How ruthless."

The inside of Wren's mouth tasted like ash.

"I didn't think you had it in you. I was wrong to doubt you," Isabel said. "I'm reinstating you to the Guard under Una's command. You'll resume your duties as soon as we return to Knockaine."

Wren opened her mouth, but no sound came out. She waited for the excitement. The thrill. The *relief*. After everything she'd endured these past few weeks, she had what she wanted. But all she could see was Hal, blindfolded, his head hung low.

She'd spent so many years chasing her aunt's approval. So many years searching for a way to prove that she could be rational. That she could be ruthless. Now she'd done it. So where *was it,* that spark of joy? The sudden burst of self-love? The fulfillment she'd always imagined? Her whole life, she'd been accused of feeling too much.

Now she felt nothing at all.

All her life, she had thought she would be loved if she managed her emotions. That she would be worthy if she became impressive, indispensable. Now, she saw it for the lie it was. Earning Isabel's love would mean becoming the girl Isabel wanted her to be. It would mean taking a knife to her bleeding heart once and for all.

Approval meant nothing if Isabel didn't love *her*. It certainly didn't mean a damn thing if Hal was going to hang.

Wren shook her head. "Your Majesty, I'm incredibly grateful. But I have a few things to say first, if you'd allow me to speak freely about the matter of Hal Cavendish."

"Spare no details."

Wren reached into her bag and pulled out a file. "This contains everything you need to know."

Isabel's rare jovial mood shattered beneath her confusion. "What is that?"

Inside were three vital things. A vial full of goddessblood poison. Blood samples, the DNA of which would exactly match the Guard's records on Jacob Byers. A lengthy list of shipping records that began a few months before the first soldier went missing.

It was enough to save Hal. It *had* to be enough to save him.

"This," Wren said, "is evidence that will indict Lord Alistair Lowry in the disappearance of our soldiers."

Surprise flickered across Una's face. Anger—then impatience—reddened Isabel's.

"I see." The queen turned to the window again, the whip of her skirts washing the air cold. "Burn it."

All Wren's confident composure split like a dropped plate. "Your Majesty?"

"I'm well aware of Alistair Lowry's *predilections*." Wren watched the reflection of Isabel's face in the window freeze over. "He gave me his solemn word that he would touch none of my subjects—only Vesria's. The snake."

"You knew?" Una asked, a quiet fury creeping into her voice. "What she claims is true?"

"Yes." The admission came freely, easily. "It's true."

Una's gloved fists trembled. "For how long?"

"I knew from the first, as soon as Vesria's soldiers began disappearing," Isabel said. "I had my suspicions when the first of the Guard vanished, but their deaths are sacrifices to preserve this alliance."

"When you sent us to look for signs of them, it was all a charade," Una said hollowly, almost to herself. "You dismissed Wren for nothing."

Wren didn't understand. She *couldn't* understand. "But if you were working together, why didn't you let me accept his offer in the first place? He requested my services specifically."

"I didn't trust you to carry out this mission," Isabel said. "I knew well what he wanted, and I suspected your feelings would get in the way of your duty. You have one last chance to prove me wrong."

Wren knew a warning when she heard one, but she couldn't bring herself to heed it. "Tell me where exactly I've failed to carry out my duty as a soldier. With all due respect, Your Majesty, it seems to me that I've done better on this mission than you ever could have hoped. I've given you all the evidence you need to stop a war and punish Lowry for his crimes against Danu. If you'd just *look*—"

Isabel rounded on her. "I thought I made myself clear. I have no interest in your evidence. I don't expect a child like you to understand."

"There's nothing to understand! If you pursue this case against Lowry, there will be no war to fight. You won't need him anymore," Wren pressed. "We can prove that we've committed no acts of war against Vesria. How can you turn your back on that?"

"Because this was our agreement." Isabel lifted her chin, deepening the shadows on her face. "Lowry would orchestrate a break in the armistice. And with Cernos's support, we'll win once and for all."

It was exactly as Lowry had said. Their evidence meant nothing. And if she executed Hal, it would be the final straw. The war Isabel wanted would finally come.

"You can't do this!" Wren hated the pleading edge to her voice. "Hal is trying to make amends. If you work with him, you can band together *against* Lowry. You can finally put this rivalry to rest."

"And what message would that send?" Isabel's eyes glittered, as cold as cracked ice. "I will *not* look weak. The Reaper of Vesria must be brought to justice for what he's done. Need I remind you of the atrocities he has committed? What are the lives of three soldiers against all those he has already killed? How many families are still grieving because of him? I'll not deny my people what they are owed."

"And what are corpses against the living?" Una snarled. "You'll send us to die for nothing!"

"Enough!"

The clock *tick, tick, tick*ed in the silence.

"You're a soldier, Captain Dryden," Isabel said, eerily distant. "Just as those who disappeared were. It is Danu's divine purpose—*my* purpose—to crush the Vesrian heathens. It is *your* purpose to obey, and if the Goddess wills it, it is your purpose to die. I will finish what my ancestors could not."

Una had dedicated her life to the queen—even loved her. Wren watched a rift tear open within Una. Watched it consume all the light, all the fire, in her eyes. Watched the exact moment she realized everything she'd stood for, everything she'd given, amounted to nothing. Her shoulders curled inward. Her head lowered, and the spill of her dark hair concealed her anguished expression.

Una's voice was softer and more defeated than Wren had ever heard it. "Yes, Your Majesty."

"I'll forgive your insubordination once and only once," Isabel said. "As for you, Lieutenant Southerland, understand you are on provisional terms. My tolerance for your disobedience has run dry."

"I don't care about my position," Wren snarled. "I won't sit idly by while you destroy our country."

"Wren," Una growled, a warning.

Once, Wren might have obeyed that implied order. Tonight, she had nothing left to lose. She took another step closer to the queen. "When you kill Hal, you'll get your war. But as soon as you defeat Vesria, Lowry will betray you. Then what will your precious legacy be? Nothing but ashes."

"You overestimate him," Isabel said icily. "I can dispose of him as easily as I can dispose of you."

"I'll take what I know to Parliament. They'll force you to release him when they hear you've sold out your own people."

Slowly, all the anger drained from Isabel's face. What remained was a sanctimonious glimmer in her eyes and a small, cruel smile. Of all the reactions Wren expected, it was not this. "I see. You're more like your mother than I thought. Both of you were undone by misplaced affections. I can't decide if you're more of a traitor or a fool for loving that monster. Either way, I'll ensure you're there to watch him hang."

Something snapped within Wren. A feral, desperate rage unlike anything she'd ever known blackened her mind. Without thinking, she lunged, her magic blazing like cold fire in her hands. But before she could reach the queen, Una grabbed her by the elbows and wrenched them behind her back. The queen did not even flinch.

Wren thrashed uselessly against Una's ironclad hold. "Let me go!"

She heard herself—recognized the unhinged shrillness of her voice—but she couldn't bring herself to care about her dignity anymore. All that remained within her was a single conviction, burning hot as coal. The queen would not get away with this.

"It seems my niece isn't well, Captain Dryden. I believe she needs rest after today's events." Isabel folded her hands primly, her face triumphantly, cruelly blank. "You'll ensure she remains safely in the Tower until the Reaper's trial."

"Yes, Your Majesty," Una said.

"Good." As Isabel turned away from them, her three-pronged circlet silhouetted darkly against the moon, she looked to be crowned by horns. "Now get out of my sight."

The carriage door clicked shut behind them with grim finality.

Everything was silver inside the carriage. The plush cushioned seats, the delicate filigree curling like leaves across the ceiling, the stitching in the pillow at Wren's side, the tassels on the drapery over the tops of the windows. It was as sterile as an operating room.

Una, meanwhile, was a dark, jagged slash in the moonlight-pale interior. For the first time, she looked out of place and utterly lost in the queen's trappings. "Can we talk?"

Wren turned away to hide the first hot spill of tears on her cheeks. "I don't have anything to say to you. Although now that the queen has made me your prisoner, you can do as you like."

"What else do you expect me to do?" Frustration edged into her voice. "My hands are tied."

"Your hands are tied? Is that really your excuse?"

"Fine. Accuse me of cowardice if you must, but I won't let Cavendish walk away without facing justice. Considering where your loyalties lie, I have no choice but to treat you like a prisoner."

"Are you accusing me of treason?" Wren asked, unable to keep the venom out of her voice. "Everything I've done, it's been to *save* Danu."

"I'm accusing you of fraternizing with the enemy."

"You don't know anything—"

"How stupid do you think I am, Wren?" Una curled her hands to fists. "He surrendered and lied for you, that knife you have is Vesrian made, and you're wearing his jacket."

"What's your point?"

"My point is that you're not seeing things objectively. You're not thinking clearly. I saw how it gutted you to turn him in. I saw how you looked at him in the ballroom."

She refused to dignify Una with a response. Their relationship wasn't any of her business.

"So the queen is right." Una regarded her with open revulsion. "You do love him."

"I *don't*." It wasn't a lie, was it? It wrung something out of her to say it. "Goddess above, Una. What does it matter if I did, anyway?"

"Because he's a monster!" Una's eyes flashed with hurt. "He's killed hundreds of our countrymen. Or have you conveniently forgotten that?"

"I haven't forgotten," Wren said. "Nor have I forgotten that Lowry's killed three without remorse. There will be thousands more."

The silence between them was a wall, impassable.

"Neither Cavendish nor Lowry is a good man," Una continued, softer now. "No matter what we do, one of them goes free. I have to put my faith in the queen's judgment. I have to believe Lowry is the lesser of two evils. Can't you understand that?"

"I understand perfectly." Bitterness coated her every word. Wren turned away from her and wrapped herself tighter in Hal's jacket. The smell of it—of Hal—nearly wrecked her. "Are you done talking yet? The queen says I need my rest. You wouldn't want to disobey her orders, would you?"

She expected another argument, but Una only sighed. Wren

didn't know what to make of the hoarseness in Una's voice when she said, "Yes. I'm done."

With those three words, Una abandoned her. How had she been so foolish to believe Una would help her, that justice could be stronger than hatred? Maybe Lowry was right. Maybe they could never escape this cycle of war, this inherited violence. They were cursed to bleed and bleed and bleed until nothing and no one remained. Wren felt herself falling into some dark place inside herself—so dark, she didn't know if she could find her way back to the light again.

She'd failed her country.

She'd failed Hal.

She'd failed herself.

It's easier to feel nothing, Hal had told her once, a strange kind of wistfulness in his eyes. Now she understood so perfectly why he'd become the Reaper of Vesria. How she wished she could cut out her every emotion, to sink into oblivion. But even now, she couldn't harden herself to suffering. She'd never been able to, and maybe she never would. This sorrow and pain at the core of her—it gave her purpose. It gave her strength. No, she couldn't let herself sink any deeper. She'd made a promise to Hal that she'd save his life.

I believe you, he'd said, with more trust and affection than she thought she'd ever deserve.

Now she had to believe in herself.

CHAPTER THIRTY-ONE

The road to the royal palace was paved with people. Crowds jeered and hissed as the Guard's carriages rolled over the slush-slick cobblestones. Wren was grateful she couldn't make out what they were saying over the clatter of the wheels and the clop of hooves. Through the foggy windows, their faces were contorted and gore-red with cold and a terrifying, ravenous hunger. This wasn't a celebration, despite the market stalls doling out hot rice milk and pickled oysters. This was a spectacle.

It was fitting. Today marked the first time Isabel had opened the palace gates since she surrendered the war a year ago. Hal Cavendish's trial, so long anticipated, warranted a setting to match its breathless gravity. Wren's stomach hadn't stopped turning since she'd first received the summons. All members of the Queen's Guard were required to attend.

She'd been home for two days now, locked in a bedchamber in the North Tower as Isabel's "honored guest." Two days spent agonizing and worrying. Two days wasted. Although she fantasized about breaking down the door, about freeing Hal from his cell some stories above her, she was still no closer to a concrete plan to save him.

Una sat beside her in the silvery chill of a carriage. Although she was effectively her jailer, they hadn't spoken since they had left Colwick Hall on the night of the ball. Whenever Wren glanced over at her, she could see the tense set of her jaw and the brutal tightness of her fists. A war raged within her eyes.

The carriage rattled to a halt, and Wren climbed out without a word.

As soon as she stepped into the rheumy winter air, the crowd's energy changed. Their jeers melted away into a hush—and then, the shouting began anew, exultant and barely articulate. Through the overwhelming noise, through the blood roaring in her ears, she could make out a single word: *hero*.

It struck her like a stone.

"You look ill." Una stood shoulder to shoulder with her. "You'd better hide it."

Wren grimaced before forcing herself to wave at the crowds. As they passed the main gates, she numbly registered the featureless, cheering masses, the sparkle of sunlight and flash of camera bulbs. Colors swam in her vision. Once, she had dreamed of this.

Admiration. Her reputation restored. Her position secure.

It was all so hollow now.

Una—her head held high and her sleek braid swinging like a gallows rope—walked alongside Wren up the pristine white stairs of the royal palace. She led them through halls and up stairs to a balcony filled with the black-capped heads of the Guard. From her vantage point, Wren could see the throne room stretched before her like a theater. Terraces and boxes and tiered seats buzzed with courtiers and wealthy business owners. Isabel so rarely held court, everyone was dressed for the occasion in their finest: bold Cernosian-flag red in support of their new ally, elaborately beaded gowns, and expensive fur stoles draped over shoulders.

On a marble dais, Isabel, veiled and crowned, sat atop her throne.

It was a monstrosity wrought in silver, its back twisting skyward like spires of ice. A canopy of lace, as delicate and liquid as poured water, concealed her from the direct view of her subjects. Isabel, as always, hurt to look at with her glass-sharp beauty, but Wren could only focus on Lowry.

He sat at the place of honor on the right hand of the dais. More extravagantly dressed than she'd ever seen him, he wore a red brocade cloak fastened at his throat with a solid gold brooch. A circlet of gold, a jaunty mockery of a crown, rested atop his neat black curls. His cloak spilled onto the floor, the exact color of blood. Even from here, she could tell something was *wrong* about his wide, exhausted eyes. Everything about him—from his fingers drumming on the arm of his chair to his bouncing knee—radiated a restless, hungry energy. As if the inevitability of his success tormented him, haunted him.

He looked like a snag in stitching. Something that would unravel if pulled too hard.

But then, as someone caught his attention across the room, his smile slipped effortlessly into place, and Wren saw not a monster or a madman, but exactly what he wanted everyone to see. Someone charming and unassailable and visionary.

"Um, excuse me." A voice yanked Wren from her thoughts. A young Guardswoman, no older than thirteen and too small to fit into her standard-issue uniform, was gaping at her from the adjacent seat. "You're Lieutenant Wren Southerland, aren't you?"

"I am."

Her eyes bulged. "You're the one who saved Lord Lowry."

Wren felt ill. The crowds outside were easy to ignore, easy to dismiss, but she saw herself in the earnest openness of the girl's face. It was a painful reminder of how naïve she'd once been. What she'd done was nothing to admire, nothing to aspire to.

"I am."

"What was it like? Facing the Reaper?"

Before Wren could even begin to formulate an answer, the doors banged resoundingly shut. A glasslike quiet followed, ringing and fragile, as two soldiers paraded a prisoner down the central aisle and shoved him toward the dais. The tether of her magic pulled taut, snapped against her breastbone.

Hal.

As if she'd called him, he turned his head toward her. Longing and fear and hope welled up in her all at once. He was *here*—painfully, tantalizingly close. She wanted to throw herself from this balcony and run to him, to tear through every soldier that stood between them. Her thoughts churned restlessly, searching for any possibility, any opening. But she found nothing. Nothing that didn't end with both of them dead before she even reached him.

She'd never felt so powerless in her entire life.

"Your Majesty," one soldier said with a deep bow. "We bring you Hal Cavendish."

The room exploded into chaos: gasps of horror, shouts of fevered delight. Hal's head hung low, and his arms were twisted and bound at a sharp angle behind his back. His once white shirt was torn and spotted with oxidized blood.

Anger and horror clawed their way up her throat like bile. Hal wouldn't have fought them, so they must have hurt him only for sport. They'd even left her makeshift blindfold fastened. It wasn't only a precaution to keep him from using his magic. The blindfold, its sequins glittering darkly, almost mockingly, was a humiliation tactic, forcing him to stumble blind into this den of wolves.

This wasn't a trial. It was sick, cheap theater.

The queen did not move. The lacy sleeves of her gown sparkled like frost in the faint sunlight. From behind her veil, Isabel said, "Hal Cavendish. How long I've waited for this day."

He remained silent.

"Show some respect," the soldier snapped.

He delivered a blow to the back of Hal's knees with his sheathed sword. Hal crumpled, and a strangled sob escaped Wren's throat. Mercifully, it was drowned out by the laughter of the spectators. He looked so small and defeated. Not at all how she knew him to be.

"Today, you shall receive judgment for war crimes committed against the Queendom of Danu, as well as the attempted murder of Lord Alistair Lowry. Have you anything to say in your defense?"

Hal kept his head down.

The room fell into a tense, vibrating hush.

"Speak when you're addressed!" The soldier cracked the hilt of his sword against Hal's back, sending him sprawling across the floor.

This wasn't happening. This wasn't real. This was a nightmare she'd surely stir from. At any moment, she'd awake somewhere else—anywhere else. But she found herself out of her seat, her fingers digging into the balcony's cold iron railing. Slowly, Hal heaved himself to his knees and spat a glob of blood onto the floor. It was shocking crimson against the white tile. The crowd jeered again. Although he remained impassive, Wren could see his dread in the tension of his shoulders, the firm set of his jaw.

"So be it." Isabel's voice dripped disdain. "I, Isabel of House Southerland, by the blood of the Goddess queen of Danu, sentence you to die. You will face execution by hanging tomorrow morning. May the Goddess have mercy on your soul."

As the crowd broke into raucous cheers, Lowry eagerly leaned forward in his seat. Isabel held up a hand, and the room fell deathly silent.

"Lord Lowry, as you are now a friend to the crown, I would like to extend a gesture of goodwill. You deserve restitution for the attempt on your life. What will you have?"

Lowry did not hesitate. His eyes gleamed black in the sunlight.

"Before the platform drops, I want his eyes."

The courtiers tittered with laughter. Wren wanted to scream. Did they think this some petty aestheticized justice? Nothing but his typical dramatics and macabre eccentricity?

"And I want Wren Southerland to remove them for me. I do, after all, owe her a debt for saving my life."

Every head on the balcony turned toward her, but Wren kept her attention trained on the dais. Isabel was staring at Lowry, and

although she couldn't see her clearly through the layers of lace and
pomp, Wren knew she was hesitating. She'd never agree to his demand; it was complete madness—and far too much to ask for after
the soldiers he'd already taken.

"Very well. You shall have them."

No. Wren wanted to throw herself at Isabel's feet and beg. *Please,
no. You can't do this. You can't make me do this.*

Whether or not Isabel's decree satisfied the crowd, Wren didn't
know. She heard only the frantic sound of her breathing, and as
her vision constricted like the tightening of a noose, she saw only
Lowry as he smiled. It was a slow, terrible smile that split open his
face like a knife drawn across flesh.

If she did this, Lowry would possess the very magic that had
turned the tide of war in Vesria's favor. Now that he had the queen's
trust, it would take only a glance to plunge the government into
utter chaos. The havoc he could wreak on Danu . . . Wren didn't
want to imagine it. *And I won't have to,* she thought. Getting Hal
safely to Vesria would delay the outbreak of a war that would doom
them all. From there, they'd figure out how to dislodge Lowry's
hold on Isabel. They'd save their people together.

But first she'd have to free him.

She had no allies. No combat skills. No plan. She needed at
least one of those things—and quickly. No matter what happened
or what Lowry took from her, he'd never stop. Until he had what
he wanted, he'd never let her go. She'd escaped Colwick Hall, but
now there was nowhere left to run.

CHAPTER THIRTY-TWO

In a secluded turn on the palace's marble staircase, Wren curled into herself and listened to the dull roar of the crowd. It wasn't far enough away to feel safe, but at least it was dark. In the throne room, it had been too bright, too overwhelming.

Here in the stairwell, a single point of light streamed through the sliver of a window at her side. It reminded her of a confessional, cramped and airless, like the ones she'd spent so many hours of her childhood huddled within. She'd once found it difficult to dredge up failures and sins to lay bare. Now, it was too easy. She had far too many to name.

The cold stone beneath her and the glass at her cheek grounded her. But her thoughts still came in a panicked rush, all of them spiraling into the same inevitable images.

Hal's hanged body swinging to the *tick, tick, tick* of one hundred clocks.

His eyes like gems in her bloody hands.

If she dwelled on it a moment longer, she was going to be sick.

Once, she'd dreamed of the day Hal would stand trial for his crimes. Now, she could only wonder at how thoroughly she'd un-made herself, caring for the Reaper of Vesria. She'd always known what they had couldn't last. She'd tried to protect herself from the pain of losing him, of wanting him when duty would inevitably call him away from her. Time and time again, she'd measured out the distance between them. And just as many times, she'd run head-long toward him.

Her stupid, reckless heart.

If only she could despise him as she was supposed to. It would be far easier to hate him than to feel the way she did for him. And yet, it had been so easy—too easy—to love him. She couldn't have fought it.

Despite her best efforts, he'd changed her, smeared all her black-and-white beliefs into gray. Now she'd carry him with her forever, a bright, tender flame to keep safe. Even now, she could still feel the warmth of his arms around her, the shyness of his smile against her mouth. Still heard the gentleness of his voice when he spoke to her, the dry wit when he indulged her. Still saw all those hidden, bril-liant blues in his eyes—and deeper still, such sadness, such hope.

Hal had let her believe, for the first time in her life, that it was alright to feel passionately, fiercely. And oh, she did. She *did*. If any feeling would kill her, it was this one. She was in love with Hal Cavendish, and he would never know it.

Wren let out a shaky breath and buried her face in her hands. She couldn't do nothing, no matter how afraid she was. She couldn't lose him. Every path—try or try not—led to death. It led to war. She might as well go down fighting.

Down two flights of stairs, a door creaked open and jerked Wren out of her thoughts. It admitted a wash of noise from the throne room, fever-pitched jeers and stomping feet. Then it slammed shut, muffling Wren in imperfect silence—until the footsteps began, a staccato, determined beat.

They were coming toward her, but Wren was resigned to her fate. She lifted her eyes. Through the haze of tears and the wayward tendrils of her hair, she saw Una standing on the flight below her. Her face was impassive, as hard as granite, but Wren knew exactly where to look for the fault lines in her military polish. As well as she hid it, Una looked exhausted.

Neither of them spoke. Wren wasn't sure how they could ever shove off the weight of everything unsaid between them.

At last, Una asked, "Can I sit?"

Wren only turned her face toward the window and lifted one noncommittal shoulder in response. From here, she could see the glittering, black band of the River Muri as it snaked through the city. It felt as if those murky, frigid waters were filling the space between them. She'd never felt so cold, so distant, as if she were seeing Una waver from thirty feet below.

Una sat on the stair beside Wren. "We need to talk."

Wren had no energy to talk, but she had no energy to tell her to leave, either.

"Fine. *I'll* talk. You listen." In profile, Una's eye was washed golden in the late sunlight, her shadow cast long and jagged down the stairway. "Back at Colwick Hall, I was angry. Ever since you deserted, I've been so angry and confused."

She trailed off. Even now, it seemed Una could not help skirting around the raw, impossible admission: *You hurt me.* But Wren could hear it plain, and the barest slither of guilt coiled around her heart.

"I was ready to forgive you. But when you told me about Lowry, I couldn't let myself believe you. I couldn't let myself believe the queen would ally herself with a monster." Wren waited for the apology. None came. "What was I supposed to do?"

"You were supposed to trust me! You were supposed to help me. If you'd believed me, none of this would be happening."

"If you'd sabotaged that alliance like you sabotaged everything else, the queen *would* execute you." Una's anger rose to meet hers. "I was trying to protect you!"

"Protect me?" Wren snarled. "Is that what you did back in Cernos, when you called me weak? Or when you yelled at me when our prisoner attacked me?"

"I didn't yell at you. Are you still angry about that kid?" Una asked impatiently. "You could have gotten yourself killed."

"I was suffocating, Una." An unwelcome, shameful heat burned behind her eyes. She refused to cry in front of her again. "Sometimes I think I've been slowly dying for years. I healed that boy because I was following my gut. My *heart*. I don't understand how kindness can be so wrong."

The muffled noise of the crowd filled the silence between them.

"You know," Wren said slowly, "now I'm beginning to doubt that my feelings are actually what's gotten me in trouble. Maybe it's because I was too busy second-guessing myself and criticizing myself. Hating myself. Maybe that's what made me weak."

Una's steely expression fractured into a thousand pieces. "I didn't want you to get hurt, Wren. You were always so easily hurt."

I was trying to protect you. When had love become a weapon with which to destroy each other? She hugged her knees and squeezed tight. If she didn't hold herself together, she would fly apart. She just knew it.

After an eternity, Una said, "I'm sorry."

Wren flinched in surprise. "What?"

"Don't make me repeat myself." Then, she sighed, a defeated, anxious sound. "I should have listened to you. I should have trusted you. And I shouldn't have said all those awful things to you at the ball. I was wrong, and I'm sorry."

Wren watched the dust swirl through thick bars of sunlight. She pressed her hands into the cold stone beneath her. These were real things, solid things. What she was hearing . . . She had to be imagining it. In all the years they'd known each other, she could count on both hands the number of times Una had ever apologized to her. She was too stunned to answer immediately. But Una was waiting, and in the uncertain slant of her eyebrows was something unfamiliar. Vulnerability.

"You were following the queen's orders," Wren said. "I understand why you did what you did."

"Following orders. I've spent my whole life following orders.

I thought that was the best way I could serve Danu. What's a country but the strength of its queen?" Bitterness crept into her voice. "But it's clear to me now that I've kept my eyes half shut. What the queen wants for Danu isn't what's best *or* what's right. If she executes Cavendish, bloodshed is unavoidable. I won't sit idly by while that snake Lowry encourages her to needlessly sacrifice lives. Not when those lives are in my hands."

"Why are you telling me all this?" Wren's voice wavered with uncertainty, with stubborn hope.

"I know you've got some kind of scheme," Una said. "I want in."

Wren could only stare at her. This was *Una Dryden,* the queen's most loyal servant. Unwavering in her pursuit of order and justice. A future general. The Una Wren knew did not choose Hal Cavendish as the lesser of two evils. And she certainly did not encourage any of Wren's harebrained schemes.

"Why should I trust you now, after everything we've done to each other?"

Una crossed her arms. "I don't blame you if you don't trust me, but frankly, it'd be wasted effort to sabotage your plan from within. It's you and Cavendish against the entire country. The odds aren't good."

"Thanks," Wren muttered sourly. At least she could always count on Una's honesty. More tentatively, she said, "You joining us doesn't exactly improve our odds much, you know. Why would you throw away everything you've worked for?"

"I don't want success if innocent lives are the price. Besides, what kind of commanding officer . . ." Una shook her head, drawing in a deep breath. "What kind of friend would I be if I let you do this alone?"

Wren squeezed her eyes shut, desperate to hold back tears. "I don't know, Una. They have him under constant surveillance of the Guard in the Tower, and it's not like we can just waltz in there. . . ."

Or can we?

"I recognize that look in your eyes," Una said dryly. "What're you thinking?"

"You and I are the ones who captured him, which means we're the queen's favorites in everyone else's eyes."

"Right."

"And you're a Captain of the Guard."

"Right," she said, more hesitantly.

"Which means no one will question us if we visit his cell. It'll be easy to get in, and as long as we time it right and disguise him, we'll be able to walk out the front door."

"That is the most absurd, incautious plan I've ever heard."

Wren braced herself for rejection.

"But since his execution is tomorrow," Una said, "it's the only one we have."

Wren let out a shaky breath. While they could easily clear the North Tower's security checkpoints, she wasn't as sure they could get *out*. If they slipped up, they would hang alongside Hal. While it was a sentence Wren was willing to face, she couldn't ask Una to do the same. "This is far from guaranteed success. You'd really die for Hal Cavendish?"

"I would gladly see him hang. But for today, I will put aside my feelings and tolerate his existence. What matters is the truth and the greater good. But you seem to think he's worth saving for his own sake."

"I wanted to hate him. I did hate him." Wren lowered her gaze. "But then I got to know him. He's patient and perceptive and . . . good-hearted, deep down. Nothing can ever change what he did, but he wants to make things right. I have to put my faith in him and believe there's another path for Danu and Vesria."

"And what is that? Without justice, we have nothing."

"Justice got us here. Justice will kill us all."

"So what do you propose instead?"

"Forgiveness."

"Forgiveness?" Una scoffed. "That's a pretty thought, but we can't change centuries of war. It's in our blood now."

"Dialysis, then. One person at a time."

"Impractical as ever." Una laughed tonelessly, a broken sound that resolved into a sigh. "I'm sorry, Wren. I really, really am."

In the end, that was what broke her. Those quiet, childlike *really*s.

"I forgive you. And I'm sorry, too. I never meant to hurt you. I never meant to put so much on you. After I was suspended, I was so scared I wasn't thinking straight. I just couldn't give up on Byers, and I was so worried you'd be next. There was a part of me that still—"

Una winced. "You don't have to say it."

"I *need* to. Not talking about it never made it go away, as much as you wanted otherwise. I still loved you, Una."

"I know," she said hoarsely. "But I never could have given you what you needed."

No, she couldn't have. For weeks now, she'd known that. At Colwick Hall, she'd been too busy to think much of Una—and when she did, she realized, it wasn't with the same lovesick pining she'd felt in Danu. Wren still loved her. Just not in the same way anymore.

"I know that now," Wren said. "I just wish we could have had this conversation sooner."

"I was a coward." Una bowed her head. "I always believed nothing scared me until . . . Wanting you made me more vulnerable than I was ready to be. Maybe it makes me selfish, but with the fraternization laws, I couldn't put you before my job."

"I understand."

Just like that, everything between them was laid bare. The horrible tangle of hurt and anger and confusion between them tugged a little looser. Wren thought she could see a wobble in the firm line of Una's mouth.

The day Una cries, I will crumble. The whole world might.

"That settles it," Una said gruffly. "We've both done wrong. We're moving past it."

Wren knocked their knees together. "Although if we're

quantifying this, technically I've done worse. I probably broke every article in Danu's Code of Military Justice."

Una snorted a laugh before catching herself. She lifted her shoulder and brushed it across her lips, as if she could wipe her smile off. "I missed you."

Wren couldn't help but grin back. "I missed you, too. Friends again?"

"Friends again."

Warmth bloomed within Wren's chest, sparkling and light. But almost immediately, Una's expression hardened again. She stood and extended her hand into the space between them. "As much as I'd love to properly catch up, we have a war criminal to free."

Wren took her hand, and as Una pulled her to her feet, she felt as though she were emerging from frigid waters. All her doubt, all her hurt, streamed off in heavy rivulets. Everything still ached, but with Una at her side, Wren felt as if she could truly breathe again.

CHAPTER THIRTY-THREE

The weight of her military uniform felt heavy and familiar. Still, Wren had almost missed its dour plainness: black tunic and black breeches tucked into perfectly polished black boots. She'd almost forgotten the delightful jangle of her medals and the jaunty sashay of her epaulettes.

"You look far too *enthused* to be on duty," Una had said as she pinned Wren's slouchy, silver-banded cap in place.

"Allow me my moment in the sun."

Una had only sighed.

But as soon as they stepped through the gates to the North Tower, all her giddiness melted away. She wished she weren't so bitterly surprised by how easy it was to navigate the Tower's security when everyone believed them to be the queen's golden children. Every Guardsman they passed snapped an eager salute.

Una wore her authority easily, her chin held imperiously high and her eyes coldly sweeping over the ranks. Their comrades kept their gazes determinedly disinterested, their backs rigid, but Wren sensed their strain. It was the little things, the stutter of their pulses as Una prowled by, the glitter of sweat in the lanternlight. Everyone on duty was restless and distracted tonight, she noted. All of them felt the pressure of protecting a high-profile prisoner—or perhaps envied their off-duty comrades, who were likely reveling tonight in honor of Hal's imminent demise.

Wren and Una climbed staircase after staircase, wound-tight helixes that dizzied Wren. Her breaths came harder with nerves and exertion, too loud in the cramped darkness. It was broken only by hazy squares of stained-glass light, reflections of haloed saints and warrior queens. At last, the stairwell emptied into a circular corridor, the outermost layer of a prison laid out like the concentric rings of a tree. At its heart, like the rotten pit of a fruit, was Hal's cell.

A small contingent of soldiers stood watch at the gate. They were young, as most of the Guard was, but these ones looked particularly green. They radiated the tense, frenetic energy of a puppy learning its first trick, their postures too rigid, their eyes too eager. They would slaver over the prospect of impressing their new captain. It was almost mortifying to remember herself like that, so hungry to please her superiors.

Una strode forward with purposeful confidence. Even the shadows shrank back from her and her lantern's leaping light. The Guardsman in charge, a boy Wren recognized as Sergeant Wilson, regarded Una with strangled awe. His boots clacked together as he saluted her. "Captain Dryden. What can I do for you?"

"You're relieved of your post, Sergeant." She spoke with an icy superiority to rival the queen herself. "Lieutenant Southerland and I have orders from the queen to make preparations for tomorrow."

"The eyes are a very delicate part of the body," Wren added gravely. "One that can suffer significant trauma if mishandled. You wouldn't believe amount of fluid in the eye."

One of the younger Guardsman went positively green with nausea. Wilson maintained his salute, his lip twitching, his pink skin flushing, as if he'd forgotten how to move. "Do you have the queen's written order?"

"I just left a meeting with her," Una said. Then, with practiced condescension, she asked, "Are you questioning Her Majesty's judgment?"

"N-no," he stammered. "It's just . . ."

"Just what?"

"W-well, it's only that she always communicates by written order. DCMJ article eighty-seven (a) s-says . . . any person who abandons their post for any reason can be court-martialed."

With the certainty of rules behind him, the familiar rhythms of recitation, he found a new steadiness to his voice. He sounded *devout,* as if he'd been entrusted with some divine purpose. Wren pitied him as much as she envied him. Her life would be much easier if she had such respect for authority.

"Major Herman told me this was a special mission, and I was not to leave under any circumstances," he added. "With such a high-profile charge, I can't trust anyone."

Una's smile sharpened. "Are you accusing me of something?"

"What?" He blanched. "No! I mean—no, ma'am. Never."

"Then need I remind you that, according to DCMJ article seventy-six, any person who willfully disobeys the lawful order of a commissioned officer or who behaves with disrespectful deportment will be court-martialed? So what will it be, Sergeant? A court-martial for insubordination or for abandoning your post?"

At this, the rest of his unit muttered anxiously behind him. Wren watched the gears turn behind the sheen of Wilson's glasses and saw the very moment he came to the realization that no protocol existed for this situation. He looked utterly despondent.

Una made a show of surveying his uniform and clucked her tongue at a single missing button on his tunic. "Just who is your commanding officer? Major Herman, you said? I ought to tell her she needs to run a tighter ship. You wouldn't pass snuff under my command with that out-of-regulation uniform."

Wilson clapped a hand over the offending empty space. "I was going to get it sewn tomorrow! I swear."

"And what do you suppose Major Herman will do when she hears that her subordinate not only disobeyed his superior's orders, but also did it as a slovenly embarrassment to her unit?"

A sheen of sweat broke out on Wilson's upper lip, a wet twin to his patchy blond wisp of a mustache.

"I respect you, Wilson," Una said with a calculated lilt. "You follow policy as religiously as the Goddess's decrees. That's rare these days. It would be a shame to see you disciplined for such a tiny mistake."

His throat bobbed. His face sagged. Then, with great resignation, he said, "Thank you, Captain. I'm so sorry for the miscommunication."

"Enjoy the rest of your evening."

He saluted as if that were an order. "Yes, ma'am. We will."

Sergeant Wilson and his unit vacated their post like frenzied ants. The heavy doors banged shut, swallowing the sound of their footsteps.

Una curled her lip. "Pathetic."

"I think you scarred him for life," Wren said.

Una tossed her hair over her shoulder. "Or maybe this will be a lesson in fortitude."

"Maybe."

Una pulled out a set of keys and began to unbolt the locks on Hal's cell. With every clang and whine of loose metal, Wren's anxiety climbed higher. Una ran her fingers uncertainly along the door's handle. "You may not like what you see."

"I don't care."

Una pushed open the door. What lay beyond was a windowless room that smelled of stagnant water and the dull tang of blood. The light of her lantern pushed back the darkness and illuminated a still figure in the corner.

Hal.

Wren's heart leapt in sheer relief, and she all but ran to his side. He was hunched over in a chair, bound at the ankles and wrists. With his head hanging, his hair fell over his face and concealed most of him from view. All she could see was the feathered, purpled edges of a bruise that crept like ivy from underneath the frayed blindfold.

"Wren." She didn't have to touch him, didn't have to speak, for him to recognize her. His voice was thick with relief and rough with strain. "I thought maybe I'd imagined the feeling of you close by."

"You didn't." She couldn't help gently tracing his jaw with trembling fingers before she found the edge of the blindfold. "I'm here."

Little by little, she peeled it away, as if readying to expose a festering wound to air. When she'd bared him, the sight turned her stomach. His left eye was swollen almost completely shut. Mottled bruises streaked his face, and thin lacerations notched his cheekbones, like the skin had split open from the force of the blows.

Her anger razed all her joy, all her relief. Hal was a war criminal, but this . . . How could they do this to him? This wasn't justice. It was vengeance, stolen and enacted in the moments when no one was watching.

She swallowed her fury like a hot coal. She could feed this feeling later. For now, she needed to assess him for any critical damage— and then get him out. The pupil of his good eye was a pinprick. The other swallowed his irises entirely. He was concussed at the very least, but he was *alive.*

He offered her an uncertain smile. Wren shook her head, fighting the urge to throw her arms around him. "You look ghastly."

Hal's gaze drifted downward and snagged on the gleaming medals adorning her uniform. She couldn't tell if he looked impressed or mournful—or maybe a bit of both. "So do you."

"Save the teary reunion for later," Una cut in. "We only have an hour until the next shift arrives and finds the post deserted."

At the sound of Una's voice, Hal tensed.

She crossed the room and made quick work of the chains binding him, easing them onto the floor in rattling coils. Wren swore the room temperature dropped several degrees as Hal glared at the side of Una's face.

"Do you have something to say to me, Cavendish?"

Una had agreed to rescue him, but Wren supposed she couldn't expect her hostility to fade immediately. And although Hal was trying to improve his relationship with the Danubian people, Una *did* order his arrest.

Wren grabbed their shoulders. "Save it. Both of you. If this plan is going to work, I need to make him look like he hasn't been dragged a mile from the back of a carriage."

Una sneered but turned away. She paced the room, her hair billowing out behind her like a war banner. Heaving a sigh of relief, Wren crouched by Hal's side and began to tend to the worst of the bruises on his face.

"How did you . . . ?"

"Una helped." Exhaustion and overuse made slow, painful work of it, but Wren watched his face smooth out under her magic's silver glow. "I know she's thorny, but I promise you can trust her."

Hal looked entirely unconvinced but said nothing.

Once she finished, she rested her hands on his cheeks and turned his head from side to side, inspecting him for any further visible damage. "How does that feel?"

"Better." He frowned. "But they'll still recognize me."

"Only if they look too close." Wren opened her bag and dropped a neatly folded uniform in his lap. "But with Una and me, they won't. We're going to walk out the front door."

Hal lifted the black greatcoat as though it would bite.

"What?" Una said peevishly. "Too proud to wear Danubian colors?"

He remained implacably blank, and then with frosty derision said, "No. Only to share colors with you."

Una barked out a bitter laugh. "So he does speak."

Wren wanted to shake him, to beg him to let Una see even a *glimpse* of what he'd shown her, any scrap of kindness, any scrap of remorse. He wasn't exactly making her case easy, even if it had been Una's idea to free him in the first place.

"Can you *try* to be nice?" she muttered.

"For you," Hal said tersely, "fine."

He began to remove his tattered shirt. Wren averted her eyes, trying to ignore the *pop* of buttons and the *shush* of discarded fabric.

Finally, he said, "I'm ready."

When she turned, she bit down on her lip to stifle an embarrassing response. Even if he hadn't always wanted to be a soldier, Wren had to admit he was born to wear a uniform. As she admired the crisp lines of his shoulders and the braided silver aiguillette draped across his chest, heat spread across her cheeks.

"You look . . ."

"Please don't finish that sentence," Una said.

"I was going to say *ready*." Wren huffed. "We're ready."

From a shadowed corner of the room, Una's eyes were as dark and cold as the underside of a stone. "Before we do anything, Cavendish, understand this. I may be serving as your glorified bodyguard until you're safely home, but once this is over, you will pay for your crimes. Whether it's two weeks or two decades from now, I will make sure of it."

"You speak with such conviction, but I have seen officers like you before," Hal said icily. "You cling to an image of yourself as impartial and cold, but you're governed by your grudges. I doubt you will last long enough to see your promise through."

Una unsheathed the sword at her hip. "Insult me again. I dare you."

"That's enough!" Wren growled. "Both of you, stop it."

"Yes, go on!" Una snarled. "Hide behind her. Hide behind all your goddessdamned shields like the coward you are."

"I said—"

"Captain Dryden is right." Una lowered her sword at the same moment Hal bowed his head. "I don't expect or deserve your acceptance. Please forgive me for my rudeness."

"Ah." As Una slunk closer to him, her boots tapped out a deadly rhythm on the floor. She placed the hilt of her blade under his chin, forcing him to look at her. There was a predatory glow in her eyes, as if she intended to carve out the flicker of vulnerability he'd shown. To study it. To destroy it. "There it is. Weak for a girl, like the worst of us."

The acid in her voice, however, couldn't disguise her fear.

Of course she was afraid—Una had risked *everything* to be here.

She could have turned a blind eye to the evidence and kept the promotion she'd always wanted. She could have killed Hal on sight back in Cernos. But Una had always done the right thing, even if it was the hard thing. And after everything Una had seen in the war, after everything she'd lost, maybe saving Hal was the *hardest* thing.

"You expect me to believe someone like you is capable of caring for her—for anyone? You've wiped out entire Danubian units single-handedly. You've killed children. Healers. Your own comrades. What you've done is unforgivable."

"Yes. I know."

"You know." Una let out a bitter sound. "Then you know you don't deserve her."

"I know that more than anything. But I will try to. I swear to you that I'll work to restore peace between our nations and repair what harm I've caused."

"How can you possibly fix what's been done?" With a single motion, she flipped her blade so that the point rested a bare inch from his throat. "For people like you, there is no justice but death."

"When Vesria and Danu are stable, I will gladly face a tribunal for what I've done." Hal met her gaze steadily. "But for now, let's agree that there cannot be another war. Not for my sake."

Neither of them moved.

Then, with a tortured twist of her mouth, Una lowered her blade. She sheathed it with a high, ringing sound. "Fine. We can agree on that much."

Wren heaved a sigh of relief.

Hal busied himself with readjusting the cuff links on his jacket. "Where do we go from here?"

Una crossed her arms. "The abbey."

The Order of the Maiden had often been a safe harbor for the needy and destitute, but Wren wasn't sure if her Sisters' devout generosity extended to dangerous fugitives. Aside from train hopping or boarding the next boat to the mainland, packed in with people who'd sell them out for the promise of coin and glory, what other choice did they have?

"We'll stay until nightfall tomorrow. Then we'll take you to the Vesrian border," Wren said. "Everybody knows our faces, so I don't like the idea of traveling by daylight."

Hal seemed to turn it over, nodding. "What do you need me to do?"

"As soon as you're home, call off your dogs," Una said. "If you can convince the magisterium to hold their fire until Wren and I deal with Lowry, we should be able to avoid any unnecessary bloodshed."

A thin, almost confused crease appeared between Hal's eyebrows. "Thank you for this."

"Don't thank me. It's for Danu, not you."

"Even so, I'm grateful for your help."

"You're *grateful*. Aren't you a saint?"

"Una, please," Wren groaned, burying her face in her hands. "Can we focus?"

"Just follow my orders." Una scowled. "Both of you, and stay close."

"Captain," Hal replied dutifully.

Outside the cell, the *tick, tick, tick* of the clocks intensified, counting the too-long spaces between Wren's anxious breaths. They walked in a single file, Una leading the way with the rickety sway and bob of the lantern. Hal followed close behind her, his eyes downcast and the brim of his hat pulled low across his brow. Through the tether, Wren could feel the wild race of his heart.

As they passed a window, she caught a glimpse of the crescent moon and felt all her blood run cold. It matched the sinister curve of Lowry's smile, the memory of it burned behind her eyelids like a scar. But he wasn't here, and soon enough, she would be safe.

Her thoughts, however, took on the playful lilt of his accent.

Can you be so sure?

CHAPTER THIRTY-FOUR

It was remarkably easy to disappear in Knockaine.

Winter had raked its claws across the River Muri, dredging up thick curtains of coal-laced fog. Along the riverbanks, it coagulated so thick that drivers dismounted from their carriages and led their horses by torchlight. Traffic slowed to a crawl because of collisions, and eerie, disembodied voices echoed in the alleyways. Wren kept her eyes fixed on the grime-caked streets.

"There is so much mud," Hal said.

"It's not mud," Wren and Una muttered in unison.

He coughed and pulled his jacket collar up around his nose.

The cold here was nothing like the sharp, thin air of Cernos. This was a wet cold that filled Wren's lungs like phlegm. Every moment in the open wore her ragged. She ached for home, her wide selection of teas, the floral smell of her apothecary, the familiar sound of the creaky old floorboards. But the moment the Guard discovered them missing, her flat—or Una's—would be the first place they'd check.

So Wren let her feet carry her to the only sanctuary they had left. A few miles down the road, where the buildings grew short and petered out into empty fields, Wren stopped at the abbey gates. Its enormous rose window was illuminated like a harvest moon.

Wren rang the bell and took a cautious step backward. After a few minutes, the gates rattled open and Mother Heloise stepped out of the shadows. Time slowed to a crawl as she took them in one by one.

For Una, guarded surprise.

For Wren, concern and fear braided together.

And when she recognized Hal, her face twisted into something unrecognizable.

"You." The Healing Touch glowed on her hands, as razor-sharp as a scalpel.

Wren threw herself in front of him, her arms outstretched. "Don't! I can explain everything."

"How dare you bring *him* to my door? Do you have a death wish?"

"It's only until tomorrow night," Una said, her hand on the hilt of her sword.

"I don't care if it's one hour or one day—"

"You have every right to hate me," Hal interjected. "I understand I have done things even your Goddess cannot forgive, but I ask for your mercy."

The silver light continued to flicker like a pale flame.

"Please, Mother," Wren pressed. "Let me explain."

"Go on, then."

Heloise's face remained impassive while Wren laid out everything they'd uncovered, from Isabel's collusion with Lowry to his sinister plan to expand Cernos's reach with stolen magic. "If we don't get Hal out of the city, we're all lost. We don't have anywhere else to go."

"You want to end these wars?" Heloise asked Hal. Her hand was still leveled at his axillary artery at the lateral margin of his rib. He'd bleed out in minutes if she cut it.

"Yes. More than anything."

Heloise did not respond at first. They must have looked like a ragtag bunch, all of them exhausted and afraid, because Heloise's resistance gave way to numb acceptance. The Touch faded from her hand and plunged them into darkness. With a long sigh, she stepped aside to let them pass. "Hurry. Before someone sees you."

Wren could have sobbed in relief. "Thank you."

The three of them piled inside, and as soon as the doors banged shut, Heloise rounded on Hal. "If a single one of the girls in my care is hurt because of you, I will show no mercy."

"I understand," he said. "I owe you my life for your hospitality."

Heloise grunted dismissively, clearly already tired of him. "Come on, then."

For an old woman with a lurching gait, she could *move* when she wanted. Wren fell into step beside her. Heloise's silence weighted down her shoulders like a cloak of lead. Even years removed from her apprenticeship, one sharp look was enough to make her wither. But when she snuck a glance at Heloise's face, there was cool assessment in the thin press of her lips—no judgment.

"Saving that man is among the worst of your ideas, Sister Wren," she said wearily, as soon as she'd pulled them ahead of Hal and Una. "And I have seen you through the fallout of many."

"Without a doubt. I'm ready for my lecture."

"I haven't much breath left in me to waste," Heloise said snappishly. "I did advise you to burn that letter."

"In retrospect, that might have been wise." They walked through the halls, the light from the low-burning chandeliers running down stone pillars like melted wax. "That mistake has cost me and my friends everything. Even if we survive, everything is ruined. Lowry still has the queen's ear. She'll still go to war if Parliament doesn't check her."

Heloise let out a disbelieving sound. "Truly, you have never listened to a single word I've said. What does the Goddess teach us?" When Wren didn't respond immediately, she said, "It is not until you have lost everything that you can begin anew."

Wren did not know what to say.

"Times are changing," Heloise said after a beat.

"I think so, too." Wren stole a look over her shoulder at Hal. He walked just a few paces behind Una, his shoulders stiff as he gazed solemnly up at the ribbed ceiling. "I can only hope for the better."

Heloise stopped in front of two doors. "You may stay here for now, but I want you gone by sundown tomorrow. May the Goddess keep you."

"Thank you, Mother. I can't repay you for—"

"Think not of it until this is over." Heloise hobbled straight ahead, the steady *thunk* of her cane announcing each stride. "Good night."

The three of them lingered uncertainly in the hall, attended only by the sound of fire whispering in torches. The air was redolent with the smells of smoke and frankincense. Una broke the uneasy silence first. "Try to get some sleep. We've got a long day tomorrow, and you look like you need it, Cavendish."

"Yes." Hal cut her an irritated look. "Your men made it quite difficult to sleep."

"Good night!" Wren cut in brightly. "Sleep well."

"Good night." With a last, withering glare at Hal, Una disappeared into one of the rooms. Their journey to Vesria would be long—even longer with these two constantly sniping at each other. After everything they'd survived, they'd better not kill each other on the way.

When she turned over her shoulder, she caught Hal regarding her as if he wanted to ask her a question. Although his expression was soft, she could see his exhaustion. He wore it like the weight of a thousand years. Understandable, when he'd been sentenced to death only earlier today.

That was when it struck her. They'd escaped from the North Tower. They were fugitives. They were alive. He must have come to the same realization, because the air grew thick and magnetic between them. Moonlight filtered through the latticed windows like water through a sieve, washing everything soft and shimmery.

"This is impossible," Wren whispered.

"It is."

At first, neither of them moved, paralyzed by the weight of it. She worried that he would shatter if she touched him. She feared he would vanish if she so much as blinked. But she needed to make sure he was real. She needed to hold him. If not now, then when?

They stepped toward each other in unison, and all her hesitation evaporated. Wren flung her arms wide and latched herself around his middle. His warmth seeped into her, and she wanted nothing more than to drown in the comfort of it, the knowledge that he was safe and here with her. He pressed his lips to the top of her head.

"Goddess above, Hal. I can't . . . I was so . . ." What word could sufficiently capture what grief he'd put her through? Wren stifled a sob, caught somewhere between anguish and relief. "I never should have let you go through with that plan!"

"It went better than expected," he offered. "I'm alive."

"This isn't the time for jokes!" She pulled back enough to glare at him. "They hurt you. I should have made it to you sooner. I should have done something at that trial, or—"

"Please don't worry about me. I'm fine."

"Don't worry? Do you want me to quit drawing breath? Quit thinking? That's what you're asking of me. This never would have happened if not for me."

"This was not your fault. It was my choice. One I would gladly make again if it meant protecting you." He cupped the side of her face, his thumb tracing the line of her cheekbone. "Besides, I've endured worse."

Wren shook her head, her throat stinging with a sudden rush of emotion. She swallowed it down. *Not yet.* "You have an unmatched talent for minimizing things, Cavendish. It's impressive."

When she dared to look up again, his expression was wide open. How could she ever have thought him unreadable? Right now, his eyes were clear, shining blue, and she saw her own heart reflected back at her.

"Come on," she murmured, twining her fingers with his. "I'll show you where you can wash up."

The air tasted bittersweet. Like salt and smog and home.

After she'd unbuttoned herself from her uniform and changed into a nightdress, Wren pressed her face against the cracked-open window beside the bed. She sucked in gulps of cold, polluted air. If she died for her country, she wanted to remember it well. Through the thick black fog, she saw only the faint glimmer of the city lights and smelled little but ash and sheep. But she felt the precious heartbeat of lives all around her.

This, she told herself. *This is what I'm doing it for.*

The door creaked open, drawing her out of her reverie. Silent and steady as the night, Hal entered the room and slid into bed beside her, as though it were the most natural thing in the world. Wren leaned back into him, breathing in the clean smell of soap: honey and herbs.

"Have you ever been to Knockaine before?" she asked.

"I haven't."

With a wry smile, she tipped her chin up toward him. "And how do you like it?"

She swore she could hear his brain churning as he grasped for something polite to say. "It's lively."

"You can say it. It smells here. We all know it." From here, she could see a storm rolling in off the sea, black as fog. It reminded her of the Vesrian raids she'd seen as a girl. Another one could come at any moment. Desperate to shove that thought aside, she said, "What's it like in Greine?"

Hal hummed pensively. "It is still rebuilding, but there's less ironwork, less poverty. If Knockaine is gray, Greine is white. There are arcades filled with stores and cafes and universities. In the afternoons, people walk in the parks."

Wren closed her eyes, imagining a city washed in golden sunlight. "A paradise, then."

"Hardly. Your government is far more liberal in affording rights and positions of power to those without magic." He paused. "There's corruption in the government. War hawks and religious fundamentalists keep the populace in fear. For any hope of change, I'll have to burn it down."

"You're going to make a lot of enemies." Wren threaded her fingers into his again and squeezed.

"I already have a lot of enemies," he said wearily. "It will be a long and gradual process. Someday, I hope you can see it."

She did, too. A small, new part of her longed to help him make it better. But all she said was, "I know I will someday."

As the silence settled, Wren turned toward him and placed her hand on his chest. Silver light veiled her palm as she swept his system for any lingering damage. Anything that remained, however, was beyond her power. The last of his sickness had cleared, and his injuries were the kind she could not see and could not reach, the ones he kept locked away. If only the Healing Touch could go deeper than bone.

The magic faded from her hand, and the bond between them sizzled. It grew fainter each day now that his body had healed itself enough to push her energy out.

In the stillness, Wren thought of tomorrow. If she could not fix what her people had done to him and she could not fight alongside him, then maybe she could do something else.

"Hal?" When he looked up, she wrung her hands together. "Will you let me finish healing your eyes? In case something happens tomorrow, I want to make sure you can protect yourself."

He hesitated. "Don't exhaust yourself for my sake."

Wren knew this would be close to the end of what her ravaged *fola* could endure. Although she'd used her magic sparingly since she'd returned to Danu, three days was hardly enough time to recover completely from the strain she'd put on her system in Colwick Hall. But right now, she couldn't bring herself to worry. "I'll be fine."

"It seems we both have a talent for minimizing things."

Wren laughed, startling herself. "I suppose we do. Make yourself comfortable."

As she leaned against the headboard, Hal laid his head in her lap. It would never fail to astound her how he'd transformed healing from something so clinical, so practiced, to something so intimate. It hurt less to use her magic now. It was all numb, all sputtering and soft like a low-burning candle. As she bent over him, nearly touching her forehead to his, her hair came loose from its messy chignon. Behind this makeshift curtain, there was nothing and no one but Hal. Nothing but the sensation of her magic binding them up, tighter and tighter, like a row of sutures. To lose him now would rend her open.

I love you, she thought. *Let nothing tear us apart again.* But she couldn't say it. Already, she wasn't sure if she could let him go when they made it to Vesria.

When her hair fell onto his face, he tucked it behind her ear. It broke the spell, just a little, and let the world back in. By the time she finished, his face had relaxed. The pain, harbored secretly for years, finally receded. He opened his eyes, and in them was the same emotion as the first time she had dared to gaze into them. Awe.

Goddess above, would she ever get used to the way he looked at her?

"Thank you," he said.

Her throat went dry. "It's the very least I can do."

The magic flickered from her hands, and when she tried to call on it again, the air was breathless and still, the dark unbroken. It did not answer her. So this was it. Her magic for his.

Wren had always known this was a possibility, but it still felt like something had been stolen. There was a void in her heart where her magic once slept. Rationally, she knew another healer could restore it. It might even come back with rest alone. But it didn't stave off the raw panic. If it never came back, she would never plumb the depths of that emptiness. She would never be whole again.

She would be just Wren. *Nothing.*

But she was still here. Still alive and breathing and fighting, even when she'd been stripped of the one thing she believed defined her. It shook something loose in her. Was this what Hal felt, too, when it happened? Fear that bloomed into acceptance—into relief? She was not her magic. Her worth—her existence—was more than the sum of her talents. Being just Wren was enough.

"It's gone," she said exultantly.

"Gone?"

Wren tore herself away from the guilt in his eyes. "I still feel it, I think. If I really pushed, I think maybe I could still . . . Anyway, as long as I rest, it'll come back. Once you're safe, I'll find a healer to fix it."

"You shouldn't have—"

"It's alright. Really." Wren looked down at her shaking hands. "For so long, I thought my magic was the only good part of me. That it was all I could offer the world."

She found understanding glimmering in his eyes. But if she lingered on it, if she let him comfort her, she would fall apart. She couldn't fall apart yet.

"We should get some rest," she said.

"We should."

It rang hollow. Something shifted in the air. This felt like a goodbye, and Wren was far from ready to give him up. After tonight, they'd never have a moment alone again. It lit her with a desperate, frightening desire.

To her mortification, she found herself tracing the curve of his lower lip with her gaze. She wondered if he knew what effect he had on her. He surely had to, or he wouldn't have that quirk to his mouth, vaguely pleased with himself. Hal lifted himself onto one elbow. Cradling the back of her neck, he drew her closer and kissed her throat, lingering and warm.

With a soft sigh of pleasure, Wren rolled her head back. A figure of the Maiden mounted on the wall landed directly in her eyeline. She was smiling so *knowingly.*

"Oh, no. We can't. She's watching."

Hal followed her gaze and smirked. "Do you want me to cover it?"

"It won't work. She'll still know."

The breathiness of his laughter tickled her ear, and Wren treasured the rareness of the sound. "I see."

"It's a sin, you know." Wren jabbed a finger into his chest. "Strictly forbidden in this Order. You shouldn't even be in here."

"How many ways are we bad for one another?"

"You really want to count the ways?"

His gaze, none too subtly, slid down her body. "None, I believe."

"None?" Wren angled his chin up toward her face again. "Really? Who would have guessed you're a romantic? You don't suppose the reality of our situation is at least *one* strike against our relationship?"

"Maybe." The corners of Hal's eyes creased into a smile, and he slid off the bed to kneel in front of her. The man who would rule Vesria was on his knees, and he regarded her with pure devotion. "Should we survive this, if you will have me, I will follow you wherever you go. Whatever use you have for me, I am at your disposal."

Wren stared down at him, unable to draw a breath. "Why?"

"Because you are the only person who has seen me for something beyond my magic. As anything but a monster. Because you've shown me I know how to do other things than hurt people." Hal's voice, usually so steady, wavered. "Because I . . . care for you."

She heard his true meaning in his hesitation.

"Oh." Wren blinked away tears. No response could be sufficient. She wanted desperately to tell him something, anything, to communicate how much he'd taught her, how much she *felt*. But her panicked mind supplied only one humiliating platitude. "That's the kindest thing anyone's ever said to me."

"I'm glad." Hal rested his chin on her knee. "Although I don't feel much like talking anymore."

She could taste those words like honey spooned into her mouth. There was something so vulnerable, so plain in his yearning, it narrowed her world to the sensation of his skin on hers. To this moment, where she could convince herself they had forever instead of this stolen night.

She carded her hand through his hair. "Maybe we could do something else instead?"

"Something else?" he asked huskily.

He began to draw up her dress, and her breath hitched. With him brushing kisses up her thighs, she couldn't seem to remember why the statue had bothered her anymore. She wasn't even sure she remembered her own name when she felt the heat of his mouth against her. Her head fell back uselessly, and a helpless sound escaped her throat. It was too much. She'd fall apart—she *was* falling apart, the backs of her eyelids shining golden. It was all she could do to ground herself: her fingers buried in his hair, his name on her lips like an incantation, and—

He pulled back, eyes glittering with something like mischief. He left her gasping as she crashed violently back into her body. Before he could say anything, she pulled him in by his lapels and kissed him. Desperation roughened her. Her nails dug into his shoulder, her teeth into his lip. He sucked in an audible breath, equal parts pain and desire. She tasted blood, copper, and adrenaline. A painful reminder that she'd almost lost him and that she might again.

How dare you leave me? she wanted to ask. *What would I have done?*

He held her close, steady. His palms were warm on her waist, his thumbs tracing the arc of her ribs. *I'm here now,* he seemed to say. *I'm with you.*

Wren drew back, panting into the bare space between their lips. In his eyes, she saw her own yearning mirrored: *more.* He gathered up the edge of her dress and said, "Can I take this off?"

"Please."

Hal lifted her nightdress inch by inch over her head, the thin fabric a caress against her skin. Next came her chemise, each layer removed as carefully as the last. When he cast everything aside, leaving her naked under his gaze, Wren had to look away from him. His admiration embarrassed her as much as it thrilled her.

"What?"

"You're so beautiful."

His hands grazed her waist, then the curves of her breasts, with such tenderness, it was as if she were something to be worshipped. She couldn't bear it. She was too impatient, too close to crying that he should make her *hope* like this. Pulling his face back to hers, she kissed him again, clumsily, and fumbled to undress him. His buttons were too-complicated puzzles. His belt clattered too loudly on the floor. Every barrier between them was cumbersome, destructible, as she searched for his bare skin. He let her do it patiently, his eyes hungry and wanting.

At last, she succeeded, her hands splayed out against the solid warmth of his chest. The moment she removed everything between them, Hal pulled her against him as though he couldn't bear being apart from her a moment longer than necessary. His weight settled over her, everywhere they touched hot and aching.

His usual confidence faded as he stared down at her. In its place was something strange on him. Nervousness. She couldn't reassure him, really. Not when her heart thrummed against his with equal parts anxiety and anticipation. She brushed his hair back from his face.

"You're certain?" he asked.

"I've never been more certain of anything," she said. "I want you."

Hal sighed, a ragged sound. Surrender.

He was gentle—everything between them *sorry,* then *yes, there,* then *wait,* until at last it settled. As she lost herself in the darkness of his eyes, she realized something she'd known for some time. It was one of those inarticulable, unquestionable truths of the universe, glimmering in the depths of his wonderstruck gaze. Hal Cavendish was *hers,* and he would do anything she asked of him. And she would do the same.

He was so impossibly still, and she swore she was flying.

"You're not hurting me," she whispered hoarsely. When he kissed her, she tasted his relief like a sugar cube pressed onto her tongue. No, he couldn't hurt her. Not on purpose.

Afterward, Wren stayed awake long after his breathing slowed. It was a vigil her body demanded she keep. She couldn't rest until she made sure he wouldn't be taken from her again.

CHAPTER THIRTY-FIVE

Wren jerked awake from a nightmare. But when she opened her eyes, it was only to a darkness muffling her like a quilt drawn over her head. The soft shadows were dappled by the faint glow of lamps outside the window. Her breathing evened out, even as her stomach churned.

I'm in the abbey, she told herself. *I'm safe.*

But her every nerve bristled with dread. Through the cracked window, the cold air carried a charge that prickled the hairs on her arms. It promised a thunderstorm. Beyond that, she *felt* something—something fast-approaching and malicious. In wartime, she'd trained herself to startle awake at even the crack of a twig. Right now, it felt too much like a battlefield, with unseen dangers lurking at the edge of her vision.

As her eyes adjusted, she noticed Hal sitting upright beside her. The blankets pooled around his waist, leaving him bare. Pale moonlight painted the ridges of his muscles with deep blue shadows. Wren reached out to him, the pads of her fingertips brushing his spine. His entire body went rigid at her touch, but when he turned over his shoulder, relief softened him.

"Do you feel it, too?" she whispered.

"Yes." His eyes were impossibly tender beneath the concern. "We should get Dryden."

By the time they dressed and gathered their things, three sharp knocks on the door sounded. Una stepped through the doorway, her face drawn. "We need to move."

A cold fist of unease clenched around Wren's heart. "You think it's the Guard?"

"It's likely," Una said, her expression steely. If she was at all afraid, it did not show. "We'll put some distance between us."

They crept through the darkened corridors and emerged into the main hall. Only the most tenacious moonlight squeezed in through the stained glass. Through the lingering haze of ceremonial smoke, it patterned the floor like waves. Wren could only focus on the long streaks of red. The color of blood. The color of the rubies always glittering on Lowry's hands. It reminded her far too much of Colwick Hall.

Wren followed Una through the gloom and out the main doors of the abbey. The doors banged shut behind them like the fall of a gavel. Outside, it was too quiet. Nothing stirred but a gust of wind that ruffled her hair and slipped into her jacket like a blade. Una took one step forward—then came to a dead halt.

It took Wren a moment to see them. In their black uniforms, the squadron of Guardsmen were daubed across the courtyard like shadows, but the dim moonlight scintillated on their silver buttons. They gleamed like rows of monstrous, beady eyes.

In an instant, all of her hope crumbled like ash. They were undone.

A woman stepped forward, her uniform marked with the single, glistering star of a brigadier general. Her voice rang out, amplified in the cold air. "Una Dryden, Wren Southerland, and Hal Cavendish. You're under arrest for conspiracy against the crown."

No one moved. No one breathed. Piecing her own experience

into anything coherent was like reassembling a broken mirror, every shard a fragmented sensation, an eternity condensed into a moment.

The feeling of Hal's hand sliding into hers.

The resignation that smoothed his face into cold impassivity.

Una tracing the symbol of the Goddess on her forehead.

"Very well," Una called out. "You've caught us."

The Guardsmen shifted in front of them. Some of them hesitated. Although Wren could not make out their features in the viscous darkness, she knew some of them had to be familiar. How many of them had worked under Una? How many of them had fought in the war alongside them?

Una held up her hands, angled her chin skyward. Almost too quietly to hear, she said, "We will die as traitors, but we will die doing what's right."

"Una—"

She couldn't do this. They were too outnumbered.

But Una stepped in front of Wren and Hal and advanced toward the Guard. Each unhurried footstep echoed through the courtyard.

"Seize her," the brigadier general said.

Everything happened in a rush.

Two soldiers approached Una and, with a ferocious shout, she cracked the hilt of her saber into the closest soldier's skull. The resounding crunch was like the fire of a starting pistol. They descended on her like wolves, and Wren lost sight of her in the flurry of black coats.

No. Her magic was gone, but she could not—*would* not—let them take Una.

Her body moved of its own accord. She sprung forward, but before she could land a blow, hands like claws ensnared her from behind. They dragged her backward, and she flailed wildly against their grip.

Then, suddenly, the hands around her went slack.

She whirled around in time to see her assailant frozen mid-stride. His face was white and horrifically twisted. Every tendon corded in his neck. Every vein bulged in his temples. He staggered backward, his mouth tearing open in a scream. It was a broken-glass sound. It crawled underneath her skin, so deep, she couldn't ever slough it off. He collapsed in a heap of tremoring muscle, his breaths high-pitched wheezes.

Hal.

Someone shouted, "Don't look at his eyes, damn it!"

Wren turned to see the silver glow receding from the *fola* around Hal's eyes. The moment's glance cost her. A sharp pain wrenched a startled cry from her throat.

There was a syringe embedded in her shoulder, the vial draining pale green liquid into her veins.

Wren knew it instantly. A potent general anesthetic composed of boiled herbs, from morning glory to ginseng to crow-dipper. As icy numbness bled down her arm, twilight bloomed across her vision. The last thing she saw was Hal reaching out to her—and a black hood pulled taut over his face.

CHAPTER THIRTY-SIX

Wren blinked open her eyes to the steady rhythm of *tick, tick, tick*. There was no gap between recognizing herself—her throbbing head, her churning stomach—and jerking violently with the realization of where she was.

The Tower.

Her wrists and ankles were bound to a chair, and her skin was already red and chafed from where the damp rope bit into her. She tugged against it experimentally but found it painfully secure.

"You're awake."

She gasped, nearly wrenching her neck in surprise. Lowry sat in an armchair in front of a rain-streaked window. Droplets steadily drummed on the roof—a strangely calming contrast to Lowry's voracious gaze. "I was beginning to worry you'd died in your sleep. How unfortunate that would have been."

She was still woozy from the anesthetic, but even with her blurred vision, there was no denying he looked awful. Against his all-black formalwear, his face was ashen, and his eyes were so hollow, he looked as if he hadn't slept in days. Sweat plastered his curls to his temples like seaweed dashed against slick ocean rock. His experiments had clearly taken a toll on his system.

"Where are they?" Her voice was ragged.

"Are you always so impatient? It's maddening." He rose from his chair. "You'll see them soon enough."

Step by agonizing step, he circled her like a stalking beast. She couldn't turn her head enough to follow him when he slipped out of her peripheral vision. Only his footsteps echoed in the emptiness of this chamber. When he at last stood behind her, he grabbed the back of her chair and turned her around. The wooden legs scraped against the stone floor with a high-pitched squeal.

The light from the wall sconces was orange as rust. It caked the sharp edges of the surgical instruments lined up on the surface of a wheeled cart. Beside it was a slab of a table, and on it, a shape draped in a white sheet. The shock of it emptied her out, left her dizzy and reeling with fear. She did not want to see what was underneath, although she already *knew*.

"Shall we take a look?" Lowry pulled off the cover, and the blood drained from her face.

A thousand feelings careened through her, but she couldn't manage a single word, a single movement. Hal lay outstretched on the table, strapped down with leather belts around his forehead, chest, and limbs. An intravenous drip punctured his arm like a plant taken root, steadily feeding him an anesthetic. Judging by the plum-purple marks streaking his forearm, he'd fought its insertion.

Lowry turned a crank on the operating table and, with a tinny whine, the platform lowered until Hal was nearly level with her knees. "Everything's already set up for you."

The full, horrible weight of his expectation threatened to crush her. She hardly felt it as he took a scalpel and cut one of her restraints. It broke with a clean *snap,* as easy as paring viscera. "Remove his blindfold."

"No."

"You're hardly in a position to deny me."

She wasn't. "My magic is gone. I can't."

"Do it."

Wren flinched at the ferocity in his voice. With her jaw locked, she reached out with trembling hands and carefully unfastened the blindfold. He looked so peaceful, she could almost believe he'd dozed off there.

"Tell me. I'm curious. How does this procedure work, Ms. Southerland?" He was so casual, he may as well have been inquiring about the weather. Lowry ran his gloved fingertips almost lovingly along the instruments on the surgical cart and chose a speculum.

Wren felt sick. Two thin blades would be inserted into the eye socket, slotted in alongside the conjunctival fornix. Once cranked, the speculum would pry back the eyelid and hold it during the enucleation procedure. The clinical facts came easy to her. But the reality of it now . . . It was unthinkable. The very thought of Hal beneath her scalpel made her want to sink into the earth.

"It seems quite easy to plunge them in too deep." Lowry unhooked the locking mechanism and wrenched the speculum apart. It clicked and rattled, a sound like a windup toy. "Or stretch too wide."

"Stop."

"Even damaging the cornea would be so painful. I'm afraid my supplies aren't as advanced as what you'd have in a hospital. . . ."

He was threatening her. Sincere or not, the image of him so coldly, clumsily gouging out Hal's eyes . . . "I said *stop*! This is madness. You can't possibly—"

"I understand my limitations." Lowry placed the instrument on the armrest beside her free hand. "If you'd be so kind, you could spare us any accidental mutilation."

Through clenched teeth, she growled, "I would sooner die."

"We'll see what we can do about that stubborn streak, won't we?" Lowry snapped his fingers. "Bring her."

A door opened with a rattling creak. A figure emerged, and as it approached, the shadows pulled back from its face like a veil.

Isabel stepped into the candlelight. She wore a diaphanous gown made of layers and layers of delicate fabric. Her silver-blond hair was unbound, spilling down her back so long and straight, it pooled on the stone floor like liquid mercury. Now more than ever, she looked like something born of the divine, cruel and cold. In her small, fragile hands, she held a thick rope that bound Una. She was gagged, and her arms were twisted behind her back, but her eyes blazed with determined fury.

"Una!" Wren lurched against her restraints, but they held fast, tearing at her wrist.

"Now," Lowry said. "What was it that you were saying? You'd rather die than help me?"

He traced a slow path to Una and untied the gag. As soon as she was free, she rounded on Isabel without sparing Lowry a glance. "Your Majesty! You must stop this, this . . ." She trailed off, casting her frantic gaze at the scene in front of them.

Isabel, however, remained impassive, as if she'd disassociated entirely from what she was witnessing. "I am the queen. I *must* do nothing at your behest." Isabel lifted her chin. "You abandoned me, betrayed me. Just like the rest of this country."

"I haven't left you! I'm trying to help you. How can you not see that Lowry is using you?"

"Are we still on this old song and dance?" Lowry reached into his breast pocket. "I'm afraid my patience has run out."

He unsheathed a small knife, serrated as a jawbone. Wren didn't have time to scream before he grabbed a fistful of Una's hair and drew the blade across her throat. Una's eyes stretched wide. Blood gushed from her neck. It burbled over her lips and splattered on the ground with a steady *drip, drip, drip.* Lowry let her go, and she collapsed in a heap.

"No!" Wren's shriek was feral, half drowned by a sob. "Isabel! Please, do something!"

Isabel stood frozen. Her face was ghostly white as she stared down at the girl at her feet. Una looked so broken and small as the puddle of blood spread around her, staining the hem of

Isabel's gown. Isabel's lips soundlessly formed the shape of a word: *no*.

Lowry raked a hand through his hair and shrugged, the picture of nonchalance. His fingers broke his curls into a frizzy black halo. "I haven't cut anything major, but do act quickly. It would be a shame to have her bleed out because of your indecision."

"I can't! It's gone. *Please*. My magic is gone!"

"For your friend's sake, I suggest you find it," he hissed.

Una was drowning in her own blood. It was spilling so fast—too fast. It sank into the pores of the stone and slickened the floor with brilliant red. Wren had to do something. She couldn't lose another friend.

She couldn't lose Una.

Una's eyes, matte and lightless, met hers in a warning. She couldn't speak with that wound, but she'd never needed to when it came to giving orders. The meaning in her glare was clear: *Don't even think about it.*

But Wren *had* to think about it.

I don't want to decide who lives and who dies. Wasn't that what she had told Una all those weeks ago? How could she tally up the value of lives like this? How could she weigh her love for Una against her love for Hal? Her heart against the lives Lowry would take once he had Hal's magic?

Lowry dropped the knife into the spreading pool of blood. His eyes were wide and wild as he approached her. His boots stuck to the floor with every step. "Make. Your. Decision."

Wren still didn't want to decide who lived and who died, but she'd never forgive herself if she did nothing. Her overuse injury was severe, but if she performed the transplant manually, she could summon enough magic to rewire Lowry's *fola* to Hal's eyes.

Frantically, Wren called to her magic. It sputtered, an agonizing spark that tore a gasp of pain from her throat. It was enough. But could she do this to the man she loved?

Hal had done so much wrong in his life and still hoped to fix it, but this would destroy everything he'd worked toward. Without his magic, he had no hope of ruling Vesria. His people would never accept him. But without his *life,* he had no hope of ruling Vesria, either. If it would save him—if it gave them a fighting chance—she would have to try.

"Alright. I'll do it."

Elation cracked Lowry's face open.

Wren's hands were shaking too hard to be able to do this quickly, much less cleanly. She picked up the speculum and carefully pried open Hal's eyes. His irises were so beautiful, strands of obsidian pigment braided with indigo. She remembered looking into them last night, when they were bright and wanting and full of love.

Biting down on her lip to stifle her whimper, she slid the blade of the speculum beneath his eyelid with a wet squelch. Slowly, she tightened the instrument until the whole of his eyeball, round and glassy, was exposed on a bed of shiny pink tissue.

The procedure was, in theory, simple.

She'd take the scissors and perform a limbal conjunctival peritomy to remove a strip of the clear tissue that encased the out-side of the eye. Then, she'd sever the thin capsule of fascia that sheathed the eye and separated it from the orbital fat and oblique quadrant muscles. She'd pin back the recti muscles with metal hooks and shear their fibers at their insertion to the eye. Clamp the optic nerve with a hemostat and snip it, like an umbilical cord. Only then could she lift the fluid-filled globe of the bulbus oculi from the hole of exposed tissue and nerves and muscle.

This was insanity. She'd save Una's life, and for what? Hal would still be executed. A war would still break out. It wasn't a life worth living when she'd doomed them all herself.

Wren picked up the second speculum, but her eyes lingered on the sharp point of a scalpel. When she licked her lips, she tasted salt and blood. "Before I go on, I'll need both my hands."

Lowry hesitated only a moment before reaching down and cut-ting her other hand free. He must have seen her gaze dart to the cart, for he immediately seized her hand in a crushing grip. The speculum clattered to the ground as she cried out.

"You'd let her die." It was disbelief, teetering on astonishment. Then his lips peeled back in a snarl. "You *will* do it." He spat with every word. "Do you think there's nothing left for me to take? Shall we pay a visit to the old woman in the abbey?"

Wren reached out with her free hand, fumbling over the instruments. The scalpel nicked her hand, drawing a hiss from her, but she seized it and drove it into the back of his arm. He tore himself away from her grasp with a guttural howl, clutching at his arm to staunch the blood spurting freely from the wound.

"Kill the girl, Isabel." The veins on Lowry's neck bulged. "Now!"

Isabel crouched beside Una's heaving body, her skirts puddling in her blood. "Do not give orders to me."

Lowry laughed—actually laughed. It was a raw, unhinged sound, as if he couldn't believe what he was hearing. "I swear, you will reel from how quickly I withdraw Cernos's support from your war."

Isabel hesitated.

Una was still breathing. But so slowly, interrupted by air-hungry gasps. Her skin was a pallid, waxy blue. Death lurked over her now, one skeletal claw already dug into her heart. They didn't have time for hesitation.

"Isabel, *please.* I know you're hurting." Wren wobbled over the words. To show kindness to the woman who'd made her so miserable—it was maybe the hardest thing she'd ever done. "I know you want to make our family proud. I know you want to finish what they started. But you're not like them. We don't have to continue the things we've inherited. We can be better—"

Isabel's head snapped up. "You know nothing of loyalty or duty. I was entrusted this nation by my mother and her mother before her. It was given to me by the Goddess, and I will not see it ruined. I will not abandon their legacy."

"You haven't," Wren pleaded. "I know how awful it is when it feels like everyone rejected you. When you've tried your best, and it's not enough."

Isabel said nothing. Lowry, for the first time, stilled.

"But you locked yourself away. You've pushed away everyone." Wren reached out. "But you don't have to be alone."

"I *am* alone." Isabel's voice cracked. "I'm the Paper Queen. Who would love her?"

"I would have loved you, if you let me!" Wren choked back a sob. "I wanted to—so badly. I wanted you to love me, too. After you sent me away, I never stopped hoping you would come for me. And after I got out, I never stopped hoping you would change your mind about me. I never stopped trying to impress you."

The ferocity in Isabel's glare faded.

"I needed you, and you weren't there," Wren said. "But now your people need you. It's not too late for them. Revenge won't bring prosperity. It won't bring back their families. It won't bring you their love or acceptance, and it won't make our ancestors proud. They're all dead. But no one else has to die for their war."

"Enough of this," Lowry growled. "Isabel—"

"Don't listen to another word he says! He's manipulating you. Exploiting your hatred for Vesria. As soon as you give into it, he will wrest your power away from you. Una and I—even Hal—we're trying to do right by Danu. And I know you are, too. Together, I believe we can make it better. We can create a new legacy. So please . . ."

Her voice broke off as Isabel lowered her gaze to Una, crumpled and bleeding on the floor, and sagged. Her hair enfolded her, closing around her like a waterfall. Isabel had always been thin, but now she looked gaunt. Exhausted and drowning in fabric.

"How touching." Lowry retrieved the knife from the pool of blood. He lurched toward Una. "Now out of my way—"

"Don't take another step toward her." Isabel thrust her palm forward, silver light glimmering at the center of her palm.

The Healing Touch.

All her life, Wren had assumed her magic was her father's gift. But it was from her mother. As the queen laid her hands over Una's neck, Wren realized there was something beyond their resentments that bound them.

Una squeezed her eyes shut with relief as the wound sealed. A solid, angry purple line cut across her throat. It was patchy and amateurish, but it didn't matter. With the bleeding stopped, she had a chance to survive.

The silvery light still illuminated Isabel. When she spoke, her voice was deathly quiet. She did not deign to look up. "It's over, Alistair."

Lowry's face crumpled from fury, to bitterness, to—finally—fear. For once in his miserable life, he had no leverage over anyone in the room.

He ran.

Wren swore, struggling against the rope at her ankles. At last, she managed to slip the bloody scalpel underneath the knot and saw until the restraints came free. "We have to stop him."

Una propped herself up on her elbow. "I'll go."

"No!" Wren and Isabel said in unison. Their eyes locked for a moment before they both awkwardly glanced away. Wren cleared her throat. Had they ever been in agreement before?

"Absolutely not," she continued. "You're far too injured."

Below her, Hal groaned softly. Thank the Goddess, he was alive and whole and—

And he had a speculum wedged in his eye.

Cringing apologetically, Wren removed it and tossed it onto the ground. Metal rang against stone as it skittered across the floor. Then, she set to work unfastening the buckles that bound him and slipping the IV from the crook of his elbow.

"Let me." His words slurred together. His eyelids drooped. "I can do it."

"Oh," Wren said almost fondly. "I don't think so."

Even as he fought to sit up, the anesthetic reclaimed him. As she laid a hand on his cheek, he sank back into unconsciousness. It seemed disposing of Lowry fell to her. For once in her life, she would have to be ruthless.

CHAPTER THIRTY-SEVEN

Her whole body ached. Her movements and thoughts were muddy with lingering anesthetic. But she was angrier than she'd ever been. She clung to it, nursed it like the last spark of a dying fire. It gave her purpose, clear and simple and driving.

Alistair Lowry would pay for what he'd done.

It would feel so good to kill him. *Justice,* some dark part of her slavered. Justice for all his servants. Justice for Byers. Justice for Hal and Una. Justice for *her.*

In the gloom, over the rumble of distant thunder, the North Tower was as terrifying as Colwick Hall. Grabbing a lantern from a hook outside the door, she chased the echoing sound of footfalls on the main staircase. Over the rush of blood in her ears, the yawning space of darkness past the railing whispered, *Fall.* With every step, she propelled herself deeper into the bowels of the Tower—so deep, she worried she'd never find her way to the light again.

She stumbled on the last stair and threw her hand forward to catch her balance. The rough scrape of the wall against her palm steadied her. In the snatches of light from her swaying lantern, Wren saw the walls were inlaid with bone, femurs and humeri layered like brick, shattered fragments like tiles.

She stood at the entrance to the catacombs. The Tower was built into a cliffside, and the tunnels housed not only bodies of queens and saints but functioned as an escape route to the sea. A precautionary measure for a monarch fleeing an invasion—or a runaway lord evading Wren's fury. She did not hesitate. She slipped into the shadows, and the hiss of the tide swelled around her.

After what felt like miles, the passage emptied onto a bluff. Slick stone stairs were carved into its side and led down to the docks. Tonight, in the stormy darkness, the ocean was made of ink. Waves crashed against the rocks, bursting into frothy white peaks. Rain fell steadily, draping everything in a sparkling liquid veil.

Wren stepped into the downpour and gasped at the shock of the cold. The air smelled of salt. And something else—something terrifyingly familiar. Burning things, like gunpowder and coffee. And beneath it, the vinegary sterility of formaldehyde.

Cold metal pressed to the base of her skull.

"How gallant," Lowry said. The safety on his pistol clicked off. "You've come after me all alone."

Wren's shoulders bunched around her ears. "Are you so afraid I'll hurt you?"

"You *are* quite unpredictable. And frustratingly resilient. At any rate, you're a convenient shield should anyone else decide to be a hero tonight."

If he wanted her as a hostage, she had at least a few minutes to live. It was time to end this.

Hal's knife was tucked into her belt. For one weak moment, she remembered the sled driver she'd knocked unconscious. Imagined him blue and stiff, buried beneath the ice because of her. It was one thing to kill in self-defense. It was another thing entirely to mete out justice. Could she forgive herself if she did this?

She thought of Jacob Byers, who had died brutally and all alone.

She thought of Una, her life pouring out of her onto the cold stone floor of the Tower.

She thought of Hal, pale and bruised on that operating table.

Yes. He deserves it.

Wren unsheathed the blade and slashed it across Lowry's shoulder. She carved out an arc of blood that spattered into a pool of rainwater. He hissed in surprise. Wren jumped back, but he caught her hand too fast. His pistol came down hard on her arm, and she screamed at the burst of agony, the snap of bone.

As her vision blackened, she doubled over and dropped the knife. It clattered to the ground, gleaming with water and blood and poison. Wren cradled her arm, her eyes watering with pain and hatred. The poison would already be making its way into his bloodstream. She just had to survive longer than him.

"You could have ushered in the beginning of a new era. One of peace." He retrieved the knife. "You stupid, selfish girl."

"How?" she shouted. "In what world would this bring peace?"

"How can you not see that Danu and Vesria will never end this of their own accord?" He trembled with the force of his rage. "No matter what you believe you can do, you cannot throw off the weight of centuries of violence. Look around you. Your land has been burned and salted. Your economy ruined. Your children orphaned. This world is a mess. Do you think your people will forgive Vesria without the proper guidance? Do you think we can ever see progress without intervention?"

She thought of Hal. The brightness of her love for him, the hope he filled her with. If two people like them could love each other, then maybe one day their broken nations could learn to coexist, too.

"Yes, I do." Cold sweat and rainwater streaked down her face, and adrenaline set her to shaking. But she lifted her chin and stared evenly into his eyes. "I know we're better than our ancestors are. I know we can heal from this. But only if we set aside violence. Only if we stop meeting wrong with wrong. Your way isn't superior. It's only more of the same."

"More of the same? You've slaughtered each other for nothing. I'm doing this for the greater good. I will be remembered as a hero. A visionary. My people have hidden themselves away for too long, but *I* will make a difference in this world."

The horrible truth of it struck her. He believed it—every word of it.

"Can you really be so heartless?"

"Spare me." Lowry sneered. "Now be a good hostage and get up."

Wren dragged herself to her feet, ignoring the steady pulse of pain in her broken arm. The gun was an insistent pressure at her back, urging her forward. Over the edge of the bluff, a tethered steamboat bobbed in the battering surf. As soon as he was finished with her, he would pitch her into the waves. She could imagine the taste of the water as it filled her mouth, her nose. How the salt would burn all the way down.

But he'd be dead before that happened.

They descended the stairs slowly. Lowry's steps were heavy and staggering against the weathered dock. Then, suddenly, they stopped. She turned over her shoulder just as he collapsed.

"What did you do to me?" There was a feral, desperate look in his eyes now, like a wolf trapped in a snare. "What did you do?"

His fear filled her with cold satisfaction. Was this how it felt on the battlefield? It felt so right. She could lose herself in this rush of power. Finally, she understood why generation after generation had signed up to die for Danu. She understood why everyone called her weak. She'd never been ruthless, but it was so easy to surrender to this hatred.

Too easy.

At her feet, so desperate and pale, Lowry looked like a frightened child dressed in too-fine clothes. How could she preach forgiveness and then watch him die by her hand?

Mercy is the most difficult thing.

Killing Lowry would not bring Byers back. It wouldn't erase the horror of these past few weeks. It wouldn't make her hate herself less. She couldn't do this. Hurt begat hurt over and over again, and she was so *tired*.

She was so tired of death.

Wren dropped to her knees beside Lowry and with her good arm she rummaged through her medical bag for the antidote, one of the last vials of it she'd prepared. She pushed up his sleeve and plunged the needle into his arm. The look he gave her as the serum emptied into his veins was baleful.

"Why?"

"Because killing you solves nothing."

"Is this the part where you forgive me?" he wheezed bitterly. "Where I repent?"

"No." She could see the fire fading from him, the exhaustion beginning to take over. His heart steadily slowed as sleep struggled to claim him. "I will *never* forgive you. Not for as long as I live. But I won't kill you, either. This ends with us."

Then—a pain worse than any she'd ever known. When the spots cleared from her vision, she saw Hal's knife buried to its hilt in her stomach.

He'd *stabbed* her. In numb disbelief, she touched the wound, and her fingers came away slick.

Lowry grabbed her medical bag and threw it. It skidded across the dock and teetered on the brink, just above the hungry suck and lap of the waves. With a panicked, animal sound, Wren scrambled for it, but Lowry's hand locked around her shin.

He dragged her back. The knife twisted in her gut, and the fragments of her broken arm ground together. Her every nerve burst into flame, blinding her with white light. She would black out from the pain if she so much as moved. The salt and blood coating her tongue threatened to gag her.

She couldn't do anything. Her magic was spent. She was going to die here. But at least Hal and Una were safe. Vesria and Danu would know peace.

She lay nearly forehead to forehead with Lowry. He looked wicked and triumphant as streaks of rain glimmered on his pale skin like tear tracks. "After all your efforts, all your struggles, how does it feel to fail?"

Wren struggled to form words. Her body was useless, broken. And it was so, so cold. Through chattering teeth, she growled, "I only feel sorry for you."

"How precious. Thinking of others, even as you die."

"I saved my country. I saved my friends. You dream of progress, but what have you really accomplished? In five years, no one will even remember your name."

Something flashed in his eyes—both anguish and longing.

Over his shoulder, a dark figure approached.

Hal.

He didn't say a word. He didn't have to. His eyes, solid black and threaded with silver *fola,* were as vicious as the ocean. He crouched beside them and turned Lowry onto his back. Rain beat onto Lowry's upturned face, and horrified recognition parted his lips.

Their eyes locked.

Lowry opened his mouth to scream, but no sound came out. He broke into convulsions, and his fingers, stiff as claws, scratched at his own eyes. Then, with a dull *crack,* his head struck the pier and lolled toward her. Pink foam poured from his mouth.

Alistair Lowry was dead, his lips pulled back in a final, terrible smile.

CHAPTER THIRTY-EIGHT

Her existence was nothing but pain and glimpses of Hal as he carried her, spray dripping from his hair, worry burning in his eyes. He set her down clumsily beneath an overhang in the cliffs and began rummaging through her bag. She heard glass vials clinking together like wind chimes. For the first time since she'd met him, all his defenses were down. He was hurried, nearly frantic, as he tossed aside gauze and gloves, scalpels and forceps.

Somehow, it was . . . endearing.

He caught her looking. "Wren."

"Mm?"

"Tell me what to do," he said hoarsely. "I don't know what to do."

Although her eyes were already falling closed again, medical instruction flowed as easily as breathing. "Don't take out the knife until another healer can stabilize me. That is very important. In the meantime, inject the antidote. Intravenous is ideal, but intramuscular will work. Don't give me an embolism."

Hal let out a soft, frustrated sound. "You need to stay awake."

"I am awake," she said indignantly.

"Which one is it? You have too many vials in this bag."

"It's the greenish one."

There was an interminable pause. More rustling. He swore.

"Goddess above, Hal, they're labeled. It's the one that says *antidote for Hal* on it."

The last thing she saw, as darkness swirled through her vision, was him fumbling to affix a vial to a syringe.

By the time Wren woke again, she decided that dying would have been preferable to this. The light was too bright, and the air too heavy, too full of broken ice. The pain in her stomach, at least, was mostly gone.

As she rolled over in the bed she'd been tucked into, she realized two things. She was back in the North Tower, and someone had dressed her in one of Isabel's nightgowns.

She kicked the thick blankets off and pulled up her dress to examine the stab wound. Her skin was white-splotched red, still angry and streaked with cold, but underneath the flush was a thick band of shiny scar tissue. It was a slapdash job if she'd ever seen one. She'd done better work as a child.

Then, memories of Isabel's palms washed in silver flooded back. Wren ran her fingers over the scar and fought back the wave of emotion. Her aunt had given her many scars over the years, but this one . . . Maybe it wasn't so terrible after all. Wren was too tired to fix it now, anyway.

Not that she could.

If she reached deep inside herself, she felt her magic sleeping like it was imprisoned beneath a thick layer of ice. It was distant, but thank the Goddess, it was there. Maybe someday it would forgive her for all the abuse she'd put it through. Wren blinked back a teary wave of relief and instead drank in her surroundings.

Compared to the rest of the Tower, this room was homey. It glowed with warmth from the fire, which washed the room in the soft orange of a sunset. She buried her nose in the wool trim of the blanket and inhaled its comforting scent.

When the door opened, Wren turned to see Hal in the threshold. He froze when he noticed her awake, as if she were some precariously perched ceramic that would fall and shatter if he moved too quickly. Steam lazily curled from the two mugs in his hands. "Wren."

"Hi," she said hoarsely. Hal placed both mugs on the bedside table and sat beside her. She twined her fingers in his. Her hands were still bone-white and stiff with cold, but his were so *warm*. Wren squeezed him tight. "You saved me."

"The other way around, I believe."

She decided not to argue with him. Not when he was being so affectionate.

He bent over and placed a kiss on her forehead, and from this angle, it was too easy to slip her hands beneath the hem of his untucked shirt. She laid her palms flat against his stomach, relishing the solid warmth of his body.

He winced. "You're freezing."

"I *did* almost die." Wren grinned wickedly. "And you're hot. So share."

Hal shook his head fondly and climbed into bed beside her, letting her nuzzle close. She tucked her head against his chest, just above his beating heart. It was something true and grounding, now that the whole world lurched around her.

Lowry was dead, but like the scar Isabel left behind, he would always be with her, no matter how desperately she yearned to forget.

"I almost killed him, but I was too much of a coward to go through with it," she murmured. "You shouldn't have had to intervene that way."

"No. You were brave." Hal brushed the hair out of her face. "We all were raised to be cruel. It takes incredible strength to be kind in this world. To endure suffering instead of further it."

Wren was too stricken to say anything.

"Without you, I would be a different man," he continued. "Without you, the sun may have risen on a very different world."

Wren had to laugh, if only to keep herself from crying. "You can't mean that."

"I do."

He spoke with such reverence, she couldn't help letting out an embarrassing whimper. Somehow, he always managed to say exactly what she needed to hear. Because of them, Lowry would never hurt anyone again. Because of them, Danu and Vesria would finally have peace. And Hal . . . He'd be the kind of leader his country needed, kind and fair.

Assuming, of course, her people let him go.

Wren swallowed thickly. "What will happen to you now?"

"I expect a tribunal will decide my fate tomorrow."

"They can't!" She shot upright, only to wince at the sharp pain in her stomach. She flopped back down. "Ow."

"Don't think about it now," he said softly.

"How can you possibly be so calm about this?"

"I have hope." Hal frowned. "I don't expect a pardon, but if your government truly wants peace, they'll have to send me home."

"True." Wren closed her eyes, sighing. "I bet you'll be happy to see home again. What'll you do first?"

"My answer is conditional."

"On what?"

"You."

"Me?" She picked at the fraying wool of the blanket. For so long, she'd thought of nothing but what came after all this. Now, she could think of nothing but this moment, nothing but her cheek against Hal's chest and the uneven stutter of his heartbeat. She dared to look up, and his eyes brimmed with hope. "What are you getting at?"

"If you would consider it . . . If you'd like . . . If I'm allowed to leave . . . I wondered if you would come to Vesria with me."

Hal Cavendish had *stammered*. At first, it was so absurd, so endearing, she didn't register exactly what he'd said. When it sank in, she blinked. "Wait. What?"

"I want you with me," he said with more conviction. "If that's what you want, too."

Of course she did.

There was so much good to be done in Vesria. She could picture it so clearly: teaching medicine to their healers, maybe even beginning to make amends by helping to rehabilitate the veterans wounded in the war.

But she was home. After all this time, she was home.

She couldn't just leave, even if the thought of returning to the Guard made her feel distorted and cramped, like she was trying to fit herself back where she didn't belong anymore. That thought was too terrifying to linger on. Nothing in her life had ever been certain but her yearning. Now that she had exactly what she wanted, she was too afraid to let it go.

As if sensing her indecision, Hal said, "Please don't decide now. And know the only thing I want is for you to be happy, even if that means leaving without you."

"What about you, though?"

"What about me?" Hal traced the line of her jaw with his thumb, his eyes warm and impossibly fond. "You've taught me how to begin again. For that, I will always love you."

"You love me? But I'm . . ." There were too many *buts*. She was too much. Too reactive and reckless and stubborn and peevish. "I think I'm hallucinating," she mumbled. "What did you say again?"

"I love you, Wren Southerland. All of you."

The words she'd waited so long to hear. Her eyes filled with tears, and the sheer effort it took to hold them in made her chest burn. She opened her mouth. No sound came out.

I love you, too.

She needed to say it. She needed to ask him where to find him to give her decision.

But the Tower was so dark, and staying awake was so *hard*. The world closed in around her like an embrace, and he last thing to vanish were his eyes. Two points of darkness on which everything bright and beautiful converged.

CHAPTER THIRTY-NINE

Wren blinked into consciousness again.

A garden bloomed around her: pink roses and daisies and chrysanthemums in bright, riotous colors. But the first thing she thought was *Hal.* She remembered speaking to him, but she couldn't remember how long ago that was. Had it been hours or days? Her memories all blurred into a smattering of silver light and injections, strange faces and snatches of droning conversation.

Her body still ached, but within her . . . She could feel her magic. With a rush of hope, Wren channeled her energy and watched silver spiderweb faintly beneath her skin. She closed her fist, drawing a shaky breath of relief.

"You're awake."

Startled, Wren turned toward the door. Una clutched a bunch of drooping lilies, starbursts of orange and pink with spots of bright yellow. She placed the bouquet in one of the empty vases on the nightstand. The arrangement was artless—and all the more endearing for its imperfection. Wren turned her bleary eyes to Una's face as she sat. She had tied her hair into a loose queue at the nape of her neck. It revealed the jagged scar that crossed her throat like a collar—or maybe a necklace, with how proudly she wore it.

"How do you feel?" Una asked.

Wren flexed her fingers, letting the glow of her magic go faint and shimmery in the sunlight. "Miraculously fine, all things considered."

"The queen had healers in here day and night."

"Oh." Wren dropped her eyes to the floor. It was a kindness she didn't anticipate. Healers didn't usually treat nonfatal wounds as part of emergency care. "I see."

Neither of them seemed to know what to say next.

Una helplessly looked at the flowers. "They looked nicer when I bought them."

It was enough to break Wren. Without preamble, she burst into tears. "How did you know they're my favorite?"

Una groaned. "Please don't cry. I have no idea what I'm supposed to do."

"Goddess above." Wren hiccupped a laugh. "Just sit there. Or hug me."

"I'll sit here." Una, mercifully, pulled a handkerchief from her breast pocket. It hung between them like a flag of surrender, limp and white.

While Wren composed herself and blotted her tears, Una told her what happened while she'd been unconscious. With the evidence presented at a parliamentary hearing, Una and Wren had been pardoned of all the crimes levied against them. By nightfall, Vesria had sent their guarded gratitude for rooting out their soldiers' abductor—and for Hal's continued survival. The press, apparently, had slavered over the political drama of the past few days. Little else had been printed in the newspapers.

"So it's really over," Wren said.

"Yeah." Una eased herself onto the edge of the bed. Silence

descended over them, soft as a blanket of snow. "I'm so glad you're alright."

"Are you getting sentimental on me, Captain Dryden?"

"No." Una shot her a warning look. "I was just worried I would never get the chance to give you a better apology."

"For what?"

"For trying to change you." Una tucked a wayward strand of hair behind her ear. "All this time, I thought I was protecting you by telling you to be harder, colder. The world isn't a kind place, and I . . ."

"I know, Una." Wren rested her hand on her arm. "You did your best."

"Did I? I was a bad commander to you. And a worse friend."

"Don't say things like that. I don't care about any of that right now."

"I'm not good at this," Una grumbled. "Will you let me finish?"

"You're absolved. Happy?"

"Yes." Una smiled—one of her rare, cracked-ice smiles. "I'm happy."

Wren leaned her head against Una's shoulder. For the first time in a while, Una let her. "Me, too."

And despite everything—the horrible, rain-drenched memories of the other night and the bone-deep chill she still couldn't shiver away—she meant it. Magic coursed in her veins, sunlight gilded the room, and Una was here. There was nothing more she could want. Nothing but—

"There's something I need to tell you," Una said. "It's about Cavendish."

Oh. She sounded so *grim*. "What is it?"

"Parliament refused to pardon him. The best compromise the queen could get was to send him home and bar his reentry into the country."

Wren's heart sank. So it was too late to give him an answer. He was gone.

She managed a wobbly smile. "That's great."

"Is it?"

"Of course it is. I'm glad he gets to go home. Everything can go back to normal now. Why wouldn't I be happy?"

"Because you cared about him."

"I'm in love with him."

Goddess, she was so foolish. Saying it aloud reopened the wound. Tears stung her eyes, but she breathed, long and even, until the worst of it subsided. She couldn't cry over this. From the very beginning, she knew it couldn't last. Even without a war to separate them, they each had duties they couldn't abandon. She had to cherish what they once had, rather than cling to what could have been.

"I never got to tell him."

"That's tragic." Una said it so flatly, so uncomfortably, Wren wanted to laugh.

"Maybe. But I'll live."

"Of course you will. He's just a boy." Una crossed her arms. "There's one other thing."

"*More?* Have some pity for my fragile constitution."

"Your . . . aunt is here."

"Oh." The flood of emotion at the word *aunt* was dizzying.

Wren flopped back against the pillows. She was exhausted, and everything was still too fresh, too raw. She didn't know if she had the energy to cope with Hal's departure and also survive a visit from the queen. As she opened her mouth to protest, her gaze fell on Una's neck again, where the scar gleamed like a crooked smile. The very sight of it rocked her with a breathless wave of fear. If Isabel hadn't been there . . .

Wren owed her at least the courtesy of an audience. "Send her in."

Una gave her a lingering, sympathetic look before leaving the room. Within moments, Isabel appeared in the threshold, as bright as the first break of daylight. Her hair was braided loosely and woven through with white flowers. Although she wore no crown, she still looked royal with the proud cant of her chin, the train of her elegant white dress. Somehow, she looked less severe than usual.

The sunlight softened all the harsh edges of her face and sharp angles of her bones.

She carried a glass vase overflowing with pink-speckled lilies and cottony wisps of baby's breath. Isabel placed the bouquet on the nightstand and sat primly in the chair beside the bed. From here, Wren could smell her perfume, lavender and the sweet vanilla of aging books.

Silence stretched out until Wren shifted nervously under her gaze. She touched one of the lily's stamens, which was sticky with pollen. "Thank you. These are lovely."

"You worried me."

Wren tried to hide her surprise. "Your Majesty . . . ?"

Isabel kept her eyes lowered, her voice quiet. "When you brought me Lowry's letter, you looked so much like her in that moment. My sister. You *are* very much like her. Too much like her. Impulsive. Hot-tempered. Moody. But kind." She paused. "How you must resent me."

Wren had imagined this day so many times. For so long, she'd fantasized about what it would be like to get an apology—and then how satisfying it would feel to reject it, to savor Isabel's guilt. But now, all she could think to say was, "I did. But I understand."

"No, you don't have to understand. You were only a child. You needed someone. I did, too." Isabel closed her eyes. "I came to say thank you. And I'm sorry. Neither is sufficient, but perhaps it's a start."

No, it wasn't sufficient—but what would be? They'd each lashed out at each other for too long. No flowers, no words, could give them that time back. Nothing could heal those wounds. But for now, this tentative thing between them . . . Their relationship was an unset bone, healing crooked but true.

It was enough.

"I forgive you," Wren said. "And I'm sorry, too, for all the trouble I've caused."

"Yes . . . trouble." Isabel pursed her lips. "Let's discuss that."

Wren cringed. Maybe she'd forgiven her prematurely.

"I've struggled with the question of what to do with you in the aftermath of all this. You're ill-suited for both the Order and the Guard."

"But I—"

Isabel held up a hand. "So I will be issuing you another assignment. One you are uniquely qualified for. I believe it is time to lay old grudges to rest. We plan to open communication with Vesria, and I will need someone to speak on my behalf."

Wren waited for the punch line, but slowly, it sunk in. "You mean me?"

"Yes."

Wren touched her collarbone, croaked when she tried to speak. "Why?"

"You have . . . a friend in high places." Isabel smiled, just barely, before rising from her chair in a rustle of silk. "Think about it. When you've made your decision, send word. I'll send the royal carriage to your flat, should you choose to accept."

She did not turn back as she walked out the door. Wren was still reeling when Una returned. "Did you know about this?"

"I did."

Wren rested her face in her hands. "What do you think I should I do?"

Una hummed pensively, as if she were carefully turning over the question. "Well, the future leader of Vesria will be on his way out of the country by train soon. I think it would be a gesture of goodwill to send an escort."

Wren's breath left her in a rush. So it wasn't too late. He was still here.

"Why would you . . . ?"

"Because I want you to be happy, even if it means you have to leave."

I want you to be happy, Hal had told her. *Even if that means you staying here.* Stay or leave, a piece of her heart would be ripped out. It was an impossible choice.

Una absently plucked a petal from a wilting flower and tore it in half. "If we're really going to change things, we need someone like you over there to build the relationship. Someone kind."

"I just got back," Wren whispered. "How can I leave you again?"

Golden sunlight warmed Una's eyes like honey. "You're not leaving me. You're doing your job."

Una held out her hand, but Wren couldn't take it. Una had been her first love. Her best friend. Her whole *world*. It was too much to walk away from. She hardly knew who she was without her. Wren shook her head. "So much has changed already. I'm afraid."

"It doesn't have to be forever," she said firmly. "You can always come back. I love you, Wren. No matter how far you go, that, at least, won't change."

"I love you so much." Wren threw her arms around her, breathing in the familiar woodfire scent of her hair. "And thank you for—for everything."

"Don't thank me yet. You only have about an hour and a half to catch him."

"I can work with that," Wren breathed. "Help me pack?"

"Of course." Una bowed her head. Her hair curtained her face with shining darkness. When she looked up again, her amber eyes were glittering and her cheeks were wet with tears. With forced disgust, she said, "How do you manage this all the time? I feel ridiculous."

"You're not," Wren whispered. "It's not ridiculous."

Una grinned at her, raw and unguarded and sad.

It was the most beautiful thing Wren had ever seen.

CHAPTER FORTY

Agreeing to take the royal carriage, in retrospect, might have been excessive.

It was a three-ton, silver-gilded monstrosity. Luminous gas lamps crowned each corner of the roof and shone on the elaborately painted phases of the moon on the solid black cabin. Between the front wheels, their spokes glittering silver in the sunlight, was a sterling statue of the Goddess, her three faces serene and imposing.

Eight white horses pulled it down the cobblestone streets. It lurched like the hulking beast it was, like a boat tempest-tossed. As if anxiety hadn't soured Wren's stomach already. She pressed her forehead to the window and watched her breath condense on the glass, the same color as the fog thickening the air outside. Four footmen in their finest livery and four Guardsmen leisurely walked in formation beside the coach, for it crawled along from its sheer weight and the heavy flow of traffic.

"Make way!" the coachman called ahead of them. "Make way!"

Another driver was barking expletives as a man shepherded a small family of goats across the street. Even the horse drawing the carriage beside them snuffled impatiently.

Wren could relate. High above them, the clocktower read 3:45. In twenty minutes, Hal would board a train to Vesria. Although she was certain she could get a letter to him eventually, the prospect of all of this fanfare, all of this nervous hope, amounting to nothing . . .

Wren bit off a hangnail, her spine tingling at the sting. "How far are we to the station, sir?"

"Another mile yet, my lady."

At this rate, it'd take them another thirty minutes to go that far. That settled it. She could run a mile in ten minutes, even with her suitcase weighing her down. "Thank you for the ride! I've got to go now."

"My lady?"

Wren opened the door to the carriage and launched herself out. Her knees absorbed the impact. She nearly crumpled at the pain—none of her wounds were *entirely* healed—but she was fueled by desperation. All of her attendants gaped at her, but she only weakly lifted a hand. "Sorry for the trouble!"

She ran faster than she ever had. Her lungs, still healing from the poison, burned with the effort. She dodged through the crush of traffic and over the slurry of rainwater and urine and ale. She wove through people making their way home from work and darted past the pubs serving honeyed liquor, past the market stalls in the square filled with early springtime produce, past women with woven baskets spilling with wildflowers and berries. All around her, winter had begun to give way. Tentative new growth budded on the trees, and the faint sounds of birdsong filtered through the air.

The clocktower tolled four times, each chime echoing in her skull.

Five minutes left.

The train station loomed over her, its steepled glass ceiling supported by iron beams. As she shoved through the front gates, elbows and shoulders and briefcases jostled her from every angle. But all she could feel was the wild, giddy race of her heart. All she could see was platform two ahead of her like the bright, guiding glow of a lighthouse.

Wren tumbled onto the platform, just in time for a train on the opposite side of the tracks to whir by. The clatter of its wheels rattled her bones. The gust of wind left in its wake whipped her hair across her face and filled her nose with the ashy smell of creosote.

She was here. She'd made it.

But her relief was quickly chased by dread. There were so many people, all drab and nondescript in dark hats and dark coats. They gathered in clusters like drifts of thick, black fog. How was she going to find Hal like this? What if he'd changed platforms? What if he'd already left on an earlier train? What if she never saw him again? What if—

But then, though faint, she felt the tug of the tether.

Look, it whispered. *There.*

Near the edge of the platform, she saw him.

It took her the space of a blink to recognize him. He wore a scarf around his chin and a wide-brimmed hat to conceal his features. But she would recognize that preoccupied expression anywhere. Above him, dripping icicles hung from the roof, each a shard of frozen sunlight. Her whole world shuddered and cracked like winter in thaw.

Wren forgot how to move. How to breathe.

Then, he glanced up and met her eyes.

His face, from what little she could see of it, drained of color. Then it warmed, pinkened. The last fragments of the magical bond between them went taut, and Wren obeyed its pull without hesitation.

She dropped her suitcases and closed the gap between them in two bounds—and as she crashed into him, she flung her arms around his neck. Hal grunted at the impact, but as soon as he wrapped his arms around her waist, she felt her feet leave the platform. She let out a breathless, helpless laugh as the toes of her boots scraped the pavement.

How had she ever hesitated to surrender to this? How could she ever have denied this heady, sun-bright feeling? She melted into the scratchy fabric of his jacket and his warm springtime smell.

"You were going to leave without me." Her voice was muffled in his chest. "I should shove you onto the tracks for even considering it."

"You're coming with me?" He sounded so soft, so struck, Wren couldn't help grinning.

When he set her down again, she slid her hands down to his elbows. "You sound so shocked. I assumed my new position was your idea. Did you honestly expect I would turn you down?"

"I hoped you wouldn't." Hal twisted a lock of her hair around his finger. Then, with mock formality, he said, "It will be my honor to present you to the magisterium, Lady Southerland."

Wren wrinkled her nose at the sound of the title. "What if they all hate me?"

"You won me over. I could think of no one more suited to the job."

"You really think so?"

"Of course I do," he said quietly. "I need you."

If she let herself imagine it, excitement bubbled up within her. He wanted her there with him. In Vesria, she could be useful *and* loved. She wanted to curl herself up in this feeling. This, here and now—this felt like belonging. It felt like hope. Theirs was already a world where a Danubian and a Vesrian could be something other than enemies.

Somewhere in the distance, the whistle of a train tore through the air. Everything but Hal slipped away. There was nothing but his scarf in her hands as she unwound it from his neck. Nothing but the heat of his face against her trembling palms.

She lost herself in the darkness of his eyes. They were filled with wonder.

"I should have said this so much sooner. I love you, too."

His breath hitched. "You do?"

"Of course I do. Do you need to hear it again to believe it?"

"Maybe," he whispered.

"I love you, Hal Cavendish, and I'm not letting you go."

Hal rested his forehead against hers. His smile was shy and full and *happy.* "I don't know what to say."

"You don't have to say anything." Wren stood on her toes and tangled her fingers into the hair at the nape his neck.

Their train rolled into the platform. Steam poured from the smokestack and pooled at their feet like still, moon-white water. Although passengers hurried by them and the conductor shouted over the huff and sigh of the engine, Hal cradled her face like they had all the time in the world.

He bent down and kissed her.

It was as fierce as a promise, more binding than a treaty.

ACKNOWLEDGMENTS

It's often said that writing is a solitary endeavor, but I don't believe that's entirely true. Ever since I was a kid writing fanfiction on the internet, my writing has brought me community. This book is no exception—it would not exist without the hard work, support, and love of a whole lot of brilliant people. I don't know that words will be sufficient to express my gratitude to them, but I'm going to try.

First and foremost, to my agents, Claire Friedman and Jessica Mileo. I could compose another book's worth of thanks to you, but this paragraph will have to do for now. You two are my heroes and my champions, full of wit and patience and spot-on editorial insight. Thank you for making my dreams come true and always having my back. I couldn't ask for better partners on this journey.

To my editor, Jennie Conway. From the moment I got off the phone with you for the first time, I knew that I'd struck gold. I'm grateful every day for our mind-meld of taste and vision. Thank you a thousand times over for bringing this book to new heights, for your tireless hard work and enthusiasm, and for loving Wren and Hal (and his collarbones) as much as I do.

To the entire dream team at Wednesday Books. I can't articulate what a privilege it is to work with y'all. Thank you for believing in this book, making sure it is beautiful inside and out, and getting it into the hands of readers. My special thanks to DJ DeSmyter, Lexi Neuville, Brant Janeway, Mary Moates, Olga Grlic, Sara Goodman, Eileen Rothschild, Melanie Sanders, Lena Shekhter, Devan Norman, Michael Criscitelli, Kim Ludlam, Elizabeth Catalano, and Lauren Hougen.

To Mitch Therieau. Thank you for loving me, reading all of my work, and hardly batting an eye when you find me on the floor wailing about my uncooperative characters. You give me the stability to dream and the kind of steadfast love I hope to capture even a glimmer of in my stories.

To Christine Lynn Herman. You believed in me first, and without you, I wouldn't be tearfully writing these acknowledgments. Over the years (!), you have guided me with wisdom, humor, brutal edit letters, and occasional tough love. You are a fantastic mentor, but more than that, you are a cherished friend. Here's to many more years of writing books we have zero chill about.

To Alex Huffman. We've been together since day one, and every day since then, I've marveled at how lucky I am to call you my friend. You are a rare, beautiful soul who makes the world brighter just by being yourself. Thank you for our three-hour-long calls about life, art, anime, and our fictional children. This book wouldn't be what it is without you, and hell, neither would I.

To Ava Reid and Rachel Morris. Where do I even begin with y'all? Ava, thank you for saving my life multiple times with your comments and memes. Rachel, thank you for all the hours we've laughed, cried, and played video games together on my couch. Thank you both for adopting me, loving me, and making California finally feel like home. The GSJ squad has made me a better writer and a better person.

To my critique partners, who have touched my life and work in profound ways. Emily Feldman, without you I would not have survived AMM and everything that came after. You're going to take the literary world by storm. Courtney Gould, there's no one else I'd rather be publishing twins with. Thank you for never letting me wallow, for writing books that make me weep, and for your graphic design skills. Cat Bakewell, your kind heart and stories give me hope that this world can be better. I can't wait to hold your books in my hands. Zoulfa Katouh, I'm so glad I crashed into your DMs. Your warmth, generosity, and talent inspire me, and your comments never fail to make me cry from laughter.

To Katie Stout, Elisha Walker, and Audrey Coulthurst. Y'all kept me sane while I was writing this book and working full time. You are all immensely talented, side-splittingly funny, and all-around gems.

To my mom. You are one of the most practical people I have ever met, but you never once discouraged me from pursuing my dreams. I love you so much!

To Author Mentor Match, which kickstarted my career and introduced me to so many wonderful people. Thank you so much to Allison Dillon, Alex Higgins, TJ Duckworth, Joanne Weaver, and Brittney Singleton for reading this book—and for trusting me with your work in return.

To the online communities that raised me and taught me to write. A special shout-out to Stephanie Ash-Perry and Alex Perry. Once, we were a bunch of confused teens on a constellation of forums. Look at us now!

To all the authors who've reached back and the independent booksellers—especially Cristina, Laura, Tori, Cody, and all the folks at Kepler's—who've been early champions of this book. I appreciate all of you so, so much!

Lastly, to Masashi Kishimoto. We will never meet, but thank you for creating a world that I found refuge in. I've dedicated over a decade of my life to shipping two of your characters who never once spoke to each other, so that says a lot about your work (or me). This one's for you.